Acclaim for
THE VAULT BETWEEN SPACES

"HopeWell—a place where no one is as they appear to be. A dwelling of dismal grey that's visited by a great light in disguise. Where hope and love is crushed, beaten, and murdered only to rise up even stronger than before. The analogies just never stop in *The Vault Between Spaces* and author Chawna Schroeder never fails to excite my imagination. Sometimes heart-wrenching, frequently edge of your seat, this is one read you will NOT want to miss."

—MICHELLE GRIEP, Christy Award-winning author of the Once Upon a Dickens Christmas series

"Chawna Schroeder has a gorgeous way with words. Her delicious descriptions transported me straight into the fantastical world of *The Vault Between Spaces*. The world building is reminiscent of C.S. Lewis but with a flair all its own. *Vault* is perfect for fans of Christian fantasy who are looking for a unique, intriguing tale packed with beautiful spiritual metaphors and deep redemptive significance."

—LINDSAY A. FRANKLIN, award-winning author of *The Story Peddler*

"*Vault* shows that beauty can be found in places of suffering. Love is often reflected in sacrifice. Freedom can be celebrated within the constraints of service. Chawna paints unseen realms amid an alternate history of our own world and invites us to watch them intersect. Imaginative, heart-wrenching, and soaring with hope."

—SHARON HINCK, author of *Hidden Current*

THE VAULT BETWEEN SPACES

Books by Chawna Schroeder

Beast
The Vault Between Spaces

THE VAULT

BETWEEN

SPACES

CHAWNA SCHROEDER

The Vault Between Spaces
Copyright © 2020 by Chawna Schroeder

Published by Enclave Publishing, an imprint of Third Day Books, LLC

Phoenix, Arizona, USA.
www.enclavepublishing.com

ISBN: 978-1-62184-113-5 (printed hardback)
ISBN: 978-1-62184-116-6 (printed softcover)
ISBN: 978-1-62184-114-2 (ebook)

Cover design by Kirk DouPonce, www.DogEaredDesign.com
Typesetting by Jamie Foley, www.JamieSFoley.com

Printed in the United States of America.

I dedicate this book first to
my Lord, the Creator of the universe.
Thank You for reminding me to stop and play a little.

And secondly,
to my parents, **Jim and Barb Schroeder,**
who gave me the freedom to play.

Without you, not only would there be no book,
there would be no author.

1

SHE APPEARED OUT OF NOWHERE.

One minute all was quiet at the country estate of the *archeras*, the high commander of Anatroshka. The next, an alarm in his private office tripped. When soldiers burst inside two minutes later, they found a young woman perched on the edge of the desk, swinging her legs as if she were waiting for them. Nothing had been removed from the office. Nothing was destroyed. The doors were still locked, the windows unbroken, and the safe untouched. Even stranger, the young woman didn't bother to resist arrest. Yet when interrogated, she refused to answer a single question, leading the chief agent on the case to declare her a dangerous skolops and a member of the Underground.

Or so the story in her file went.

The commandant of HopeWell eyed his newest prisoner over the top edge of the papers. Young woman? That was an exaggeration at best. The slender girl of porcelain skin might pass for fourteen years, fifteen at a stretch, but eighteen, the legal age of an independent adult? Never. But despite her young age, she showed none of the normal signs of a new arrival at the prison camp. Whereas others would defy him with glares or tremble before him in terror, this girl merely studied the uneven floorboards of his office with a quiet serenity that contradicted both her youth and her position.

With a scowl, the commandant shuffled again through the file, which had been delivered, along with the girl, by the curvaceous woman sitting opposite of him. Torrents of rain pounded against the tin roof, the noise filling the otherwise quiet room. A lightning bolt flashed outside the window; thunder shook the building with impatience.

Finally, the commandant tapped the papers into a neat pile and squared them with the corner of the battered desk. "Everything appears to be in order." His voice tightened at the word *appears*, making him sound none too pleased with that fact, and as if to underscore his displeasure, his lips pressed into a hard, flat line. He scrutinized the girl again. The tall, muscular sergeant guarding her only accentuated her youth. "She looks sickly."

"Looks deceive." The curvaceous woman tossed out the careless rejoinder on a cloud of cigarette smoke and leaned back in her chair. Though dressed in a well-fitted military jacket and skirt, she flaunted convention by crossing her legs at the knees, emphasizing their length. "You'll get plenty of miles out of her before she's boxed up. If nothing else, she's young, fresh, spirited, just the way men like them." Rising, she sauntered over to the prisoner, a feline grace marking each movement. She brushed a lock of limp ash-blonde hair from the girl's cheek, exposing her neck, and jabbed the end of the cigarette against the tender skin.

The girl flinched, yet her voice remained silent.

"You've made your point." Clipping the edges of his words, the commandant pressed his knuckles into the scarred desktop.

The woman stubbed her cigarette out and flicked it across the room and strode toward the door, her heels clacking like the report of a machine gun. "I'll return at my usual time to check on your progress." She lifted a black umbrella from the coat stand in the outer office and stepped into the stormy night. A bolt of lightning flashed, highlighting her dark form beneath the umbrella's hood. Then oily darkness swallowed her whole.

The commandant slammed the door on both the night and the woman. Over the years, headquarters had brought him the intellectual dissenter who threatened the state as well as the violent rebel who threatened society. But this newest prisoner, this *girl*, seemed incapable of endangering either.

Marching back to her, he grabbed her jaw and yanked it up. "Children! Is this what we hunt these days?"

Eyes blinked back at him, as unperturbed as a placid mountain lake and luminescent as stars. A pink blush blossomed across her cheeks, bringing with it a fiery heat and the spicy scent of cinnamon. Cursing, the commandant snatched his hand away, redness searing his fingertips as if he had grasped a live coal, not human flesh. He shook his hand to cool it off.

Outside, the pattering rain seemed to laugh at him. Blood rushed into his face, and his right hand flew upward, cracking against her cheek.

Her sharp inhale cut through the room.

The commandant narrowed his eyes. Was that all?

Slowly she raised her right hand, letting her left dangle from the handcuffs binding them together, and her fingertips probed the crimson streak etched into her pale skin. She shivered slightly.

With a snort, the commandant stalked back to his desk. "Whatever you knew, whatever you were no longer matters. You are now"—he glanced down at the top page of the stacked papers—"Prisoner 304, and I am your ruler, your master, your god. You will do what I say, when I say, how I say." He looked at her again. "Understood?"

The girl's slender shoulders rose, then fell.

"Answer me."

A hard glint flashed through her eyes, and a boom of thunder rattled the rafters. Then the glint vanished, leaving behind undisturbed tranquility. "I understand, sir." The soft words, her first since arriving, flowed from her mouth with the same unwavering confidence of a mighty river.

His eyes narrowed. "No, I think not. You still believe you'll return to the outside. You still believe there's hope. But no one has ever escaped. No one ever will." The commandant turned to the sergeant, who had observed the entire scene in silent stillness. "Take her to the Cellar. I'll deal with her tomorrow."

"Yes, sir." The sergeant snapped out a salute, then grabbed the girl's upper arm and marched her toward the exit.

The commandant, preceding them, opened the door and then stood back at mock attention. "Welcome to HopeWell."

AS MORNING DAWNED OVER HOPEWELL, IT REVEALED a monochrome landscape. Maybe vibrant colors once graced the camp, but if they had, they bled together long ago, painting the whole world in shades of dreariness. Ramshackle buildings constructed of weathered wood huddled beneath the low-hanging clouds of autumn. Transparent droplets tumbled from sagging roofs. The chain-link fence clanked out a death knell in the damp wind.

The prisoners of HopeWell fared no better. Forming two ragged lines in front of their cabins, men on one side and women on the other, they blended into their surroundings, resembling lumps of clay more than living creatures with their pale faces and faded clothing. Oh, a few—the healthiest of the group—stomped their feet and rubbed their arms in attempt to keep warm, but most merely stood with their shoulders scrunched and hands tucked beneath their arms. Even the commandant and the sergeant, when they finally made their appearance, were bundled so heavily they were more gray wool than flesh. As if fearing the loss of what little color they yet possessed, they barged through roll call, barking the next number before the previous one could account for his presence.

Reaching the end of the row, the commandant pivoted to

return to his office, where a fire waged war with the cold. But three steps into his journey, he stopped. The wind changed. While still seasoned with damp decay and the sting of smoke, the air carried something else—a sound, one which had never before breached the fence of HopeWell: singing. And if that weren't odd enough, this song didn't slide downward in broken lament or hammer at the world with rage. No, it floated and glided with the smooth grace of contentment and an occasional twirl of joyful abandon.

The commandant glared at the nearest prisoners. All devotedly studied the mud seeping through the cracks in their shoes, their lips sealed tight. Still the song flitted from note to note, the rattle of chain links and scraping of barbed wire unable to manacle this music made of pixie dust and fairy wings.

Turning on his heel, the commandant stalked away from the cabins. The sergeant, after dismissing the prisoners, scrambled after him, mud splashing his coat hem, scarf flapping behind. But even hurrying, he didn't catch up until the commandant halted at a cinderblock shed sunk into the ground. With a tin roof that almost touched the earth, the Cellar offered no way in or out except a single, squat door of reinforced steel, whose use required the humiliation of crawling on the knees. Despite all this, the airy music floated within.

One minute, then two ticked off as the commandant stood, unmoving at the paradox of any cheerful sound emanating from the Cellar. Only when the song ended did the commandant point at the door. "Open it."

The sergeant thrust a key into the lock and dragged the door open, allowing weak light to reveal the other side of the cinderblock. Identical to the outside, the blocks extended down to a cold cement floor sunk several feet below grade, reached by iron rungs bolted into the wall.

"304!"

Nothing stirred. No sound responded. Each breath, each

heartbeat mocked the commandant's order. The prisoners, crouched in the shadows of nearby buildings, exchanged looks. Some were open mouthed in wonder at such bold defiance. Others—those who had endured prison life the longest—shook their heads at such arrogant stupidity. One grizzled old man leaned against a wall and folded his arms across his chest, eyes watchful and expression guarded.

The commandant stepped closer to the Cellar just as the top of a head covered in ash-blonde hair poked out of the door. The rest of the girl followed, and with a lightness that defied explanation, she rose to her feet without making a sound. Only the brown smears on her palms and knees bore testimony that she touched the ground at all as she crawled out.

She turned her head, gaze methodically traveling across the surrounding area, as if to catalog all the details missed the evening before. At the sight of the grizzled old man, she dipped her chin ever so slightly in greeting.

The commandant tensed, daylight confirming the previous night's impression. This prisoner was nothing more than a pale girl of fragile bone structure, which would shatter under the slightest force. A child. One who should be trembling in fear, easily intimidated, easily broken. Instead, her relaxed posture conveyed neither defiance nor fear.

What was he to do with this? He had broken the rebellious. He had terrorized the cowardly. He had intimidated the strong and crushed the arrogant. But what to do when there was no defiance to break, no arrogance to crush, no fear to cultivate? Yet terrorize, crush, break he must. The commandant grabbed the girl's jaw, his glove providing a thin barrier between them. "All singing will be punished."

Silence.

"Understood?"

"Yes, sir." Her words flowed out smoothly, void of any spark of anger or crack of fear.

He tightened his grip until she drew in a quick breath, then shoved her away. "Lock her back up. No food for the rest of the day." He marched past the sergeant, sending the other prisoners scurrying around corners and into shadows.

The sergeant faced the girl. Rattling the keys, he broadened his stance, muscles coiled to meet any resistance. "Inside."

She searched his face, and the depths of her gaze thrust him back a full step. "I'm so very sorry." Her soft voice extended not an apology, but sympathy. Then turning, she disappeared into the Cellar as quietly as she had emerged.

2

AFTER THE GIRL ARRIVED AT HOPEWELL, LIFE continued on much as it always had. Gray skies oppressed. Damp, autumn winds chilled. Prisoners woke each day to sharp words, tasteless food, purposeless work, and an endless misery escapable only by death.

Yet after she arrived, everything changed.

Not that the changes were obvious, not at first. Upon her release from the Cellar, she was assigned work and a bunk in a drafty cabin, just like other new prisoners. And like other prisoners, she received the scanty rations of food with a side of cutting remarks from the guards. But unlike the other prisoners, not a word of complaint crossed her lips. In fact, few words left her mouth at all as she moved among the prisoners with the silence of an apparition. Except apparitions were supposed to be invisible and she was anything but, an awareness of her presence infiltrating the consciousness of each and every person.

When she walked into a room, shadows retreated. When her hand brushed another's, a flare of warmth eased the cold. And though she had not sung since her first morning at HopeWell, both prisoners and guards often paused in their work when she passed by, certain their ears overheard a soft strain of lilting music. For the first time in his career, the commandant eyed the mountain of paperwork required to transfer a prisoner. Instead, he sent her back to the Cellar on a technicality.

When she was released three days later, two other prisoners

awaited her. Without a word they escorted her across the camp. Without a word she submitted to their lead as others watched, guards smirking and prisoners concerned. Even the commandant monitored their progress until they entered Cabin Twelve on the men's side of the camp.

At first glance, Cabin Twelve resembled every other cabin in HopeWell: a patched tin roof, dirt floors, a rickety table, and two benches surrounded by even more unstable bunk beds. It was an old place, a cold place, and very cramped. But during this midday break, one dark form lingered in a corner. The grizzled old man. Rising, he approached the trio and waved away the girl's escort.

The girl fixed her gaze on the ground according to her custom, leaving the old man free to inspect her at his leisure. HopeWell's toll on her could not be missed. Clothing, which fitted ill at the start, swamped her slim body. The lack of proper care had dulled her hair's luster. Cheekbones jutted out even more prominently than before, and dark smudges shadowed her eyes. Yet the beating of HopeWell extended no deeper than the physical. The same serene expression softened her face, and her bearing still exuded calm assurance.

"Look at me." The old man's voice rasped, but the grating tone, rather than undermining his authority, added weight to it: he'd seen it all and survived. Still, she hesitated a moment before she raised her eyes to him.

Although this was his first meeting with her, he'd heard the rumors about her unsettling gaze; gossip was one of the few things that thrived at HopeWell. But while others had laughed it off as the crazed imaginings of a few, the old man had listened. Now he faced that gaze himself, and it proved to be all that others had purported—and nothing like what they had said. Hers were ancient eyes, far older than any human should have, carrying the maturity and wisdom of time without the weight of years. Unsettling could not begin to describe such an encounter. Even so, the old man refused to blink first.

At his refusal, a smile brightened her eyes. The old man frowned. "Who are you?"

Instead of lowering her eyes as she was wont to do, the girl tipped her head in consideration. "That is a many-sided question, Mighty Prince of men."

"Your name, girl. I want your name. And without the flattery. That will get you nowhere."

"I am called . . . Oriel, Mighty Prince." She dipped her head in some strange bow of honor. "But in what have I spoken false sweetness?"

"I am not mighty nor a prince. I am a prisoner, the ninety-seventh prisoner. Nothing more." The old man dropped onto one of the wobbly benches by the table.

Her hand alighted on his shoulder, something troubling the depths of her eyes for the first time since she'd arrived at HopeWell. "But Mighty Prince . . ."

He grabbed Oriel's wrist, and with a twist, shoved her away from him. "Do not *ever* touch me again."

A red handprint stained her skin where he'd grabbed her, and Oriel rubbed her wrist absentmindedly. "Then it's true. You have forgotten."

"I have survived. And if you want to survive, you'll forget too." Turning his back on her, he pulled out a block of wood and a crudely filed piece of metal, one end wrapped in a rag. He began to whittle, flaking off small curls of wood. "Do you know why you were brought here?"

Quiet answered him.

"You're disturbing the commandant. When the commandant is disturbed, prisoners die. Lots of prisoners." The impromptu knife sliced deeper into the wood. "That's not happening on my watch."

"And what would you have me do, Mighty Prince?"

Stabbing the knife into the tabletop, he whirled around. "Stop calling me that."

"No." The single word echoed through the cabin, strong and uncompromising.

He leaned back, as if not sure how to respond. Then he shrugged. "You will not last the winter. Do not expect me to shed tears at your departure." Facing the table again, he tugged at the knife, but his anger had buried it deep into the wood, and it refused to pull free.

"I do not expect any tears, least of all from you." Reaching around his shoulder, Oriel slid the blade out of the wood as if it was butter softened by a summer's sun. Then she laid the knife on the table and walked out of the cabin.

He picked up the knife, still warm from her brief touch, and light glinted off the metal. The dinted and uneven blade shone smooth, polished, and honed to a razor's edge.

THE AFTERNOON'S WORK ASSIGNMENT PLACED ORIEL with the rock movers.

Like most prisoner tasks at HopeWell, it was a pointless job. The pile of boulders might look important, stacked at the south end of camp, but it existed solely for moving to the north side and back again, a way to determine if evening rations were deserved. With each rock weighing twenty-plus pounds, the grueling work was usually reserved for the healthier men—unless the commandant wished to punish a particular person or drive a wedge between prisoners.

Today, both seemed intended. Time after time the guards directed Oriel to the larger boulders. Time after time Oriel did as told, not uttering a word of complaint despite the cold rain numbing the fingers and making the boulders harder than normal to handle.

The overseeing guard stopped another prisoner hefting one of the larger rocks. "Not you. Her." He pointed to Oriel just trudging up, her slipshod shoes sliding on the soggy mud.

The prisoner set his jaw and held the rock out to her. She accepted it with a nod—even a thank-you could be punishable when the guards felt surly—and turned northward, the overseer shadowing her.

Oriel passed the Pits, where the grizzled old man removed mud from a waist-deep hole with a flimsy scoop. His eyes tracked her progress rather than his work, his hands conditioned by years of repetition to dig out what another would fill.

Reaching the north pile, Oriel added her boulder and turned to retrace her steps. The overseer blocked her way. "Not down here. Up there." He pointed to the crown of the heap.

She looked up at a pile taller than she.

"Hurry up."

Oriel hoisted the stone and began to climb, her brow furrowed in concentration. Her foot skidded, slamming her shoulder-first into the pile, but she managed to hold onto both the rock and her cry.

"Faster!"

Oriel struggled up, face pale and arms trembling. Prisoners and guards alike paused to watch. One, two, three steps. Almost there. She leaned into her next step, raising her load to dump it on the top. The boulder beneath her foot broke loose. Her shoe slipped. Down she tumbled, her body crashing into the rocks again and again before landing in an awkward heap at the bottom.

A collective gasp spiked the air.

"Is she—"

"It's an act." The overseer stalked toward Oriel's unmoving body. "Get up." He kicked her side. "Now."

Prisoner Ninety-Seven drove his scoop into the mud. "I

wouldn't do that if I were you."

"Silence, old man, or you're next."

He shrugged and leaned against the edge of the pit. "Your life."

The overseer glanced around. Over three dozen prisoners circled the scene, most of them able-bodied men with clenched fists and folded arms. Several bore various tools like the scoop, which despite their flimsiness could still inflict plenty of damage.

"Fine. Take her to the healers' cabin. Then finish your work and hers." The overseer shoved past the circle of prisoners.

Prisoner Ninety-Seven climbed out of his hole and knelt beside Oriel, resting a palm on her chest.

Another prisoner edged forward. "Is she—"

"She lives." He gathered Oriel in his arms. "Get back to work." Cradling her against him, he crossed HopeWell with a speed and agility that defied his age.

As they neared the healers' cabin, Oriel's eyes fluttered open. A small smile appeared among the grime. "Mighty Prince of men." Her words came out more a murmur than anything else, yet clearly bore the satisfaction of an I-told-you-so. Then her eyes closed, her body once more going limp.

With utter gentleness, Prisoner Ninety-Seven laid her on a bed in the healers' cabin and pulled a blanket around her shoulders. The back of his hand brushed a strand of hair from her face. Then he left, spine straight and head held high.

3

AT THE OPPOSITE END OF HOPEWELL, BEHIND THE
commandant's office, knelt an elderly woman working among the
twisted vestiges of a summer garden. Harvest had ended weeks
ago, but for Maggie, the stalks crumbling toward the earth only
signaled the next stage of the garden's care. Today that meant
digging holes along the muddy trenches where she buried bits of
rotted food to prepare the soil for next spring's seedlings.

Though not a prisoner at HopeWell, Maggie spent more time
inside the wire than outside it. She slept among summer's vines
and stalks, lullabied by the crackling of her precious charges'
growth. During autumn's colder days, Maggie displayed a strange
reluctance to leave, curling up in any corner she could find—an
empty bed among the prisoners, the seat of an unlocked truck, a
dark corner of the office. Only when the commandant wearied
of her wanderings and mutterings would she be escorted out of
the camp. But whenever the sun once again warmed the earth,
Maggie would show up at the gate in her dress that was more
patches than material, a basket of seedlings upon her arm.

That expulsion, however, had not yet come this year, and
until it did, she worked, her pace slow but steady, though the
rain pounded her bent back and dripped off—and through—her
sagging straw hat. Like its mistress, the hat had seen better days,
but its lack of protection didn't bother Maggie. Rain went with
dirt and plants and sunshine, which meant it went with her.

Then mid-row Maggie stopped, arrested by the same tension

immobilizing the rest of the camp. The rain alone ignored the strain and continued to fall unheedingly.

A snarl of indistinct words lashed out against the brittle restraint, shattering the stillness. Other words followed, and soon normal sounds picked up where they'd left off. Yet while activity resumed elsewhere, Maggie remained unmoving, her head cocked, listening to something no one else could hear.

Brandon Toxon, the young sergeant, strode along the southern perimeter of the garden. "Of all the miserable, rotten weather . . ." He tugged his coat collar higher, then paused, squinting at Maggie. "Old Mags?"

She didn't stir.

Brandon scanned the surrounding area, and upon seeing no one else about, crossed the trenches until he was within an arm's length of her. "Mags? Are you all right?"

Maggie continued to stare, not acknowledging his presence in any way.

He reached out to her, but before he could touch her, Maggie lurched forward with a gasp: Out from between two buildings appeared HopeWell's longest resident carrying the petite form of HopeWell's newest. Maggie stumbled to her feet and hobbled toward them. Brandon, after another furtive glance, followed her.

As Maggie reached the door of the healers' cabin, Prisoner Ninety-Seven stepped out. His eyes flicked from Maggie to the young sergeant shadowing her, then back to Maggie. She raised her face in inquiry. He nodded once before striding away.

"The rumors be true?" She shuffled toward the worksite in pursuit of Prisoner Ninety-Seven, only to stop again. A melody, inaudible yet inexplicably present, called from the interior of the healers' cabin. Like one drawn by a siren's song, Maggie hobbled inside, the dim interior lit by a stark bulb.

At Maggie's entrance, a woman leaning over a nearby bed straightened up. "Old Mags?" Setting aside the rag she'd been using to clean off Oriel's face, she wrapped an arm around the older woman and put a steadying hand under her elbow. "Is something wrong?"

Maggie waved the woman off with a flutter of her hand, thin and gnarled like the roots she worked among. She knelt at Oriel's bedside, eyes never leaving the girl.

When neither stirred further, the healer returned to cleaning up Oriel, stitching up a gash and bandaging others, with an occasional sideways glance at Maggie. "Can I get you anything, Mags?"

She shook her head.

"Okay, I'm here if you need anything. Just say the word." The healer moved down a few beds to check on another patient moaning in delirium.

Another minute passed. Maggie stretched a hand toward Oriel and brushed a knobby knuckle against the girl's pale cheek. Warmth flared at contact, drawing a gasp from Maggie.

"Mags?" The healer hurried back to the elderly woman's side.

Maggie lifted her face to the healer, weak light glinting off dampness on her cheeks. "She's real."

"Yes, yes. She's real." The healer guided Maggie to the bed nearest Oriel's and rubbed Maggie's back like a mother soothing a child. "Let me get you something to drink while you rest. It has been a tough day for everyone." She scurried toward the other end of the cabin.

If Maggie heard, it didn't show. All her attention rested on Oriel, who now returned her gaze. A tear wended its way through the furrows of Maggie's cheek. "Ye don't belong here."

"Neither do you." Oriel's eyes burned brightly in the dim light.

"I belong nowhere." Maggie picked at the edge of a patch almost as old as the dress itself.

"He has not forgotten you. He cannot, especially His Jewels."

Her hands stilled their picking.

Oriel reached across the narrow aisle, her fingers stretching just far enough to rest on Maggie's wrist. "Don't be afraid. He has heard and treasured every word."

Maggie's head lowered, her hat hiding her face from view. "It's been too long. It's too late."

"He's never late."

"They'll never let ye go."

"They cannot hold me."

At Oriel's confident pronouncement, the cabin door creaked. But the healer brought Maggie her drink at that moment, leaving Brandon free to escape the scene unnoticed.

THE NEXT DAY, THE WEAK SUNSHINE OF LATE autumn stepped at last from the heavy blanket of clouds. Though its threadbare rays offered little warmth, HopeWell's residents gravitated toward any patch of sunlight they could find. Soldiers spent inordinate amounts of time checking the camp's perimeter. Rock haulers veered from their normal paths to trudge through bright strips between the cabins' shadows. One of the healers set up a bench with a couple of crates and an old board for those well enough to totter outside.

Oriel sat at one end of the bench, a splinted leg extended before her and head swathed in bandages. Despite the apparent injuries, warmth and the song she never audibly sang flowed around her, causing a hitch to the gait of any person who passed by, be it prisoner or guard.

Near midday, the other patients retired inside, leaving Oriel alone on the bench, her head bowed over the sock she was darning; even illness and injury did not excuse a prisoner from working.

A shadow fell across her work. It was the young sergeant.

Though Brandon didn't speak, his broad stance and folded arms demanded she acknowledge him.

Instead, Oriel brought the sock closer to her face, peering at the tiny black stitches as she wove her needle among them. "You're in my light."

Brandon's face grew red. "I could have you thrown into the Cellar for that."

"You could." Oriel knotted the thread. "But you won't." She clipped the end and set the sock aside with the others she'd already finished.

"Are you certain of that?"

"I am, for words would now be action rather than the only action being words." Oriel pulled another sock out of the pile and wiggled her hand inside it, fingers poking out the hole in the toe.

Brandon pressed his lips together and turned away.

"She needs you."

Oriel's voice halted the young sergeant in his tracks.

"You need her even more."

Brandon's shoulders grew taut. "What are you talking about?"

"Who."

"What?"

"No, not what. Who. Maggie."

"Old Mags?"

"She prefers Maggie."

"Don't tell me about the preferences of my—" He snapped his mouth shut.

Oriel raised her eyes to him. "Your grandmother?"

"One of my village's crazies," Brandon said, wheeling about.

Oriel neither flinched nor looked away. Rather, sadness troubled the depths of her eyes.

Prisoner Ninety-Seven rounded the corner of the cabin, a small tray in his hands. At the sight of the two silent combatants, his step hitched. "I brought you dinner." Although his words were directed toward Oriel, his frosty tone sliced toward Brandon. Oriel laid the sock aside so she could receive the tray. Beside a chunk of stale bread and a bowl of broth, a handful of wood slices were heaped in a small pile. Oriel fingered one as if not sure what to do with it.

Ninety-Seven shifted. "I have"—he cleared his throat—"had a friend like you once. He said sucking on those helped restore his strength."

Oriel put one into her mouth and sighed; a light flush blossomed across her cheeks. "Thank you, Mighty Prince. Just what I needed." She slid the rest of the wood into her pocket.

Brandon stared at them. "You're as crazy as Old Mags."

A smile curled one corner of her mouth. "Crazier." She cupped her hands around the bread, eyes closing.

Brandon shook his head. "The whole world's gone mad." He pivoted to walk away once more.

Oriel broke off a bite of bread. "I still plan to, by the way."

Brandon ground to a halt. "Plan to what?"

"Escape."

At her announcement, Prisoner Ninety-Seven's head reared backward. Brandon stiffened into a statue.

Oriel sipped some broth to wash down the hard bread, showing no sign she had just uttered the unthinkable. "That's why you sought me out, was it not? To dissuade me?"

A harsh laugh burst forth from Brandon's mouth. "A waste of time, I see. But you'll learn." He adjusted the gun slung across his back. "If not now, then with your last breath."

4

AFTER BRANDON'S DEPARTURE, A TENSE SILENCE
settled into the void left behind. In the distance, doors slammed
and voices called to each other, but between Oriel and Prisoner
Ninety-Seven all conversation crumbled to dust.

Yet as Oriel munched on her bread, a smile hovered on her
lips. Unlike Prisoner Ninety-Seven. Turbulent shadows brewed in
his eyes, darkening his scowl with every passing second. "I forbid
it." His words struck at Oriel with all the fire of a lightning bolt.

Which she absorbed without a quiver. "I thank you for the
food, Mighty Prince." Finishing the broth, she placed the dented
bowl on the metal tray with the care of handling porcelain. "It
strengthens the body and lightens the spirit." Picking up the
unfinished sock, she resumed her darning.

Prisoner Ninety-Seven stepped closer, casting a shadow over
her work. "Did you hear what I said?"

She peered at the sock's toe, pulling dark threads across the
hole. "I heard."

"Good." He snatched up the tray, causing the dishes to clatter.

"But I will not—cannot—do as you request."

Her refusal caused him to sputter. "Of all the fool—are you
determined to cost us our lives?"

"I intend to cost no one anything." Though Oriel's words
were soft and firm, her hands trembled, and she struggled to
weave the needle through the stringy web.

"Intention or not, that is what will happen. So banish that
notion from your head once and for all."

Oriel's shoulders sagged "Have you never wished, Mighty Prince, to go home?"

His fingers tightened around the tray. "I have no home."

"Surely there is someone—"

"No one." Then he muttered, "Not anymore."

Oriel pursed her lips, then nodded as if in agreement to some unspoken word. "What happened?" She poked her needle through the sock.

"None of your business."

Oriel pushed the needle over and under, waiting. At the lack of reaction, Prisoner Ninety-Seven flattened his mouth further. "I killed a man."

Oriel's needle wove over and under, over and under.

"I do not regret it."

She packed her weave tighter together before starting the needle's return trip.

"If I could do it over, I would kill again."

She knotted the thread and clipped the end.

"Have you nothing to say?" he demanded. "Too disappointed in your mighty prince?"

"You are not the first prince to kill." She added the socks to her mended pile and rose, leaning on her crutch. "You will not be the last."

THE WIND STRUCK HOPEWELL AS WITH A mighty hammer.

The weather had been dreary all week, but now icy drafts triggered bone-rattling shivers in prisoners and guards alike. With the night's descent, the attacks grew more vicious still. The beams groaned at each strike, threatening to collapse. The men of Cabin Twelve pulled blankets to their chins. Not that the ratty cloth would provide any protection against the chilly night or structural implosion, but such pretenses were necessary if anyone hoped to sleep.

After one particularly brutal hammering, the wind retreated with a shriek, and an ear-ringing silence wrapped around the camp. One by one the men relaxed against their hard pallets. Maybe a little sleep would be possible . . .

Flesh thudded against wood. The men whose bunks flanked the door pushed onto their elbows. "Did that sound like—"

"Yeah." A man flung aside his blanket and rolled out of bed. He yanked the door open.

Cold air barreled through the opening. A round of curses spewed from the other prisoners, but the man ignored them. The door banged against the wall as he stooped over the crumpled shadow huddled on the threshold. "Old Mags!"

At the mention of HopeWell's wanderer, men scrambled from their beds. As Maggie was brought inside, two men wrestled the door closed against the raging wind while a candle stub was unearthed. Others helped Maggie to the table. Several men offered her their blankets. Prisoner Ninety-Seven pushed through the knot of activity. "Quiet!"

Instantly questions about Maggie's wellbeing faded, and the men retreated to provide the pair breathing room.

Prisoner Ninety-Seven crouched in front of Maggie. The flickering flame of the candle twisted and warped the shadows around them, further accentuating the grim lines of Ninety-Seven's face. Maggie had visited Cabin Twelve only once before, a night that had devolved into one of HopeWell's worst.

Maggie rocked back and forth, hands covering her face. "Gone, gone, gone." Her old hat flopped in time with her words. "Gone, gone, all gone."

"Old Mags." Prisoner Ninety-Seven cupped her icy hands in his.

Maggie continued to rock, eyes squeezed shut.

"Maggie."

She stilled, and after a moment, raised her face to his. Her eyes glinted with fevered mania.

Prisoner Ninety-Seven leaned forward, keeping a firm hold on her. "What happened, Maggie?"

Tears spilled down her weathered cheeks. "She's gone. All gone."

"Who?" He squeezed her hands, as if that would keep her mind from drifting. "Who's gone?"

"*Her.*" Pulling away from him, Maggie wrapped her arms around her middle, her bony frame shuddering. She hunched forward, rocking harder than before.

Prisoner Ninety-Seven rose. "Get her warm if you can. I'll be back." Heading to the door, he added under his breath, "I hope," and stepped into the night.

The old man crisscrossed the compound; his many years at HopeWell had familiarized him with the camp's patterns long ago. With ease he dodged both searchlights and patrols, and soon his knuckles rapped against the door of Cabin Nine, where Oriel had returned two days before.

A wide-eyed woman peeked out, and upon seeing him, opened the door. He scanned the cabin. Women huddled around the table, faces ghostly pale in the light of their single candle. The woman who opened the door shook her head, confirming what his eyes already saw.

Oriel was not there.

Ninety-Seven pushed back into the night. Where to now? He hovered in the shadows between the cabins, feet spread against the buffeting wind. The searchlight passed by once . . . twice. Yet he remained where he was, his head turning in measured increments as if probing for things far beyond his vision. At the direction of the commandant's quarters, Prisoner Ninety-Seven paused in his searching. If Oriel's disappearance were reported now, the rest of the camp might be spared the commandant's wrath. Maybe.

Instead, Ninety-Seven continued his scan of the night. When his focus reached the northern section, he hesitated again, then stepped from between the cabins.

The wind lunged at him. He ducked his head and plowed forward, not slowing again until he reached the last cabin.

The searchlight swept by, illuminating a guard on his rounds along the fence. Prisoner Ninety-Seven pushed back into the shadows. He counted slowly to three, then edged out once more. The guard was far enough along the perimeter to overlook him. Ninety-Seven sprinted for the lone building in this section: the Cellar.

The wind howled, gust after gust pummeling him, its chill flaying every inch of exposed skin. He grunted. "I'm not here to hurt her, you fools."

The wind died, and at its sudden withdrawal, he stumbled a couple of steps before regaining his balance. A dozen more steps and he pressed a trembling hand against the wall of the Cellar. Around the corner curled the scent of cinnamon carried on a strand of warmth and an impression of music.

He rushed to the north face of the building, nearly tripping over Oriel tucked deep in its shadows.

Oriel ignored his arrival, intent on studying a section of the fence. Yet its poles, chain links, and barbed wire matched the rest of the poles, chain links, and barbed wire surrounding HopeWell.

Prisoner Ninety-Seven grabbed her arm. "Time to go."

"Go?" Oriel looked up at him. "No, not yet." She allowed him to lead her back toward the cabins but cast one last glance over her shoulder at the fence. "But soon, Mighty Prince. Very soon."

THE SCENE IN THE COMMANDANT'S OFFICE A WEEK later mirrored the tableau from the night of Oriel's arrival. The commandant sat behind his desk while Oriel stood before him, hair bedraggled and clothing sopped from working in the rain. Brandon once again guarded her, silent and motionless as a wood post. And Agent Kasam, the woman who had delivered Oriel to HopeWell, smoked a cigarette from the same chair as before, her long legs once more crossed at the knees. Although rain hammered against the roof, just like on that memorable night, the light of a gray afternoon filtered through the windows, and the redness of simmering anger tainted the commandant's face.

He thumped a three-inch stack of papers on his desk and shoved them toward the woman. "I've done all the necessary work. Now get her out of here." He sank back into his chair with the weight of one completing an arduous task.

The woman lazily spewed a stream of smoke into the air. "You should have spoken to me first, Commandant."

He glared at her. "I cannot be talked out of this."

"Has she stirred the prisoners to riot?"

"No."

"Has she sabotaged any property?"

"No."

"Has she turned your men against you?"

"No."

"Has she attempted to escape?"

"Not yet, but I have it from different sources—*reliable* sources—that she plans to."

Agent Kasam laughed. "Many plan, few execute, Commandant. Which means she stays."

"Stays?" The commandant half rose out of his chair.

"Stays. As you would know if you had consulted me first."

"But the paperwork—"

"Irrelevant." Agent Kasam waved his protest away. "She's a Class One."

"Class One?" Color drained from the commandant's face, his gaze darting toward Oriel. She, of course, found the floorboards infinitely more fascinating. "Her?"

"I told you before. Appearances can be deceiving. She cannot be transferred from HopeWell for any reason short of burning down the camp, and if she succeeds in that, more than her will be transferred." Agent Kasam ground out the cigarette against the arm of the chair and flicked the remaining butt away.

A light sheen of sweat accumulated on the commandant's forehead.

Uncrossing her legs, the woman stood. "Of course, if you are having difficulties breaking her, I'd gladly assist." She scraped a long nail across Oriel's cheek. Though she applied no obvious pressure, a ridge of scarlet welled up in her nail's wake. A small smile twisted Agent Kasam's lips. She gathered the blood on her nail and sniffed it, like one testing the quality of wine before drinking. The metallic aroma carried the sharp scent of fire, widening her eyes.

The commandant also rose, the taut muscles along his jaw declaring his refusal. "I'll keep your offer in mind."

Agent Kasam's fixation broke. Lowering her hand, she retrieved a handkerchief and wiped off her nail.

"We can inspect the rest of the camp at your leisure." The commandant waved toward the door.

"Yes, I suppose we must." Agent Kasam's gaze lingered on the scratch she had inflicted. Then she lifted her chin and strode out of the office.

The commandant circled his desk to follow, but after a glance at the doorway, he leaned toward Oriel. "I'm not the idiot they suppose. There's no way you can be a Class One. Who are you really? Whom do you work for? Did *they* send you?"

Rain pounded against the tin roof, emphasizing her silence. The commandant backhanded her. "My patience thins. Why are you here?"

Oriel pressed a hand to her inflamed cheek. "My Master is greater than you know. It is His purpose I have come to fulfill. And what He purposes, He does, for His will cannot be thwarted."

What color remained in the commandant's face drained away. Then the outer office door opened. "Coming, Commandant?" called Kasam.

At her query, the commandant inhaled again. "Coming!" Then lowering his voice, he turned to Brandon. "Take her to my quarters, Sergeant. We'll finish this conversation there."

5

THE INSPECTIONS OF HOPEWELL ALWAYS FELT
laborious to anyone involved. But the inspection following the
commandant's attempt to transfer Oriel would have given a
snail enough time to traverse the entire length of the camp and
return again, as Agent Kasam insisted on inspecting the *entire*
camp. Which meant every door had to be opened, every corner
examined, every mattress poked, every prisoner interviewed.
Minutes crawled by. Hour inched into hour. The rain let up,
but heavy moisture clung to everyone and everything within
reach. More and more often the commandant swiveled his head
toward his quarters where Oriel awaited.

When he lagged behind the sixth time, Agent Kasam asked,
"Something the matter, Commandant?"

The commandant snapped his attention back. "Of course
not." He strode forward, launching into the next droning spiel
about the current balance of food supplies.

Finally, after nine hours, long after the sun had surrendered
to the night, Agent Kasam climbed into her car and drove away.
The bar thudded across the gate; the entire camp released a
collective breath, guards slumping at their stations and prisoners
collapsing to the muddy ground after their extra-long workday.
Only the searchlight continued its relentless hunt for escapees,
never mind that all were sprawled out on the ground too tired to
contemplate crawling to bed, much less climbing the fence.

Then the commandant marched across the compound,

snapping out commands. "Get those prisoners into their cabins. Start the night patrols. Secure the perimeter."

Guards slogged back into motion, and soon orders rang throughout the camp as prisoners were herded toward bed.

The commandant scaled the porch steps and rested his hand on the door to his quarters, but instead of barging inside, he tightened his grasp on the knob. Finally, after several seconds, he thrust the door open and entered the front room of his quarters.

Though not large, the lit room compensated for its size with unexpected coziness. Thick rugs softened the wooden floor. A narrow table to the right held a bowl of colorful apples and his now-cold dinner, while a sideboard offered an array of maroon- and amber-toned drinks. To the left, a deep wingback chair, a half-read novel splayed on its arm, sat at a right angle to a blanket-draped sofa boasting a collection of plump pillows. A fire danced in the hearth, providing warmth and a rosy glow. And at the far end of the room, opposite the front door, stood Oriel, facing an old grandfather clock.

The commandant slammed the door. Oriel kept her back to him, neither jumping nor facing the noise. A confident and fearless position—or one hopelessly foolish and naïve. Which was she?

The young sergeant stepped out of the shadows, ready to aid the commandant with his coat. The commandant waved him away, hanging his coat on the wall hook for himself. "Leave us."

Brandon saluted in acknowledgement and departed, seemingly unnoticed by the commandant, whose gaze never strayed from Oriel. Moving to the sideboard, he poured some of the amber liquid, stepped over to Oriel, and extended the glass to her.

Oriel remained fixated on the clock's face. "I prefer the fruit of the vine, sir."

Fire reddened the commandant's cheeks; the pendulum ticked off seconds. One . . . two . . . three. At the fifth click, the commandant marched back to the sideboard and reached for a different decanter.

"Don't bother." A small sigh escaped her lips. "I'll only be disappointed."

His fingers strangled the neck of the decanter. "Why are you here?"

"Why do you persist in asking questions to which you already know the answer?" The murmured words, unguided by any alteration in body language, tumbled about the room, making it unclear whether Oriel spoke to the commandant, the clock, or the world in general. Then, "I am here to escape, sir."

"I knew it! Headquarters sent you to test me, didn't they? What kind of fool do they take me for?" He downed the drink he fixed for Oriel. "Two can play at this game."

"You are indeed being tested, sir, but not as you think."

He halted his pouring of a second drink. "Explain."

"An explanation will do no good; you will not believe it or accept it."

He rocked back on his heels, as if to physically halt his mental self-congratulations. Then he leaned forward again and finished pouring his drink. "You almost had me there, trying to confuse me with headquarters' doubletalk." He toasted her with his glass. "But I am onto you now. Your ruses will no longer work on me." He waved toward the door. "Dismissed."

Oriel turned to obey, looking at him for the first time since he arrived. Light sparked within her eyes. "Careful, Commandant. You're almost out of time."

Then she left, the clock striking eleven behind her.

DARKNESS GRIPPED THE MOUNTAIN. NO MOONLIGHT illuminated the rocky slope. No starlight danced around its peak. Only the headlights of a lone car pierced the inky night as it wended through treacherous switchbacks, and even then, the blackness, as thick and inescapable as a tar pit, ceded no more ground than absolutely necessary.

From the rear seat of that long-nosed vehicle, Agent Juliet Kasam stared at the impenetrable night. If its stranglehold perturbed her, her vacant expression masked the disturbance. Her makeup, however, was not nearly as successful in its role of maintaining a placid appearance. While applied flawlessly, the cosmetics could not conceal the dark circles beneath her eyes or the irritable pinch of her lips. A fortnight with almost no rest was taking its toll, and if she couldn't find the answers she sought tonight, sleep deprivation would force her to retreat until her body could recuperate. A small delay in theory—except retreat tasted like defeat, bitter and difficult to swallow.

The car turned up a gravel road to a wrought-iron gate set into an imposing stone wall. The gate opened, and the driver circled around to the blocky stairs of an ancient country manor. Its crumbling stonework and massive girth, more than twice as long as its towering four stories, bespoke of old wealth, yet its paned windows were as dark as the world they watched.

Opening Juliet's door, the driver offered her a hand. She ignored him, even though she wobbled as she stood. The driver frowned but held his tongue. His cheek already bore one set of scratches from the last time he expressed concern.

At the top of the stairs, a door swung inward, casting an electric glow across the steps and onto Juliet. She winced as if the illumination caused her physical pain, but she trudged upward, dismissing the driver with a flick of her hand.

Inside waited a butler, a skeleton shrouded in cracking skin. He bowed stiffly as Juliet entered the spacious foyer, which boasted a grand horseshoe staircase and an antique crystal chandelier converted to electricity. None of this opulence, however, attracted a second look from Juliet. She merely dropped her clutch purse on a chair, pulled off her black gloves, unpinned her hat, and handed over her coat with a routine matter-of-factness. "My supper?"

"Being laid out in your private library as we speak." Another bow followed his words, though Juliet was already crossing the foyer.

She ascended the stairs and walked down an unlit hall to a pair of mahogany doors left slightly ajar. Flickering light and the low crackle of a fire beckoned her inward.

Disarray and disorder dominated the library. Books were crammed into the floor-to-ceiling shelves at odd angles. Volumes and volumes wobbled in precarious towers on every surface available. Overturned tomes were scattered across the thickly carpeted floor. Whatever organization once held court here had long since fled, testifying to a growing frustration with a fruitless search.

Metal clinked, drawing Juliet's attention toward the fireplace opposite her. A young woman, her back to the door, arranged a tray of food upon a table beside a wingback chair. Her woolen skirt and coarse blouse stood out as rustically old-fashioned in comparison to Juliet's fitted jacket, knee-length skirt, and heels.

Upon seeing the younger woman, Juliet gave her first smile of the night, a twisted thing that darkened her face rather than brightened it. She stepped farther into the room and cleared her throat.

The young woman whirled, revealing a startling resemblance to the agent, despite a lack of makeup. They shared the same chestnut locks, oval face, delicate nose, slender mouth, and long, dark lashes. Yet their differences were as striking as their similarities. Juliet's eyes smoldered black. The young woman's sparkled a clear gold. Juliet's complexion was flawless. A puckered scar marred the younger's skin, forming a jagged ridge from hairline to jaw along the left side.

The young woman ducked her head and backed away. Bare feet and a dull metal band peeked out beneath her skirt's hem, and a metallic clank punctuated the fire's crackling. Cringing, she slowed her steps toward the door.

Juliet watched, bemused at this attempt to circumnavigate her. "Come here."

Steel undergirded the soft command, demanding instant obedience. Yet the young woman wavered for the minutest of moments, eyes darting to the open door and the hallway beyond. Then she shuffled toward Juliet and knelt at her feet, tugging down long sleeves over forearms crisscrossed with hairline scars.

Juliet ran her tongue over her lips as if savoring the taste of the young woman's fear. "You hesitated."

The young woman hunched forward, her fingertips digging into her thighs.

"I should send you down to Doctor Minio for such blatant disregard."

A sharp inhale stiffened the young woman's body.

The fire popped in the hearth; a flare of flames cast distorted shadows over the books. "Unfortunately, I haven't time to watch his experiments tonight. So . . . three days without food. That should be sufficient punishment. This time." Juliet flicked her finger in dismissal.

No further encouragement was needed. The young woman scrambled to her feet and darted out the door, heedless of how much noise she made.

"Witless shall be your name." Juliet tore a bite from the bread on the tray. "Someday I will enjoy draining your lifeblood drop by drop."

After washing down the bread with some wine, Juliet picked up a book on the table nearest her, a text on poison. She leafed through, then tossed it aside, choosing the next one in the stack, this one on the "humours of blood." That soon joined the first, and Juliet wandered along the bookshelves, finger running along the spines. "The answer is here. I know it. What am I missing?" She pulled book after book, only to shelve it again after a glance at the cover. "Smoke and blood. Blood and smoke. What would make blood smell like smoke? Smoke and fire and . . ." Her gaze fell on the hearth. "Could it be that simple?"

Striding to an ebony cabinet tucked in the corner, Juliet withdrew a small, silver key from under her blouse and unlocked the door. Inside, each narrow shelf bore a single, ancient tome. She slid out a particularly fat volume, its leather binding brittle and cracked with age, its pages threatening to crumble to dust. Faded block lettering filled the sheets with foreign words illuminated with starbursts, swirls of water, and lightning bolts. She reached a section adorned with flames.

Her long fingernail scraped down the text, her smile broadening with each successive line. She turned the page, revealing an illustration of a humanlike man engulfed in fire. His lower body smeared into one solid blaze. An aura surrounded his head and torso. Behind him the artist had drawn hundreds of individual flames.

Below the picture a caption read, "An Ishir."

6

THE DAYS CREPT BY AT HOPEWELL IN A MONOTONOUS blur. A week passed, then a month, with little to distinguish one unmemorable day from the next. Temperatures dipped, chilling both bone and ambition. Maggie left for the winter, returning to her home beyond the wire. Snow fell, adding a fresh layer of misery to the camp. Coats and hats were handed out to the prisoners, and Oriel accepted hers along with the rest, as if she had every intention of staying the winter. Gossip meandered onto new subjects with the delivery of a fresh batch of prisoners, leaving the commandant and Prisoner Ninety-Seven to watch the quiet girl.

Yet endless monotony dominated even their observations. Oriel rose at the same time as the other prisoners, ate when they ate, and retired when they retired. She arrived promptly to whatever task was assigned and worked through the day with nary a complaint, no matter how hard or tedious the labor.

Another month passed. Three more layers of snow accumulated atop the first. Tempers shortened with the days. The overall mood of the camp plummeted with the temperatures.

Hefting a rock, Prisoner Ninety-Seven turned from the pile of stones that the prisoners relocated there the day before, and he trekked back across the camp to return the rock to its former location. Breaths escaped his nose in small white puffs, their frequency the solitary sign of the labor's strain. A new prisoner cursed as he passed by. Prisoner Ninety-Seven shook his head. Cursing was a wasted expenditure of warmth and air.

Reaching the rock pile, the new prisoner hoisted an icy boulder and bumped shoulders with another man. The rock plunged from his numb fingers. With a new—and louder—string of curses, he leapt back, only to collide with Henri, one of the older prisoners.

Snarling, Henri wheeled on him. "Watch it!"

"You watch it." The younger man blew on his fingers, trying to warm them.

"I'm not the rag doll here."

The new prisoner stilled, then narrowed his eyes on Henri. "What did you call me, old dog?"

Henri leaned forward and over-pronounced his words. "Rag. Doll."

And with that, the first fist flew.

Immediately, five, six more men charged into the fray. The guards folded their arms and let the prisoners fight, tossing out comments to egg them on. "Come on, show a little backbone. You aren't going to let a little pain stop you, are you? He's not a man; he's a chicken. Hey, are you going to let him get away with that?"

News of the fight spread. Work halted. The circle of spectators grew. Guards herded over their charges so they could watch without neglecting their posts.

Prisoner Ninety-Seven scowled at the scene. Unchecked by the guards, the fight only gained momentum. But why should they stop it? They were bored, the brawlers provided free entertainment, and in the end, the guards wouldn't suffer the punishment for disorderly conduct.

He shouldered his way through the crowd. Most clung to their hard-earned spots, slowing his progress, but he was Prisoner Ninety-Seven, not some lightweight jockeying for a better position, and inevitably they ceded their position to him. Finally, he broke into the impromptu fight ring.

"Enough!" His voice sliced through the insults and yelling, grunts and jeering. The noise from the crowd—prisoner and guard alike—tapered away, leaving only the thuds and scuffs of the fighters.

Several brawlers paused mid-strike. Prisoner Ninety-Seven leveled each with a glare. The men hung their heads and slunk into the crowd, opening a clear path to the four men still battling it out.

Arriving at the first pair, Ninety-Seven shoved them apart. They whirled on him with fists raised, but when they saw who confronted them, they backed away. Which left Henri and the newbie.

Prisoner Ninety-Seven grabbed the shoulder of each. An elbow jabbed at him. He dodged it and pulled back the new prisoner. "Break it up."

The newbie shrugged him off. "Mind your own business."

"Henri—"

"Someone has to teach the pup a lesson." Henri swung at the younger man, who ducked and threw a return punch.

Around them feet shuffled, and a low murmur rippled through the crowd. News of the fight had extracted the commandant from the warmth of his office. No time for words remained. Prisoner Ninety-Seven dove between the men, and before anyone could do more than gasp, the two opponents made their acquaintance with the ground—Henri doubled over on his knees, nursing a bloody nose; the newbie sprawled on his back, gaping at the sky as if unsure how it got there. Ninety-Seven nodded at the men along the ring's front edge. They hauled the two defeated prisoners into the crowd.

Not a moment too soon, either. The next instant the commandant breached the perimeter on the opposite side. "What's going on here?"

Prisoner Ninety-Seven clasped his hands behind his back. "Nothing, sir."

The commandant poked at the blood-splattered snow with the toe of his boot.

Ninety-Seven cleared his throat. "An accident, sir."

"An accident." Icicles of sarcasm hung from the commandant's words in the frigid air.

"Yes, sir. An accident." The older man held his gaze steady.

"They're being treated now and will return to work within the hour. Sir."

The commandant bored his glare into Ninety-Seven, and when he didn't flinch, he scanned the crowd. Neither prisoner nor guard spoke up. "Humph. See that they do."

"They wi—"

A gust of wind smacked Prisoner Ninety-Seven in the face, freezing his words. The wind had been biting all day, but this . . . this stung with a temperature a dozen degrees colder than before. He jerked his head toward the north. "She didn't."

The commandant leaned forward. "Who didn't do what?"

Ninety-Seven ignored the commandant, his eyes probing for what couldn't be seen.

"Prisoner Ninety-Seven!" An extra layer of warning iced the commandant's words.

Ninety-Seven, instead of responding, shoved his way into the crowd. Guards and prisoners alike startled at his uncharacteristic behavior, which would be sure to earn him a painful reprimand later. It didn't matter. His course never deviated, his gait never hitched. Indeed, his speed even accelerated when he finally broke free of the crowd.

Only after reaching the Cellar did Prisoner Ninety-Seven slow his stride. But no extra heat warmed the air; no strain of music lingered nearby. Oriel's midnight hiding spot along the Cellar's north face was deserted. He leaned back, as if being dragged where he did not want to go, and raised his eyes to the fence.

Near the top, one of the crossbars hung askew, its charred end wafting smoke. As a result, a narrow opening gaped between chain links and barbed wire. And there, in the snow just beyond the barrier, two almost indistinguishable footsteps merged with the path of the beyond-the-wire patrol. At the sight, Prisoner Ninety-Seven curled his fingers around the chain links and pressed his forehead to the fence. He was too late.

Oriel had fled HopeWell.

7

THE NEWS OF ORIEL'S ESCAPE RICOCHETED THROUGH the camp. From the sickest prisoner in the healers' cabin to the night watchman still abed, all heard that the unthinkable had occurred.

A prisoner had breached the fence unseen.

Within minutes a blizzard of activity engulfed the camp. Off-duty guards were summoned and night sentries roused. Every building was thoroughly inspected and every prisoner interrogated. The commandant dispatched two squads to hunt for Oriel beyond the wire.

Prisoners clustered together, whispering resurrected plans of revolt. Guards barked at them to disperse, but orders couldn't eradicate the stubborn tilt to their chins or squelch the fire in their eyes. As soon as the soldiers turned their backs, conspiratorial whispers resumed.

The commandant ordered all prisoners confined to their quarters, but even there the rush of rekindled hope refused to die. Women chatted together in hushed voices. Men paced cabins as they plotted. Adrenaline surged through the veins of all at seeing the impossible become reality.

Except for Prisoner Ninety-Seven.

He returned to Cabin Twelve with shoulders bent, even though any punishment for his earlier erratic behavior was stayed until the commandant recovered Oriel, and he shook his head at the celebratory backslaps he received. He stretched out on the hard mattress of his corner bunk, back to the rest of the room.

The other men shrugged and continued their contemplations of what might be possible. Prisoner Ninety-Seven crossed his arms and closed his eyes, muttering to himself, "This changes nothing."

One hour extended into two, then three. The initial rush bled away, replaced by tense waiting. Oriel made it outside the wire, but how long could she evade the commandant? One girl on foot and ill-equipped, hunted by truck full after truck full of well-armed and highly trained guards? The prisoners' pacing altered rhythm from confident exaltation to coiled agitation. Yes, Oriel had breached the fence, but that was only the beginning. Now she had to elude every soldier combing the surrounding woods for her.

The cabin door banged open. Those lying down bolted upright. Those pacing halted. Brandon scanned the gaunt faces scrutinizing him. "Prisoner Ninety-Seven?"

The old man materialized from his corner. "Here."

"Follow me." The sergeant wheeled about.

Prisoner Ninety-Seven paused on the threshold. Clouds, which were depressing before, had darkened to an ominous shade of charcoal in the dwindling light, and plummeting temperatures dug icy claws into any bare skin. Thunder rumbled in the distance. The lines of his face tightened. "You brought her here; *you* protect her." He stomped after Brandon, snow cracking beneath his boots.

Brandon motioned Prisoner Ninety-Seven ahead into the main office, and then remaining outside, closed the door, leaving the prisoner alone with the commandant.

Leaning over his desk, the commandant flattened his palms along the edges of a local map. Lines and circles crisscrossed its surface, marking the progress of various units dispersed over the area. Such a scattering meant the guards had not found Oriel's trail yet, otherwise they would be converging on a centralized area.

The commandant's head snapped up, cold menace freezing

out every other emotion. "Where is she?"

Prisoner Ninety-Seven studied the window. Frost covered most of the panes, but not enough to obscure the increasing gloom outside. A storm was brewing. "You tell me."

The commandant shoved away from his desk. "You knew she planned to escape."

"So did you."

"She must have told you something."

"She told me nothing." One corner of his mouth twisted upward. "She wasn't the talkative type."

The commandant slammed his palms against the desktop, making pencils jump. "Tell me something I don't know!"

"What do you know?"

"That you skate on thin ice." The commandant's lip curled. "Or do you want me to line up the prisoners and shoot them one by one until I get some answers?"

"Dead bodies require explanation."

"I require answers."

Prisoner Ninety-Seven held his stance in disciplined stillness, a man made of stone, not flesh. The commandant stretched a hand toward the telephone on the corner of the desk.

A board creaked under Prisoner Ninety-Seven. "The girl seemed to have a special bond with Maggie." He returned his gaze to the frosted glass. A burst of snow veiled the world from sight.

"Maggie?" The commandant wrapped his fingers around the telephone's handset.

"Old Mags."

No response from the commandant.

"The villager woman who oversees your garden."

The commandant lifted his hand from the telephone. "Does the girl know where she lives?"

Prisoner Ninety-Seven shrugged.

"Does she know?"

"Unlike you, Commandant, I do not listen to private conversations."

The commandant's face reddened. Marching to the door, he jerked it open. "Sergeant, get him out of here."

Brandon saluted and stepped aside so that Prisoner Ninety-Seven could leave ahead of him. The older man strode out, ignoring the whiteout conditions created by the snow burst. By the time they reached Cabin Twelve, another truck rumbled toward the gate. Prisoner Ninety-Seven grasped the door, then glanced back at Brandon. "Warn your grandmother if you can. They're on their way."

THE FOREST CREAKED AND MOANED IN THE deepening twilight. How long must they stand shackled in this way, encased in snow, entrapped by cold, ensnared in darkness? Creator made them for warmth. Creator made them for light and life. Not for this death, this endless bondage to inescapable decay.

A wind swirled through the trees, and they strengthened their complaint. Oriel, skimming between them, winced and rubbed her ear. "I hear you, Ancient Ones, but even I cannot loose what Creator has bound." In the distance thunder rolled. Oriel nodded once and quickened her pace, steps light and a warm song trailing behind her. "Not long now."

A clattering rumble pinballed among the trees, drowning out their protests. Oriel ducked behind the substantial trunk of an old pine as a yellowish glare sliced through the forest; a military truck lumbered down the rutted road. Oriel pressed her back against the pine, hands flattened against the bark, as if willing the tree to absorb her into itself. Snow slid down the branches, bending them into a shield about her.

The truck clattered nearer and nearer . . . then passed by without slowing. Darkness settled in again. The rumble faded. Snow slipped off the branches, allowing them to spring up to their normal positions. Oriel rested one hand on the trunk and fisted the other over her heart. "Thank you." She paused. A glance at the surrounding forest confirmed she was alone. "I don't have much, but what I have, I give." Stooping, she pressed her palms against the ground. The snow melted and seeped into the dirt. A sigh rippled through the pine's boughs.

Oriel smiled up at the branches as she rose. "You're welcome." Brushing off her hands, she resumed her trot through the woods.

A feathery snowflake swirled by, then another and another until they peppered the air. Oriel merely plowed ahead, angling her path until it intersected with the road. The ruts, frozen into jagged ridges, threatened to snap the axel of any vehicle pushed too hard and the ankle of any creature running too fast. Oriel carefully picked her way along the left edge. Yet despite her close encounter with the truck, neither stealth nor haste marked her movements. If it weren't for her grayed prison clothing, she would be easily mistaken as a stranded motorist trying to return to town.

As she crossed over to the right side of the road, thunder rumbled overhead. Oriel frowned. "He will not fail." She glanced back toward HopeWell, though it was long out of sight. "He cannot." She veered into the forest again.

The falling snow thickened, filling her faint tracks as fast as she made them. Her gait never deviated, despite the low visibility, every step firm and sure as if guided by a sense other than sight. Then Oriel stopped, her brow wrinkling. She looked right, left, then right again, like a hiker deciding which fork to take of a path that split unexpectedly. She moved one step to her right.

A gunshot fractured the air.

Oriel stiffened. Stillness smothered the forest; even the trees complained no longer. A minute passed. Two. Oriel nodded.

Turning left, she accelerated into a sprint.

The wind picked up as well, pushing her along through snow falling denser than before. She dodged a low-hanging branch and leapt over a log half-buried in the snow. Neither obstacle slowed her steps. Then with a rustling shudder, the trees released her into open air. Oriel skidded to a stop, as if smacking into an invisible wall. With a gasp, she twisted and stumbled sideways, barely catching herself from landing in the snow. Doubling over, she braced one hand against her knee and pressed her other hand against her chest.

Thunder rumbled a third time, more distantly but with a driving sense of urgency. Face contorted in pain, Oriel stumbled up the small ridge of earth. Here the snow flew not as profusely, and between swirls of white, a small town was visible, hunkered down against the thundersnow in the earthen bowl below. Most of the buildings huddled together were dark, though one building near the center spilled light into the night.

A brittle wail drew Oriel's attention back to a shack several yards away, just beyond the lip of the bowl, the weathered boards illuminated by a truck's headlights. Maggie knelt in the midst of strewn clothing and furniture, her hat missing and hair disheveled. She clawed at the snow near an overturned basket. Around her, HopeWell guards dumped more of the shack's contents before a pacing corporal. Oriel staggered toward Maggie. "Grant me strength, Creator."

The corporal growled. "This is getting us nowhere." He jerked Maggie to her feet. "Where's the girl?"

Maggie rocked forward, clutching recovered seeds to her creased cheek. "My babies, my poor little babies."

The corporal shook her. "Answer my question, old woman."

"My poor little . . ." Maggie squinted at the ridge, as if sensing that Oriel raced to her rescue, though Oriel was far beyond the circle of light.

"No!" With unexpected strength, Maggie wrenched free.

"Away, away!" Scattering the seeds she'd collected, Maggie stumbled toward Oriel, past the beams of the headlights, flapping her arms to shoo the girl into the forest.

The corporal followed after Maggie but hesitated at the edge of the headlights' glare, the brightness diminishing his night vision. What if an ambush awaited? He readied his gun and waved at the soldiers. "Get some light over there, now!"

Flashlight beams bounced, and an engine rumbled as a soldier scrambled to turn the truck. Oriel wavered. Stay or go?

Then Maggie fell. Oriel rushed to the older woman's side. Maggie pushed her away. "Wolves be here. Fly away, quick!"

Before Oriel could respond, light spilled over them, stripping away the night's protection and contorting the corporal's face into an expression of demonic pleasure.

8

THE RUMBLE OF TRUCKS SOUNDED THE FIRST CALL of defeat. With their clattering heard in the farthest corners of HopeWell, their return could not be missed, even in the pitch-coated night, a return which could mean only one thing: a victor had been determined.

Prisoners clustered around windows and peered into the darkness. They twisted their heads at odd angles for a better view. A few of the braver men cracked open their doors. Whispers darted around the cabins, batting around various interpretations of the fractured shadows jostling amid scattered lights outside. Prisoner Ninety-Seven alone remained abed, his back turned to the rest of the room. His eyes stared blankly at the wall. A single teardrop trickled down a crease in his cheek. He had resided at HopeWell too long; he knew what the others did not. The commandant did not give up. If the trucks returned already, they returned with either a captive, or more likely, a body.

Shouts echoed outside. Lights converged on the front gate. Guards swarmed forward to disbar and pry it open. The hinges protested the midnight disturbance, and the cabins groaned in sympathy. But all eyes were fastened on the first truck lumbering through the gate. Prisoners poked and elbowed those with the best view. "What do you see? What's going on?"

A soldier broke away from the swarm, the bouncing ray of his flashlight darting toward Cabin Twelve. The men dove for their bunks. The door banged open. Brandon stomped across the threshold and snorted at the prisoners trying far too hard to look sleepy. He flicked his beam toward the back corner of the cabin. "Prisoner Ninety-Seven."

The older man entered the beam's grasp and squinted at the young sergeant, whose face was overhung with shadows. Ninety-Seven's shoulders drooped. "Let's get this over with." He passed Brandon, then paused a short distance from the cabin, his hands hanging limply at his side.

Thwack! Brandon's fist connected squarely with Ninety-Seven's jaw, snapping his head back. The older man grunted, then doubled over as the sergeant's flashlight struck his midsection. Brandon stepped back, allowing the prisoner to catch his breath and straighten up. Ninety-Seven squared his shoulders and readied for a second attack. It never came. He peered at the young sergeant, who scowled at him but was no longer rigid with tension. "That all?" Ninety-Seven probed the spot where Brandon's fist connected. "Maggie's resilience never ceases to amaze."

"No thanks to you." Brandon spun on his heel and strode toward the commandant's.

Prisoner Ninety-Seven followed, albeit at a slower pace, until he neared the trucks. Then he stopped altogether.

In front of him, a soldier leapt from one of the trucks. "Come along." He yanked out a smaller form—Oriel.

She stumbled, then regained her balance. Swaying unsteadily, she frowned at her cuffed hands. She tried to separate them, as if not understanding they were bound together.

"Keep moving." Brandon prodded Ninety-Seven forward, but he might as well have been trying to move a mountain.

Oriel's head lifted, and when her gaze met Ninety-Seven's, the murky confusion in her eyes dissipated. She leaned toward him, then gasped. Her eyes rolled upward, and she collapsed.

"Get up." The soldier poked her with the tip of his rifle. "Now!"

Oriel didn't move.

The soldier swung his boot at her, but instead of connecting with the girl, it struck Ninety-Seven, who had thrown himself over Oriel.

The soldier growled. "Why you—"

Prisoner Ninety-Seven surged upward, the odd lighting transforming him into a dark force of nature. The soldier choked on his words and clutched his weapon to his chest.

"You will not touch her." With each rumbling word, Prisoner Ninety-Seven seemed to grow taller and more powerful, causing the soldier to shrink backward. "Have I made myself clear?"

Brandon reached out to stop him. "You can't . . ." His words died at the glare he received—fiery, unflinching, the kind that belonged to a dragon protecting his horde of jewels. The sergeant retreated. One did not trifle with dragons.

Stooping, Ninety-Seven cradled Oriel in his arms and headed for the healers' cabin, guards parting before him without a murmur. Reaching the healers' he barged inside. "Blankets! I need blankets, as many as you can spare. And a length of rope, if you can find one."

"Rope?" A woman turned on the light, the healers' cabin the only one allowed electricity at all hours.

"Rope! The sooner the better." As she darted away, he gently transferred a shivering Oriel from his arms to an empty bed.

She began to thrash, forcing him to hold her down. "Let me go! I must go. I must get to the Vault before they breach the Wall. Let me go!"

Gritting his teeth, Ninety-Seven pinned her down.

With a shriek, Oriel reared her head. "Levioth! So close . . ." She slumped back onto the mattress, over-bright eyes fixed on some indeterminable spot. "I just wanted to help—oh Creator, mercy!"

Ninety-Seven bent over her, putting his mouth close to her ear. He began to croon, his voice's timbre rough and dry, but the tune of a lullaby distinct. *"Day is over, night is here. Sleep, sleep, sleep. Rest is needed, gift most dear. Sleep, sleep, sleep."* Oriel's body relaxed, breathing evening out. *"He is watching, do not fear. Sleep, sleep, sleep. Through the darkness, He is near. Sleep, sleep, sleep."* She blinked once, twice. Her eyes closed, her chest rising and falling in a steady rhythm. Ninety-Seven eased back, and when she didn't stir, he released his grip. Straightening, he turned to the women clustered behind him, their eyes wide.

A small, burning hand snagged his wrist.

Ninety-Seven twisted around to restrain Oriel again. But he stopped short when their gazes met. Although her face was flushed and hair was plastered against her head, her eyes were clear, their light bright and warm. "Mighty Prince, they have almost breached the Wall."

Ninety-Seven paled, years crashing back on him. "Let the other guardians—"

"There are no others." Her grip tightened, and she pulled herself upright in bed. "Don't let pride fell us, Mighty Prince. This is the boon I ask." She drew his hand nearer and pressed her lips to it. Her trademark cinnamon scent, this time underscored by a dark sappy smell, wafted around them, and a fiery red mark, like a severe burn, seared his skin, then faded.

Suddenly, she grabbed her stomach, curling over on her herself. "So black, I can't . . ." Her skin clouded into an ashy gray, and she rolled onto her side, body going limp.

"Oriel? Oriel!" Ninety-Seven seized her hand.

It was now ice cold.

9

TWO MONTHS OF WORK–OBLITERATED.

Seated stiffly on the wingback chair of her private library, Juliet twined the metal chain of her necklace around and around her fingers, its wooden heart pendant thumping against the file on her lap. For a month, she reviewed and scrutinized every shred of information she possessed on Oriel to scrounge up sufficient grounds for a fresh interrogation. Then before she could compile her request, another assignment at the capitol busied her for over two weeks. When she at last submitted her request, her superiors dithered away another fortnight before approving it.

And now the weekly report had arrived from HopeWell, complicating matters further. The girl attempted escape, and almost succeeded, though the report didn't admit as much. The result? She suffered from an unidentifiable malady which rendered her unconscious.

Unconscious prisoners weren't easily interrogated.

A soft knock interrupted, its hesitant timbre apologizing for the intrusion. Juliet did not answer, the fire-cast shadows seething and snarling around her in the darkened library. A second apologetic tap went unacknowledged as well. The door swung open. Witless, Juliet's scarred look-alike, poked in her head. From the door, the room appeared deserted, the wingback chair hiding Juliet from sight. Witless crept in, carrying a heavy package wrapped in brown paper. She slid it onto a central table, nudging aside some of the other books to make room for it.

"I told you to never touch those." Juliet's voice struck from the depths of the chair.

Witless stumbled backward and tripped on a stack of books. The chain between her ankles snapped taut. She hit the floor hip first.

Pocketing the necklace, Juliet rose from the chair, a dark phantom backlit by fire. Witless scuttled backward. Too little, too late. Dropping the file on a table as she passed by, Juliet strode forward and drove a heel into her look-alike's hand. "You never learn, do you, Witless?"

The young woman dug the fingers of her free hand into the carpet, her breathing ragged.

Juliet pressed even more weight onto the trapped hand. "This is your lot. There is no escaping it. For it falls to the children to atone for the sins of their fathers—and Father's sins were many." She pressed a palm against the chest of the young woman, whose body stiffened unnaturally.

Fire leapt behind them. Juliet inhaled sharply, face contorting. "Stop that." She glared at the hearth.

A split second later, Juliet's back arched as her head snapped backward. She broke away from Witless and retreated toward the chair, rubbing her temples.

With the physical connection severed, Witless's body slumped against the floor, spasms coursing through her.

Juliet picked up a glass bottle from the mantle, and uncorking it, breathed in its fragrance. Her forehead relaxed. After placing the re-corked bottle on the mantle, Juliet returned to inspect the package Witless brought in. The dark pleasure that had filled Juliet's eyes a minute before hardened into black ice. "Report to Doctor Minio immediately."

A violent shudder rattled Witless, a choked whimper escaping her throat.

Cutting the package's string with her nail, Juliet examined the tattered book inside—an ancient text on medical lore from

Anatroshka and Camdon. "I'll be there in ten minutes. You don't want me to arrive before you like last time."

Witless swallowed another whimper and scrambled to her feet, the chains clanking.

A glint of renewed pleasure flashed through Juliet's eyes, but her gaze remained fastened on the book as she flipped through the pages. "And shut the door on your way out." Juliet stopped at a chapter entitled *The Uses of Fireblood.*

The door clicked closed.

Juliet's tongue skimmed over her lips, tasting the saltiness that fear left behind. The fire snapped again. Irritation hardened the planes of her face. "I'm coming."

After locking the door against further intrusions, Juliet picked up an earthen vessel from beside the fireplace. A black, grainy powder filled the pot. Juliet threw a handful onto the fire. Flames flared and black smoke boiled over into the room, piling up into a giant man whose head brushed the ceiling. His eyes glowed like two coals, and behind him, wisps of smoke spread out like extended wings.

Juliet crossed both arms over her chest and bowed deeply at the waist before the smoke creature. "You wished to speak to me, O Great Zarbal?"

Sparks flickered among the smoke, and a crackling roar vibrated the walls before molding into identifiable words. "You grow careless."

"Witless wouldn't be an issue if you'd let me handle her properly." Juliet's tone fluctuated with childish petulance.

"Silence!" Smoke roiled and coal eyes flashed. "She has a purpose yet, therefore you'll do as I say. Unless you've changed your mind?" Zarbal held out a hand, flames springing up from the palm and melding into a glowing crown of gold and rubies.

The crown's light reflected off Juliet's eyes, filling them with the red haze of unquenchable desire. "Don't worry, balai. I won't destroy her until you say. But her father ravaged me, stole my innocence, cast me aside; I *will* revisit the sins of the father upon her in the meantime."

"As long as breath and dust remains united, do as you wish." Zarbal snapped his hand closed, the crown vanishing. "How long until you cross into Echoing?"

For the first time during the conversation, Juliet squirmed. "There's been a complication . . ."

"The blood moon is less than three weeks away. You must breach the Wall soon." The room trembled at the indictment rolling beneath his words.

"Then tell me where the gateways are."

"Some laws even I can't defy."

"So *you* say." Juliet's eyes smoldered.

"Then go to the gateway at—"

The shriek of a hundred kettles blowing off steam pierced the air. Juliet doubled over, hands clamped over her ears. The shriek died. "That is why," Zarbal said.

Sliding her hands from her ears, Juliet bowed in acknowledgement of the proof, though her jaw retained its stubborn set. "Nonetheless, I would make faster progress if your minions would quit interfering. My best lead in months is lying unconscious because of one your traps, isn't she?"

Smoke swirled, choking the air as the giant grew larger. "You question my wisdom?"

"I question"—her voice hitched as she sought the right words to maintain her precarious position—"the wisdom of your minions."

Her answer calmed the churning smoke, and a thick cloud of it sank to the ground. "Don't worry. They have been . . . disciplined."

Juliet tapped a finger, obviously still dissatisfied. "So, since your minions brought this about, any *wisdom* you wish to impart?"

Zarbal waved his hand, the motion of which created an upside-down tornado of smoke. "The path forward lies in the past." The tornado spun across the room, collided with the door, and disintegrated.

"But—"

Smoke billowed outward as another crackling roar surged through the library. The cloud burst apart, dissipating into little puffs that drifted up the chimney. Zarbal was gone.

"This would be easier if you weren't so cryptic." Juliet snatched up the file from HopeWell and thumbed through it again. "Forward is in the past." As her eyes skimmed the papers, her fingers toyed with the necklace again like a special talisman. A handwritten note at the bottom of the page snagged her attention. Her lips twitched, and her thumb rubbed the surface of the pendant's intricate carving. "So, you haven't died after all. But are you desperate enough that you'll go back to save her?"

A WEEK LATER JULIET KASAM STOOD ON THE PORCH of the commandant's office with the icy calm of a chess player evaluating her next move. Her fingers rolled around a cigarette, its thin wisp of smoke tainting the morning air. Her unfocused eyes shifted back and forth, as if visualizing the potential consequence of each move. And like any good chess player, she seemed intent on taking her own sweet time with her decision, despite the winter chill seeping through even the heaviest of wool coats.

Behind her the commandant waited, his body unconsciously rigid from years of military service. Although duty dragged him outside, he lingered near the door, telegraphing his desire to escape into his office as soon as possible.

"You were wise to inform me of this, Commandant." Juliet raised her clutch purse. "Driver."

The lanky man beside the long-nosed auto altered his stance from general surveillance to alert attention. At a slight nod from Juliet, he opened the front passenger door and withdrew a lumpy package, wrapped in brown paper and tied with twine. A plain envelope was tucked under the knot. The driver presented the bundle to the commandant.

Juliet inhaled a long drag from her cigarette, and a stream of smoke spilled out with her next words. "See that these instructions are carried out to the letter. Miss one, and my next report will have a few . . . errors of its own."

Keeping his stony mask in place despite the threat, the commandant snatched the package from the driver and marched inside, a slammed door solidifying his escape. The driver, unperturbed by his reception, tucked his hands behind his back, waiting for his next instructions.

Juliet flicked aside the remainder of her smoke and descended from the porch. "Ready the car. I shall return in a moment." And with that she crossed HopeWell's compound.

At her approach, guards saluted. Prisoners, on the other hand, stood to the side, black loathing filling more than one pair of eyes. Juliet's reports had sent more than half of them to this desolate place. Yet she ignored both salute and glare, never deviating from her target: the chest-deep trench where Prisoner Ninety-Seven hefted boulders onto the edges.

Fingering the chain of a necklace mostly hidden beneath her jacket, Juliet bypassed the row of boulders, lined up like giant withered potatoes waiting to be skinned. She reached the edge of the trench just as Ninety-Seven heaved another rock upward. For a moment, he held the boulder above her feet, threatening to crush them. Juliet retained her position, daring Ninety-Seven to let the stone fall.

His nostrils flared at the challenge, hands adjusting their grip. Then he dropped the stone beside her, letting it hit the ground with a warning thud. He stooped for another rock.

Juliet's mouth twitched, and she moved to the next place in the row, as if this too was part of an elaborate chess match. Prisoner Ninety-Seven shoved his stone into the spot she'd just vacated.

Crouching, she rested her black clutch purse across her knees. "Conscientious as ever, I see."

He shoved another stone onto the ledge.

"And powerful, too." She ran a finger down his arm.

He froze, eyes fixed straight ahead, jaw muscles twitching.

Juliet leaned forward, lowering her voice to a throaty whisper. "What about this girl has caused you to go all soft again, Gareth?"

He jerked away from her. "Gareth is dead." Dullness ironed all emotion from his voice, and when he turned, his half-lidded expression shuttered every window to his soul. He dropped his next boulder on the opposite edge of the trench.

Juliet sat atop a boulder, placing her back partially to Ninety-Seven. Withdrawing a compact from her clutch, she raised its mirror high enough to watch him as she applied a fresh coat of lipstick. "I once thought the same, but this latest report makes me think my people weren't as thorough as I thought they were." She rubbed her lips together to smooth out the lipstick, and the tip of her nail carved off a smear of crimson that bled too far. "Tell me about her."

Prisoner Ninety-Seven worked his way down the other side of the trench in silence.

Juliet slid her compact and lipstick into her purse. "She must be pretty special." She dropped into the trench behind him. "They say you visit her every day." She trailed a hand along his back.

Another rock hit the frozen ground with a thud.

"Perhaps I should reexamine her myself." She sauntered toward the wood ramp leaning against the mouth of the trench.

Ninety-Seven snagged her arm. "Leave her be, Juliet. She's just a child and a very sick one at that."

Her smile widened, teeth peeking out with a predatory gleam between the blood-red lips. "So Gareth *is* alive and well."

He snatched his hand away.

With the confidence of a chess player who knows checkmate is one move away, Juliet ascended the ramp. "Thank you for your cooperation, Gareth. You have been most helpful."

AS SOON AS THE GUARD RELEASED HIM FOR THE midday meal, Gareth charged up the ramp and bolted for the healers' cabin. He covered the ground in half the normal time and barged inside, the door banging the bunk behind it.

"Is she . . . ?" His gaze fell upon Oriel. Though the rope with which he'd bound her the first night had been removed, gray continued to discolor her skin as if smoke coursed through her veins. But she was still here. Gareth blew out a deep breath and plowed a hand through his hair.

"I'm sorry." The head healer wiped her hands on a rag, compassion softening the lines of her face. "Nothing's changed since your last visit."

Gareth knelt at Oriel's bedside and wrapped his hands around her icy fingers. Oriel's face relaxed, the mere presence of her mighty prince enough to chase away her nightmares.

The healer shooed the others back to their duties, then came up behind Gareth. "We continue to feed her the woodchips and sing to her whenever we dare, but signs of improvement remain scarce."

"Not your fault. Can't give her what you don't have." He scanned Oriel's face, then her body for fresh scratches or bruises.

"Has anyone else—anyone at all—been in to see her?"

"No."

Visible tension drained from Gareth's body.

"Is there anything—?"

"Nothing." The gruff word smacked the air. He softened his voice. "No, but thank you."

The woman began to move away, but she paused to place a light hand on Gareth's shoulder. "There's still hope, however slender."

"Hope is for fools."

"Then would we all be such fools, for without hope there is no life." She left to attend her other patients.

Gareth's breathing slowed to match Oriel's, a whisper of ghostly music floating nearby. While it faded to inaudible each time it was focused on, its challenge was unmistakable. Gareth shook his head. "I can't." Emotion roughened his voice. "Too many watch."

A smile flickered across her lips, as if she found his words amusing. Then the smile vanished. With a strangled cry, she wrenched away and thrashed about, kicking off blankets, clawing at her clothing.

Gareth lunged forward, wrapping his arms around her. "Shh, all's safe. Levioth hasn't crossed the Wall yet." He hummed a lilting melody. Her thrashing abated, and she relaxed against him, a tinge of pink warming her cheeks.

A shadow fell over the pair. "Prisoner Ninety-Seven." Brandon's voice, sounding unusually dissonant, disrupted the song.

Gareth stiffened, his hold on Oriel tightening for the merest fraction of a second before he released her. He tucked the blankets around her and faced Brandon.

The young sergeant stepped backward. Gareth's face no longer looked weighted with years, but with experience—a warrior tested by many battles.

Gareth eyed him. "Did you want something?"

Though Brandon still stood with proper military bearing, respect had replaced his earlier dominance. "The commandant has requested to see you."

Gareth snorted. "Don't flatter me, Sergeant. We both know the commandant requests nothing around here."

Redness tinted Brandon's ears. "Follow me please." Pivoting on his heels, he led Gareth through camp and veered toward the commandant's quarters instead of his office. Gareth edged inside, muscles coiled at the unusual proceedings.

The commandant stared out a window, swirling a drink in a glass. "You're free to go." Even in profile, his scowl was evident.

"Go?"

"Your papers are on the table along with civilian clothes."

Gareth poked at the brown paper, which curled around a stack of folded clothing, and then picked up the typed document beside it. *Release papers of Gareth Aberson.* He flipped to the bottom sheet. It bore the day's date and a signature of authorization: Juliet Kasam.

"No." Gareth crumpled the papers. "I refuse to leave." He tossed the wad across the table.

"For once, it appears we are in complete agreement." The commandant tipped his head to empty his glass, then slogged over to the sideboard. "Nonetheless, orders are orders—and mine are to release you. Forcibly if need be." Behind him, the clock chimed the half hour. "Sergeant, escort him to his cabin to change, then see him to the front gate. Immediately."

10

PRISONER NINETY-SEVEN LEFT. ALIVE. AND THROUGH the front gate.

The shock of it all immobilized the whole of HopeWell. This wasn't supposed to happen. No one ever *left* HopeWell. Attempted escaped, yes, but left? Never. Yet that was exactly what Ninety-Seven did. He walked *out* the front gate, upright, breathing, under his own power. How could this have happened? Prisoner and guard alike gawked at the miraculous event.

Then the crossbar thudded back into place across the gate, jumpstarting the heartbeat of HopeWell. Normal routines resumed. Patrols paced their routes. Prisoners moved rocks. Guards oversaw.

Brandon alone seemed unable to recover. After escorting Prisoner Ninety-Seven to the gate, he returned to the stoop of the commandant's quarters and stared at the closed door. More than once he raised his hand to knock. Each time it dropped to his side without so much as brushing the coarse wood. After all, he wasn't summoned. Disturbing the commandant unsummoned— such an act would almost guarantee punishment, especially if the commandant were in a bad mood. And with the forced release of a prisoner, the commandant's mood did not bode to be good.

Brandon turned from the door and tugged homemade mittens out of his pockets to layer over the thinner, military-issued gloves. A metal medallion tumbled out with them, hitting against the wooden planks. Brandon snatched it off the porch and glanced around the camp. Everyone proceeded as normal, oblivious to him.

He opened his hand to inspect the piece for damage. The old memento bore no additional dents. A twelve-pointed ruby remained embedded in the tarnished metal. No fresh scratches obscured the four words engraved in a circle around the ruby star: *Tolmone, Dynamis, Eleos, Elpis*—boldness, strength, mercy, hope. It was a Protector's Star, once regarded as the highest honor given in Anatroshka, but now scoffed at as antiquated idealism. Brandon fingered the Star a moment longer before sliding it away. Stuffing the mittens into the other pocket, he confronted the door and rapped his knuckles on it.

At first no one responded, though someone shuffled within. Finally a muffled "Enter!" beckoned him inside.

The scene awaiting him was not an encouraging one. The commandant sat slouched in his armchair, little visible of him except his left hand clutching a half-empty glass. "What do you want?"

Brandon clicked his heels together and saluted, though the dying fire held the commandant's gaze instead of him. "Former Prisoner Ninety-Seven has left HopeWell, sir."

"You disturbed me to report *that*?"

A board creaked under Brandon as he shifted his weight. "I also came to request your permission, sir."

"Permission? For what?"

"To follow him. Sir."

"Why? He's no longer a prisoner here." The commandant lifted his drink to eye level, contemplated the sloshing liquid, then lowered it without taking a sip.

"Prisoner or not, he's a known revolutionary and convicted killer. He will strike again."

"So? That could take weeks, months, even years."

"It could . . ." Brandon pressed a hand over the Protector's Star. "But I don't believe it will. Prisoner Ninety-Seven didn't want to leave. How better to return than by repeating his previous crimes?"

The commandant raised his head. "An interesting theory." He slumped forward again. "But a theory nonetheless. Besides, he is no longer our responsibility."

Brandon edged nearer, securing a direct view of his superior's face while remaining well outside striking distance. "Forgive my boldness, Commandant, but it should be our business. No one escapes HopeWell. No one escapes *you*. This agent has undermined that work."

The fingers of the commandant tightened around his glass.

Brandon slowed his breathing. One wrong word and a minefield would explode in his face. "If you catch Prisoner Ninety-Seven in the act, you will prove yourself inescapable—even beyond the wire. Moreover, your claims that he shouldn't have been released will be upheld." He leaned forward, lowering his voice. "Agent Kasam will be called to give account and likely be . . . reassigned."

A gleam lit the commandant's eyes, and a ghost of a smile flitted across his face. Still, he said nothing.

"One week. That's all I ask, sir. One week to unearth proof that he remains a threat to state and society."

The commandant rolled the glass between his fingers. His expression hardened. Downing the rest of his drink in one swallow, he staggered up and over to the small desk in the corner. He set aside his empty glass and scribbled a leave of absence, then thrust it out to Brandon. "Make it happen."

Relief relaxed Brandon's stiff posture. "You can count on me, sir." He grasped the edge of the paper.

The commandant held on. "But if anything goes wrong, if Agent Kasam receives one word of your activities, I will deny any knowledge of them. Your leave was for a family emergency. Am I clear, Sergeant?"

Brandon met the commandant's eyes without flinching. "Abundantly."

"Then I suggest you get going." The commandant released the paper. "Dismissed."

Brandon saluted and returned to the porch. There he reread the leave of absence before tucking the paper in the same pocket as the Star. *"Tolmone, Dynamis, Eleos, Elpis."*

THE GATE'S CROSSBAR FELL INTO PLACE, THE THUD reverberating through the woods with terrible finality. Outside the fence Gareth stood alone. He now wore the thin shirt and slacks provided, along with the expression of a man facing the Grim Reaper. With the way behind literally barred, he had no choice but to go forward. Yet how could he go forward when all he expected for the future lay behind? So he neither advanced nor retreated. As still as granite he merely stared into the woods, hand pressed against his bulging right pocket.

A soldier patrolling the fence jeered at him. "You can stand there all day if you want, but we're not letting you back in."

A burst of heat reddened the skin on Gareth's right hand, then faded as rapidly as it flared. Though not much or long, that moment of warmth was enough to thaw him. Gareth inhaled deeply and began to make his way down the rutted road.

Soon the forest closed in around him. The road narrowed. The ruts deepened. Thick-needled limbs bent farther and farther into his path. A squirrel scolded him from the safety of a tall oak's branches. Deeper in the woods on both sides, creakings and groanings bounced back and forth conversationally, like might be heard on a windy day—except no wind ruffled even the topmost branches. The air was frozen.

The road sloped upward, promising an end to the forest. A promise the trees loathed to see fulfilled. The creaking and groaning crept nearer; pine branches, weighted with ice and snow, blockaded the road, preventing Gareth from progressing further.

He looked at the trees. "I don't like this either, but returning will get me shot. What good would that do her?"

A murmur passed among the trees.

Gareth turned in a full circle, gaze still fastened on the treetops. "Grant me passage, and I *will* find the help she needs—or lose Creator's breath trying."

Stillness enwrapped the forest. Gareth waited.

A pack of snow slid off a branch, hitting the ground with a plop. A second clump followed, then a third. Branches sprang up, shaking more snow loose until a clear path laid before him once more.

He clasped a fist to his heart and bowed his head. "Thank you."

As Gareth crested the ridge, the sun touched the edge of the world, setting the snow aflame while plunging the village below into shadow. Lights flicked on, inviting him onward. Instead, he waded through the snow toward Maggie's home. Hesitating at the entrance, he touched the lump in his pocket. A lump that Maggie alone would know what to do with. He rapped on the weathered door.

No one answered.

Gareth knocked a second time. That also failed to rouse a response. "Maggie, it's me."

Two more clouds escaped Gareth's mouth before the door squealed, and Maggie peeked around its edge. Her eyes widened. "Be ye ghost?"

He poked his arm. "I don't think so." A branch cracked in the distance. "But I should get out of sight before I become one."

Maggie swung open the door, and Gareth stepped inside.

Despite the house's dilapidated appearance on the outside,

the interior of the one-room home was snug. Dry herbs hung from roof beams. A fire danced in the hearth. A thick blanket blocked the cold trying to seep through the single window, while on the opposite side a crazy quilt adorned a four-poster bed. Throughout the whole room, trays of dirt and labeled jars filled every available surface—the ratty trunk at the bed's foot, the fireplace mantle, a lopsided table.

After shutting the door, Maggie shuffled toward the fireplace and lifted a blackened kettle from its hook.

Gareth rested a hand on her shoulder. "I can't stay that long. I only came to ask a favor." He pulled out a small bundle from his bulging pocket and unfolded a rag, revealing his whittling knife and a palm-sized, coiled whistle carved from wood. He held out the whistle. "I finished it this morning but didn't get to use it before they forced me out." He looked at Maggie. "I know I'm asking much, but would you . . . ?"

Maggie's eyes clouded as she focused on some unseen point. Soon a smile warmed her face, dissipating the clouds. She patted Gareth's cheek as if he were a silly little boy. "Spring be early this year." She slipped the whistle into a pocket and lifted a wicker basket onto the bed.

"Thank you, Maggie." Gareth carefully rewrapped the knife and slid it away.

Humming a wandering tune, Maggie started to fill the basket with seed jars.

Gareth backed toward the door and grasped the latch. "I'll be leaving now."

Maggie spun around. "Not like that, ye won't be." She cleared the top of the old trunk, piling jars on the floor, and shoved open the lid.

"There's no need—"

"Hush. My Hiram won't mind one bit." She set aside another quilt and a simple, white dress with a high neck and puffy sleeves.

A long, wool coat followed, its double-breasted style far out of date, yet the fabric showed no wear. Maggie thrust the coat, along with a hat, scarf, and mittens, at Gareth.

"My Hiram were knowing." Tugging Gareth down, she pulled the hat crookedly onto his head and wrapped the scarf around his neck. "Said I'd be needing them one day. I reckon he be thinking of you." She patted his cheek again and returned to the trunk.

Gareth slid on the coat, tucking the mittens into the pockets. The coat settled onto his frame as if tailored for him. Maggie nodded in approval and stuffed a leather pouch into his hands, metal clinking against metal.

At the weight of the pouch, Gareth thrust it back. "Maggie . . ."

She waved him away. "Scat." She placed two more jars into the basket.

Gareth tucked the pouch into a pocket and stepped up behind her, resting his hands on her shoulders. Maggie leaned into his touch, eyes closed and face uplifted.

"Stay safe." He dropped a kiss on her head and then abruptly walked out, leaving Maggie standing alone with tears in her eyes.

BRANDON PEERED THROUGH THE BINOCULARS AT his grandmother's home and frowned. Wearing dark-colored civvies, he perched in a tree at the forest's edge, clutching a chunky limb for balance. Shadows lengthened around him, masking his presence further, but the camouflage cost bitterly; the temperature bowed before the invading darkness lower and lower in subservience.

Brandon shifted his weight, seeking a better position, only to resettle into his original spot. Comfort would not be found in this treetop lookout.

"Come on, come on." His muttered words hung in the icy air, threatening to expose his position. Then the air shivered, and the impatient words fell to the ground, shattering into nothingness.

Not a moment too soon, either. The door to his grandmother's house opened, hinges squawking in protest. Prisoner Ninety-Seven exited, wrapped in old-fashioned winter wear. Brandon bent forward. The branch beneath him moaned.

Ninety-Seven eyed the tree line.

Brandon stilled. There was no way the old man should be able to see him without aid, but Ninety-Seven had done much that should not be possible.

A thick cloud of breath puffed out of Ninety-Seven's mouth. Then he trudged away, down the hill toward the village. Brandon scrambled to the ground and plowed through the snow to his grandmother's home. Passing the door, he rounded the corner to the window. A rag poked out of a broken pane. He pulled it out, pushed his fingers through the hole, and nudged aside the quilt, pressing his face to the glass.

Humming tunelessly, Maggie shuffled in and out of his view as she packed an old basket. Not only did she appear unharmed, but she was in a chipper mood. Brandon lowered the quilt, restuffed the hole, and released a slow breath. His grandmother was not the prisoner's way back into HopeWell. Circling around the house, he resumed his surveillance, tracing Ninety-Seven's steps into Koma.

11

THE CHILL OF THE NIGHT SETTLED DEEP INTO THE bones of the town.

Wooden buildings huddled together as if to share each other's warmth, their doors locked and heavy curtains pulled tight. Nonetheless, the wind clawed at boards and pried at cracks, causing windows to chatter and a hanging sign to creak in protest.

Despite the air's sting, Gareth ventured down Main Street toward the center of Koma. Not that anyone noticed. No other steps crunched ice and gravel, every house sealed up, every storefront dark. The whole town had turned its back, refusing to interact with the outside world, except for a single brick building near the town's center, the local artoikos. That structure spat light, voices, the smell of food, and an occasional person into the night.

Gareth stood across the street, watching the strange display of a building ingesting a man, only to disgorge another as easy prey for the darkness. Five minutes stretched into twenty. A footstep scuffed behind him. Gareth's head tilted slightly. Then, burrowing his hands into his pockets, he crossed the road.

Inside the artoikos, coffee and cheap beer vied for the strongest odor amidst the thick haze of smoke curling around the room. Men squeezed themselves around the tables crammed into the too-small space and sat peering into the depths of steaming coffee as if the dark brew contained the courage to face the world. All donned faded variations of Gareth's clothing, except for a central table of soldiers, where tankards clanked and voices rose higher. In the corner, a curvy woman crooned off-key about love lost.

Gareth hung his coat on a peg and cut through the swirl of conversation, his shadow severing sentences and choking off words as it fell across each table. Newcomers were rare in town. Those that did pass through inevitably had ties to the government or the Underground. Both invited trouble, and trouble was to be avoided at all cost.

As stillness overtook the room, the soldiers' attention swung toward Gareth. The youngest of the group slapped a companion on the shoulder. "Watch this." He swaggered toward Gareth.

Gareth leveled a look in the new recruit's direction. Light glinted off his dark eyes, adding dragon fierceness to his silent gaze. The soldier halted, his skin absorbing the yellowed glare of the lights. As Gareth continued his trek, the soldier slunk back to his seat.

His friend elbowed him. "Watch what? I didn't see nothing."

"Shut up." The young soldier slumped deeper into his chair. "You know nothing about nothing." He slammed down the rest of his beer.

Gareth reached the table in the back without further disturbance and squeezed his frame into the corner chair, placing his back to the wall, in order to provide him a view of the entire room. A pinched-face waitress sauntered up. "What'll ya have?"

"Coffee. Miner's black." Gareth pronounced the words distinctly, scanning the room. When no one reacted to the unusual order, he added, "And two helpings of whatever you have cooking that's hot and filling."

"Two?" She glanced at the door.

"Two."

The waitress shrugged and ambled off. As long as he paid his bill and caused no trouble, what did it matter whether he was an innocent traveler, hardened criminal, or government informant? She placed his order with the cook and returned to pour his coffee.

Gareth sipped the bitter brew, studying the room over the rim. A few patrons still eyed him with suspicion, but at the lack of noteworthy activity, the attention of most had already drifted back to their own tables. One man paid his bill and left. Several more arrived and ordered coffee.

The waitress slid two plates laden with sliced potatoes in front of Gareth. A heavy, dark gravy was slathered across the top, dotted with chunks of unidentifiable meat and vegetables. "Anything else?"

"No." Gareth poked a fork into a potato covered in gravy and put the steaming food into his mouth. His face relaxed, and his eyes closed at his first taste of non-prison food in almost twenty years. He shoveled in a second and third bite, stuffing his mouth to capacity, and in record time, cleaned the entire dish of food.

Gareth swapped plates and dug his fork into the second mound of potatoes. A horn blasted outside, and over half of the men in the artoikos scrambled for the bus waiting to transport them to their night shift at a factory. Soldiers also rose and left, albeit more leisurely. Continuing to eat, but at a slower pace, Gareth examined the remaining half dozen customers.

A bespectacled man entered the artoikos. He was maybe in his thirties, yet with the stooped shoulders of a man bearing twice as many years. Gareth finished his meal as he scrutinized the newcomer, who settled at the same table the soldiers had vacated.

The waitress approached the new arrival. "What'll ya have?"

"Coffee, miner's black."

Gareth pushed away his second plate and fished around in the pouch from Maggie.

The waitress set a mug before the bespectacled man. But instead of drinking the steaming sludge, he twisted the cup between his hands, as if following a forced routine with no heart.

Gareth pulled out a couple of paper bills from the pouch. Rising, he offered them to the waitress. "I assume this will cover the bill."

"Of course." She snatched the money from his hand.

"Good. Keep the change." He paused, then added, "Never know when a little extra will help."

The newcomer's gaze darted toward Gareth, but Gareth shrugged into his coat and tromped into the night without giving him a glance.

FROM ALL OUTWARD APPEARANCES, KOMA'S recruitment center was deserted for the night. Its dark windows mirrored the unlit storefronts on either side. A quick jiggle of the doorknobs would find them locked. No one had entered or left the building in hours. But just beyond the edge of the second-story window waited Juliet, keeping a silent vigil over Main Street. Some work simply could not be relegated to business hours, especially when success could pivot on a few crucial minutes.

Therefore, she watched and waited, carefully guarding this vantage point that allowed her to see without being seen, especially now the pieces had begun to move. Two minutes ago, per her instructions, the mole entered the artoikos, which in this backward town was little more than a glorified bar that served food. What happened next, though, would determine the course of her evening's remainder.

Gareth exited the artoikos—alone—and crossed the street. Halfway over, he glanced up at the second story of the recruitment center, as if sensing Juliet's presence. She pressed into the gloom, just another shadow among many. Normally, no one would be able to detect her presence, but normality had never been well acquainted with Gareth.

Gareth disappeared into the alley between the recruitment center and the store next door. His next move had been made . . . but what did it mean?

The door to the artoikos opened again, this time revealing her mole. His gaze darted side to side, fingers twitching, every inch of his being a nervous Underground skolops. His fake spectacles further enhanced the impression of timidity. Juliet leaned forward. If he was still entrenched in his role, he must have a reason.

Mopping his forehead, he shuffled in the opposite direction from which Gareth arrived, toward the shell house used for various operations. Gareth emerged from the alley and followed. Juliet's lips twisted into a half smile. The pied piper leading a child to his doom.

She started to turn away from the window, but a shadow sprinting between the buildings captured her attention. Another tailed her quarry, someone younger than Gareth or her mole, judging by its speed and agility.

"Interesting." Juliet pulled on her gloves and descended to the street, leaving the center by a back door. She traversed a street paralleling Main, not bothering to cloak her movements and yet making no noise.

"We want no trouble around here." The mole's squeaky voice pierced the quiet night. "Koma is a peaceful town."

Juliet slowed her steps and crept up an alley toward Main. Gareth, with his back to her, had chosen to brazenly confront the mole, who was cleaning his glasses with erratic motions.

"Trouble comes, wanted or not." Gareth's voice rumbled clear in the icy air. "But I've been away. Tell me, does anyone still offer their extra bed to strangers these days?"

The mole jerked, the handkerchief fluttering away from his

fingers. "I suppose, though not as often as they were once wont to do. It attracted all sorts of unsavory types."

"I imagine so." Gareth's chuckle was hoarse from disuse.

The mole stooped to retrieve his handkerchief and peered past Gareth. Delay further or close the deal? Juliet edged out and nodded once before melting back into the shadows.

The mole tucked the handkerchief into his pocket. "I don't have much to offer, but it's warmer than out here."

"Sounds heavenly." Gareth waved for the mole to lead on.

"Your age is showing, Gareth." Hastening up the side street, Juliet slipped into the back door of a deserted home opposite of the shell house. She ascended the stairs to the upper bedroom.

Gareth and the mole entered the shell house. Lights flicked on, and the men disappeared into a back hallway. A second later, the tail she spotted earlier paused before the house. Juliet stood on the balls of her feet, nose almost touching the window. The man glanced around, as if memorizing the location, and turned away. Amateur. He let the moonlight fall across his face, unmasking his identity. The young sergeant from HopeWell. As he hurried off, Juliet tapped a fingernail on the windowsill. "What game are you playing, Commandant?"

The mole emerged from the back room. With Gareth no longer at his side, the man had transformed dramatically. Gone were the stooped shoulders, erratic motions, and spectacles, leaving behind a stony-faced man in complete control of himself.

At the sight, Juliet's fingers stilled.

The man went over to an empty birdcage hanging in the front window.

He latched its door shut.

12

A KNOCK ON THE BACK DOOR ECHOED THROUGH THE vacant house.

Sitting on the steps to the second story, Juliet frowned at her compact mirror. Only one person knew she was here, and he was under strict orders not to contact her except under the most extreme of circumstances. Otherwise, Gareth would notice. Juliet finished applying her lipstick and tucked the cosmetics into her clutch purse. Had things gone awry already?

Juliet smoothed her skirt, pressing away the few wrinkles acquired from her overnight stay, and headed toward the back of the house. On the other side of the door stood the mole, sans spectacles, his skin glistening with a pale sheen in the early morning light.

"He has vanished," stated Juliet.

To the mole's credit, he didn't flinch at her lifeless pronouncement. "Yes."

"Show me."

He circled the building and crossed the street, Juliet in his shadow all the way. Entering the shell house, he motioned down the back hall to a plain interior door. "It's as I found it this morning."

Juliet rubbed her fingers along the edge of the door. With no knob or handle on the inside, scratches or other signs of tampering would be expected. Yet none marred the wood. She looked around the room, which was little more than a closet. On the right, a small table bore a washbasin and a neatly folded towel. Against the far wall was wedged a cot, the blankets smooth— apparently no one had sat on the cot, much less slept upon it.

Whenever Gareth had left, it was hours ago.

Juliet paced the narrow room, heels clacking evenly against wood. She examined the floor, but no scuffmarks indicated the moving of furniture. Her fingers probed the boards; no dents revealed that any had been pried up. She checked the walls next, tapping knuckles against them, her head tilted to catch the slightest deviation of sound.

The mole stood rigidly. "I assure you, the room was sealed. There's no way he could have escaped."

"Yet he is not here." She ran her hand down the door's edge again, this time pausing at the lock.

"He must have had outside help—help you said he wouldn't have."

Juliet dug into her purse. "He had paper money on him?"

The mole blinked at the abrupt change of subject. "How did you—"

"Logic." Juliet walked back into the room, but her heel caught, forcing her to steady herself against the jamb. Straightening, she snapped at the mole, "Close the door."

"I told you. It's inescapable."

"Close it."

The mole shook his head but obeyed.

Juliet pressed a palm against the door. It swung open. From inside the jamb's strike plate a crumpled paper peeked out. The mole's jaw sagged at the simple trick that allowed Gareth to escape the room unseen.

Retrieving the paper, Juliet put it in her purse. "He knew you were a mole."

"But my cover was perfect!"

"Like the room was inescapable?"

He swallowed hard.

"He knew and returned with you so that we would relax our guard." Juliet strode down the hall and into the chilly air. "Well played, Gareth. Well played." Her breath clouded the air.

The mole tailed her outside, face red. "Say the word. I'll track him down."

"Track him down?" Juliet coughed a short laugh. "You couldn't hold him for one night; you'll never find him. No, it's time to call in some real hunters."

THE NARROW ROAD WOUND THROUGH THE GORGE, the epitome of isolation. No houses dotted the byway; no side roads broke off from it. No animals scampered along the rock walls; no birds flitted among the scrubby bushes clinging to the ledges. And though the last snowfall was well over a fortnight ago, neither tire track nor footprint marred the path. A place ignored, forgotten by a world intent on surviving modernization. Even the sun had turned its face away so that a pale orb, obscured by a thin veil of clouds, was all that hung in the sky.

Such desolation could both bless and curse Gareth. The isolation lowered the risk of unwanted encounters. But should anyone uncover his trail at the gorge's mouth, he would be easy to track. Would the blessing supersede the curse? Time alone would reveal that. He could only continue to climb, clinging to the blessing for however long it would last, using it to spur him forward despite being on the move an hour after following his duplicitous host home. Both coffee and adrenaline wore off hours ago, and the lack of sleep was taking its toll, hunching his shoulders and lining his face with the grooves that aged him into an old man again.

A low rumble intruded upon the quiet. Gareth stopped. Though the bitter air hampered the ability to gauge the precise distance, the noise grew steadily louder, solidifying after a few seconds into the distinct thrum of a car motor. Someone drove at a reckless pace in his direction.

Gareth rubbed his chin and faced the rocky cliff on his right. It offered little shelter, but even a little was better than none. He hauled himself onto a narrow ledge several yards above the road, a few bushes clutching at the rocky soil. Not great cover, but if the car moved as fast as it sounded, the driver might fly by without noticing him.

Mere moments after Gareth hunkered down, a long-nosed car skidded around the curve, taking the icy corner at a treacherous pace, smearing black against the white background. Gareth held still. The car zoomed by without slowing. A few seconds ticked by. Gareth breathed again.

Brakes screeched.

So much for going unnoticed. Gareth withdrew his whittling knife. A poor defense against bullets, but he wouldn't go down without a fight.

The motor puttered nearer as the car U-turned and ascended the gorge again. When it reached the spot where Gareth's tracks veered off, the vehicle shifted into park. Gareth crouched lower, a mountain cat preparing to pounce.

On the far side of the car, the front door swung open, and the driver climbed out. A wide-brimmed fedora obscured the man's face, flattening it into a featureless shadow. A heavy woolen coat added girth to his hulking frame. Warmth bubbled around him, and the air quavered with a low strain of music. Or was that the idling motor reverberating off the rocky walls?

Rounding the nose of the car, the stranger knelt beside Gareth's tracks. He picked up some snow, which melted instantly, and rubbed the water between his gloved fingers. Then he angled his chin, sniffed the air, and lifted his face toward Gareth's hiding place. Russet-colored eyes peered out from under the hat's brim. "You're out of practice."

The bell-toned words deepened Gareth's scowl. "You shouldn't be here, Jaki."

"Neither should you, Gareth."

"I had no say." An acidic tang was embedded in his words.

Jaki rubbed his chin as he eyed Gareth's defensive posture. "When the vigils reported a disturbance, I believed Creator had raised up a new guardian in our time of need."

"Sorry to disappoint."

"Surprise? Yes. Disappoint? Never." He walked to the driver's side and placed a hand on the roof. "Coming?"

Gareth compressed himself against the cliff, the grip on his knife never easing. "Eager to see my death?"

"You know I never agreed with Sarish's order."

"Instead you arranged for me to be locked up," he shot back.

"You still dwell among the living, do you not?"

"Death would have been preferable."

"Then why are your breath and dust still joined? You would have had opportunity to separate them, I am sure."

Gareth's jaw twitched. "Did it work?"

Jaki curled his fingers around the door handle as he transferred his weight to his heels. "Sarish is . . . hard to read."

"So no." Gareth massaged the back of his neck. "Go home, Jaki. Sarish's wrath is against me, not you."

"Surprise is powerful. I can get you through the Wall before the vigils can identify you."

Gareth toyed with his knife, then slid it away and descended. As he faced Jaki, he stuffed his hands in his pockets. "Last chance."

"You can't stop me from being there."

Gareth flicked out a hand. The knife flew toward Jaki.

With inhuman speed Jaki snatched it out of the air. "Stubborn Adam." He spun the knife back across the car's roof. It stopped an inch from the edge in front of Gareth, handle toward him. "Get in, Gareth."

The cloth wrapped around the knife's base had hardened into a glistening white hilt, but Gareth didn't move to take it. "Why risk it?"

Jaki shrugged a shoulder. "Bad company corrupts. It seems I've become a bit of a rebel myself."

Gareth finally tucked the knife under his coat and yanked open the passenger door with a huff. "We're wasting time." He ducked inside and slammed the door.

Jaki folded himself behind the steering wheel and glanced at the grumbling figure beside him. Chuckling, he shifted the car into gear. "I've missed you too, old friend."

WITH ONE NOTE, GARETH'S WOODEN WHISTLE immobilized the entire camp of HopeWell.

It wasn't that the sound pierced the air shrilly. Quite the contrary. The instrument gifted to Maggie rolled out a note that rumbled so low and throaty it growled a warning to retreat or face dire consequences. Prisoners paused in their work. Guards tightened their hold on their weapons. Even the commandant, crossing the porch to his office, paused and searched the compound for the sound, which seemed to come from everywhere and nowhere at the same time.

With everyone's attention gripped, the whistle's pitch glided upward before tumbling into a sorrowful melody that pleaded with the listener to come home. The gatekeeper's gaze turned distant. A sigh escaped the lips of a washerwoman. The door of the healers' cabin creaked open, and Oriel's head poked out, her ash-blonde hair dangling in dull clumps after so many days abed. Like one dreaming, her eyes darted back and forth behind closed lids.

The song ended. Oriel's pale face twisted in confusion. Go forward like the song beckoned . . . or retreat? Deep stillness enveloped the camp, all awaiting the decision.

The trees beyond the fence groaned, and the branches began to thrash. A blast of unnaturally warm air charged into the camp.

Chain links rattled. Barbed wire grated. The hot wind slammed into Oriel, banging the cabin door all the way open. *Go back, go back!* She fell to the ground in a protective ball, arms wrapped over her head, as the wind hammered at her.

An earsplitting blast sliced through the whirlwind's racket. The air convulsed with a snarl. The whistle responded with another long blast, followed by three shorter ones. The wind whipped around Oriel once more and died.

But Oriel remained curled tight, rocking back and forth, arms clamped over her ears. Gareth's lullaby curled around her. *He is watching, do not fear. Sleep, sleep, sleep. Through the darkness, He is near. Sleep, sleep, sleep.* Oriel's rocking stilled.

When the final note faded, a breath of calm rested upon the camp. Then notes scurried upward and burst into a lively tune. The song reeled and whirled, calling, *Come, take a spin with me!* Even the brief breaks seemed like nothing more than an out-of-breath laugh extending an invitation to dance. But inevitably the listener would hesitate, and the music would twirl away with a shrug of the shoulder.

Nonetheless, feet tapped of their own accord, and smiles crept onto faces unawares. Oriel's arms slid from her head.

The song paused.

With eyes still closed, Oriel nodded and extended an arm as if to grasp the proffered hand of an invisible partner. She rose. The tune resumed. Immediately she whirled into a set of steps, familiar yet not quite recognizable as any dance past or present. Reels glided into a waltz before accelerating into a tarantella. A few patterns even hinted at more recent crazes. Prisoners and guards alike watched, fascinated, as she avoided every obstacle, human or otherwise, though her eyes remain closed. It was as if the dance had been choreographed around them. And despite the song's reckless pace, her movements flowed fluidly, a smile on her lips.

As she reached the commandant, standing shell-shocked on his porch, she paused and took a breath with the music. The commandant stared. Oriel's pale cheeks glowed rosy, and her hair glistened with a golden sheen. She turned her head to one side, as if sensing his presence within her sleep-dancing. Then the music resumed, carrying her around the corner of the building.

The song coalesced, centering around its single source. In the midst of the dead garden sat Maggie, her old straw hat once again perched upon her head. Beneath its sagging brim peeked the strange coiled whistle from Gareth.

The music slowed. Oriel twirled to a stop less than two feet in front of Maggie. Sliding one foot behind the other, Oriel extended her arms and bowed before the older woman. The music faded. Oriel rose. Her eyes opened, fire illuminating her golden irises. A puzzled expression creased her face as if she was not where she expected to be, and she blinked several times at the cold, hard-edged world around her.

Maggie rose from the ground and cupped a hand around Oriel's cheek. The girl's skin radiated warmth. Maggie smiled broadly. "Ye back?"

"Aye." Oriel looked around the area loosely ringed by prisoners and soldiers, a mixture of scowling disgust, slack-jawed awe, and teary-eyed joy upon their faces. In the rear, the commandant stomped around the corner of his office. Oriel's brow furrowed. "Where's Mighty Prince?"

"He's not here, but he left ye this." Maggie wrapped Oriel's fingers around the whistle.

Her eyes widened, and her face lost a shade of its glow. "He went back?"

"He didn't say, but yea, I 'spect so."

Oriel sank to her knees.

Maggie stooped beside her. "Is that not what ye wanted?"

Oriel shook her head. "Not now, not in this way." Pressing the whistle to her chest, she lifted her face to Maggie. Unshed tears glistened in her eyes. "Without me, they'll kill him."

13

THE YOUNG MAN IN BLACK MELTED INTO THE shadows lingering between the houses, the last of six elite hunters to be dispatched after Gareth. Juliet slid her hands into her coat pockets and headed in the opposite direction. She'd hand-selected these hunters. If Gareth yet walked in Terrestrial on this side of the Wall, the hunters would find him. Unfortunately for her, that was a big *if*.

Either way, Juliet could do nothing further about it. She strode down the streets toward the heart of Koma. Late morning sunshine breathed a promise of spring, softening snow and ice into slush wherever it squeezed between the buildings.

Evading both sunshine and slush, Juliet hugged shadows until she entered the recruitment center. A lone soldier tended the front desk. "Agent Kasam." He rose with a salute.

"As you were." She bypassed him to climb the stairs to the office she used the night before. Locking the door behind her, she hung her coat on a peg and crossed the room to pull the shade, plunging the room into darkness.

The sharp report of her shoes moved toward an interior wall. Wood scritched against wood; the metallic clicking of a combination lock filled the room. With a pop, a safe door opened, and after a brief shuffling of papers, the noises reversed. A lamp clicked on.

Sitting at a desk, Juliet lit a cigarette and withdrew a stack of papers from an overstuffed, unmarked folder. *Operation Diadem* headed the top sheet, handwritten in heavy, bold strokes. The rest of the page was typed:

```
A moon shows full his face,
Blood glows in every place.
But where the darkness all shall bend
A door to regions with no end,
Torment to never cease
Nightmare without release
When from a vault not here or there
Is gained a key both black and bare.
```

Juliet laid the poem aside, revealing a calendar beneath. Most of the first three weeks were crossed out. On the last week, a circled day bore the notation *blood moon*.

A complex set of calculations followed. Juliet flipped through the pages. She leaned forward. Snuffing out her cigarette with one hand, she reached for a pen with the other. A quick line struck one set of numbers, and a similar equation was penned in above it. Juliet continued making corrections as she went. On the final page, half-filled with notes, she added more calculations until she reached a final pair of numbers. Those she circled. "Got you."

With the last page in hand, Juliet proceeded to a large wall map of Anatroshka. She found the coordinates corresponding to the circled numbers and stabbed the map with a pin—piercing the very heart of HopeWell.

THE CAR'S TIRES SPUN USELESSLY AGAINST THE ICY snow. It didn't matter what Jaki tried, the car refused to creep another inch up the gorge's road. The wheels merely whirled around and around, unable to gain any traction.

Gareth folded his arms and glowered at the wet flakes falling so fast that they formed an impenetrable veil of white. "They aren't going to let you through." Thunder rumbled above them as if a demigod practiced his dark arts.

Jaki slammed the car into reverse. Again the wheels rotated without achieving momentum. He snatched off his hat and tossed it onto the seat, exposing a tense bronze face topped with unruly spikes of coppery hair. He shifted back into drive, his gloved hands strangling the steering wheel.

"Might as well walk." Gareth reached for the handle of the door.

"Don't do it, Gareth."

"I may be out of practice, but even I can recognize Dachi mischief." He pointed to the snow. "A nuisance but harmless."

Jaki put the car in park. "Once true. No longer." He turned off the engine; the ensuing silence rang around them. "Levioth turned them."

A boom of thunder punctuated the quiet words. Gareth rubbed his ear. "You said the Dachi couldn't ally with anyone."

"We were wrong."

Gareth's eyes sparked. "How many?"

"Enough."

The single word rushed blood into Gareth's face. A stifling thickness weighted the air. Snowflakes splatted against the windshield and instantly liquefied. Jaki adjusted his position, rocking the car.

Gareth flattened his fist against his knee. "What else has changed?" Each word strained to present itself as self-controlled.

"You, I'm beginning to see."

"Not as much as you think." A guttural snarl boiled up, adding veracity to his statement. "But news?"

Jaki twisted his fedora around in his hands. "The number of Levioth's hunters has increased exponentially. Our enemies stockpile at an alarming rate. My people weary of guarding the Wall, and yours have almost breached it a dozen times in the past year."

"Sarish's thrilled, I'm sure."

"Do *you* wish the Adam of this age to breach the Wall?"

"I wish for the peace of the ancient tales." Gareth kneaded his neck. "Any other surprises?"

"You're the last trained guardian in this quadrant. All others are dead or missing, and the other sectors aren't faring much better."

"Oriel said as much."

The hat in Jaki's hands stilled. "Who?"

"Oriel." When Jaki's face remained questioning, Gareth added, "Young girl, pale skin, blonde hair? At least in her human form. Bears a light, lyrical song and a cinnamon scent undercoated with a dark sap smell."

"You mean you've seen . . ." Jaki's skin lost some of its luster. "When, where?"

Gareth waited a moment before stating the obvious. "HopeWell."

"She breached *Terrestrial*?" He crushed the fedora into a felt ball. "How could she after . . ." He bolted upright. "Do the hunters know?"

"One suspects . . . but no. They don't know they hold one of yours, much less a healing cantor."

Jaki choked and sputtered. "Gareth, she's no cantor. She's the Key."

"*The* Key? No. Not possible." Gareth's face froze in a mask of horror. "Fool!" He shoved open his door, breaking through the shell of ice forming around the car. Snowflakes cascaded over him, melting then refreezing. Gareth plowed forward, shielding his face with his arm.

A car door slammed. Jaki blocked his way, his uncovered head gleaming and eyes ablaze. "Don't. We need you alive."

Gareth just swerved around Jaki and continued his winding

path down the gorge. Or was it up? The whiteout conditions distorted any sense of direction.

The storm redoubled its fury. A creaking, cracking rumble filled the air.

Jaki grabbed Gareth's arm and dragged him downhill. "Avalanche!"

Gareth stumbled after him, sliding on Jaki's half-melted trail through the knee-deep snow. The rumbling roared closer. Jaki shoved Gareth ahead of him and whirled around, peeling off his gloves. He flung up his hands, palms out, skin glowing brightly. A wave of snow crashed against a wall of heat. Jaki stumbled back at the impact, but the melted snow refroze into an ice dome around them. Another sheet of snow slammed into it. Fissures spread through the ice.

Gareth backed against the cliff, then leapt away from it, eyes wide in alarm. Seizing Jaki's shoulder, he yelled, "I can't travel through a crack."

The ice dome popped and groaned. Jaki's arms quivered under an invisible load. "No choice. Can't . . . hold." Snapping his hands shut, Jaki whirled to face the cliff. He smashed a fist against the stone. The rock trembled and a black fissure split its face, bordered with a thread of light. "May Creator see fit to add another miracle to this day!" He dove into the fissure, pulling Gareth in after him.

The ice dome collapsed, burying the spot in snow.

LIKE A VULTURE SEEKING CARRION, THE COMMAN-dant circled around Oriel, seeking something at which to pick. But he kept coming up empty. Her hair gleamed healthy. Roses blossomed in her cheeks. Strength exuded from her body. Not at all what would be expected from a person who had suffered a long and debilitating illness. Indeed, miraculous would best describe her sudden recovery—except the commandant didn't believe in miracles.

For the third time in the last minute, Oriel's gaze flitted toward the closed door, ready to fly at the slightest provocation. The muted clacking of a typewriter from the outer office assured that the secretary was hard at work. At least one person was accomplishing something on this bizarre day.

The commandant's scowl deepened, and completing another circuit, he struck Oriel across the face. She didn't utter a sound, but Maggie gave a little cry from a nearby chair, clutching her basket closer.

Oriel shifted her weight, face distressed for the first time during the interrogation. "Please, sir." Her soft voice stretched out with the pleading that her hands dared not express. "Hold her no longer. She has only done good, restoring me to you."

"She goes when I say." The commandant stomped to his desk and dropped the confiscated whistle into a drawer. Oriel tracked his every move; he twitched under her scrutiny. Slamming the drawer shut, he raised his voice. "Old woman, you're dismissed."

Maggie rocked back and forth unheeding of the command.

"Maggie."

At Oriel's whisper, the older woman stilled, and she blinked blearily at the room around her. Oriel nodded toward the door. Maggie shuffled toward it but paused at the threshold. "Promise ye won't leave without saying yer fare-thee-wells?"

Oriel hesitated, then crossed an arm over her chest. "I promise." As if to seal the vow, warmth and the spiciness of cinnamon filled the room, bearing a whisper of hopeful music.

The commandant grimaced, but Maggie smiled, and she shuffled out. When the door clicked shut, Oriel sighed, the music and heat dissipating.

The commandant pressed hands against his desk and leaned forward. "What are you? Mage? Witch? Wielder of the dark arts?"

Oriel looked at him. "Now you ask the question you should have asked at first—now that the end stands at your gate?"

"I asked you a question. I expect an answer."

She bowed her head, and for a moment, her pinched lips seemed to indicate she would refuse the commandant's demand. Then the words came, tight and low. "The truth will find no soil in your heart, though you are made of dust. But so that you may be without excuse, what you request I give." She pulled back her shoulders and met the commandant's scowl head-on. "I am what your stories call an Ishir."

At her mention of the legendary fire beings, Oriel's appearance transformed. Her skin was no longer pale but white like the hottest fire. Her hair wasn't messy but aflame. Her eyes didn't glisten but radiated light.

The commandant blinked. The vision vanished. Oriel was just another pale-faced prisoner at HopeWell. A shudder rippled through him anyway. "Your illness has destroyed your sanity, what little you had left." He thrust open the door and waved a waiting guard toward Oriel. "Take her to the Cellar. I'm going to dinner." He exited the outer office.

The guard escorted Oriel out. She pulled to a stop; a stench of decay polluted the air. She turned toward the commandant. "It's not too late."

"Late?" He paused with his hand on the door to his quarters. "For what?"

"To turn from this path." She strained against the guard gripping her arm. "To escape the coming destruction."

"Destruction?" The commandant snorted. "Get her out of here." He entered his quarters and slammed the door behind him, dismissing Oriel and her words.

As the guard led her away, a long-nosed car pulled up to the gate, followed by two trucks. A guard approached the car. The driver passed him papers. At Agent Kasam's name, the guard's eyes widened. He waved for the gate to be opened. The three vehicles pulled inside and around to the commandant's office.

The driver of the car opened the passenger door, and Juliet climbed out. Behind her the trucks emptied a dozen under-agents into the compound, and they dispersed throughout the camp on pre-assigned tasks. Juliet ascended the porch steps and banged open the door. The secretary startled, scattering papers from a file she held. Juliet paid her no attention but marched to the inner office. It was empty. "Where is he?"

The secretary snatched up the last renegade paper and clutched the pile to her chest. "The commandant? He returned to his quarters for—"

Juliet was already outside, striding across the porch to the adjoining quarters. She threw open the door without knocking.

The commandant sat at his table, a bite of roast partway to his mouth. Behind him, the grandfather clock began to chime.

"Agent Kasam." Pushing back his chair, he wiped his mouth with a napkin and tucked it under the rim of his plate. "This is . . . unexpected."

Juliet put her hands in her coat pockets. "Where is the girl?"

"Girl—Prisoner 304? In the Cellar—"

"That is all, Commandant. You are hereby relieved of your command." Withdrawing a hand, she aimed a pistol at him and fired.

Wide-eyed, the commandant clutched his chest and collapsed in his chair, then slumped forward over his unfinished dinner. The clock struck the twelfth bell.

In the Cellar, Oriel curled into a tighter ball, eyes squeezed shut. "Creator, mercy."

14

THE CRACK THREW GARETH INTO LIGHT AND AIR. Blindly he grabbed for anything solid. His hand brushed stone—a boulder—and he threw an arm around it like a drowning man. He needed to breathe. He needed to breathe *now*. But his lungs, deprived of oxygen for far too long, tried to inhale and exhale simultaneously. Instead, they locked up, doing neither. His muscles turned rigid and eyes glazed, his grasp slipping.

A warm hand pressed against his back, and a marching melody flowed around him, as tangible as a summer breeze. "Shalom le-atah, ben Adam." Jaki's voice rumbled close to Gareth's ear. "Breathe, Gareth, and live."

Gareth drew in a wheezing gasp, a dying man's last, then stuttered out an exhale. His breathing eased into a normal cadence. His body relaxed, and with a groan, he rolled onto his back, eyes still closed. "If I'd wanted to die, I could have done it without your help."

"Says the man on a suicide mission. But desired or not, Death's hand has been stayed; you've successfully traveled a crack into Echoing!"

At Jaki's pronouncement, Gareth opened his eyes. The snow was gone, as well as the car and the entire gorge he'd stood in a moment before. In its place stretched a long, narrow hall. Rocky walls glinted with intricately intertwined veins of gold and silver and with precious stones placed in a pattern so random it seemed deliberate. Several yards above his head, the walls transformed into thick trees, whose leafless branches meshed together into a lattice roof, allowing golden light, softer yet more brilliant than normal sunshine, to penetrate the hall. Not that such light was needed, for everything here gave off a shimmer of its own: stone, gems, trees, even the air itself.

Gareth looked up at Jaki, who had undergone an even more startling transformation. While he retained a vaguely human shape, his skin had been stripped away to reveal a being of molded fire. His arms and face radiated light like molten metal. Short flames replaced his spiky hair.

He had shed his bulky clothing as well, now wrapped in woven rainbows that melted into an upside-down cyclone of golden flames, obscuring his body below the waist; it was impossible to discern whether he possessed legs or feet. Both rainbows and cyclone draped upon him like clothing yet melded with his body as well. Behind him spread a triple layer of fire wings, the flames almost feathery. Overall Jaki presented a sight both mesmerizing and terrifying.

Jaki extended his hand to Gareth, a smoky oak-and-cloves scent wafting through the air. Gareth hesitated, then grasped his friend's hand. Against the fire, his own hand appeared thick and cold, a muddied shadow scarring the surrounding beauty. As soon as Gareth gained his feet, he pulled his hand away.

On his left, the wall sparked with an electrical build-up and hummed with perfectly tuned harmonics. A flash of light followed, and a tall woman wielding a sword stepped out of the rock. The smell of a warm autumn day and a throaty melody of bold determination accompanied her, yet despite the contrast to Jaki's song and scent, hers melded seamlessly with his.

"Shalom." Jaki bowed his head to her. "Danger is past, though I thank you for watching over our passage, Warrior."

Her sword sagged, and she sighed. Her flames softened into a pale yellow, which accented the vibrant red hair cascading across her shoulders like fresh lava. Gareth shaded his eyes against such brilliance.

At his movement, the female Ishir's eyes widened. "He lives?"

"No, I'm a breathing corpse," Gareth muttered.

She winced at the dissonance of his voice but gave him a half bow of respect before sliding her sword away. The blade blended into the surrounding flames, the crystalline hilt alone visible near her waist. "Forgive me, Prince of Guardians. I've never met one of your kind able to walk the webbing. You are most favored indeed."

"Or most cursed." A new voice, mixing the timpani's roll with a shofar's call, rattled the air, and the ground vibrated in echo.

The trio turned. Another Ishir man, even more imposing than Jaki, glided toward them. His flames roiled so intensely that Jaki's fire flickered like a match before a bonfire. The Ishir warriors and Gareth draped both their arms over their chests and bent forward, the gesture of highest respect.

The newcomer gripped the hilt of a sword at his side. "What do you want, man of blood?" His voice set off another ground tremor, and above their heads, the trees groaned.

The spot of Oriel's kiss flamed hot and red upon Gareth's right hand. Gareth straightened, transforming into Oriel's Mighty Prince. "Peace to you too, Sarish."

With a streak of lightning, the point of a double-edged sword pressed against Gareth's throat. The thinnest layer of glass encased the blade, preventing the gold and blue flames from doing any harm, but fiery heat rolled off the weapon, a promise that the flames weren't just for show. "There can be no peace while a slayer shadows this place."

Jaki glided forward, but Gareth raised his hand, stopping his friend from interfering.

Heat boiled around Sarish, raising the temperature a few degrees with each passing second. "I ask again. Why are you here, man of blood?"

"To help."

"We do not need or want help from one such as you."

"Then why am I here by boon?"

Sarish's flames brightened, and he grew several inches, causing Jaki and the female warrior to flinch. "Has your tongue become forked as well, slayer? We made no request of you."

Hairline cracks spiderwebbed across his blade's casing, the flames churning.

Beads of sweat gathered on Gareth's skin, though his expression did not reveal whether that was due to fear or the intensifying heat. "*You* did not, but the Key of Everything did."

"Impossible. The Key is in the Vault."

"You can taste a lie. Does any such rottenness foul the air?"

Sarish swished air in his mouth, and his eyes flickered, his grip on the sword's hilt tightening. "Then you are deceived."

"You tell me." Gareth stretched out a steady hand. The mark burned brighter, as if it knew it was under scrutiny.

Sarish pressed his fingertips to the mark, eyes half closing. A drop of sweat rolled down the side of Gareth's face.

"It is hers." Shrinking several inches, Sarish lowered his sword and drifted backward. The temperature dropped several degrees, and both Sarish's flames and his melody lessened, now churning in confusion. How had Gareth come by a mark from the Key? "I ask you a final time, man of blood. What do you want?"

The haggardness of Prisoner Ninety-Seven resettled over Gareth, and a shadow wrapped him like a second skin, darkening and muddying his form further. "I deserve death." He closed his fingers over Oriel's mark. "Let me use that death for good."

WITH THE NEW DAY'S DAWN, THE SUN SQUEEZED blood-red light through the crack between charcoal clouds and frozen earth. But though that chased away the night's darkness, the cold refused to budge, clinging to both ground and air. Brandon tugged his hat down further on his head against the iciness clawing his skin and tried to hasten his ascent out of Koma. There simply wasn't any reason to linger. For over twenty-four hours he had scoured the town and the surrounding area in search of Prisoner Ninety-Seven. Nothing. The man's trail had gone colder than the snow swathing the world. Even eavesdropping at the recruitment center and the artoikos produced nothing fruitful.

Cresting the hill, Brandon paused to catch his breath. His gaze strayed to Maggie's home. He still had a few days left on his pass. He took a step toward the ramshackle house, then shook his head as if to clear it. "What am I thinking?" He returned to the road leading back to HopeWell.

The clouds swallowed the rising sun, and light flattened into a depressing gray. An unnatural calm overshadowed the forest. No birds hopped among the tree branches. No wind rustled the pines boughs. Nothing moved, nothing impeded the silence except the crunching tread of Brandon's feet. He unfastened the buttons of his coat despite the cold and moved the handgun beneath. He rounded the final bend, bringing HopeWell into sight. He abruptly halted.

Where activity should dominate, stillness. Where men should be stationed, emptiness. No soldier marched along the fence, no guard tended the gate, and though the prisoners should be well into their workday, no noise echoed within the wire. Smoke didn't even drift up from chimneys to mesh with the clouds.

With leaden steps Brandon drew near the gate, still barred to the outside world. Neither greeting nor command arrested his approach. He curled a hand around a post and peered through the chain links. Not a soul in sight.

"They're gone."

Brandon whirled, pressing his back against the gate. Maggie sat on a tree stump at the edge of the forest, her hat shadowing her face and the wicker basket beside her.

"What are you doing here, Grandmama?" His voice was terse but quiet, though no one else was around to hear.

"Night fell. The trucks came. They took them all away." Her words drooped under the weight of sorrow.

"What are you talking about?"

"Only *she's* left." Maggie's voice dropped to a whisper. "Her and evil." She shuddered.

The hair along Brandon's neck prickled. "Go home, Grandmama."

Maggie looked up at her grandson. "Can't. She needs me."

"Nobody needs you." His remark smacked the air, and Maggie crumpled, hand to her heart.

Brandon winced. "I didn't mean it that way."

"Yer right. Nobody needs me." Maggie inhaled deeply and opened her eyes, tears sparkling within. "But I am wanted, and that is enough." Rising, she set her jaw. "So I go, not because I need to, but because He wants me to." She reached HopeWell's gate and lifted her face skyward. "But I can't be doing this alone, Ye know."

Brandon spread out his hands helplessly. "The gate's barred. From the inside. Even if I wanted to—"

The clouds ripped apart, and a blinding light flashed. Brandon threw an arm over his eyes while Maggie smiled in greeting. Then the clouds mended themselves, sealing away the light, and an unnaturally warm wind barreled past them. Wood cracked; the crossbar splintered, allowing the gate to swing in a few inches. The wind died.

Maggie grasped the gate, still looking heavenward. "I thank Ye." Then she inclined her head to her right and left. "Ye too."

Lowering his arm, Brandon squinted at the space on either

side of Maggie. Nothing but air. Then at his grandmother's expectant look, he obediently opened the gate wide enough for them to slip through. On the other side, Maggie paused to straighten her hat while Brandon examined the broken bar. The wood was charred at the break. "How . . . ?"

"The Ishir helped. A Qolet too."

"Grandmama." Brandon looked at her with exasperation. "There is no such thing as an Ishir. Or a Qolet or a Dachi. They're fairytales, the product of somebody's imagination."

"Even fairy stories must begin somewhere, Brady." Maggie patted Brandon's cheek, the nickname for her grandson softening the chiding tone.

"She's right." Juliet materialized from behind a leg of the watchtower—a leg which shouldn't have hidden her from sight.

Maggie paled to the deathly gray of weathered wood and curled over like a withered leaf. Brandon stationed himself between the two women, his spine stiffening like a rod of iron.

Juliet sauntered toward them, hands buried in the pockets of the heavy coat hugging her curves. "Aren't you going to introduce us, Sergeant? Your grandmother seems like a real *jewel* of a woman."

Maggie shuddered and squeezed her eyes shut, lips moving soundlessly. Brandon broadened his stance. "With all due respect, I'm sure you've more important duties to attend to, Agent Kasam."

"I doubt that." Juliet stretched out a foot as if inspecting the shoe for scuff marks. "Besides, stories can enliven a gloomy day, and it sounds like Grandmama knows some good ones."

"Just the normal bedtime tales." Brandon crept a hand toward his gun.

Juliet sidestepped him and whipped out her own weapon, aiming it straight at Maggie. Brandon froze. Whatever move he made would only endanger his grandmother further.

"I thought you'd reconsider." Juliet came closer, aim unwavering. "I would hate for her to have heart failure. The commandant's untimely passing yesterday was tragic enough."

Brandon's gaze flicked toward the commandant's quarters, then the office. The windows of both were dark, their chimneys smokeless.

"Yes, he's dead." The punctuated words implied the fact should be obvious. "Why else would no one be here? Without someone to run the camp, I had to transfer everybody."

"Not all, not all." Maggie huddled closer to Brandon.

"I couldn't transfer *her*, could I? The other commandants aren't trained to handle nonhuman prisoners."

The fabric of Brandon's coat stretched taut, straining to contain his building fury. "You're mad."

"Am I? Then perhaps you'd better tread with care, Sergeant." Juliet caressed the gun's barrel with the tip of her finger. "For if you're right, I'm a madwoman wielding a gun, and mad people aren't known to act predictably."

A forced calm relaxed his posture, though tension still pinched his lips. "What do you want, Agent Kasam?"

"That's right. Humor the madwoman, and you might live. Or not." Juliet shrugged a shoulder. "But let's talk someplace warmer, shall we?" She waved them toward the commandant's office.

Brandon slid his arm around Maggie's shoulders and helped her along as Juliet trailed behind them.

As they reached the porch, a man in a black uniform exited the office. The silver dragon crest embroidered on his sleeve identified him as a hunter. Stopping before Juliet, he clicked his heels together and bowed at the waist.

"You have news?" Disinterest flattened Juliet's voice, but her nostrils flared in anticipation.

The hunter straightened. "We tracked the guardian to a gorge a few miles away."

Maggie gasped and clutched Brandon.

"You secured him then?"

The hunter shuffled his feet. "No. We found an abandoned car."

"A car?" Juliet's voice rose. "I don't want another car. I want *him*."

Despite her anger the man held his ground. "We traced a path from the car to the canyon wall where the trail ends." He glanced at Maggie and Brandon, then leaned closer to Juliet, voice lowering. "We suspect a gateway."

15

"DID YOU BOTHER TO SLEEP AT ALL?"

Jaki's unconventional greeting rang out among the leafless trees, harmonizing with the birds' chatter despite his chastising tone. Though clouds grayed the sky, the world glowed with early morning light, no shadow marring the treed hillside. No shadow, that is, except for Gareth himself. Wearing the same clothes with a few extra wrinkles, he sat on a rock in the hilltop clearing, flipping a pair of long-bladed knives between his hands. Dark circles had deepened under his eyes, testifying that his second night away from HopeWell contained as little sleep as the first.

Jaki folded his arms across his broad chest, sparks cascading through his flames in disapproval. "You shall drain all your strength before the battle begins if you continue like this."

"I can rest when my breath disperses." Gareth twirled the knives one last time. Unlike Sarish's fireblade, Gareth's weapons appeared to be made of steel engraved with gold scroll patterns. He stashed them under his coat into sheaths strapped at each hip.

"At this pace, my friend, the lack of rest will disperse your breath." Jaki scrutinized the knife peeking over the top of Gareth's new boots—his one upgrade in clothing—and then eyed the tomahawk strapped to his small pack of food, next to a water skin. "At least you visited the armory."

"They refused me my guardian daggers."

"That is indeed a pity, but it's a refusal I can understand. Guardian weapons belong to guardians."

"And I am no longer one, am I?" Gareth tightened a strap on

his pack with a jerk.

"Gareth, guardian is more than a position. As you very well know."

"Do I?" He swung his pack over his shoulder and inspected Jaki. The flames of his Ishir companion burned hotter and brighter than before; the scent of pine and an intertwining contralto harmony lingered around him. "I see, however, you availed yourself of Cantor Avviel's healing song."

"Unlike you," said Jaki. "I plan to face the battle with all the strength Creator will grant." Compressing his flames into an arc, he leapt across the entire clearing to a deer trail grooved into the snow and headed the opposite direction from which he arrived. "Cantor Avviel is the best Ishir healer in Echoing, her gift unmatched."

"And her flame the brightest?"

Jaki's fire intensified to a brilliant red. "Your lack of sleep has befuddled your brain."

"And love yours." Gareth came up beside him. "Why not ask her to meld flame and song, and end your agony? At least one of us should have that joy." His smile faded, the shadow around him deepening.

"It wasn't your fault." A sympathetic lilt was added to Jaki's melody. "She walked away, not you."

Gareth ignored him and started down the trail. "Are we planning to reach HopeWell by nightfall or not?"

Jaki's fire flickered in concern, but he spread a pair of his wings and glided after Gareth. Gareth pressed onward without acknowledging him.

The trail steepened, the ice-glazed rocks and roots warping the path into a treacherous climb. Gareth continued upward at the same brutal pace, but after he slipped for the third time, Jaki cleared his throat. "Perhaps we should—"

"No."

The path flattened out, and forest succumbed to barren fields swathed with snowdrifts. In the distance, an arched distortion marred the sky much like a heat mirage, though the chill of early spring still nipped at the skin. Gareth cut across the lumpy furrows of the field toward it.

Jaki flapped his wings to propel him to Gareth's side. "Perhaps we should have waited for the car we were offered."

"More efficient . . . to meet at . . . the gateway."

"Slow down, Gareth." Jaki touched Gareth's arm, and Gareth flinched at the heat penetrating his coat, though Jaki's flames didn't scorch the cloth. "It aids no one if you weary yourself in the first hour."

"It aids no one if we are a single minute late."

Jaki shook his head. "Understanding eludes me concerning the impenetrable shadow surrounding you."

"Of course a shadow hangs around me," Gareth retorted. "I'm made of dust and breath, not fire and song like you."

"That is not the shadow of which I speak. Creator Himself holds time in His hand and bends it to His will, yet you march as if you have forgotten this."

Gareth's shoulders caved. "You're right. I have forgotten." Reaching a split-rail fence separating two fields, Gareth stopped and leaned against it. "But I had no choice. Forgetting was the only way to live."

"Yet if you must forget Creator in order to live, what is left to live for?"

"Sometimes I wonder if even He is worth living for." Gareth expelled a heavy sigh. "That must sound blasphemous to you."

"Your imprisonment has been hard."

Gareth hefted himself over the fence, movements stiff and cumbersome. "It erased any envy of your long life." He dropped to the ground on the other side, splattering slushy snow and mud everywhere.

Jaki vaulted over, his flames arching well above the rough-hewn rails, and he landed in front of Gareth. He pressed his palms together. "Do I have permission to speak forthrightly, Guardian?"

Gareth made a face at the formal title. "You have always been free to speak your mind with me, Jaki. That hasn't changed."

"Thank you." Jaki steepled his fingers and closed his eyes, melody softening.

Above them a bird wheeled, and the dripping trickle of melting snow promised that spring was nearing.

Jaki raised his head, renewed intensity burning in his eyes. "You forget, not to avoid dying, but to avoid living."

Gareth propped himself against the fence, folding his arms. "You always enjoyed a good riddle. Care to explain this one?"

"Forgetting may have kept Creator's breath joined with dust, but that is not *why* you forgot. You forgot because remembering would require you to act."

Gareth's shoulders stiffened. "Not all darkness is repulsive." He shrugged off his pack and detached the water skin. "No one expects a man to work at night. No one expects the sick to doctor the well."

"Or the prisoner to protect the treasure?"

Gareth's hand tightened around the water skin.

"You do not stop being what Creator designed you to be because you no longer do what He created you to do." Jaki moved into Gareth's peripheral. "You are a guardian, Gareth. You do not cease to be a guardian because you refuse to perform the duties of a guardian."

Gareth took a long swig, then meticulously reattached the water skin to his pack. "I can't make myself desire what Creator desires."

"Yet here you are."

"Not willingly."

"Then ask Him. Ask for the will. Creator has promised to

provide all we need—including the desire to do His work."

Gareth shrugged the bag onto his back and resumed traversing the field. "You make it sound easy."

"Simple, Gareth, not easy." Jaki skirted a cluster of puddles. "Creator's ways are rarely complicated but often require everything we have to give."

Gareth trod through the water, the splashing his only response.

Around them, the air warmed, and the distant smudge of a distortion enlarged into a transparent archway, a blue-gray shimmer against the cloudy sky. Jaki snagged a small branch and chewed on it as Gareth trudged forward at a steady pace.

Crossing a road, Jaki pointed at the archway with the charred tip of the branch he held. "How do we proceed once we reenter Terrestrial?"

"The plan is to have no plan."

Jaki chuckled. "It's a pleasure to know some things haven't changed." He consumed the rest of the wood with a crunch.

"Hard to predict the unpredictable." An almost-smile lightened Gareth's shadowiness a shade.

Mist spiraled up from the ground, stringing beads of moisture together. "Predict the unpredictable. Predict the unpredictable." Disembodied voices singsonged the words from every side. The mist thickened into swirling white eddies, the echoing voices cascading into childlike giggles.

Gareth cautiously pulled out his knives and backed up to Jaki. "Do we run for it?"

"And which way would you go?"

Gareth looked around. The mist had become so dense that it obscured even the tips of his knives. "I see your point."

"If you can see my point, your eyesight exceeds mine." Jaki's fire dimmed amongst the abundant dampness. He raised his voice and thrust out a fiery hand. "Neru!"

The command rumbled through the air, and the mist

sighed. Moisture bunched together into several small clouds before condensing into two dozen water children—the Dachi. Collectively they looked at themselves and groaned. "Aww."

The boy nearest Gareth perked up. "New game—waterball!" He rolled his hands together, and a watery sphere formed between them. He lobbed the ball at Gareth.

Gareth raised his arm defensively. The ball splattered against it.

A fresh round of giggles spread through the group. "Waterball, waterball!" Wet globes of every size were launched from all sides.

Ball after ball struck Jaki and Gareth. They deflected many of them, but dodging all of them was impossible. Jaki's fire, no longer protected by the skin of his human façade, died a little more with each direct hit. His flames near the ground grayed to ash. "Gareth . . ."

"Working on it." He struck out with his knives; two more globs hit the flats and burst. Water soaked his clothing and dripped off his hair.

"Work faster, would you?" Jaki blocked a ball only for another to sneak past his guard, striking him on the shoulder and dousing the flames there. They reignited a second later, but not as strong as before. Strands of smoke snaked toward his chest and the core of his fire.

Gareth slashed through another watery orb, but that merely divided it into two smaller spheres. "In Creator's Name, stop!"

The barrage ceased. The Dachi glanced at each other, arms still poised, then at Gareth and Jaki. The nearest Dachi, a girl of three feet, smashed her ball into the ground already muddy from the water dripping off of her. "Fire and Dust no fun." At her emphatic head shake, her turquoise braids, decorated with snowflakes, swung about, spraying water droplets around her.

"They never have time to play." The girl beside her stuck out her lip and folded her arms over a dress still made of snow and ice.

A boy stomped his foot, muddying the ground further. "They don't like to play."

"Except Levioth." The first girl perked up. "She plays with us. She teaches us new games."

"Like waterball!" Several Dachi tossed their balls.

Gareth shielded his face with an arm. "Levioth is a he."

"Not the new one. She's a girl. A girl who likes fun."

A massive waterball struck Jaki square in the chest. He staggered backward, his flames sputtering in the fight to rekindle.

"Jakkiel." Gareth sheltered him a best as he could.

"At least . . . we know . . . how Levioth . . . turned them." Jaki wheezed, smoke dominating his form. One strong gust of wind and much of him would dissipate. "Who knew . . . the childish . . . that powerful."

Gareth's face cleared, and he wheeled about. "Who wants to learn a new game?"

The Dachi hesitated, arms raised to launch the next round. The boy who spoke first lowered his hand, eyes narrowed in suspicion. "What does Dust know about games?"

"Creator made us like Him. He taught us to make up things like He made up the world. How else would Levioth know new games? She . . ." Gareth frowned at the feminine pronoun. "She is Dust too."

A girl combed her fingers through her braid without messing it up, water passing through water. "Dust is right. What games do you know?"

Gareth knelt, putting him at her eye level. "Many games. But you see, I have a problem. Your last game hurt my friend. I need to get him to a cantor soon or he could lose all his fire."

"You just tricking us. Dust knows no new games." The boy leader swung back his arm.

"Then Levioth has taught you skipping stones?"

"Skipping stones . . . skipping stones?" A brook's babbling

rippled through the Dachi as they whispered excitedly to each other.

The boy leader scowled. "No. You are tricking us." But his words curled up at the end, revealing doubt underneath.

"Follow us to the cantor's. Once there, I'll teach you skipping stones."

The boy considered the ball perched on his hand, then Gareth's solemn expression. He closed his fist, reabsorbing the orb. "What else?"

"Else?"

The boy held up fingers. "One Fire. One Dust. That makes two games."

Gareth skimmed the landscape. "If you promise to never play Levioth's games except with each other, I'll teach you *three* new games."

"Three?" The boy's watery body rippled.

"Three."

The Dachi's babbling murmur surged into the chant of a pounding surf. "Do it, do it, do it."

The leader hesitated a moment longer, then clapped his hands. "Deal!" A geyser of water gushed out between his hands and crystallized midair, falling upon Jaki and Gareth as snow.

"Deal." Gareth scooped up a handful of mud and blew on it. It dried into dust and sprinkled over the Dachi.

Giggling, they scattered backward. "Dust, that tickles."

Gareth smiled begrudgingly and helped Jaki rise. Despite his weakness, rainbows cascaded through his flames, expressing the amused pleasure of being proven right. "Neither you nor Sarish may want to admit it, but even after all these years you are the Prince of Guardians. You cannot escape what Creator has made you to be."

16

A BLACK CAR GROUND TO A HALT BEHIND THE ONE Gareth and Jaki abandoned, now half-buried in the remains of the avalanche. Three men and one woman stood a few paces away, their gazes as black as their clothing. Juliet climbed out from her vehicle, ignoring how her feet sank into the snow. Skipping all formalities and greetings, she simply demanded, "Show me."

The Alpha hunter trudged over to a half-collapsed ice dome a dozen yards down the gorge. Juliet followed him into the crater and examined a small section of ice yet clinging to the cliff. While crystals prickled the outside, the inside was glass smooth—the work of an Ishir. She transferred her attention to the four shoeprints embedded in the snow by the cliff, preserved by the still-standing ice. "Two men"—Juliet glanced back at the abandoned car—"retreating . . . but from what?"

"We haven't uncovered any evidence of a pursuer," offered the nearest hunter, "but the avalanche may have obscured their trail."

"Avalanche?" Juliet tapped a finger against her chin before satisfied realization spread over her face. "So they *can* be turned." She looked up at the cliff again. "But why flee here?"

She slid her hand across the rock face several times before centering over a spot near the middle of the dome's protection. Pressing her left palm against the cliff, she muttered three words, spoken too low for the hunters' ears. She couldn't have them stealing her secrets.

For a moment nothing happened. Then the stone darkened, like a shadow falling upon it, and Juliet's hand sank into the rock. The newest hunter gasped. A dark gleam filled Juliet's eyes as she pushed forward. Her forearm disappeared, then her elbow.

The cliff shuddered. Juliet's triumphant expression evaporated. Stepping backward, she tugged on her arm. The stone refused to release her. Blood drained from her face. She yanked again and again, digging her heels into the snow in the struggle to free herself. Another inch of her arm vanished into the shadow. Juliet's scream reverberated off the gorge's walls. "Don't stand there, fools. Do something!"

The hunters sprang forward and latched onto her, trying to drag her backward. The wall groaned, then let go, sending the group sprawling into the snow. The shadow faded from the rock.

"Off of me. Off!" Juliet disentangled herself and clawed her way upright. She cradled her left arm against her chest, hand dangling at an odd angle. Her forehead glistened from pain.

The Alpha scrambled to his feet and bowed deeply before her. "I am sorry. I thought it was—it won't happen again."

"No, it won't." With one swift movement, Juliet withdrew her gun with her good hand. A shot rang out. Redness splattered the snow. "You." Juliet pointed the gun at the female hunter. "You're in charge now. Dispose of the body and continue the search."

The woman bowed to Juliet as she passed. "As you wish."

Juliet reached her vehicle, where the driver opened the door for her. She paused, glancing back at the three remaining hunters. "Next time, verify it's a gateway, not a crack. Otherwise I will send each of you through—feet first." She got into the car, and the driver closed her door.

He returned to his spot behind the wheel. "Where do you wish to go?"

Juliet drummed her fingers against the arm rest. "HopeWell.

I've a prisoner to interrogate."

LAUGHTER RANG THROUGH ECHOING, ALL THE
Dachi finally occupied.

One group tossed a flat rock between them by skipping it
off the watery surface of their being. A short distance away, the
leader hunted for his friends hiding among mud puddles and
snow piles. A third group played leapfrog, each trying to arch
higher than the last one. Water droplets scattered rainbows over
the scene.

Gareth watched nearby, seated beside a heap of boulders
hand-picked from the surrounding fields. The Anatroshkan
government might boast how modern they were, but most farmers
still worked the ground the way their fathers and grandfathers
had before them. This rock pile bore testimony to that, and the
Terrestrial farmer probably left them here for that reason—in
mockery of Anatroshka's "advanced" society and the State that
claimed these lands as its own.

Whatever the reason, the rocks formed the perfect spot in
Echoing for the fire-reviving work of the cantors, with its nearness
to a gateway an added bonus. Only a dozen yards away the
archway shimmered and sparkled, beckoning Gareth onward.

"Surely you do not think to charge back to Terrestrial without
me, old friend?" Flames and lava squeezed out between the
rocks and coalesced into Jaki's fiery form at the edge of the pile.
Although the warmth rolling off him was cooler than when they'd
first set out that morning, neither smoke nor ash bound him any
longer, and his melody glided along without gasping breaks.

"To my shame, think is all I've done."

Jaki's melody and flames flickered merrily. "That *was* concern
which darkened your face."

Gareth shouldered his pack. "Too much joy song again, I see."

"Never." Settling his sword at his side, Jaki surveyed the Dachi's play. "I've not seen them this content in decades. Maybe even centuries. How did you do it?"

"Children's games, amusements every human child learns at a young age. Nothing brilliant."

"Thus you may say, but to feel the laughter of Creator ringing through the air—it heals almost as well as the cantor's songs." As if to verify his words, giggles cascaded around them, and Jaki's flames leapt up like fire refreshed by a burst of oxygen.

Gareth gave a half grin, but then he refocused on the gateway. "We need to go."

"What perturbs you, old friend?" Sparks of concern crackled around Jaki. "An extra shadow has cloaked you since the Dachi mentioned a new Levioth, yet I cannot illuminate why. Creator limits even the unnaturally long life of Levioth, and the last one had already seen two centuries when you grasped your guardian daggers, now how many years ago?"

"Too many." Gareth cinched his pack's straps tighter. "But a new Levioth doesn't bother me. A woman as Levioth bothers me." He started toward the gateway.

Jaki coasted alongside him. "Why? A female Levioth is rare but not unheard of."

Gareth's hands clenched around his pack's straps. "Unless things have drastically changed since I was active, only one woman wielded enough power to become Levioth. And that woman has Oriel."

FROM CAPTOR TO CAPTIVE IN LESS THAN TWO DAYS. How could plans go so wrong so fast?

Brandon circled the cramped space of the prison cabin again

and again, as if boots could pound answers from the floor. A losing cause. What did wood and nails know about the mechanisms of a madwoman? Because Agent Kasam was mad—had to be, even more than his grandmother—to believe the things she said. Right?

"Sit yerself down, or ye shall wear before the battle's begun," Maggie admonished from the bunk where Brandon insisted she rest. He pounded the floorboards harder as he passed by.

"Your grandmother speaks true." Oriel sat atop her old bunk, knees hugged to her chest. After Juliet's departure, the two remaining hunters confined her in the cabin with Maggie and Brandon. Oriel leaned forward, the ticking crackling beneath her. "Battles extract a high cost; you will need all you possess for the time ahead."

Brandon sneered at her. "And what would you know of war and battle?"

"Only that which can be known through the Ancient Writings." She lowered her head, the cloth of her pants scrunched in her fists. "But knowledge gained from others' trials does not render that knowledge invalid." She dropped to the floor, landing in the midst of Brandon's path, and locked eyes with him. Their depths once again dispelled the notion she was a child. "You cannot serve two masters. You must decide what is worth protecting." She pinned her gaze to his right pocket, where the Protector's Star resided.

Outside, an engine rumbled.

Twisting toward the door, Brandon reached for the gun he no longer possessed. Maggie wrapped her arms around herself. "Levioth," she whispered.

Oriel skirted around Brandon to crouch before Maggie. "Al-irah, Margaret. Don't fear." She took Maggie's gnarled hands in hers, warmth curling around them. "Can a mother forget her child? Even though she forgets, He cannot forget you. Like rubies and diamonds in a crown are the prayers of a Jewel in the ear of Creator."

Maggie sighed. "He be my strength and my shield."

"That's right. Breathe His words, for they are life."

"Thank ye for staying." Maggie cupped a hand around Oriel's face. "I know it be hard for ye."

Brandon huffed. "Like she had any choice in the matter." He stalked over to the window and tried to peer through a crack between the shutters' boards.

Pressing her lips together, Maggie snatched her hat from the end of the bed and smashed it down on her head. A fresh tear spread through the brim near the crown. "It's never wise to deny an Ishir's strength, Brady."

"More fairy talk!" Brandon plunked down onto a bench, his back to the other two. "Why do I even try?"

Oriel stood. "Because truth calls and your heart leaps, though your mind won't let it answer."

Brandon shot her an icy glare. "Why can't you speak plainly like normal people?"

"In what way do I speak unplainly?" Oriel was now perched on the other end of the bench, legs folded under her.

"Yer talking's not the problem." Maggie shuffled over. "It's his hearing."

Brandon crossed his arms. "There's nothing wrong with my hearing."

"Then why there be wool stuffed in yer ears?"

"There's nothing in my . . ." He blinked, his words dying as his fingers extracted a wad of wool from his right ear. In the left he found a second tuft.

Oriel scooted near him, confusion on her face. "Odd. He doesn't usually . . ." Her mouth formed a small o. "Free the prisoners, not prisoner. Forgive my blindness, Creator."

Brandon edged away from her. "What?"

"My mission—it wasn't complete. That's why Creator

sent me back."

"You make less sense with every word you speak."

Maggie poked at the wool, childlike wonder filling her face. "It's real!"

"Of course it's real." Oriel took one of the wads and closed Maggie's fingers around it. "Creator gave you eyes to see what others cannot. Relish the gift rather than fearing it."

Maggie opened her hands. Instead of wool, she held a pair of old-fashioned spectacles. She stroked them in awe, then slid them on; a warm glow bathed the cabin, and flames haloed Oriel. When she removed them, the room returned to normal. "Thank ye."

Oriel held out her hand for the rest of the wool, which Brandon had crushed in his fist. "May I?"

He tossed it onto the table. "If you want. It's just wool."

Pinching the tuft between her thumb and forefinger, Oriel twisted it side to side, like one inspecting a gem. "Creator has offered you a rare glimpse beyond the Wall. What you do with that glimpse—that is the choice before you." She cupped her hands around the wool and rested her forehead on them, the scent of cinnamon and frankincense swirling around her.

Brandon glanced at Maggie for an explanation, but her eyes were fastened on Oriel.

Lowering her arms, Oriel kept one hand close to her body and slid the other away. A wood shaft materialized between them, and when she opened her fingers, an arrow rested upon her palms, notched with vibrant golden feathers. She extended it to Brandon.

He reached for it but jerked back before his skin brushed the wood.

"Take it." Though soft, her voice urged him on, compelling him. "Every protector needs a weapon."

Brandon stretched out his hand again. For several seconds, it hovered above the arrow, then his fingers closed around the shaft. He sucked in a breath. His skin reddened from a surge of heat, but he held onto the arrow and the shaft cooled to room temperature.

Oriel smiled, light dancing within her eyes. "Creator's choice is true, as always." Then her gaze darted toward the door. "Levioth comes."

Brandon positioned himself between Maggie and the door. The arrow he tucked into his belt behind him, out of sight but accessible. Oriel rose, her skin flushing.

The door swung inward, and outside light tumbled into the room. Juliet crossed the threshold. Her left arm, splinted and bandaged, hung in a sling. Pain had hardened her face into a determination to unleash that same pain on another. Seeing Brandon blockading her way, Juliet snapped her first three fingers together. "Kagor."

Brandon collapsed, unconscious.

Oriel leapt forward, but before she could near Juliet, the older woman repeated the motion with Maggie, who also crumpled to the floor unconscious. Oriel jerked to a stop, an invisible leash yanked taut.

Juliet smirked. "That's right. I'm no longer a threat to them, so there's nothing you can do." She closed the door, plunging the room back into shadow.

A willed calm relaxed Oriel's posture.

"How'd he do it?" spat Juliet.

Oriel only looked at the closed door.

Crossing the open space between them in two strides, Juliet shot out her hand and grabbed Oriel's throat, forcing her chin up. Oriel's skin reddened, but Juliet didn't release her. "Your Ishir tricks won't work with me. How did Gareth pass through a crack?"

"The Adam can't use cracks." Neither the tremor of terror nor the boiling of anger rippled the surface of Oriel's voice.

"Two trails led to the crack."

"And one of them must be his?"

Juliet squeezed her lips together, eyes flicking back and forth in review of the memory.

"Ever looking but never seeing, ever listening but never hearing." Oriel's words were unmistakable despite their quietness. "You cannot obtain what you desire for your desire has already obtained you."

Juliet jerked her attention back, and she broke into a sharp laugh. "Says the one who has power but cannot use it." She leaned forward, the odor of stale cigarette smoke tainting the air. "Where is the nearest gateway?"

Oriel fixed her gaze over Juliet's shoulder.

"Many people think death is the worst that can happen. But we both know that's not true, don't we?" The threat fouled the air as much as stale smoke. Then Juliet released Oriel and turned toward the others. "She's old and frail. Him, on the other hand . . ."

Oriel remained statuesque.

"The question is who to start with? Will it be more fun to watch him lose his grandmother inch by inch . . . or for her to lose her grandson? Or better yet, maybe I'll alternate so I might enjoy the best of both."

Oriel's nostrils flared.

It was the tiniest of movements, but Juliet needed nothing bigger to spur her on. "Terrible, isn't it? All that power, more than enough to stop me, but *He* won't let you interfere in human affairs without permission, unless one of us is in immediate danger."

"You're right. I can't interfere." Despite her admission, Oriel's face relaxed. "But that doesn't stop me from leaving." She flicked her hand toward the door, and it burst into flame.

"No!" Juliet lunged for her.

But Oriel leapt forward and plunged her hand into the blaze. Melting into the fire, she passed through the door on the flames.

She emerged on the other side, skin molten and hair fiery, until she broke contact. Then she resumed her human manifestation unscathed, neither clothing singed nor the scent of smoke clinging to her.

At Oriel's appearance, the hunter standing guard stumbled back, fumbling for his gun. Oriel paid him no attention. She held out her palm and closed her fingers. The door's flames extinguished, leaving behind charred, smoking wood.

The hunter fired his gun one . . . two . . . three times, each bullet striking her chest, ripping through clothing and skin. But instead of falling, Oriel merely grimaced, fireblood oozing from the punctures. She pressed a hand over the holes and sprinted toward the gates.

Drawn by the gunshots, several other hunters converged on the scene and opened fire. Several shots hit their mark. Oriel's gait hitched, but she kept going: Bullets were designed to remove an Adam's breath, not douse an Ishir's fire.

She reached the gate. The bar hadn't been repaired since Maggie and Brandon's arrival. She shoved the barrier aside and continued her sprint down the road. Trees soon veiled her from sight.

The hunters ceased their pursuit, guns lowering to their side. Juliet emerged from the scorched door, rushing toward them. "What are you standing around for? We must catch her before she passes through a crack!"

"But the prisoners . . ."

"Secure them in another cabin and leave them. They won't wake for a couple of hours yet, and fear will hold them here after that. And if they do escape . . ." Juliet shrugged a shoulder. "I've more important quarry to track."

17

A FEW RAYS FROM THE AFTERNOON SUN WERE squeezing past shuttered windows by the time Brandon stirred. Transferred to another cabin before Juliet's departure, he had lain deathly still upon the bunk where the hunters had dumped him. Only an occasional flicker of eyes revealed he fought the darkness binding him.

Maggie shuffled over to check on him. His hand began to twitch. Then he pried his eyes open, only to immediately close them again, groaning.

"Easy, Brady." Maggie sat on the edge of the bunk and pressed a hand to his forehead like a mother checking a child's temperature. Brandon's skin didn't burn but was cold and clammy. She softly clucked her tongue. "He mayn't know it, but he's needing Yer help."

A moment passed, then Brandon's skin warmed, color returning to his cheeks. "Grandmama?" He squinted up at Maggie, then rolled his head to the side. A row of shadowed bunks stretched before him. He groaned again. "It wasn't a nightmare."

Maggie squeezed his hand. "No, it weren't. A nightmare would be a mite more frightening." She moved out of his way. "Can ye rise?"

Brandon gritted his teeth and propped himself onto his elbows. The effort wrung beads of sweat from his forehead, but he kept going, pushing himself into a sitting position, legs over the edge of the bunk. Resting elbows on knees, he clutched his head between his hands, his chest straining to draw in sufficient oxygen.

Maggie rubbed his back. "Give yerself time."

"I don't think time can fix this."

"Then it don't need fixing." She hobbled to the door and rattled the knob. "Locked."

"You still don't understand, do you?" Brandon kneaded his neck. "We're prisoners now."

"Pishposh." Maggie fluttered a hand, batting away his reasoning as nonsense. "Prisoners don't make doors locked. Keys make doors locked. And jest because it was locked don't mean it'll stay that way. Creator does as He wishes."

"Even assuming that's true, what makes you think He'll unlock it?"

"What makes ye think He won't?"

Brandon opened his mouth, shut it again, then shook his head. "You always did know how to turn everything upside down."

Maggie clucked her tongue. "It be upside down only because ye are."

"If you say so." Brandon gripped the post and pulled himself to his feet. "Where's the girl? Prisoner . . . 309? 304?"

Maggie's shoulders drooped. "Gone." She sank onto the bench. "Levioth too."

"Levioth—oh, Agent Kasam?" Keeping a grip on the edge of the upper bunk, Brandon wobbled forward. "How can you be sure they are gone? They could be in a different part of camp." He held up a hand before Maggie could respond. "Never mind. I forgot to whom I was speaking." He reached the foot of the bed and turned to walk back. Oriel's arrow lay on the mattress. He picked it up and fingered the smooth shaft.

"Ye needn't be fretting about her. She's Ishir."

Brandon clenched the arrow. "I'm not 'fretting.' As a prisoner she deserves whatever she gets."

Maggie hummed, which conveyed doubt better than any

words she could have offered.

His face flushed. "Think what you will, but it doesn't change my opinion." He tossed the arrow toward the table.

It glanced off the edge and returned to him, the tip embedding itself in the floor less than an inch from his foot. Maggie ducked her head, hiding her face beneath her hat's floppy brim, but a chuckle emanated from beneath it.

"Not funny, Grandmama."

"Only because it was *your* toes," commented a gruff voice behind him.

Brandon spun back toward the door, which—miracles of miracles—had opened soundlessly. Two men stood in the opening, their features indistinguishable against the waning light. With a gasp Maggie pushed past Brandon. "Yer back!" She drew the nearest man's head down to bestow a motherly kiss on his forehead.

Gareth dropped his own kiss on the crown of her hat. "Hello, Maggie."

The two men entered the cabin, backing Brandon up against the table. Though the first was unmistakably Prisoner Ninety-Seven, youthful power radiated from him, and many of the lines had faded from his face, as if he'd lost fifteen or twenty years during his two-day absence from HopeWell. The second man was Jaki, once again sporting his Terrestrial form, complete with heavy coat and wide-brimmed fedora. An imposing pair.

"How—how did you get in here?" Brandon stammered.

Gareth arched his eyebrows. "Through the gate."

"But the others—"

"There are no others. HopeWell was deserted, except for you two." He lifted the sagging brim of Maggie's hat with his index finger. "The whistle, did it . . . ?"

"Ye worry too much." Crinkles gathered at the corners of Maggie's eyes as she patted him on the cheek. "She's strong. Music was jest the thing to help."

"And now?"

The crinkles drooped, and her eyes glazed. "Gone. Don't know where. Levioth . . ."

"She means Agent Kasam." Brandon edged along the table toward Maggie.

Gareth's brow knotted at this latest confirmation that Juliet and Levioth were the same. "What happened, Maggie?"

She rubbed her arms. "Cold, black, everywhere. Then both gone . . . all gone." She swayed.

"Carry no shame, Creator's Jewel, for the blame is not yours to bear." Jaki's voice rang through the cabin, the sound warming the air.

Maggie blinked, then squinted over Gareth's shoulder. "Can it be?" With trembling hands, she patted her pockets until she found the spectacles from Oriel. She slid them on and gasped. "Ye are!"

Jaki chuckled. "Yes, I am, and it has finally pleased Creator to grant me the joy of meeting you, Honored Jewel." Lowering himself to one knee, he fisted his hand over his chest and dipped his head in respect. "Your steadfastness to Creator and the work He has given you is legendary among the Ishir."

"I knew I saw ye that day, but all said I was not right in the head."

"Your head was the most right of all." Jaki placed a hand upon her, calming the tremors cascading through her body.

"I told them ye rescued him, not me. But their stubbornness wouldn't let them hear." Shaking her head, Maggie tucked the spectacles away.

"They didn't know it, but they spoke truth. I was there to see, not act. Creator wanted me to observe a Jewel at work in order that I might remember He is the source of all. I did nothing except watch Creator answer your prayers Himself." Jaki raised his head, the light in his eyes chasing away the shadows that the fedora cast. "I still remember my shock when I realized you, a mere child, could see me, even though I stood on the other side of the Wall. I had heard stories of Jewels who could see beyond, but you were the first I witnessed with that rare gift."

Brandon finally reached Maggie's side and put a protective arm around her. "We thank you for your help, but I need to get my grandmother home. She has had an exhausting day." He drew Maggie toward the open door.

Gareth stooped and plucked the embedded arrow out of the floor. "We're not mad."

The words stopped Brandon cold. "I didn't say that."

"Didn't need to." Gareth balanced the arrow on his fingertip, then jerked his hand from under it and snatched the shaft before it could fall.

Brandon broadened his stance, provoking a huff of exasperation from Maggie. "They mean us no harm, Brady."

"That might be," Brandon said, "but mad people don't tend to act predictably."

Gareth whipped the point of the arrow at him. "So you do think us mad."

Brandon sputtered for a moment, his face a burning red. "Yes, I do think you're mad. How can I believe otherwise with your talk of walls and Levioths and Ishir? None of them *exist*."

Jaki roared with laughter. "Do you hear that, old friend? I don't exist!"

"That is indeed a shock." Gareth rubbed his chin thoughtfully as he considered Brandon. "Perhaps you're right. Perhaps it is madness, but it's a madness Creator has asked you to join." Gareth held out the arrow to him. "He's called you to be a guardian."

Brandon began to reach for the weapon, then shook his head. "I've no need of an arrow, especially one without a bow." He took Maggie's arm. "Come on, Grandmama. Let's get you home."

"But Brady—"

"You don't want to be here when Kasam returns, do you?"

Brandon didn't wait for an answer. "Me neither." He guided her toward the gate.

Jaki and Gareth stood at the door and watched the pair depart. Jaki clapped a hand on Gareth's shoulder. "May Creator grant you the patience of Job with that one."

Gareth rubbed the arrow between his fingers absentmindedly. "No riddles, Jaki."

"You wield another guardian's weapon. Creator has selected you as his trainer."

Gareth dropped the arrow like a hot coal. Its point embedded itself in the ground an inch from his foot.

Jaki laughed. "Too late, old friend."

Gareth snatched up the arrow from the ground and tucked it into his belt beneath his coat before starting out across the compound. "We need to be going."

Jaki matched him stride for stride. "And where would that be? After we retrieve the car, that is."

Gareth glanced back toward the eastern horizon, already a navy blue in the dying light. "The one place I planned never to go again."

"You know where the Key is?"

"I know where she will be, if Juliet has her."

They reached the front gate. Jaki continued on, but Gareth slowed, then stopped at the threshold, just inside HopeWell's perimeter. He had left once before but only under compulsion. Never by choice. He looked back at the ramshackle cabins, the holes, the mounds of rocks. How many hours had he spent hauling those very boulders from one end of camp to the other? How many days had he spent digging holes and refilling them? How many prisoners had he watched enter these very gates, never to leave?

"Gareth?"

The shutters closing off Gareth's soul crumbled, revealing dark pools of unbridled pain. "I wanted to believe them. That I would never leave. That I belonged here."

Lightning flashed within Jaki's eyes. "You believed Creator had dismissed you just as Sarish had."

"Because I cannot regret what I did. *How*, yes, but not what." He dragged a hand across the rough post of the gate. "Every time it ends the same. Wallace had found the gateway. He was on his way to tell Levioth." Gareth's fingers dug into the post. "I tried to talk him out of it. Did you know that? But he just laughed. Mocked you . . . the Ishir . . . Creator."

"And you killed in the rage of man rather than in the righteousness of Creator."

"I was supposed to be the Prince of Guardians. I knew better—and didn't care." Gareth stared at HopeWell. "I deserve this." His voice broke.

Jaki lifted his face skyward, eyes closed. A long minute passed, wind gusting and shadows lengthening. Then his eyes reopened, golden light emanating from their depths. "Hear this word of Creator, O Gareth, Adam of dust and Creator's breath: 'Who appointed you as judge? Do I not punish those I wish to punish and show mercy to those I wish to show mercy? If I have chosen to show you mercy, who are you to say I err? *I* am Master, the Maker of ground and sky. It is I who give the Ishir his song and the Adam his breath; and it is I who take it away. Why do you seek to dethrone Me by refusing what I choose to give you?'"

As Jaki spoke, Gareth's head bowed, and he leaned against the post for support. But even that sturdy structure was not sufficient to shore him up. His legs buckled, and he sank to his knees, his forehead resting on the cold ground.

The fiery light faded from Jaki's eyes. "Remember who you are, Gareth, by first remembering who He is."

Gareth remained as he was for some time. Gradually he inhaled deeply, as if breathing in sweet air of long ago. "'The Lord is merciful, giving good gifts to His children.'"

Jaki nodded in encouragement. *"The Song of Eber the Ishir."*

Slowly Gareth sat back on his heels, though his head remained bowed. "'Guardian is not a position which an Adam seeks, but which Creator appoints, vessels of clay through whom He delights to show His Glory.'"

"*The Oracles of the Lion.*" Jaki extended a hand to Gareth. "Have you not been imprisoned long enough, old friend?"

Gareth's voice strengthened. "'Not from the deeds of the Adam, but from the heart of Creator springs hope.'" Grasping Jaki's hand, he lifted his head and rose. "From the heart of Creator."

He stepped across the threshold of HopeWell.

18

TWILIGHT DEEPENED INTO NIGHT AS ORIEL
followed an invisible path away from HopeWell, in the opposite
direction of Koma. Her light steps made no sound. They made
no print. In fact, Oriel seemed to skim over the snow more
than sprint across it, her speed never slacking, her movements
nimble. No observer would know her escape had earned her a
dozen bullets. Even the tears in her skin had already mended.
Only the rips in her clothing, edged in fireblood, verified that
she had been shot at all.

A half-moon rose, casting a silver glow between bony branches
while the stars sang their nightly praises. But as Oriel continued
to zigzag among the trees, fingers of clouds stretched out greedily,
eager to dominate the heavens. One by one the stars fell prey. The
moon eventually succumbed too, unable to force its reflected rays
through the thickening mass. Soon darkness ruled unchallenged.

Instead of slowing Oriel, the blackness drove her onward until
she entered a small clearing. With a sigh of relief, she slowed her
pace. Although the crack between HopeWell and Koma was closer
to the camp, she didn't want to reach it too soon. With no trail to
follow, Juliet would have returned to HopeWell to exact retribution
from Maggie and Brandon. Providing more time for their escape
by distracting Juliet was the best protection she could offer.

Oriel stopped at the clearing's far edge before two tall trees.
Above her, their branches intertwined to form an organic archway.
She stretched out a hand. Her palm flattened, as if she pushed

against something solid midair. "Not long now," she breathed out.

Glancing around the clearing, she seemed to catalogue every detail from the piercing cold of the wind to the sweet mustiness of damp earth. "Thank You for this time; I will treasure it always." Then she closed her eyes, and her extended hand glowed.

Light spiderwebbed away from her palm, outlining the ragged edges of a narrow crack. Oriel leaned forward. Her hand's glow brightened. Her brow wrinkled with exertion. But the crack refused her entrance.

With a gasp, Oriel stumbled backward. Her hand broke contact with the crack and the light vanished. A quick scan of the clearing's circumference revealed no other tree arches; this wasn't a decoy.

"I don't understand. You told me to leave. I'm trying to leave." Stretching out her hand again, she repeated the process—with the same results.

Oriel returned to the center of the clearing and held her hands out, palms up. "I am Your servant." She slowly rotated. A tree branch moaned. An owl hooted. When she had almost completed a full circuit, she stopped. "There's nothing for a hundred miles that way."

A passing breeze swirled around her and darted in the direction she faced.

She took a breath. "As You wish."

She left the clearing, steps heavy. The trees thinned and then were bisected by a road. Oriel paused along the bordering ditch. The owl hooted again, but this time its call wobbled, as if unsure how many whoos to string together. A footstep squelched. Oriel spun around. Several bucketfuls of water flew out of the night, drenching her. She stumbled back with a gasp.

A shadow rose behind her. "Time to bank the fire, don't you think?" A syringe plunged into her neck.

Oriel clawed at the intrusive needle but couldn't dislodge it.

Her movements grew jerky, and she collapsed to the ground.

The clouds split. Eight hunters circled Oriel, overshadowed by Juliet.

THE HAMMERING KNOCK RATTLED THE RAFTERS OF Maggie's home.

Sitting on the bed, Brandon stilled, his last bite of supper partway to his mouth.

A fist pounded the door a second time, more insistently than before.

Setting her plate atop some jars, Maggie rose from her lopsided stool and shuffled toward the door, muttering about people not learning patience these days. Brandon grabbed her wrist as she passed by. "Grandmama, what are you doing?"

"Answering the door."

The matter-of-fact response loosened his grip for a moment, but a moment was all she needed. Maggie slipped away, and although Brandon immediately lurched after her, it was already too late. She pulled open the door, and for the second time that day, the broad frame of Prisoner Ninety-Seven filled the opening.

Clenching his fists, Brandon planted himself between Maggie and the intruder. "Get out of here."

Gareth merely looked past the young man. "Grab your things, Maggie. We've not much time."

"Don't listen to him, Grandmama." Brandon put his arm in front of her. "You aren't going anywhere with him."

"Pishposh." Maggie hobbled over to a peg to pick up a dress as worn as the one she wore. "He says go. We go." She rolled a loaf of bread and a bunch of dried herbs inside the second garment.

Brandon growled. "Leave us alone." He shoved the door toward Gareth, trying to force him out.

Gareth flattened his hand against the door, preventing it from shutting. "You're not safe here."

"Obviously." Brandon leaned against the door. The wood groaned, threatening to splinter under the opposing forces.

"If you wish to face Kasam again—and she *will* look for you here—your life be on your own head. But you won't endanger Maggie's as well."

Brandon glanced back at his grandmother. She knotted a string around her small bundle, then put on her old coat and hat. "All ready."

Brandon blocked her path. "You don't have to do this. There are other . . . safe places we can go."

Maggie patted his cheek. "A Guardian Prince, an Ishir warrior—can't be much safer than that, Brady." She looked at Gareth. "He be here still, aye?"

"Waiting in the car," he confirmed.

"See? All safe." Maggie doused the fire and a lamp. Gareth wrapped an arm around her as they departed, leaving Brandon alone.

He shifted his feet, as if uncertain whether to pursue or stay. His hand slid into his pocket and rubbed his Protector's Star. His jaw clenched. Grabbing his coat, he dashed into the night after them.

A SINGLE, NAKED LIGHT BULB ILLUMINATED THE tomblike room. Not that the room was much to look at. Gray stone formed the whole of it, a raised slab of granite upon two concrete supports near the center.

Metal ground against metal. The door, comprised of reinforced steel and the only way in or out, resisted the force leveraged against it, releasing each inch begrudgingly. Finally, fingers curled around the door's frame and pried it far enough to allow entrance. Juliet stepped inside and waved for the four hunters behind her to follow. Two carried Oriel, unconscious and skin grayed due to regular injections throughout the all-night drive. They placed her on the slab, then joined the other two already mixing a batch of quick-setting cement.

Juliet stood at Oriel's head, another syringe ready if she stirred. "Hurry up!"

The command, though not loud, startled the foursome. Death himself seemed to haunt these corridors, any noise an invitation for him to come calling. Each man cast a glance toward the empty hall beyond the open door, then worked faster, avoiding any excess noise. No one wanted to be caught here should Death decide to stop in.

Soon the mixture attained proper consistency. The hunters poured the cement over Oriel, covering her from soles to waist. A band across her shoulders was added to secure her upper body, followed by two generous heaps over her hands, palms placed up in order to expose the inside of her forearms.

"That will do." Juliet flicked her hand toward the door. "Return to HopeWell and prepare for the blood moon. The Alpha there will provide you further instructions."

The four hunters saluted her and marched out single file. Their footsteps faded. Juliet's breathing synchronized with Oriel's. A vent hummed as it exchanged stale air for fresh, then retreated as soon as it performed its duty. Minutes stretched into an hour. The quick-setting cement solidified into a restraint impervious to all fire except at the highest of temperatures.

Juliet tucked the syringe away. "What is keeping the doctor?" She glanced at the hallway, then back at Oriel. "Don't go anywhere while I'm gone."

Quiet shrouded the room. As if sensing her solitude, Oriel tightened the muscles in her arms and arched her back. Her cement restraints withstood her. She pulled harder and thrashed her head. She couldn't break free. Her body quivered, then slumped against the slab. Her head continued to roll side to side, eyes darting back and forth behind closed eyelids, red and gray mottling her skin. A whimper escaped her lips.

Metal scraped against stone. Oriel's movements stilled. A scarred face framed by chestnut hair peeked into the room. Seeing no one around, Witless crept over to the granite slab, the chain between her ankles grating against the floor. She brushed a hand against Oriel's cheek. Oriel jerked away.

Witless tucked a loose strand of hair behind her ear and pressed a hand to Oriel's chest, near where a heart would be. But while a pulse throbbed there, it differed from a heartbeat—more the rhythmic whoosh of a bellows stirring up a fire. Intense heat also boiled beneath. This was no human prisoner Juliet brought back, but a legitimate Ishir.

Witless nibbled her lower lip, fingering the herbs she'd stashed in her pocket. The herbs meant to help a *human* captive. After several moments, Witless finally nodded to herself and crawled up on the slab, scooting her lap underneath Oriel's head. Then after another glance at the door, Witless bent forward and folded her hands over Oriel's chest near that core of fire.

For several minutes nothing happened. Then the bitter spiciness of incense wafted upward from Witless and spread through the room. Oriel relaxed, the faintest pink tinting her cheeks. Witless lowered her head further, as if a great burden rested upon her shoulders. A tear, sparkling like a diamond, rolled down her cheek, and she began to hum.

The splotchy color of Oriel's skin evened out, the smokiness dissipating. Her lips parted, and ever so slowly her mouth began to move in cadence with the song Witless hummed. As the tune curved back to repeat itself, the words flowed forth from Oriel.

"On the day, the first one,
"Creator molded light and word,
 "The Melakah His message to proclaim.
 "And it was good, so very good,
 "As only Creator could do.
"On the day, the second one,
"Creator molded water and laughter,
 "The Dachi His joy to bring.
 "And it was good, so very good,
 "As only Creator could do.
"On the day, the third one,
"Creator molded wind and thunder,
 "The Qolet His power to display.
 "And it was good, so very good,
 "As only Creator could do.
"On the day, the fourth one,
"Creator molded fire and music,
 "The Ishir His song to sing.
 "And it was good, so very good,
 "As only Creator could do.
"On the day, the fifth one,
"Creator molded plant and sighing,
 "The Yerek His comfort to whisper.
 "And it was good, so very good
 "As only Creator could do."

The tempo accelerated, and Oriel's voice strengthened, a glow filling out her skin.

"But on the sixth of all the days,
"Creator molded the greatest of all:
 "He fashioned dust into the Adam
 "And breathed Himself into them,

"His very nature to reflect.
"Proclaim His message, Bring His joy!
      "Display His power, Sing His song!
      "Whisper His comfort, Reflect His Nature!
"For on the day, the seventh day,
"Creator rested from His work.
         "All creatures His Glory now praise,
         "For Creator's good, so very good,
         "As Creator alone can be!"

As the music faded, tears streamed down Witless's face. She sighed and removed her hands, her skin now brightened to a sunburnt red from the intense heat radiating from Oriel.

Oriel herself lay very still except for the steady rise and fall of her chest. What would she find when she opened her eyes? Her lips formed the last line of the song again. *For Creator's good, so very good, as Creator alone can be.* Her eyelids lifted—and she flinched at the face peering down at her, far too much like Juliet's.

Witless cringed at the reaction and scooted out from under Oriel's head.

"Wait."

A swirl of warmth scented with cinnamon tugged on Witless, preventing her from scurrying away. She nibbled her lip, then faced Oriel.

Oriel's gaze brushed the scar, then locked onto the young woman's golden eyes. "A Jewel—here? And a Spliced at that?"

Witless gasped and seized Oriel's arm, shaking her head emphatically.

At the unspoken plea, Oriel nodded. She would say no more. A strand of warmth wrapped around them, accompanied by the hint of a calming lullaby. Witless took a deep breath, her secret still safe.

Heels clacked in the hall.

A strangled cry escaped Witless, and she clamped a hand

over her mouth at the sound, gaze skittering about the room. No place to run, no place to hide unless . . . Witless dropped to her hands and knees and crawled under the granite slab. Pressing her back to the support nearest the door, she scrunched her trembling body into the smallest ball possible. Above her, Oriel closed her eyes, her breaths forcibly regular.

Juliet entered and instantly recoiled, gagging. "Ugh." She yanked out a handkerchief and covered her mouth and nose with it, her eyes canvassing the room. Everything looked as she left it, except for the renewed glow to Oriel's skin. She edged further into the room. "A thick stench fouls the air . . ." Snake like, Juliet stooped, nabbed Witless's arm, and dragged her out. "Should have known." She dug her nails into the tender underside of the girl's arm, slicing tiny cuts into the skin. "What will your interference reap you this time, Witless? Isolation, injection—or perhaps both?"

Witless stared at the floor motionless, though her complexion paled.

Oriel, on the other hand, flushed a deep red. Heat boiled off her rigid body, a volcano preparing to erupt. Juliet arched her brow at the sudden rise in temperature.

At Juliet's new focus, Witless gritted her teeth. What she needed to do next would cost her dearly. But she wrenched her arm from Juliet anyway, leaving wide gashes across her skin, and sped down the hall for the nearest intersection, despite her chain-shortened stride. Twenty yards, fifteen, ten . . .

"Fool." Juliet spun from Oriel and strode to the doorway. "Kabak, gargon, charn." She thrust her palm forward.

Witless stumbled forward as if pushed from behind. She tried to catch herself, but the chain jerked taut and she tumbled to the floor.

Before she had time to right herself, Juliet was crouching over her. "Most people would consider the loss of their tongue sufficient deterrent. I see you shall necessitate something more drastic." She wrapped her fingers around Witless's throat.

The younger woman swallowed hard, eyes wide.

"Leave her alone!" Oriel's cry ricocheted through the hall.

"So, her fire *has* been restored." Juliet glowered at Witless. "I suppose I have you to thank for that." She yanked the younger woman to her feet.

Metallic clanks and grindings reverberated from farther down the corridor.

"Ah, Doctor Minio at last," Juliet observed as she dragged Witless to the nearest door and shoved her against the wall. "If you value walking, don't move." With her good hand, she finagled the door open and pushed Witless inside. "I'll return." She slammed the door, locked it, and headed back to Oriel.

Juliet reached the room just ahead of a hunchbacked man dressed in a white lab coat, his wild mop of brown hair completing his disheveled look. "Doctor Minio."

He shuffled sideways into the room, his left leg lagging behind the right. "This is her? She's the one?" His left shoulder twitched as he set a wood case on the slab.

At his arrival, Oriel strained against the concrete, trying to break free. But the concrete didn't melt, and with nothing to set afire, she had no flames with which to meld and slip away like she did with the door at HopeWell. Nonetheless, she pulled and yanked and thrashed, tidal waves of heat crashing through the room. The dark sappiness of frankincense blended with the spiciness of cinnamon.

Juliet backtracked at the pungent aroma, which was so like the one Witless stirred up, she checked the door for the young woman's presence. But the hallway was empty, and the smell definitely surged with the heat rolling off of Oriel. Juliet coughed, the repulsive odor nearly strong enough to expel her from the room. It smelled too much of the anointed and the holy.

The anointed and the holy. Juliet's eyes narrowed, and once again covering her face with a handkerchief, she approached Oriel. On the opposite side, Doctor Minio laid out his tools, undisturbed by any theatrics.

"Could I truly be so fortunate?" Dropping the handkerchief, Juliet slammed Oriel's head to one side and bent back the ear with her thumb. A red blemish was nestled underneath, unremarkable except for its shape—that of a keyhole. "And here I was all prepared to hunt you down when I reached the other side." Juliet's voice held a hint of glee. "Instead you walked right into my hands. How considerate of you." She released Oriel's head and stepped back.

Oriel sagged. Juliet knew her secret, knew who she was. She squeezed her eyes shut, her chest still heaving from her struggle to free herself.

Doctor Minio seized upon her sudden stillness to press fingers to her throat, then to pry open an eye, into which he shone a light.

That jarred her from her momentary stupor, and she tried to pull away. "You can't hold me forever."

"Actually, I could, but I have no intention of doing so." Juliet retrieved her handkerchief from the floor and folded it away, the foul smell finally abating. "In fact, I expect you to flee from me, both far and fast." Circling the head of the slab, she placed two syringes next to the doctor's other tools.

"Two?" Doctor Minio picked them up. "That is all you have left?"

"Her fire was more potent than expected." A hint of pleasure touched her lips, the reason for Oriel's stronger fire now obvious. "But your solution worked."

He bobbed his head. "Knew it would. Never doubted it." After securing the syringes in his case, he rolled up Oriel's sleeve and tied a tourniquet around her upper arm.

Oriel tried to pull away, but the concrete held her fast. "What is it you wa—"

The doctor stabbed a needle into her arm, cutting off her question. He filled a vial with the fireblood and offered it to Juliet. Light didn't merely glint off the brilliant red liquid inside but emanated from it. Juliet swept her tongue across her lips. "Victory shall taste sweet indeed."

Horror widened Oriel's eyes. "You mean to drink it."

"Not yet, but soon." Juliet placed the vial into the case along with a second one the doctor handed her. "And thanks to Witless, your fire is at full potency, rather than diluted from the doctor's solution."

"Not for long." Oriel closed her eyes tightly. "Tsunni." Instantly she fell unconscious, glow and color fading from her skin.

Juliet tensed. "Doctor?"

Without responding, he thrust a third vial at her and snatched a fourth, filling the remainder as fast as he could. The fireblood in each subsequent tube sparkled less than the one before. After he filled the final one, he paused to mop his forehead with his sleeve.

Juliet twisted the last vial, the fireblood a dull brown-red. "Will it work?"

His shoulder twitched as he secured the vials and stored his tools. "The potency of the potion may be less. The time to brew may be more."

"But will it *work*?"

The doctor snapped the case closed. "Absolutely."

19

GARETH SNORED AWAY IN THE PARKED CAR'S FRONT
seat, his head cocked at an odd angle. Midday sunlight shafted
through leafless branches of the surrounding woods, softening
leftover snow into slush and adding its warmth to the small
campfire Maggie worked a few paces away. She hummed merrily
as she fixed hot food from the stash Jaki provided upon their
arrival at the small clearing.

Standing near the automobile, Jaki had swung open the front
passenger door. After picking up Brandon and Maggie, Gareth
could no longer deny his need for rest and promptly fell asleep.
But now Maggie had food ready—something Gareth also needed.

Brandon poked a stick at the campfire. "Just give him a good
shake and get it over with," he grumbled.

"Unlike you, son of dust, I know better than to startle
a sleeping guardian." Jaki nodded to Gareth's hand, which
even in slumber clenched a weapon. Jaki slammed the back-
passenger door.

Gareth bolted upright, blindly swinging his knife. It sliced
into the car's metal frame a full inch before becoming wedged.
Jaki tossed Brandon a smirk before turning back to Gareth.
"Ready to break your fast, sleeper?"

Gareth scowled and worked his knife loose from the car.
"You should have awakened me for the second watch." The knife
pulled free. He shoved it into its sheath beneath his coat.

"Gareth, you needed the rest. If we are to breach Levioth's, I need you at full capacity."

Brandon sprang to his feet. "I thought we were going someplace safe!" He held the stick like a rifle, its blackened tip smoking.

"I said Maggie wasn't safe in her home." Gareth rolled his shoulders and accepted from Maggie a wedge of bark piled with hot food. "Many thanks." He shoveled the food into his mouth with his fingers, ignoring the heat.

"Should have known." Brandon flung the stick away and stalked over to Maggie. "We're leaving. Right now."

She planted her feet. "No."

"But it isn't safe here." He tugged on her, but she dug her heels in, her stiff posture declaring he would have to remove her bodily if he hoped to move her at all. He lowered his voice. "Grandmama, listen to me. I know you think these men are your friends, but—"

"No, you hear me, and hear me well, Brandon Elias Toxon."

Brandon startled at the use of his full name.

Maggie shook a bony finger in Brandon's face. "Ye might wear a fancy uniform. Ye might have some important title. But ye don't know nothing yet except a shadow."

A flush climbed up Brandon's neck and into his face.

"Ye mean well. I know that." Maggie's tone softened as she touched his face. "But the world ye see is not all there is." She stepped back. "If ye must go, go. But I'll hear no more talk of me leaving. I am where I'm supposed to be." She shuffled back to the fire.

Light danced in Jaki's eyes like the fire he squatted beside. "That is an introduction for training if I ever heard one."

Gareth wiped his mouth. "But Oriel—"

"Will be protected by Creator. Trust His timing. He does not err."

Gareth chewed his food slower. "You really think . . . ?"

"I do."

Setting his makeshift plate aside, Gareth beckoned to Brandon. "Come with me."

Brandon barked a nervous laugh. "Right. Go alone, unarmed with a known murderer bearing who-knows-how-many weapons to a remote location."

Turning from the fire, Maggie put her hands on her hips. "Brady—"

"It's fine, Maggie. I can handle this," Gareth assured her. But under his breath he muttered, "Creator, help me." Shoving aside his coat, he unsheathed his long knives and laid both on the ground. He removed a third blade from his boot and added his whittling knife beside that. From his belt, he lifted a tomahawk, two guns, and the arrow Oriel created. The last one he extended to Brandon. "This belongs to you."

"Little good it does me."

Gareth shot a glance at Jaki. "Do you still have stockpiles at each gateway?"

"But of course." Jaki jogged into the woods.

Neither Gareth nor Brandon moved, retaining their standoff, but Maggie resumed her humming as she dished out food for herself. A couple of minutes later Jaki returned, a bow and a quiver of arrows in hand. He held them out to Brandon.

Brandon eyed Jaki, but when Jaki didn't retract the weapon, he accepted it from him and conducted a thorough examination. When it passed inspection, he nocked an arrow, pulled back the string, and aimed. The arrow thunked in the center of a hole left by woodpeckers in an old tree a hundred paces away. He pulled out four more arrows and constructed a perfect box around the first. Maggie grinned. "My Hiram made him a bow when he were a boy. Many afternoons were filled with the sounds of practice."

Jaki retrieved the arrows for Brandon. "Do you find the weapon satisfactory, son of dust?"

"It'll do." Brandon tucked the arrows into the quiver along

with Oriel's.

"Are you ready now?" Gareth stuffed fists into his pockets, turning his back on the lure of his own weapons.

Brandon slung the quiver over his shoulders, new confidence straightening his posture. "Where are we going?"

"To Echoing."

"Never heard of it. Where's it at?"

"On the other side."

"On the other side of what?"

Gareth scowled. "Didn't you listen to *any* of your grandmother's stories?" He stomped on a fallen branch, flipping it into the air, where he snagged it. "The attraction of digging holes is growing." He tossed the branch at Jaki.

Jaki caught it easily and used it to stir up the fire. "Just show him, Gareth. That way still remains easiest."

Gareth paced away, circled a tree, and stopped in front of Brandon. "Five minutes. That's all I ask."

Brandon looked from Gareth to Jaki to Maggie and then back to Gareth.

"Go with him, Brady," urged Maggie. "Let him show you."

Tightening his fingers on his bow, Brandon nodded. "Five minutes."

Gareth retraced the path which Jaki took to retrieve the bow and arrows. Brandon followed, though every snap and creak from the trees unsettled him. After about two minutes, Gareth paused. "Follow in my footsteps." He marched ahead . . . and vanished.

Brandon froze, the grip on his bow white-knuckled. Two, three seconds ticked off. Gareth didn't reappear.

"Hello?" Brandon turned in a tight circle. "If this is a trick, it isn't funny."

A squirrel bounded across the snow and scurried up the nearest tree.

Brandon circled around Gareth's final footsteps and

waved his hand through the air where the tracks ended. His arm slashed through emptiness. He turned and scanned the surrounding forest.

"When I said follow, I meant exactly."

Brandon whirled around.

Gareth stood behind him, face stern. "Shall we try again?" He pointed at his tracks in the slushy snow. "Follow. Exactly this time." He once more vanished from sight.

Brandon clasped his bow to his chest and forced himself forward. One step to go. Closing his eyes, he dove after Gareth.

Leaning against a tree on the other side, Gareth wore a faint grin. Some things never changed. Brandon's headlong plunge through the gateway into Echoing was the same plunge every first-time guardian took, anticipating some of kind of resistance as they passed through. Resistance that didn't exist. "You can open your eyes." Gareth's amusement crouched underneath his words.

Brandon's eyes popped open. Besides the shimmering arch of the gateway, everything looked as it did before—every tree, every snow pile, every rock in the exact same place. Then again, nothing looked as it did before, every tree, snow pile, and rock glowing with an ethereal beauty despite the winter bareness.

"Welcome to Echoing." Though Gareth's voice was gruff as usual, the air here softened some of its ragged edges. "The other side of the Wall."

"It's . . . real?" The words slipped out as a whisper, for surely anything louder would dissolve the illusion. "This can't be. It's—it's . . . impossible." Brandon pressed his hand against the nearest trunk, as if the rough bark could imprint reality upon him.

"Impossible or not, it is." Gareth pushed away from the tree and motioned for Brandon to follow him back toward the camp. "And if you accept the call of guardian, guarding this world from human interlopers will be one of your primary tasks, along with the protection of the gateways and cracks."

"Gateways?" Brandon peered back at the shimmering arch half-hidden by the trees. "Is that what we just came through?"

"It is."

"Then what's a crack?"

"A thin spot between here, Echoing, and Terrestrial, where we were. Cracks are connected by the webbing, which allows the Ishir to both pass between dimensions and jump locations as well." Gareth pivoted to face Brandon, who barely kept from bumping into him. "But *never* use a crack, no matter how strong the temptation."

"Why not?"

"The webbing almost always crushes the humans caught within its strands, guardian or not." Gareth wheeled back around, coat flapping at the abrupt change in direction.

A fire popped and crackled ahead. Brandon darted forward. "Grandmama . . ." He halted, words dying.

Unlike everything else around him, which appeared more real and solid than before, both Maggie's and Jaki's forms had become semitransparent and ghostlike. Moreover, Jaki's human façade had thinned enough to reveal his Ishir fire roiling within.

Giving Jaki wide berth, Brandon slowly walked over to Maggie. "Grandmama?" He waved a hand in front of her face. "Grandmama!" He reached for her arm. His hand passed right through.

Maggie peered in his direction, but her gaze focused on the trees past him, as if he weren't there. She turned back to Jaki, her lips moving but her voice inaudible. Jaki responded with the same voiceless words.

"You might want to study lip reading. It's quite handy when walking in Echoing." Gareth crouched by the fire and spread his hands before it, absorbing its warmth.

Brandon confronted him. "What happened to my grandmother?"

"Nothing. We're just on the other side of the Wall." Gareth eyed a branch resting against the fire pit's stones. "Although Creator's physical world spans all dimensions, stabilizing and linking together Echoing and Terrestrial, the Six Races can inhabit only one at a time. At least under normal circumstances." With mischief glinting in his eye, he nudged the branch with his foot, and it tipped over, causing Jaki to spring backward. "And no, I don't know why we can see them, but they can't see us. Maybe because the other five races were commanded to serve, protect, and aid humans."

"This . . . it's almost too much." Brandon paced the clearing. "I don't understand. If these things exist, have always existed, why don't we hear more about them?"

Gareth grew somber again. "Man was not the only race the Adversary tempted during the Great Fall, but because we were made in Creator's image with His breath and were given charge of creation, we were held to the highest standard. Therefore, when we ate the fruit of knowing all things, both good and bad, our eyes were opened to know—but our hearts were blinded to understand. For Creator always fits the punishment to the crime." He surveyed the surrounding area. "After the Deluge, Terrestrial and Echoing were separated. The Wall was erected to prevent the races from destroying each other, and we forgot. The truth was dismissed as legends, fairytales."

Brandon knelt in front of Maggie. "I thought she was crazy."

"Most do, and not without reason, as her close relationship with Creator allows her to glimpse things most others can't see." Gareth crouched beside him. "Your grandmother is one of the most gifted people in the world—and one of the most resilient. The ridicule she has withstood over the decades would have crushed most other souls."

Brandon eyed Gareth with new interest. "And how long have you known my grandmother?"

"The joy she exhibited the day your mother birthed you was only second to her joy the day she birthed your mother." He clapped Brandon on the shoulder, rose from his squat, and headed to the gateway.

Brandon caught up with him. "That didn't answer my question. How old are you?"

"Impertinent youth." But though Gareth grumbled the words, bemusement belied the annoyance. He lengthened his stride at the shimmer of the gateway between the trees. "Let's just say that being a guardian comes with its own unique blessings and curses."

As they reached the gateway, a terrible shriek splintered the air. It seemed to come from everywhere and nowhere all at once, its origin unmistakably human yet its timbre of a thousand glasses shattering.

Brandon snatched an arrow from his quiver. "What . . . ?" His voice cracked.

Gareth reached for his knives, swearing when he didn't find them; they were still back at the camp. "The terrified cry of a Jewel's soul." He charged through the gateway, Brandon on his heels. When they reached the clearing, Maggie was scrunched down on her rock, spilt food at her feet and Jaki hovering over her, his smoky oak-and-cloves scent permeating the clearing.

"We heard a Jewel's scream." Gareth swiped sweat from his face.

Jaki moved aside for Gareth. "It wasn't her."

Brandon prowled the perimeter of the camp, bow ready to shoot the first thing that twitched. "What's going on?"

"I'll let you know when I know." Kicking away the dropped food, Gareth squatted in front of Maggie. She shivered uncontrollably, and Gareth wrapped both his hands around hers. "Maggie?"

She rocked back and forth, groaning. "Much too young. Too much darkness." A tear wended its way down her cheek.

Jaki straightened, focusing on a distant point. "I wonder . . ."

"If you know something, say it!" snarled Gareth.

Pulling off his fedora, Jaki mashed and reformed it in his hands. "A few years ago the incense of a new Jewel threaded its way into the Throne Room. We sought her in all realms, but despite the cries rending Echoing, an impenetrable darkness hid her location. Then two years ago, the cries died and the incense dwindled to but a ghost of its former potency."

Maggie rocked harder, the single tear now many. "*She* wants to silence her forever."

Gareth jerked back on his heels as if physically struck. "Juliet has both the Key *and* a Jewel?" Blood drained from his face. "Shirel's warning–heart of a guardian, tears of a Jewel, blood of the Key . . ."

"Lord of the Rishi." Jaki smashed his fist against the nearest tree, leaving a black scorch mark on the trunk. "After all the precautions–"

"And yet, it might not be too late. I didn't recognize Oriel as the Key. Juliet might not know yet either." Gareth bolted to his feet. "Time to go."

"Aye, it is." Sniffing, Maggie wiped her sleeve across her face and proceeded to bundle any food that could be carried while Jaki snuffed out the fire and eradicated marks of their stay.

Brandon gaped at the sudden flurry of activity. "What's going on?"

Gareth gathered his weapons, rearming himself. "An old prophecy warns that a lord of the Rishi–those Ishir who rebelled against Creator–will breach Terrestrial should a Levioth hold the heart, the tears, and the blood. Oriel is the Key, and it now seems Juliet has been holding a Jewel for several years."

"But that's only two of the three. What about the heart of a guardian?"

Gareth shoved his two long knives into their sheaths. "Juliet was once my fiancée."

20

"INTERRUPTIONS—ARE THERE NO END TO THEM?" Stalking into her private library, Juliet slammed the door. The last twenty-four hours had been unusually long, and this day wasn't shaping up to be any better. First, Doctor Minio required her help to decipher the directions to prepare the fireblood. A hunter then arrived with news that the other prisoners had escaped HopeWell, and the Alpha wanted further instructions. There was also a mix-up with some of the transfers to the other prison camps, which the commandants expected her to correct because she initiated the distribution. And now when she could finally oversee an appropriate punishment for Witless—not the usual roughing up she ordered yesterday—she had to stop again.

Crossing over to the hearth, Juliet stirred up the fire and cast the black powder upon it. Flames leapt up, and smoke boiled over into the room, molding into the dark Rishi. Juliet clasped both arms over her chest and bowed. "You summoned me, balai?"

"I am not pleased." The smoke roiled and writhed around Zarbal, restrained anger deepening the red of his eyes.

Rising out of her bow, Juliet remained void of any visible emotion. "About what, mighty balai?"

"The blood moon is only five days away." His bass voice rattled the room, and a precariously perched book tottered from its shelf, thumping on the floor.

"I will have the key to the Bottomless Regions; already plans are in motion—"

"I speak of the girl, the one you call Witless."

Every muscle in Juliet's body tightened, even the normal sheen of her eyes solidifying into stone. "What of her?"

"Are you not preparing to silence her voice?"

"She defied me. She must be made to pay."

"Find another way!" Zarbal snapped out his wings, spewing smoke and sparks into the room.

Coughing, Juliet extinguished an ember that lighted on the rug and smothered another with her palm before a nearby book could ignite.

Zarbal retracted his wings, gathering the smoke around him again. "We are too close. We cannot risk her becoming . . . incapacitated."

Tamping out another cluster of sparks, Juliet snatched a burning paper from the table. "After the blood moon, then. Promise me that I can silence her after the blood moon."

The Rishi waved his hand carelessly. "After the blood moon, you can send her to the grave any way you wish."

Juliet raised an eyebrow, the burning page dangling from her fingers. "*Any* way?"

"With the tormentors of the Bottomless Regions themselves, if you wish. After all, you will be the DragonRider."

She crushed both paper and fire in her hand. "Yes, yes, I will be." She bowed again. "As you wish. I will make sure Witless remains intact. For the moment."

"See to it." The Rishi clapped his hands and vanished in a puff of black smoke, restoring the room to normal.

Juliet studied the blackened page she still grasped in her burned hand, then tossed it into the fire. Flames licked around the paper, flaring at the easy feast before returning to gnaw at the logs. A knock interrupted the crackle of wood disintegrating into ash. "Enter."

Her skeletal butler came in. If the fresh scorch marks around the room surprised or concerned him, he gave no indication. "This just arrived." He handed her an official-looking envelope.

Juliet slit open the envelope with her fingernail and skimmed the typed document.

She was to report immediately to her superior concerning the recent death of HopeWell's commandant.

DEATH POSSESSED THE LAND.

Gareth trudged through the forbidding landscape, Echoing's warmth and light unable to soften the harsh realities of the plateau. Tinder-dry scrub brush dotted cracked earth, thirsty for more moisture than the scant powdering of snow would provide. A half dozen bleached trees raised bony hands toward a washed-out sky. White boulders, pockmarked to resemble giant skulls, gaped at the intruders. And in the distance, imposing mountains oversaw it all.

Behind Gareth, Maggie huddled against Brandon, who kept a protective arm around his grandmother's shoulders. "How much farther?" He whispered the words, although no one seemed to be around. The area could not be as deserted as it seemed. *Something* must be watching them.

Jaki, bringing up the rear, scanned the gravel road behind them. "Only a little farther."

Crossing back into Terrestrial wouldn't change the landscape, but Jaki promised that a car would be waiting for them, making their journey through the barrenness faster. Their last vehicle ran out of gas several miles back, and with no easy way to fill the vehicle in Echoing, they were forced to abandon it.

A black speck materialized on the road ahead. Gareth held up a hand, halting the group. The speck grew into a car, driven by a ghostly man.

Gareth spun around, waving for everyone to get off the road. Jaki leapt onto the nearest pile of boulders and compressed his flames to slide between the rocks. Brandon lifted Maggie and sprinted for the same pile, gravel crunching beneath his boots. Gareth crouched beside them, knives in hand. "Whatever you do, don't move," he whispered.

The car drew nearer, its low drone grinding on nerves. A bird wheeled above their heads. Gareth inhaled a measured breath. Brandon shifted his weight. A pebble spurted out from under his shoe and skittered across the ground, past the boulder's edge, as the car whizzed by, a translucent Juliet staring out the back window.

Brandon froze in horror. The pebble would be visible in Terrestrial, and a rock that moved for no apparent reason would arouse suspicion, if seen.

The car continued down the road.

Gareth growled at him. "Are you trying to kill us all?"

A red flush mushroomed up Brandon's neck, but before he could respond, Jaki's disembodied voice warned, "Watch out!"

Brandon ducked back down.

"This time, don't move." Gareth peered between two of the boulders.

Five paces away Juliet scanned the plateau, her ghostly form little more than a hazy outline in Echoing's bright light. But while her form didn't appear that solid, there was nothing undefined about her intention: Somehow from the speeding car she saw something atypical—the pebble perhaps—causing her to stop and hike back to this spot. Juliet stooped and filtered a few pebbles through her fingers while her driver scouted behind her, ready to shoot the first thing that moved.

Juliet dropped the rocks and dusted her hand off against her leg, straightening. But as she rose, so did her gaze, landing on the boulder pile. Her eyes narrowed, and her lips formed a tight line.

Her form darkened, solidifying into something more opaque and tangible than she had been a moment before.

Gareth closed his eyes, breathing rigidly controlled. His mouth shaped two simple words. *Hide us.*

The driver dropped his gun.

Juliet whirled, her body once against dissipating to a phantom. The driver scrambled for his weapon as she angrily berated him with inaudible words. A minute later they returned to the car and drove away.

Gareth surveyed the road once more and blew out a long breath. "Too close."

Brandon stood up beside him. "I thought no one on the other side of the Wall could see us."

"Rules don't apply to Levioth." After one more check, Gareth shoved his knives away.

"Why does everyone keep calling her Levioth?" Brandon bent to help Maggie to her feet. "I aced my class on chain of command, and this Levioth thing was never mentioned for either military or intelligence."

"That's because the position predates both Anatroshka's military rule and the monarchy before that, and it has nothing to do with Juliet's role as an intelligence agent. She uses that as a cover to get what she wants as Levioth." Gareth offered Maggie an arm and guided her around the brush to the packed tracks of the road.

"Which still doesn't explain what Levioth is." Brandon tried to dust the white dirt from his pants.

"Levioth is the leader of an ancient alliance between the fallen Ishir and the fallen Adam." Fire bloomed out of the rock and coalesced into Jaki. "The Rishi provide power and knowledge of the deep and hidden things. The Adam provide malleable slaves who can tread places and perform acts restricted to the Rishi, as they help the Fallen Star dominate all dimensions."

He leapt down to the road, orange flames dominating his fire in his concern. "Did you see what I saw, Gareth?"

Gareth grimaced. "I'd hoped it was a trick of the light. She found a way to cross the Wall without a gateway, didn't she?"

"Yes . . . and no." Jaki cocked his head. "She crossed over, yet not all of her."

"Not all?"

"Her breath alone breached Echoing; her dust she left behind."

"What does *that* mean?" Brandon joined the other two men, having given up on brushing himself off.

"Juliet separated her spirit from her body." Gareth drummed his fingers. "That explains how she could contact the Dachi, but why she still needs a gateway. Prolonged separation would kill her."

Jaki slowly shook his head. "I've heard legends of such things but never thought I would witness it."

"There are many things that none of us thought we would see." Gareth faced the dark, ragged peaks of the eastern mountains glowering at the plateau. "Which means the sooner we return Oriel to the Vault, the better for everyone concerned."

A FEW MINUTES BEFORE FIVE P.M., JULIET ENTERED the outer office of General Zaccharin. Her makeup was flawless, her clothing impeccable, despite the eight-hour drive to reach the capitol. Long black gloves hid the bandages swathing both hands, the sling removed for this meeting. Her bearing was military perfect.

The young woman at the desk raised her head, and upon seeing Juliet, stood in the commanded respect, though she seemed secretly pleased at something. "Agent Kasam. Go on in.

The general is waiting for you." She waved toward the closed door.

Juliet acknowledged the instructions with a nod, nothing more. The military ruled Anatroshka by virtue of its might, but its strength would soon dwindle without the fuel provided by intelligence. Juliet hadn't reached her current position through dispensing that fuel indiscriminately. She shoved open the thick oak door and strode inside with her head held high.

The inner office of General Zaccharin was a room designed to intimidate. The thick carpet spoke of luxury and wealth. The long, narrow space funneled every visitor toward the heavy mahogany desk at the far end, the bookshelves lining either side adding to the tunnel effect. Behind the desk, a large window overlooked the impressive skyline of Jaquilin, the capitol's progressive façade of concrete and steel maintained at any cost for the rest of the world to marvel at. The sight was a far cry from the wooden structures of the outer towns Juliet usually frequented.

But if her summons bothered her, Juliet didn't show it as she approached the desk, her face an expressionless mask. She stopped a couple of feet away and clasped her hands behind her. Between the desk and the window, a leather swivel chair faced away from her, hiding its occupant from sight.

Minutes ticked by. Juliet waited statuesque, not even transferring her weight in impatience. Finally, a low, over-honeyed male voice rose from the chair. "Welcome, Agent Kasam." The chair pivoted, revealing a short, wiry man encased in its depths. His black uniform accentuated his sandy hair and skin so pale it carried the pallor of living death. His granite-gray eyes held as much warmth as the stone from which they took their color.

Juliet, still expressionless, inclined her head. "Good day, General Zaccharin."

He waved a hand toward a sideboard. "I'd offer you something to drink, but as I remember, you prefer not to partake while on the job."

"You have an excellent memory, General."

"I also recall that you prefer to get right to business." Zaccharin leaned forward, steepling his fingers. "I've been informed that our most efficient commandant is dead, and his prisoners have been dispersed among the other camps, taxing the system. Would you care to explain?"

"Being a commandant is strenuous work. Being the most efficient, doubly so. His heart was giving out." Juliet's matter-of-fact words paraded before the general with the same military precision with which she conducted herself, almost monotone in their orderliness.

Eyes narrowing, General Zaccharin parsed her words for the truth. "So you mercifully put him out of his misery?"

"A necessary evil for the greater good."

"Still, this is a substantial loss. I'm not sure how we'll compensate." General Zaccharin's final word carried a stinger, challenging her to provide a worthwhile reason to overlook her role in the matter.

"While the loss of the commandant is . . . regrettable, it forced me to review the prisoners' records to redistribute them." Juliet paused, though it was unclear whether she did it to build suspense or whether she finally felt the weight of the interview, which could determine the fate of both career and life. Either way, she delivered her next words with measured renitence. "I found something of . . . great interest."

General Zaccharin's eyelids drooped to half-lidded boredom, the bait failing to reel him in. "And what did you find? The mythical Key Keeper?" His voice scoffed, but an undertow of interest added weight to the words, making them more than rhetorical. He wasn't hooked, but neither had he swam away.

"Something better." Juliet cast a second lure. "I have the Key."

"A key. You found a key." The general snorted and dismissed her words with a wave of his hand. "What good is a key without a lock?"

She stepped closer, refusing to let him escape so easily. "I can find that as well, General. But . . ."

"But what?"

"I need time. To verify my sources."

General Zaccharin contemplated his steepled fingers at the tempting bait she offered him. The caverns that the legendary Key Keeper protected were purported to contain the wealth of nations. Not a bad bribe to overlook one murder. "How much time?"

Juliet pursed her lips in thoughtful consideration. "If I focus on that *exclusively*, I might be able to track it down in a month."

"Two weeks. And I want daily reports of your progress. Progress which had better be fruitful." Hooked, he swiveled back to the window. "Dismissed."

"As you wish, General." Juliet turned on her heel and marched out, a triumphant smile on her face.

By the end of two weeks, the world would be hers.

21

THE FIRST RAYS OF MORNING FOUND GARETH
sitting at the point of a rocky outcropping, hands busy with some
whittling. It didn't matter that not enough light had invaded to
see by. He moved through habit, the shavings piling up at his
feet. Besides, Gareth's attention wasn't on his work. Couldn't be,
not when the outcropping overlooked Juliet's mountain estate.

Even with the vehicle waiting for them at the gateway, it
had taken the rest of the day to reach this point. Which led to
the debate of when they should attack, a decision made more
complicated by the awareness that Juliet was currently absent
and by the uncertainty of when she'd return. Brandon argued for
going ahead. Jaki insisted on waiting. Maggie was adamant that it
be not their decision, but Gareth's.

Gareth sent them to bed for a few hours of sleep.

But the old advice that things would look better in the morning
didn't hold true this time. While the estate had been divested
of the eerie darkness blanketing it in Echoing, the mansion
remained shadowed in Terrestrial, the surrounding mountains
shading it from the sun's dawning. Such gloom only enhanced
the forbidding atmosphere, its thick walls imposing and darkened
windows watchful. Another curl of wood joined the mound at
Gareth's feet. Surely it was folly, if not outright madness, to
believe they could rescue anyone from such a fortress.

A warm gust of wind scented with cloves announced Jaki's
arrival behind him. Still Gareth whittled, his gaze never leaving

the dark building below, every cut a reminder of the irrevocability of each choice made, no matter how big or small. Wood chips couldn't be glued back into a stick. Choices couldn't be unmade. But that reality didn't stop doubt from barging in. "Was the boy right, Jaki? Should we have attacked last night while we knew Juliet was away?"

"And face evil when it reigns strongest? No, you were wise to advise rest after our long day of travel."

"Wisdom had nothing to do with it." Gareth's eyes fell to his work; he'd started a small heart, similar to the pendant he'd given to Juliet upon their engagement. He clenched the wooden reminder in his fist.

Jaki clasped Gareth's shoulder, reassuring warmth penetrating the wool coat. "Trust Creator's leading. He will never direct you wrong."

"I don't doubt His leading. I doubt my following." Gareth tucked the unfinished heart into his pocket and brushed off a few pieces of wood clinging to him.

Jaki offered him a chunk of bread. "Creator can redeem even the worst decision for good."

"We'll find out today." Gareth accepted the bread. "Rouse the others and meet me at the shaft. I'll scout ahead."

"Be careful, Gareth."

"Known me to be anything else?" He broke off a bite.

"Frequently."

Gareth chuckled as he passed Jaki. "Risks don't seem risky to a man on his dying breath."

Jaki flicked a gloved hand at him, a bubble of warmth propelling Gareth forward.

A smile lingered on Gareth's face as he finished his light breakfast, but as the path widened and steepened, any lingering levity was wiped away with his meal's crumbs. This was still enemy territory, even if the enemy wasn't currently visible. Gareth unsheathed both of his long-bladed knives and softened his tread to reduce the noise of his descent as much as possible. The road curled around the mountainside away from Juliet's mansion. The ground flattened, and a rusty fence stretched out before him. A faded warning sign ordered trespassers to stay out, the abandoned mine unstable and highly dangerous. Gareth shook his head. The dangers that lurked beyond this fence had nothing to do with the stability of the earth and a whole lot to do with the stability of mind.

He paced along the fence several yards in both directions. No recent activity had churned up the earth. Not that this was much of a reassurance. A hunter knew how to cover tracks as well as follow them. Gareth returned to the gate and sliced through the rusted chain holding it closed. They should be long gone before anyone would notice. Should be.

Jaki arrived with Maggie and Brandon as it began to snow, greetings kept to a quick nod. Gareth pushed open the squeaky gate and led the group up a short rise to the mountainside. The gaping maw of the mineshaft punctured the vertical slab of stone.

Brandon eyed the dark entrance propped open with rough-hewn beams of questionable soundness. "Are you sure we're in the right place?"

"You doubt the Guardian Prince's path?" challenged Jaki.

"I doubt this whole venture," said Brandon. "Secret labs, underground labyrinths—it sounds like a make-believe story." He shook his head, dislodging several feathery snowflakes.

"Yet is it any stranger than what you've already seen, son of dust?"

"Don't blame him, Jaki." Gareth paused in his search for tire tracks, footprints, anything that would indicate they weren't alone. "It does seem far-fetched Juliet could build that and more without the government knowing. If I hadn't seen it, I wouldn't believe it myself."

"You've been there?" Brandon curled his fingers around the strap of his quiver.

"I have." Gareth paced off a distance from the mineshaft and squinted at the mountaintops, half obscured by clouds and snow. "After I was arrested for murder, Juliet was assigned to interrogate me. She brought me here." Gareth moved one pace to the left, then two to the right. Three points of a mountain appeared in the valley between two others. "I would have died here too, except after the way our engagement ended, she thought killing me outright was too merciful. So I was sent to HopeWell."

Gareth faced the mine again. "While I was here, rumors whispered of a back door through an abandoned mine from which you could see the whole crown of Diadem. This is the closest mine and there"—Gareth gestured to the triple-peaked mountain—"is Diadem."

Brandon still looked doubtful. "It seems too abandoned to be the back door to anything."

"Looks can deceive, son of dust, especially where Levioth is concerned." Jaki wrapped Maggie in a bubble of warmth to ease her shivering. "You'll soon learn the truest truth about her and those who serve her is that nothing they touch is as it appears to be."

"Speaking of which." Gareth caught some fat snowflakes falling so thick that they dropped in white clumps where they caught on each other. "More Dachi mischief?"

"It seems Dachi in origin." Jaki tipped his head thoughtfully. "But I sense neither malice nor ill intent."

"Because neither is meant, flame of fire." A reverberating voice behind them rattled sky and earth, each word rolling over the next like successive booms of thunder.

They whirled around, Jaki drawing his sword and Gareth raising his knives. Brandon's bow clattered to the ground at the giant apparition towering behind them some fifteen feet in the air. A fierce wind swirled around the phantom, the ever-shifting eddies of snow the only thing providing form or substance.

Jaki clasped his arm across his chest. "Sarruak."

"Time is short. The word of Creator." The gale around Sarruak accelerated into an earsplitting roar, forcing the three men to cover their ears, and thunder cracked and boomed and rolled until the mountain shook so hard that a few rocks ripped free. Then the noise faded, and the wind eased. "Let him who has ears hear." And with that the apparition collapsed, dissolving into a swirl of snow.

The storm died a moment later. Bandon picked up his bow, trembling. "What"–his voice cracked and he cleared his throat– "what was that?"

"That was Sarruak, a prince of the Qolet." Jaki turned to Gareth. "Things must balance on a sword's edge for a Qolet prince to breach the Wall."

"I didn't know they were even permitted to cross the Wall." Gareth studied the snow pile that had collected beneath Sarruak; nothing marred the white surface. "More concerning, what message were we to hear?"

Maggie slid on her spectacles and blinked slowly several times, as if to refocus her vision, before facing the mineshaft. "He told the way."

Gareth arched his brow. Jaki shrugged a shoulder. "A Jewel seems a true choice to hear clearest."

Maggie sniffed. "Ye hear better if yer ears be not stopped up."

"That indeed helps," Gareth observed wryly.

"But there be so many."

"Many what?" Brandon tightened his grip on the bow.

"The Rishi." Jaki gripped his sword with both hands. "They have a strong contingent here."

"So how do we pass without alerting them?" Gareth held his knives at the ready.

"We can't. There are too many to elude."

"We'll have to move fast."

"We're still going in?" Brandon backpedaled.

"The Rishi may no longer serve Creator, but He yet constrains them." Gareth scouted the mine's entrance, but nothing moved within. "While the Rishi can see us, alert the hunters, and even play havoc with our surroundings, they can't touch us. Not as long as they're in Echoing." He waved the others forward.

"Nor can they cross over." Jaki guarded Maggie as she approached the shaft. "Creator shields the cracks and gateways." He paused to blow on his blade; it began to glow like super-heated metal, a bright beacon against the mine's black mouth.

Brandon held his ground. "What's our strategy then?"

Gareth crossed his blades in front of him. "Move fast, keep your head down, and beg Creator for His protection— not necessarily in that order." He nodded at Maggie. "When you're ready."

She nodded. "Creator, be our guide." And she plunged into the darkness.

A moment later a sickly yellow glow illuminated damp stone, drawing Brandon forward. A string of light bulbs hung from the ceiling, none broken or unlit. Gareth grunted. "Very abandoned."

Brandon withdrew an arrow from his quiver. The arrow's shaft chattered against the bow as he tried to nock it. Jaki thumped him on the back. "Breathe, son of dust. You aid no one if you fall for lack of it."

Timbers creaked and moaned. Brandon jumped. Gareth scowled. "Skittish colt."

"Patience, Gareth." Jaki offered Maggie an arm of support. "He is just learning the world you've known for decades."

The group traveled further in. The ground shuddered, and light bulbs swayed, causing the shadows to lunge and leap. The short bursts of Brandon's breathing echoed in the tunnel. Then the shaft split into two. Maggie wavered and clutched her head between her hands. "So dark. Too dark. It strangles. It smothers."

Gareth knelt before her. "Maggie." He waited for her gaze to center on him. "I don't like it either, but that's why we're here. To rescue Oriel and the other Jewel from the darkness."

"Yes, yes, rescue." Maggie inhaled a shuddering breath and adjusted her spectacles. "Close, so very close." She pointed a gnarled finger down the left-hand tunnel. "There."

"Well done." He rose to head that direction.

She snatched his coat sleeve. "Oil be rainin' there. Black, dripping oil. Hissing, spitting . . ." She fumbled for the right word. "Drowning."

Jaki's sword dipped, its glow dimming. "Gareth, if that's what I think—"

"You and Maggie should drive the car around to the front of the estate. If things go sideways, that's where we'll come out." Gareth blocked Maggie's view of the tunnel. "Did you hear me, Maggie? You don't have to go any farther."

She sank against Jaki's arm. "Ye were always good to me."

"A reflection of what you give others," Gareth said. "But Oriel and the Jewel—where are they? What did the Qolet tell you?"

Maggie wrinkled her brow. "Arrow's path to monster's mouth. Down the throat, into the belly. Two wrongs make not a right, but two rights lead to a place of great wrong."

Gareth repeated her words. "I have it. Thank you, Maggie." He started toward the left branch.

"And whatever happens," added Jaki, "get the Key. We must have the Key. We can return for the Jewel later." He slid a protective arm around Maggie. "May the wind of Creator's breath be yours."

"May His fire be your shield."

"For all ages and beyond."

Gareth bowed his head in acknowledgment of the blessing

and motioned for Brandon to follow him deeper into the mine, leaving Jaki and Maggie behind.

The shaft angled downward, switching back to the right as darkness closed around them, the lights now farther apart. After a while, Brandon asked, "What is raining oil?"

"A Rishi trap, made of black sap, invisible in Terrestrial." Gareth sidestepped some animal droppings. "I misspoke earlier. The Rishi can't hurt us, but Jaki on the other hand—the sap would have clung to him and smothered his fire, extinguishing him."

"It would kill him?" Brandon faltered. "Are you sure we—"

"It can't hurt us. We're made of dust, not fire."

"But—"

"We're fine."

Brandon looked uncertain, but they walked on. Though the scenery didn't deviate, an eerie silence pressed around them, which felt full of noise despite the lack of sound. After the third switchback of their descent, Brandon spoke again. "Where is everyone? Shouldn't there be a patrol or a guard or something?"

"The Rishi are here, which should be sufficient." Gareth rolled his shoulders to loosen his own tense muscles; the eerie silence was getting even to him. "But the hunters aren't responding, and that's troubling. Maybe with Levioth gone, the Rishi can't rouse them. Or maybe Creator is intervening."

They reached a three-way split. "Which way now?"

"Arrows can't fly around curves . . . so straight ahead."

They descended deeper and deeper, the air cool and clammy. The shaft ended at a natural cave, its opening filled with stalactites and stalagmites like row upon row of giant teeth. Brandon stared. "A monster's mouth."

"You're catching on." Tightening his grip on the knives, Gareth ducked between a quartet of exceptionally fang-like formations and navigated around the stalagmites. The damp floor and the odd shadows slowed progress further. After several yards the mouth opened into a ledge that dropped off into an impenetrable blackness stretching as far as the eye could see in any direction. Gareth peered over the ledge. A ladder descended into the darkness. "Down the throat, into the belly."

"You're not actually thinking about going down there, are you?" Brandon held back, the whites of his eyes stark.

"No thinking about it." Gareth returned to the cave opening, sheathing his knives. On his left, a few sets of mining helmets and battery packs sat on a rock shelf. "I'm going." He put on a helmet.

Gareth clipped the battery pack to his waist and flipped on the light.

Brandon shaded his eyes from the brightness with his hand. "You could die down there."

"Not unlikely."

"Then why go?"

"Because it's the right thing to do." Gareth looked down into the chasm again. If it had a bottom, the light didn't reveal it. "I don't blame you for fearing this path. The Rishi and the hunters are powerful. I cannot guarantee that we will succeed. But for twenty years I have lived death because I would not heed Creator's call. Never again. If His call leads to my death this day, then I die alive. And that is a death worth living." Stepping onto the ladder, he disappeared down cliff.

Rung by rung Gareth descended. Seconds stretched into minutes. Muscles tightened into knots. Sweat dripped down his face. Finally his boot scuffed against stone rather than another metal rung. A quick glance around showed he was indeed at the bottom of the chasm, which extended both to the right and to the left farther than his helmet's beam could reach. Opposite the ladder, a couple dozen yards away, rose another wall of stone, even more daunting than the one he just descended.

Gareth looked up the ladder, watching, waiting. Nothing moved. Nothing creaked. The rescue team had been reduced to one. He dropped his head. "Forgive me, Creator. I have failed him."

Withdrawing his long knives, he followed the rock wall to the right. "Two wrongs make not a right. Two rights lead to a place of great wrong." After a dozen yards, the wall disappeared. He veered right into the tunnel. The ground smoothed out. The ceiling and walls squared off with each other—the work of human hands. A few paces further, thick metal doors were inserted into each side.

Gareth came to a stop, his grip on his knives white-knuckled. He swallowed. "Not the prisoner. Not anymore." Still he struggled to sheathe one of his knives, and his hand shook as he tugged on the first door.

The door was unlocked and pulled open reluctantly under Gareth's force. The narrow room reeked of death and decay and despair, but it contained nothing except a pair of iron manacles and few scattered bones. Gareth rubbed his ear. Here the keening wails and terrified shrieks from the ghosts of his past screeched incessantly.

"Creator is merciful. Creator is just. Creator is powerful. Creator is . . . Creator is . . ." Gareth gripped the jamb, grooves burrowing deeply into his face. "Creator is . . . good. Always." The words required everything for him to say here, now. But once spoken, his breathing eased. "And He will not forget, may His name be eternally praised."

At the praising of Creator, the ground convulsed as if all the evil of this place stampeded in retreat. With renewed determination Gareth slammed the door shut and proceeded to the next one. It too was unlocked and devoid of anything living. The next half dozen doors led to more of the same. Then he reached a door that refused to budge.

Gareth yanked on it several times. Still the door remained closed. Inside metal scraped against stone. The door was locked for good reason; more than dry bones inhabited this space. Gareth withdrew his whittling knife. "Hope your work is good, Oriel." He wiggled it around in the lock.

The tumblers clinked.

Shoving away the knife, Gareth jerked the door open, and the light of his lamp fell on a young woman huddled in the back corner. But it wasn't Oriel. The hair veiling half of her face was too dark, less ash-blonde like Oriel's, more chestnut like—"Jul?"

The young woman cringed, her hair moving to reveal a puckered scar running down her face. Definitely not Juliet either. Gareth stepped into the room.

Witless curled into a ball, trying to make herself as small as possible. Dark bruises colored her arms. Dried blood edged the manacles binding her ankles to the wall. She clutched her left side. Yet an almost inaudible strain of music spilled from her mouth, a hint of dark spices scenting the air. Gareth caught his breath. He had found the Jewel.

Kneeling in front of her, Gareth touched Witless on the shoulder. She jerked back, arm shielding her head, eyes squeezed shut.

"Don't fear. I'm here to help." He examined leg irons. These chains were three times as thick as the one he slashed through at the gate. "I told them I needed my guardian blades," he muttered under his breath. He grasped a link and sawed at it with the knife. It took several strokes, but the blade finally cut through, and the chain fell with a clank. "What's your name?"

Witless hung her head and picked at her sleeve.

His blade sliced through another link. "Mine's Gareth. I'm here to get you out along with another young girl—Oriel."

Witless lifted her head, and her golden eyes sparkled brighter than normal in the helmet's light.

Gareth startled. "You're a . . ." He clamped his mouth shut and refocused on severing the rest of the chain. "So any chance you've met Oriel?"

Witless hesitated, then nodded.

"Do you know where she is?"

Another hesitation and another nod.

"Will you take me to her?" Gareth offered her his hand.

She ignored it and rose on her own. But when she tried to stand erect, she gasped and clutched her side.

"May I?"

Witless studied his face, weathered and hardened by experience and yet lacking the sharpness of a cunning deceiver. She took her hand away.

Gareth tenderly probed the spot, triggering a cry of pain from her. "Could be broken. The sooner I get you help, the better. But first"—he looked at her—"Oriel?"

Witless led him deeper into the darkened tunnel, hand pressed against her ribs. But the pain she had to be in didn't slow her steps, nor did any sound of complaint escape her as she navigated the maze of halls. Finally, she backed against the wall and pointed to the door at the end of the hall.

"Wait here," Gareth told her. "I'll get Oriel out. Then we can all leave."

Witless only hugged herself tighter, eyes again on the floor.

The room, on the other hand, was not as accommodating. It took Gareth three attempts to unlock it, and even then, the door stubbornly resisted releasing the room's secrets to him. Finally, he made it inside. His lamplight fell on Oriel, half-covered in cement on a raised slab of granite. The faintest glow colored her cheeks.

"Oriel?" He hurried to her and touched her arm. "Oriel."

No movement. He was on his own to get her out. He struck at the cement with his knife, then the tomahawk. Neither cracked it. His light bounced around the otherwise empty room. "Now what?"

A metallic clanking came from the hall; the elevator was

descending. The Rishi had roused some of the hunters at last.

Gareth directed his beam toward the ceiling. "What am I supposed to do? I'm not strong enough to . . ." He redirected the light at Oriel, at the impossible cement.

He placed his hands over one of the mounds covering her. "Creator, I am not strong enough, but You are." He lowered his head. "Free her. Please."

The room began to shake. Dust and pebbles cascaded down. Stone creaked and groaned. The floor heaved, throwing him sideways, and he hit the ground. Then as suddenly as it began, the shaking stopped. Gareth stumbled to his feet, coughing and covered in gray dust. But the concrete had cracked. Clasping both arms over his chest, he bowed his head. "Thank You."

Returning to Oriel's side, he pulled away huge chunks of the cement. Soon she was free, with only a few pieces of crumbling stone still clinging to her clothing. Gareth slung her over his shoulder and exited the room. "Time to . . ."

The hall was empty.

22

BRANDON PACED THE CAVE. SEVERAL TIMES HE approached the mineshaft. And each time he turned back. "This is so stupid! Just leave." Finally he halted. "Argh!" He whacked his bow against the wall.

The bow sprang back with unexpected force, ripping out of his hand. It skidded across the floor and teetered on the edge of the chasm. Brandon lunged. His fingers brushed the tip, but before he could grasp it, the bow tilted over the edge, vanishing into the darkness below.

"Idiot." A bow and arrow might be an antiquated weapon, but it was still a weapon. One he very much needed. Brandon grabbed a miner's helmet and battery pack off the shelf and descended the ladder to retrieve the bow.

Darkness closed around him until the circle of light from his headlamp was all that remained, shimmering across the stone wall between the rungs. Reaching the bottom, Brandon found only endless stone. No bow.

He glanced up the ladder, the attraction of the lighted mineshaft growing, with or without the bow. Brandon gritted his teeth. He didn't climb all this way to return empty-handed. He scanned the ground with the helmet's beam. A dozen steps to the left revealed nothing but more stone. Retracing his path, he searched in the opposite direction. His light glinted off something—his bow, fully intact, though wedged tightly between two boulders.

Brandon examined the rocks. With their girth exceeding Brandon's height, their weight would easily surpass what one man could handle. He wrapped both hands around the visible end of the bow and, bracing one foot against the boulder, he pulled. "Please don't break."

The bow budged a little, then popped free.

He crashed backward, the helmet flying from his head. The lamp shattered, plunging the cave into darkness. The ground spasmed, and a stone smashed into the earth near Brandon, far too close for comfort. Clutching his bow, he scuttled toward the center of the chasm.

The earth quieted. Brandon exhaled. A couple of scrapes, a few bruises, but he otherwise escaped unscathed. Unlike the miner's helmet. When he used the battery pack's cord to retrieve it, he found a deep dent caved one side and the light no longer switched on. He tossed it aside.

A narrow spot of light drew his gaze upward. The entrance to the mineshaft.

Orienting himself by that weak glimmer, he crawled back to the cliff. Sweeping his hand across the stone in search of the ladder, he felt his way forward.

A soft glow bounced off the rock ahead of him. Brandon squinted. A figure—a young woman—emerged into the chasm, the glow emanating from her hands. A seemingly impossible scene, but one that remained unchanged even after swiping his hand over his eyes.

Suddenly, glaring lights illuminated the tunnel behind her. Brandon flattened himself against the cliff. The young woman spun around, the glow of her hands extinguishing. In the tunnel's mouth stood five men in black. Hunters.

Before she could dart away, the hunters circled her, and the Alpha seized her arm. "My, my. What a pretty trick." The Alpha twisted her arm behind her back, making her wince. He leaned forward. "My mistress will be thrilled to learn about this. I wonder what else you've been hiding all these years?"

Witless bit her lip, pain contorting her face.

"What? You refuse to beg for mercy?" He yanked up her arm. She moaned.

Brandon withdrew an arrow with calculated slowness, his muscles taut with needed restraint. Sudden movement would attract attention and lose his biggest advantage: the element of surprise.

"Oh that's right. You can't beg. What a pity." The Alpha jerked harder. The cracking of bone mingled with a scream.

Brandon ground his teeth. He nocked the arrow and raised the point, eyes narrowing on his target.

A scraping echoed from deeper in the tunnel. The Alpha crushed Witless against himself, backing against the wall. "The lights!"

A hunter sprinted into the tunnel, and a moment later, the chasm plunged into darkness. Brandon blinked rapidly, trying to readjust his eyes quicker.

The light of a headlamp approached toward the chasm accompanied by the heavy tread of boots. The hunters froze, the Alpha's hand covering Witless's mouth. After a long half minute, Gareth appeared, crossing from tunnel to chasm, Oriel slung over his shoulder.

A foot scraped against rock. Gareth whirled around, his lamp's beam arcing across the five hunters who blocked the tunnel entrance. The Alpha, front and center, clutched Witless to his chest, gun pressed to her temple. His face's shadows emphasized the black pleasure burning in his eyes. "Missing something, *Guardian*?" He spat the final word at Gareth.

Brandon edged forward. Encircling a finger around the arrow's shaft to prevent it from chattering against the bow, he raised the point.

Gareth inched his free hand toward his waist. The Alpha cocked the gun. Gareth's hand stilled. The Alpha's grin widened, baring yellowed teeth. "I see we have an understanding." He gestured with the weapon. "Put the Ishir down."

After hesitating a moment, Gareth lowered Oriel to the floor. He shuffled his feet against the ground as he did so, filling the chasm with the echo of boots scuffing against rock.

Using the noise as cover, Brandon pulled the arrow back and aimed at the hunters. All he needed was a moment of steady light to lock onto his target.

Without rising, Gareth tipped his head up, focusing his light on the Alpha. "Now!"

Brandon released the arrow.

The Alpha's head snapped to his right, the arrow striking him in the side with a sickening thud. He crumpled, his hold on Witless loosening. Gareth lunged forward as Brandon released a second arrow and reached for a third. Another hunter intercepted Gareth, knocking his helmet from his head. Light and shadow cavorted in strange formations as grunts mixed with clatters and cries.

Brandon hesitated, his aim bobbing from potential target to potential target. Someone deeper in the tunnel moaned. Light flared around the curled fist of Witless. A thud and a man's scream, followed by the scent of burning flesh, announced a target had been struck.

Then a gunshot ricocheted through the cavern.

23

THE LAST HUNTER DIED TWO SECONDS TOO LATE.

He should have been dead already, but from some deep reservoir—or by some dark force—he managed one final act. He tripped the alarm.

Immediately every light flicked on, and a siren began to blare.

Slinging Oriel over his shoulder, Gareth led the charge back down the chasm, but as they reached the bottom of the ladder, a jolting thud reverberated through the cavern, overpowering the wail of the siren. With a sharp command to Witless and Brandon to stay put, Gareth laid Oriel on the ground and scrambled up the ladder. Seven agonizing minutes later he returned, shaking his head. That exit had been blocked, the alarm dropping a gate between the cave and the mineshaft, which left one way out: through Juliet's mountain estate.

Shouldering Oriel again, Gareth eyed the barefoot Witless, who swayed slightly despite the rock wall she leaned against, her broken arm cradled to her chest. Brandon lowered himself before her and motioned for her to get onto his back. Witless hesitated, then climbed on awkwardly, clinging to his neck with one arm as he hefted her up.

Before another two minutes passed, they had found their way back to the tunnels and a caged elevator. Still no additional hunters had appeared. Were they waiting upstairs to ambush them? But with no other way out, they had no choice. They boarded the elevator, and it began its slow ascent. Gareth adjusted his grip on Oriel to better secure her limp body and to withdraw one of his long-bladed knives with his free hand.

The elevator slid between levels, the surrounding rock somewhat muting the alarm. Brandon leaned toward Gareth and shouted, "What's the plan?"

"To get out alive."

Brandon stared at him. "What kind of plan is that?"

Gareth shrugged his free shoulder. "A flexible one."

The elevator slowed. Witless shuddered. Gareth slid his knife between the elevator's grate, ready to flip it open.

A dim room gradually came into view. A wood door, which would normally hide the elevator, stood open, and shelves lined the walls of the narrow room, lumps of various shapes and sizes adorning them. At the far end of the storeroom a closed door blocked from sight whatever—or whoever—was beyond.

The elevator jerked to a stop. Nothing in the room moved. Gareth pushed the grate aside, the siren drowning out the rattling. Everything remained still. They quietly crossed the room, but as they reached the second door, it flew open. "About time you—"

A silver blade flashed, permanently severing the doorkeeper's sentence.

Witless buried her face in Brandon's shoulder. Gareth kept moving, charging down the stone hall beyond. After a split-second hesitation, Brandon hurried after him.

A maid exited a room farther ahead. With one look at Gareth's blade, she shrieked and fled back inside. Other doors behind them flew open.

Gareth pounded up the steps to the main level, taking two stairs at a time, despite Oriel's dead weight, and skidded around a corner. The ornate entranceway of Juliet's mansion opened before him with the front door at its end.

A bullet slammed into a mirror. Glass splintered, shards flying in all directions. Brandon's steps stuttered.

"Don't stop!" Gareth plunged through the foyer, gunfire

regularly punctuating the siren's wail. Two panes of glass shattered in the window to the door's left. Another bullet pinged off a bolt, one of three securing the front door. Gareth veered from it—the door would take too long to unlock—and instead smashed his boot into the muntins of the window on the right, scattering glass and splintered wood outward. He climbed over the low sill, debris crunching underfoot, and dashed across the front lawn, Brandon struggling to keep up.

Four hunters rushed from the cover of the halls to the broken windows, reloading as they went. As two climbed over the sill, the other two took aim. Bullets burrowed into the ground at the heels of the escaping men.

Gareth slashed through the gate's lock and rammed his free shoulder into the iron bars. He nodded Brandon and Witless through, then followed them down the road. Jaki waited with the car a few yards ahead. Maggie peered anxiously out of the back window.

"Start the car!" Gareth shouted. "Start the car!"

Jaki dove into the front seat, and the engine roared to life. Gareth yanked open the front passenger door, shoved Oriel inside, and squeezed in beside her. Brandon did the same with Witless in the backseat.

Jaki slammed the car into gear and sped off. He ratcheted it up as fast as he could while navigating the mountain's hairpins. Gareth clutched Oriel to his side. Witless whimpered. Brandon wrapped an arm around her shoulders while Maggie patted her hand.

After ten minutes they reached a plateau. Gareth twisted around to search the road as Jaki jumped the car another gear. "Anything?"

"Nothing visible. Maggie?"

She slid on her spectacles. "All be quiet."

"That was close." Brandon sank back into his seat.

"Nothing close about it." Gareth faced forward, body taut as he scanned the plateau. "They let us go."

Jaki shot Gareth a sharp sideways glance. "Are you sure?"

"Hunters don't miss. There." Gareth pointed to a bleached, dilapidated barn left behind from a failed attempt to work the barren land. "Pull in there."

Jaki slowed the car and turned down the rutted track past a broken fence.

Brandon leaned forward. "Shouldn't we keep going and put as much distance between us as we can?"

"Distance does us little good if it loses what we came for."

The car rolled into the shadow of the barn. Gareth and Brandon got out and pushed the door open, and Jaki parked inside. Light slanted through gaps between the boards, and dust motes lingered in the air, adding a haze to the stuffiness. Gareth grabbed a couple of boards and put them across the sides of a stall for a makeshift table.

Brandon helped Witless out of the car. A shaft of light glinted off her head, giving her chestnut locks a fiery halo. At the sight, Gareth clenched his jaw. Rounding the nose of the car, he knocked Jaki backward.

Jaki righted himself and massaged the spot Gareth struck. "So, you figured it out."

"I'm old, not senile." Gareth rubbed his hand, red from striking skin-wrapped fire.

"Sarish forbade us to interfere."

"Sarish is not Creator."

"She's a Spliced, Gareth."

"Did you even bother trying?"

"And do what?" Jaki snatched up his fedora from the ground where it had fallen and beat the dust from it. "I couldn't hide her. Guardians were dying faster than we could train them. You'd fallen off the face of the earth, and you know Sarish would order her death on sight, Jewel or no Jewel." He smashed his hat back on his head.

Gareth crossed his arms, his scowl not easing up. "It's not her fault, being a split-race."

"I know." Jaki glanced over at Witless, who had slipped into the shadows as Brandon offered his hand to his grandmother. But Witless's attempt to blend into the gloom only emphasized the light glow of her skin and the brightness of her eyes, highlighting her Ishir nature. "It took many days of Creator's working, but He did at last convince me. I was to do what I could rather than what I couldn't, and let Creator handle the couldn't. Therefore, while I knew I dare not attempt a rescue alone, I could search for her and verify she still lived. I started using my Sabbaths accordingly. Though I couldn't confirm the breath of life, I had narrowed her presence to this region when the vigils announced a guardian walked Terrestrial, and I found you."

"That's why you didn't question my direction."

"Indeed. It only confirmed what I already knew."

Gareth plowed his hand through his hair, scattering the last of the debris he'd collected in the quake. "You should have told me."

"In your absence, I forgot some things too."

"I thought the Ishir never forgot."

"And I thought you never wasted time." Jaki inclined his head toward the car where Oriel still lay.

"Always changing the subject." Though he grumbled the words, the tension that had bound him upon confronting Jaki had bled away. Gareth retrieved Oriel and gently laid her on the makeshift table.

Jaki placed his hands over Oriel's firecore. A deep sigh of relief dissipated some of the tension from his broad shoulders. "Her flames burn low but not from smothering. They have been merely banked."

"Banked?" Brandon had joined the other two men, Maggie shooing him away so she could talk to Witless.

"An Ishir's self-induced coma." Gareth brushed hair from

Oriel's face; her skin was cool but not clammy. "Can she be awakened?"

Jaki checked her for other injuries. "Perhaps it would be best to let her sleep until we reach the Vault."

"You don't trust her." Gareth's accusation dared Jaki to justify his suggestion.

Which Jaki promptly did. "She left the Vault. The Key isn't supposed to leave. Sarish's orders."

"So she's guilty before she can even defend herself. Wonder why that seems familiar."

Jaki lowered his head at the slicing reference to Gareth's own Ishir conviction. The one he had fervently protested. A shaft of sunshine caught dust motes, transforming them into pixie dust around Oriel's still body. The picture of vulnerable innocence.

Gareth softened his voice. "Aren't there enough prisoners in the world?"

Jaki studied his friend, eyes glinting beneath his hat's brim. "When did wisdom find a roost with you?"

"When it took flight from you."

Jaki laughed. "You win." Carefully, he pressed hands to her firecore and sang, *"Awaken, awaken, the morn has begun. Sleep no more, sleep no more, there's work to be done."*

Color seeped into Oriel's cheeks, and she stirred.

"It will take a minute for her to fully reignite, but she should awaken soon."

"Plenty of time then."

"For what?"

Gareth cocked his head toward Witless.

"Gareth, I'm a warrior, not a cantor."

The guardian folded his arms.

"Fine. I'll do what I can." The twinkle in his eye ruined his attempt at exasperation.

Sensing Jaki's approach, Witless turned away from Maggie,

only to shrink back from the hulking giant behind her. Jaki stopped a few paces from her, his hands in his pockets.

Maggie patted Witless's shoulder. "It be well, lamb. He means no harm, being an Ishir and all."

Witless bit her lip, then took a tentative step toward Jaki, looking him full in the face. Something about her expression echoed Juliet so strongly that Jaki was taken aback. "I know I judge human appearance poorly, but does she not resemble Levioth?"

Leaning against a post, Gareth began to whittle a chunk of wood he found. "Sisters generally do."

"Sisters?" Brandon backtracked a half step.

"Half sisters," Gareth amended. "Same father, but her mother was Ishir. Not that Juliet knows that. She would have destroyed the girl by now if she had."

"The same blood shared by Levioth and a Jewel? Creator's wonders never cease." Awe permeated Jaki's voice, and he stretched a hand toward her. "And what is your name, daughter of fire and dust?"

Witless hung her head, the bitterness of shame cutting through Jaki's oak and cloves.

He glanced at Gareth.

Gareth shook his head; such knowledge was not his. "It was by a slip of the tongue alone that I even knew of her existence. Juliet hated her—believed herself cast aside because their father favored the younger."

Jaki put his finger under her chin and lifted her face. He waited until she raised her gaze to him. "I cannot aid you until I know your name." His gentle tone infused warmth into the air.

Witless blinked away tears. Slowly, she opened her mouth to him.

His warmth plummeted several degrees. "Gareth . . ." Horror choked his words. "They stole her tongue."

Gareth froze mid-cut. "Stole?"

"Levioth cut it out." A silent keening seemed to rip through the air, causing the entire structure to shudder.

Hunching her shoulders, Witless swiped at the tears spilling down her cheeks.

"Levioth called her Witless."

Startled, they all turned around as one to Oriel. She now sat upright and alert, but a deep sorrow dimmed the light in her eyes. Jaki crossed an arm over his chest and half bowed to her. "Key of Everything, you have returned to us."

"Not for long." She slid off the makeshift table and stretched her back.

"Do not say that. Your fire will yet be restored." Jaki pulled a pouch from the inside of his coat and dumped a handful of woodchips into his palm. He offered them to Oriel as she approached.

She accepted them, sliding several into her mouth, but her attention rested once more on Witless—the girl with no tongue and no real name.

Maggie huffed. "This be not right. Everybody gots to have a proper name." She cupped her hands around the younger girl's face and stared deeply into her eyes, whose brightness spoke of a sharp intellect. Their golden irises were flecked with a rainbow of colors. "Ye are not witless. Ye are priceless, an Iris made by Creator's hand." Maggie tipped the young woman's head forward and pressed her lips against it in a kiss of christening benediction.

The young woman sighed as if relieved of a terrible burden. With her good hand, Iris squeezed Maggie's wrinkled one, the warmth of her touch expressing her thanks better than any words. She peeked over Maggie's shoulder, the light of hope now shining in her face.

Jaki nodded in unspoken assent. Maggie moved behind Iris, her lips soundlessly petitioning Creator, while Jaki covered Iris's head with both his hands and began to hum.

At first the song rumbled low and deep, so that bones felt the sound more than ears heard it. A cloud passed over the sun outside, dimming the light further, as if to reflect the earthy tune. Then the pitch rose. Shafts of light cut through the loamy melody, cold earth warming beneath the spring sun.

As the song grew, so did the glow of Jaki's skin, and even Iris herself gained a dim aura of many colors, as if to reflect the root meaning of her name. A rich wordless melody spilled out of Jaki's mouth, calling to mind plants emerging from the earth, leaves uncurling and flowers blossoming. Finally, he lifted his face heavenward, and notes formed words.

> "Beauty fills the wood and plains;
> "Splendor marks the iris fair.
> "But greater glory around Him rains
> "Forever praised everywhere.
> "Rainbows and lightnings flash;
> "Flames of fire hide from sight
> "The radiance that is found within
> "The matchless, untainted, pure light!"

At the last note, the glow around Jaki and Iris burst into hundreds of sparks, which slowly faded as they fell to the ground. Jaki lowered his hands and looked at Iris. "How does your arm fare?"

She rotated her wrist, and her eyes grew wide. Her arm moved with all the dexterity of a limb that had never been injured. She probed her side and then her other wounds. All had healed completely. Then she moved her jaw side to side, and disappointment evaporated her smile. Her tongue was still missing.

Jaki clasped her shoulders. "We ask. Creator answers. But our asking doesn't necessitate Him answering as we wish. He's still Creator."

"Jaki speaks truth. Listen to him." Gareth showed her the result of his whittling—a life-like iris that almost glowed in the dusty air. "Don't let the joy of the yes be marred by the disappointment of the no." He held out his creation to her.

Iris accepted the miniature flower and twirled it between her fingers. Dust motes danced around it, and the faintest hint of something floral perfumed the air. She nodded her thanks to Gareth.

Jaki turned from Iris and froze. "Where is the Key?"

The group glanced around.

Oriel was gone.

THE FIVE HUNTERS SPLAYED ACROSS THE TUNNEL'S entrance had each died differently. The first took a bullet. The second bore two arrows, one to the side and one to the neck. The throat of the third had been slit, and the fourth bore multiple stab wounds.

But as gruesome as the first four were, it was the fifth body over which Juliet hovered. This one also sported an arrow, this time to the thigh, but the face revealed the real cause of death: the right side of the skull caved in, skin charred beyond recognition. The center of the crater was the size of a small fist.

A hunter trudged up the hallway to the tunnel's entrance, and Juliet rose from her examination of the corpse. "Well?"

"They're both gone."

"Both?"

"Yes, Levioth."

"Hmm." Juliet adjusted her sling and fingered the chain of her necklace. "Why risk the extra baggage?"

"Shall we pursue?"

The hunter's question jarred Juliet from her musing over the unexpected development that Gareth had taken Witless as well as the Ishir. "No, everything proceeds as planned." Juliet strolled down the hallway toward the elevator. "My original orders stand."

The hunter, tailing behind her, glanced over his shoulder. "What about—"

"Leave them." Juliet entered the elevator and shut the gate behind her. "As a warning to others." She yanked a nearby lever, leaving the hunter behind.

When the elevator stopped again, a brightly lit, sterile hallway stretched before her. She thrust aside the gate and strode forward. One closet, two operating rooms, and a half dozen padded observatories later, she entered the door with the plaque, "Lab."

Inside, Dr. Minio shuffled among beakers full of unnaturally colored liquids. Three other tables displayed an odd assortment of test tubes and petri dishes growing alien substances. A burnt, sulfuric taste flavored the air.

When the doctor noticed Juliet in the doorway, he wiped off his hands and limped forward. "Terrible thing, this break out. Terrible."

Juliet waved away his sentiment as inconsequential. "The serum. Is it ready?"

"First batch at 80, maybe 85 percent potency. Needs six hours to finish aging."

"I can't wait that long. Will it work now?"

The doctor's head wobbled. "In theory, though less effective and not for as long."

Juliet checked her watch. "Then we will do it now."

"Most certainly, Levioth." He pulled a key from under his lab coat and hobbled over to a metal cabinet, shoulder twitching in synchronization with his steps.

Juliet slipped off the sling and unbuttoned her jacket.

Beneath that the wooden heart pendant rested against her chest. She tucked the necklace out of sight and sat on a nearby stool. "Whatever you don't use I want packed with everything necessary for additional injections."

Dr. Minio slid a rack of corked vials on the table. The first tube contained an almost clear liquid, colored by the lightest tint of yellow, with red and orange sparks floating inside. The color of the other vials deepened systematically from yellow to orange to red. The liquid twisted and writhed like flames, not merely reflecting light but emanating it as well.

As Juliet rolled up her sleeve, Dr. Minio filled a syringe with the liquid from the first vial and eyed her. "You do not wish to lie down until we know the effects?"

"An unnecessary precaution." She stretched out her arm on the table, palm up.

"As you wish." He strapped a tourniquet around her arm, then tapped the crook of her elbow until he found a vein. Piercing her with the syringe, he emptied the contents into her bloodstream.

Juliet gasped, her arm brightening to an inflamed scarlet. The doctor whipped off the band and scurried backward. The redness raced up her arm and into her face. She doubled over with a hiss, arm cradled against her chest. Still the flames spread. Juliet's breathing turned labored and wheezy, and she writhed as if in torment.

Then her color gradually evened out, an unnatural glow lighting up her eyes. A smile twisted her lips, and she flexed her broken hand, now healed. She gave a gravelly laugh of delight and stood.

"Let the hunt begin."

24

GARETH SHADED HIS EYES AND SCANNED ALL THREE hundred and sixty degrees of the horizon. Glaring whiteness spread out in every direction. No dark spots smudged the plateau. No footprints disturbed the snow-dusted ground. After two hours of searching, there simply was no trail to follow, no way to track Oriel.

A mouse scurried from a bush and dove into a hole near Gareth's feet. A bird wheeled above. Still no sign, natural or supernatural, provided him any further direction. There was nothing more he could do. Retracing his steps, Gareth wound between clumps of scrubby bushes. It was almost time for the meeting at the barn anyway, prearranged so that they wouldn't wander the plateau endlessly. He kicked at a loose rock with a growl.

The rock tumbled into a creek bed that paralleled his path, one strand of muddy melt-off meandering through the bottom. He paused. If he wanted to cover his tracks, that would be the way to do it. He squinted at the sun, then toward the barn. "I'll give it five minutes."

Switching directions again, he jogged along the creek bed toward the mountains. Five minutes stretched into ten, then fifteen. Gareth searched the horizon. Nothing. He kneaded his neck. So much for that. He turned . . . and halted. There, at a particularly narrow spot in the creek, half of a footprint dented the mud. The toes pointed east, toward the mountains. Gareth wheeled about and accelerated into a run.

After two more minutes, a slim figure materialized—Oriel

walking barefoot amid the icy water. Her boots swung from her hand by their laces. Water had wicked halfway up her pant legs.

Gareth blew out a slow breath and fell into step with her along the bank. When Oriel failed to acknowledge him, he scooped up a twig and began snapping it into small pieces. "Water can seep through skin."

Oriel continued to slog up the rivulet.

"It will affect your fire."

A shudder rippled through her slight frame, but she sloshed through the water all the same.

Tossing aside the bits of the broken twig, Gareth placed himself in front of Oriel. She swerved to circumnavigate him. He snagged her arm. "Oriel?"

She bowed her head, a wind gust teasing loose strands of hair across her face. "Do not call me that, Mighty Prince."

"Why?"

Her head dipped lower, a deep blush coloring her cheeks. "Because I spoke falsely to you."

"That so?"

"I told you that I was called Oriel—the Light of God." She spoke the meaning of her name with the wistful yearning for what could never be. "But only one named me that." She rubbed the birthmark behind her ear. "To all others, I am just the Key."

Gareth tightened his hold on her arm. "To trade one's name for a role is a terrible thing."

"A choice which was not mine. As usual." A sharp tang of bitterness invaded her words, and she pulled away. "You should return to the others." Stepping back into the water, Oriel followed its winding path.

Gareth's hand covered the hilt of his knife. "I won't leave you unprotected."

Her pace quickened, the water boiling around her feet. "I'm not a defenseless child!"

He raised his eyebrow at the billowing steam.

Oriel gasped and leapt onto the bank. The mud encasing her feet instantly dried and cracked, flaking off in chunks. Her boots dropped from her hand to the ground, and she sank onto the embankment, burying her face behind drawn-up knees.

Settling beside her, Gareth began to whittle a chunk of wood that was nearby. Chips and curls accumulated in a pile between his feet as he stared over the plain of sagebrush and limestone. "Why HopeWell?"

She lifted her head slightly.

Gareth waved the wood at the surrounding area. "The world was yours. Why leave the Vault and come to HopeWell?"

Oriel curled her toes against the hard ground. "I was lonely."

"Lonely?" He stared at her.

She fisted her hands. "The Vault supplied all my needs. Visitors were deemed an unnecessary risk."

"But Creator—"

"He was there, and I would not trade that for all the wealth of Echoing. But after decades, centuries of no other companion . . ." Despite the brilliant sunlight beating down on their heads, shadows of a moonless midnight lurked in her eyes. "Was it so terrible I longed for more? To go somewhere, to do something other than read the Ancient Writings and talk with Creator?"

The muscles along Gareth's jaw clenched. Many would—and had—killed for such a utopia as she had been gifted. Did that make her ungrateful . . . or others deluded? "An idyllic prison is still a prison." He resumed his whittling as if that put the matter to rest. "But why exchange one prison for another?" He cut a V out of the wood and flicked it into the sagebrush.

A shadow jerked away from it, drawing Oriel's gaze. Nothing more moved. The wood must have startled some small animal. She rubbed her eyes. "I was sent."

"By Sarish?"

"By Creator." She sighed. "I thought if I could prove able to protect myself, Sarish would permit visitors to the Vault. Therefore, I asked Creator for a reason to leave, and He told me to show the prisoners the way." She looked out into the distance. "And because my heart desired to be more than the Key, to be more *Oriel*, the Vault is forever barred to me."

Gareth's knife bit deeply into the wood, slicing off the outstretched wing of the bird he was whittling. He cast the ruined carving aside. "The position of Key is not for Sarish to take."

"I speak not of Sarish." Oriel picked up the discarded bird and fingered the clipped wing. "Levioth has my blood, and once she drinks of it, anywhere I go she can follow." She rubbed her thumb and index finger together, causing them to glow. She sliced the other wing cleanly from the body of the wooden bird. Now it couldn't fly away any more than she could.

Gareth took the carving from her. "You left to protect us." He began to work on the sides of the bird.

"And that is why you should return to the others." Oriel stood, picking up her boots by the laces again.

"Jaki will kill me if I return without you."

Oriel hopped down into the creek bed. "Don't threaten another Adam, and you'll be safe from him."

"Creator's limits on Ishir power don't extend to tongue-lashings." Gareth brushed a loose shaving from the remade bird, its wings tucked against its side in contented safety. He put the knife away and stepped into the creek beside Oriel. "Come back with me."

"Levioth—"

"Is not all-powerful . . . nor is flight the only way to escape." Stooping, he placed the wooden bird on the water. It bobbed from side to side, then found its equilibrium. It floated between her legs and downstream.

When the creek had carried the bird out of sight, Oriel asked, "But how?"

Gareth took in the surrounding plateau. "Isn't there a crack nearby?"

"Your memory serves you well." She cocked her head. "What path does your mind travel, Mighty Prince?"

"If you passed through a crack but stayed near it, Juliet wouldn't be able to follow you nor use you to find a gateway, even should she be able to track your path in Echoing from Terrestrial." He stepped back up onto the bank. "The rest of us will meet you there, and together we'll determine how to stop Juliet."

Oriel twined the shoelaces around her fingers. "You know with all certainty she cannot use a crack—like you did?"

Gareth gave her a sharp sideways glance. "I don't know how you learned of that, but by Creator's mercy alone do I yet live."

"That sounds like a tale worth hearing."

"Perhaps another day."

"Yes, another day." Oriel sighed, a shadow falling back over the moment of brightness. She climbed up beside Gareth and set her face to the north. "I suppose your plan bears a seed of wisdom." Sitting, she shook her feet dry and pulled on her socks and boots.

"Only a seed—" Gareth abruptly jerked his head to the left, a hand curling around his knife hilt.

"Mighty Prince?"

"I thought I saw . . ." He shook his head, releasing his grip. "Never mind." He waved for her to lead on. "We should be going."

"It's not far." Oriel jogged ahead of him across the plain, winding her way through the sagebrush. Soon it was clear she headed for a gray rock arching its back out of the limestone plain. Its unexpected size—that of a small hill—made the rock appear nearer than it was. After several minutes, they reached it.

Oriel walked along the base of the rock halfway around the circumference, paused, and backtracked three steps. She nodded once to herself, and stooping, hit her fist against the ground. A black fissure edged in light traveled out from her fist along the base of the stone. Oriel looked over her shoulder at Gareth. "I'll be waiting." She pressed her palm against the fissure and vanished down into it. The fissure sealed behind her, leaving no evidence of ever existing.

Gareth scuffed the ground with his boot to mask her final tracks, then leaned his back against the sunbaked stone. Oriel was safe for the moment. "I'll be there soon," he promised.

"You always were a sentimental fool." Derision fouled the air, and Juliet sauntered around the far side of the stone. Dressed in slacks and flats, she emanated a heat that blurred the edges of her form like a mirage.

Gareth whipped out both of his long knives, keeping his back to the stone.

Juliet snorted at the gesture and circled him, her eyes blazing with unnatural light. "Even now, after all you've been through, knowing that I'm Levioth and it's your sacred duty as guardian to kill me, you won't." She stepped within easy striking distance and leaned forward. "Because you are a sentimental, old fool."

In a blur of movement Gareth flashed behind her and wrapped one arm around her chest, crushing her against him. A knife blade pressed against her throat.

"Go on, Guardian Prince." A sneer curled Juliet's voice as much as her lip. "Prove yourself to still be a man."

He increased the pressure of his blade against her neck, and a thick line of sparkling crimson appeared along its edge. Then he lowered his weapon and shoved her away.

Juliet tilted her chin, showing off the wound like a trophy. "A fool *and* a failure." She swiped her hand across her neck, sealing up the cut. She sniffed the blood on her hand, then licked it off.

Gareth looked away, repulsed.

That only fed Juliet's delight. "I shall have to add weak of stomach to that list. Maybe your imprisonment was more effective than I realized."

"Says the girl who once fainted at the sight of blood." Gareth backed away from Juliet. No reason to fight a battle he could not win.

"And therein lies the difference between us." She matched his pace, neither closing the gap nor broadening it. "Your ways weakened you while mine made me stronger."

Juliet was too close for outright flight; to turn his back would most likely be lethal. Gareth tried to increase the distance between them. "There is no strength in madness."

"Is that so?" She thrust out a palm. A fireball hurtled from her hand.

He leapt to the side but not quick enough. The fire struck his shoulder. He dropped and rolled once to smoother the flames, then sprang back to his feet and sprinted away.

"Leaving so soon?" She whipped a hand around her head, and flames leapt up. Blocking any retreat, the ring of fire encompassed several boulders and bushes, creating an arena large enough for cat-and-mouse.

Gareth dropped into a crouch, both knives poised, as he eyed the wall of flame. How dense was it? The smoke made it impossible to judge.

Juliet clicked her tongue. "Why bother? You've already shown yourself unable to kill me, while I, on the other hand . . ." She tossed two more fireballs at him.

He blocked both with the flats of his knives, which absorbed the flames, and skittered sideways.

"Nice trick. I have some of those too." She swung her arm in a low underhand. Flames arched from her palm, and the bush to Gareth's left burst into flame, black smoke billowing into the air.

Throwing an arm across his face at the superheat, Gareth bolted to one side, toward a spot where the flames seemed thinner.

Juliet set ablaze another bush in his path, forcing him to backtrack, and then ignited a row behind him, trapping him within a flaming box. But the bushes couldn't burn forever. With enough time, the fire would run out of fuel. Gareth planted his feet defensively, poised for her next strike. "You would kill me, just like that?"

"I can't have you informing the others of the Key's where-abouts, can I?" Juliet tossed a fireball into the air and caught it with her other hand, reabsorbing the flames into her palm. "And with no one to rescue her, she'll have no choice but to go on, pro-viding me a path to follow."

Black smoke swirled around Gareth, and he again covered his face with his arm, squatting low in search of purer air. "Since you're going to kill me anyway then, answer this: did the girl I love ever exist . . . or was she an illusion too?" He edged to the left, where the fire seemed to be weakening the fastest.

She caught another fireball but didn't absorb it this time. "Oh, she existed—until you killed her." She snapped her fingers closed, and lava oozed out between them, dripping to the ground.

Tugging his wool coat around him, Gareth barreled through the dying flames.

A stream of lava spewed up in front of him, forcing him backwards. He tripped over a bush and sprawled on the ground.

Juliet stalked toward him, her face flushed and the air boiling around her. "One thing. That is all I asked of you . . . one thing. And you refused." She flung a massive fireball with both hands.

Gareth crossed his blades in front of him, blocking it—barely. "You had my love, Jul. But you didn't want it." He scuttled backward, trying to regain his feet. "You wanted worship."

"You denied me what was mine!" Juliet's voice pitched upward in a screech, and she threw fireball after fireball, alternating hands as she neared him.

Gareth gritted his teeth at the unrelenting onslaught, sweat pouring down his face, smoke searing the lungs and stinging the eyes. "You sought"—he dodged right—"to steal"—his left blade blocked—"what belonged"—another block—"to Creator."

Coughing, he rolled onto his feet, his back to the main ring of the fire. A few feet to his right the flames wavered, giving a brief glimpse of the plateau beyond.

"Belonged?" Juliet spat the word along with another stream of fire. "What right does He have to worship? He abandoned you, Gareth. Abandoned me. Left us to be used by man and thrown away."

Gareth edged to his right. "I don't pretend to know why." A wheeze invaded his words from all the smoke he'd inhaled, and a tremor rattled his arms, the blades of his knives glowing white-hot from the constant barrage. "But I do know He was there, weeping over your pain, enraged at the violations your father enacted against you, and grieving when you were abandoned." Three feet to the thin spot.

"He had a fine way of showing it." Juliet thrust her palms forward, increasing the volume of fire bombarding him.

"And because you refused to believe it, you've turned into twice the devil that your father ever was." Gareth catapulted himself through the wall of fire, tucking into a ball just before he passed through. But instead of bursting onto an open plateau, the end of the rock protruded into his path. He crashed into it, knocking the wind from him, and he lost his grip on his knives.

Before he could recover, Juliet was there and, with inhuman strength, flipped him onto his back. "Still convinced you will never bow before me?"

Gasping for breath, Gareth rolled onto his side, reaching for another weapon. Except there was no other weapon. He'd given them all away to the others. "You may . . . bend the body . . . Jul." His knives glinted about a yard beyond Juliet. "But you can't . . . steal a heart." He grabbed onto a nearby bush and pulled himself to his knees. "And Creator holds mine." He lunged forward.

Juliet kneed him in the abdomen. Gareth crumpled to the ground. Turning him onto his back, she slashed her nails across his chest, slicing through cloth and skin. "Then He can hold you while you burn. Slowly." She pressed a glowing hand against the bleeding wounds.

Gareth howled, fingers clawing the dirt, sweat spilling down his face. Juliet pushed harder, smoke curling around the edges of her hand.

Thunder cracked, and Oriel burst out of the ground, skin gleaming, hair white-hot. "Enough!" She knocked Juliet sideways, breaking the connection with Gareth.

"No." He dragged himself onto his hands and knees. "Go . . . back." He wheezed and collapsed again, hand to his heart.

Neither Juliet nor Oriel responded as they wrestled, setting afire anything flammable they touched. The inferno grew, gaining momentum as sparks flew. Soon it was visible for miles around.

Drawn by the plumes of smoke, Jaki tore across the plateau and plunged through the ring of flames, turning his skin liquid-metal hot. He charged toward Oriel, still locked in battle with Juliet.

Oriel ducked Juliet's attempt to claw her face and smashed a fist into the older woman's stomach. Juliet reeled backwards.

"Not me!" Oriel motioned Jaki toward Gareth's prostrate form. "Him!" She flung up her arms as Juliet threw flames toward her. They absorbed into her, and Oriel's own fire strengthened, brightening her face. She charged.

Jaki hesitated, then hauled Gareth to his feet. With a wave of his hand, he parted the flames and half dragged Gareth through them. Soon afterward, Oriel's glow began to dim.

Juliet cackled, the sound raspy through her cracked lips; the intense heat, both from within and without, was taking its toll. "There's no human left to protect, flame." She circled to Oriel's left, blocking her path to the crack. "Admit it. I've won."

"Not yet." Snatching up Gareth's knives, Oriel stepped into the raging fire. Immediately, her body melded with the flames, vanishing from sight.

25

THE FIRE SNAPPED UP THE DRY PLATEAU WITH hungry bites, the minimal amount of fuel unable to dent its insatiable appetite. Gray-brown smoke billowed into the sky at its growing impatience with the meager fare, warning everything movable to steer clear of its path. Yet a car barreled toward the inferno, not away from it.

Hunched over the steering wheel, Brandon held fast against the bumpy ride as he navigated the roadless plain, rocks jostling the vehicle side to side, bushes scraping the undercarriage. Crammed into the front seat beside him, Maggie clamped her flopping hat to her head, and Iris clung to the door.

"There they be!" Maggie thrust a knobby finger in front of Brandon's face.

He hazarded a glance in the direction she pointed. Sure enough, a trio of figures raced ahead of the all-consuming blaze. He jerked his wheel to the left, and as branches screeched across the side of the car, pushed the accelerator down harder. Soon the trio solidified into recognizable figures: Jaki and Oriel on either side of Gareth, hauling him along.

Pulling up in front of them, Brandon spun the car into a tight half circle, brakes squealing and dust ballooning heavenward. Oriel released Gareth's arm and darted forward to open a door. Gareth was helped into the seat as sweat poured down his red face. "Told you . . . I was on . . . my dying breath."

Jaki shoved Gareth farther inside. "Not if I have anything to say about it."

Gareth dissolved into a fit of coughing that doubled him over.

"I should go." Oriel backed away from the vehicle. "I'll meet you on the other side."

Jaki grabbed her arm before she could leave. "I can't permit you to go."

"I must." She twisted free and sprinted toward the fire.

Jaki thrust a hand toward her. "Esor!"

Her arms clamped against her side, and her ankles snapped together as if bound by invisible cords. She tumbled to the ground. "Release me, Warrior, before it's too late!"

"Don't make me stifle your flames, Key of Everything."

Brandon grew agitated as the fire filled the view behind him. "Get in now, or I'm leaving without you!"

Jaki approached Oriel, who wriggled backward. He stooped and pressed his palm to her chest. "Sheqa!"

Oriel collapsed, unconscious.

Scooping her up, Jaki put her inside the car and slid onto the seat after her. "Go!"

Brandon jerked the car into gear and headed for the road.

"You should have . . . listened," Gareth said to Jaki with difficulty.

"Save your breath, friend." Jaki reached across Oriel to grip Gareth's shoulder.

The weakened man shook his head. "Must stop." His words ended in another wracking cough.

Brandon pulled onto the road. "Which way?"

"South." Jaki squeezed Gareth's shoulder. "Rest. We'll soon have you to a cantor." Then leaning forward, he gave Brandon several curt directions.

After about an hour, the road sloped downward, wrapping around the edge of the plateau toward the main plain, leaving behind the fire. No sign of a tail emerged, and Brandon eased up on his speed slightly as he navigated the car along a narrow path winding parallel to the plateau's base. Deep ruts bounced the passengers about.

The car jerked and sputtered, then jerked again before dying altogether. Brandon turned the ignition; the car refused to restart. They were out of gas.

"Again? Of all the . . ." Jaki exhaled heavily. "Act on what you can, not complain about what you cannot." He shoved open his door. "The gateway is only a few yards ahead. We'll walk the remainder."

Brandon slung his bow and quiver onto his back, then roused Gareth to help the older man to the gateway. Maggie and Iris followed as Jaki brought up the rear, carrying Oriel, who was just starting to stir again.

Crossing over into Echoing, Brandon straightened as if an invisible load had dropped from his shoulders. Even Gareth's panting didn't seem as labored as before. He helped Gareth onto the ground, leaning him against a boulder, then turned to aid the others.

Maggie crossed over next, her ghostly form immediately turning solid, but when Iris entered Echoing, Brandon's jaw dropped. Although she retained her human form, a colorful aura danced around her, skin gleaming and a single pair of fire wings unfurling behind her. Seeing his face, Iris glanced over her shoulder and gasped. She extended her wings to their full breadth and flapped them a few times. The flames brightened, but her feet remained firmly planted on the ground, her dust weighing too much for the fire wings to lift. Gareth grunted. "Told you . . . was part . . . Ishir."

Maggie knelt at his side and wagged a gnarled finger at him. "Ye've been chancing too much."

He offered her a crooked smile. "Still . . . here . . . aren't I?"

Jaki laid Oriel on the ground beside Gareth and surveyed

the group. Iris's bare feet attracted his attention. "I shall return soon." He unfurled a pair of his wings and skimmed back along the trail they had traveled.

Oriel stirred. Her human form now replaced by blue-white flames, her "skin" gleamed bright, and her hair curled around her face like spilt sunshine. A black cord bound her arms and wings to her body. She blinked at the world around her. When her gaze fell on the shimmering archway, a keening wail rose from her throat, making all around her cringe.

"Peace, Key of Everything." Jaki, returning with a pair shoes, tossed them toward Iris and glided over to Oriel. "All will be well." He flicked a hand, and the cord around her vaporized.

"No, it is not well." Oriel rose, flexing her wings. "We must fly. Now! Levioth will soon be upon us."

His wings fluttered, the only sign of his irritation. "I understand your concern, but perhaps being long in the Vault, you may not know Levioth lacks the knowledge to find the gateways."

Lightning ricocheted through her flames. "I may be long in the Vault, Warrior, but even I know the legends about the Adam drinking of our flames, and Levioth has drunk mine." She spun away from him. "I will lead her away. Get Mighty Prince to a cantor."

Jaki leapt in front of her, arms folded and all six wings outstretched. "I can't let you go alone."

"You can't go with me. It will be the death of all."

"You are the Key."

"As if I could forget!" Her fire flared until she matched Jaki in size.

Brandon barged between them. "Decide now." He frantically pointed up at the cliff. "She's on her way." A black car descended the same road they'd traveled only minutes before.

"Dachi." Gareth struggled to sit more upright, the effort drenching his pale face with sweat once more.

Jaki retracted his fire back to normal size. "Rest, Gareth. There are no Dachi here."

Iris, standing on the outer edge of the group, furrowed her brow. Brandon leaned over and whispered, "Water people. Or so I've heard." His gaze darted to Maggie still settled at Gareth's side.

Gareth coughed and shook his head. "Find." He squeezed out the word, whatever benefit Echoing had provided waning quickly. "Play."

Iris mouthed Gareth's words, and her face lit up. Stepping toward Jaki, she started singing a twelve-note melody over and over.

"This is not the time to play." Jaki frowned at Iris, electricity crackling around him in disapproval. "Or sing."

But she didn't stop. Hands spread out in pleading, she turned to Brandon, then Maggie, and finally Oriel, still repeating the same strain of music, a fragment from an old Ishir folk tune about the Great Deluge.

Oriel's lips began forming the words to the song. "'*Water over all things lies, world is flooded, fire dies.*'" Her eyes widened, golden sparks cascading through her blue flames in sudden understanding. "Warrior, Levioth carries my *fire*. Water douses fire."

Iris smiled, and her song faded. Gareth relaxed against his boulder, nodding his thanks to her.

Jaki hovered. "Water . . . fire . . . it could work." He faced Brandon. "Son of dust."

Brandon stepped forward, his military training automatically responding to Jaki's commanding tone. "Yes, sir?"

"See that cave?" He pointed to a ledge on the cliff, just off the main road. "That's the cantor's. Escort Gareth and the elder Jewel there. I'll protect the other two."

Brandon snapped a salute and stooped to help Gareth rise. Gareth leaned heavily on him, even that simple action intensifying his wheezing. Brandon nodded to Maggie. "Lead the way, Grandmama." She patted his arm, and they ventured on.

As the trio left, Oriel's flames flickered with concern. "Will you not go with them, Warrior? You could carry Mighty Prince and reach the cantor's sooner."

Conflicting colors swirled around Jaki, as if he wanted to agree to her request but dared not to. "You are the Key. I must protect you first." He unfolded one pair of wings and sped off in search of water and Dachi. Oriel glided after him, Iris trying to keep up.

After ten minutes of the intense pace, Iris stumbled behind, forcing Jaki to wait for her to catch up. He surveyed the dry plain and cloudless sky. "Where will we find the Dachi here?" The initial jubilation of having a workable plan was fading in the stark reality of its implementation. "Not a drop of water lingers on earth or in the heavens."

Oriel closed her eyes and pointed to the southwest. "A river, three miles away."

"How could you know that?"

"The Vault contains many wonders, including vast libraries of information. Studying passed the time."

Iris trudged up the path behind them, wings drooping and smoke intertwining their flames. Oriel touched Jaki's arm and gestured toward her.

He extended his arms to the exhausted girl. "May I carry you?"

She hung back from his molten appendages.

"Do not worry. You also carry Ishir fire. My flames cannot harm you."

Iris nibbled her lip but finally nodded, even as her body stiffened for the coming contact.

Jaki wrapped his arms and a pair of wings around her, encasing her in an orb of fire. She blinked at the soft warmth and poked at the gelatinous orb. Jaki twisted uncomfortably, flames reddening. "Please don't do that."

Iris tucked her hand back at her side.

Jaki turned to Oriel. "You know the way. I will follow."

Spreading her wings, she seemed to catch a wind in this breathless place and surged across the ground, an unstoppable fire, wild and uncontainable, blazing the way to the river.

JULIET PAUSED AT THE FORK IN THE ROAD AND sniffed the air. Although her form remained human, a fiery glow veined her skin, her complexion resembling broken porcelain glued together with molten gold. Smoke streamed out of her mouth with her next exhale, though no cigarette was in sight, and her tongue flicked out, tasting the air like a serpent. She traveled down the right fork a dozen steps, a black bag bouncing at her hip, and stopped. Stooping, she examined the ground. "You paused here, then . . ." She raised her head, tracking an invisible strand to the path's left fork. "Nice try, but you'll have to do better than that." She crossed over, and after a brief hike, a river curved into view, its banks lined with bushes and a few trees.

Waist-deep in the river, Witless was scooping up handfuls of water and tossing them into the air. For a moment, the liquid coalesced into a slender, childish form, only to fall apart in a cascade of sprinkles. On the far side of the river, two Ishir, even more magnificent than the descriptions in the old books, stood with their backs to her, heads bent in consultation.

Juliet hid behind the trunk of a broken tree, watching of the scene before her. Did the skin of Witless gleam brighter? And there—when the girl turned, her back sparkled. Juliet blinked, and the illusion vanished. It must have been a trick of Echoing's strange light, glinting off the water.

The two Ishir, unheeding of the half-wit's play, disappeared around a rock pile. Or maybe they intentionally left her. Either way, Witless was voiceless and alone with a few of the Dachi, those silly water children.

A feral smile stretched out Juliet's lips. Transferring her bag to the small of her back, she stepped out from behind the tree. "Hello, Witless."

Iris spun around and paled, bubbles rising up beside her—a head of water with eyes that peeked above the surface, only to bob down again.

Juliet stalked nearer her prey. "Poor Witless. Your fire friends have abandoned you. And these water children are helpless against my power." She extended her hand. "But come along now, and I'll spare your life."

Iris crossed her arms, lifting her chin in defiance.

Juliet's face darkened. "So be it." She thrust her palms forward.

Iris dove underwater as the heat blast hit, and it rolled over her. Resurfacing, she squirted water out of her mouth.

Juliet looked at her disdainfully. "How pitiful—"

The river surged and foamed as dozens of Dachi breached the surface. Water arced toward Juliet. She raised her hands, and heat collided with water, vaporizing it. The resulting mist refracted the light, scattering rainbows in every direction.

The Dachi broke into a chorus of oohhs. "More, Fire-Dust, more!"

Iris smiled at her water companions and then focused on her half sister. Her eyes burned with an internal flame that was not human.

Juliet froze. "No . . . that can't be . . ."

Iris cupped her hands below the river's surface and flung the water at the woman. It fell short, but Juliet backtracked anyway, rage contorting her face.

Imitating Iris, the Dachi lobbed waterballs at Juliet from every direction. Juliet ignited a wall of flames between her and the river, scorching the bushes. Most of the water evaporated, but some breached her defenses and splattered against her. Steam hissed. While her human skin slowed the water's effect, without an Ishir's firecore she couldn't reignite what was being extinguished.

She retreated before the onslaught, each hit dousing her fire further. Her heel hooked on a tree root, and she crashed backward. Dozens of balls struck her, enveloping her in steam. Then even that dissipated, leaving behind a drenched but normal Juliet.

Iris blew out underwater. The waterballs stopped as the Dachi danced away from her. "That tickles, Fire-Dust."

"Thank you, little ones." Jaki stepped from the rock pile behind which he and Oriel had taken shelter during the water battle. "But we must be on our way."

The Dachi drooped. "Awwww . . ."

Iris flipped a handful of water as high as she could. Giggles spread through the group, and they crowded around her in a pile, covering her from head to foot.

Jaki chuckled. "Don't drown the girl."

The Dachi scampered away, diving back into the river with fading calls of "Play again with us soon, Fire-Dust," as the river returned to normal.

Jaki arced across the river and offered a hand to Iris as she staggered onto dry land. "Hold on." He wrapped her in his fire, singing wordlessly. When Iris emerged from his embrace, she was once again dry and haloed in fire. A pair of fiery wings unfurled behind her.

"No!" With a screech Juliet lunged at Iris.

Jaki flared up between them, knocking Juliet aside with his broad forearm. She crashed against the tree trunk, expelling breath from her lungs.

Oriel joined Jaki and looked steadily at Juliet. "You have no power in this place. The flames have been doused."

"Return to the pit from which you crawled, viper." Jaki withdrew his sword and towered over Juliet.

Behind him Oriel ushered Iris toward the path. Juliet tried to lunge again, only for Jaki to toss her backward. Iris stopped and raised a hand toward the older woman. Not in an offer of friendship. The pain was too deep and the time too short for that. More an offer of forgiveness, given in the hope of healing. Then Oriel led her away, and when they gained significant ground, Jaki skimmed after them.

After some time had gone by, Juliet rolled over and pulled out a hinged box from her bag. She lifted the lid. To the top was strapped a black-bladed knife and a jar of clear liquid. On the bottom a row of vials carried Oriel's fireblood. Three had shattered during the fight, but six remained unbroken.

Juliet smiled.

26

"WHAT IS HIS STATE?" JAKI'S BOOMING INQUIRY preceded him into the cantor's haven. Formed from a natural cave, the three-room dwelling boasted few furnishings, dominated by the tools of a healing cantor's trade: foodstuffs of wood and other flammable objects, bellows for oxygenation, tablets inscribed with various songs.

Gareth laid on a stone shelf in the back room, made slightly softer by a stash of hay and the coats of Brandon and Maggie. The skin near his heart burned with inflammation, almost untouchably hot even though Maggie kept changing the cool compresses prescribed.

The cantor responded to Jaki quietly, blurring the words into an indistinguishable murmur. Nonetheless, the somber tone declared Gareth's prognosis was not good.

Maggie changed the damp cloth, which had been icy minutes before but now was steaming. Worry deepened her wrinkles as she placed a fresh cloth over his heart. In the opposite corner near the doorway, Brandon perched on a flat-topped boulder. Earlier Gareth had ordered him to quit pacing the room, but sitting still was difficult. Tension saturated the air, infecting all who inhaled it. His left leg bounced restlessly as he shifted constantly.

The scent of cinnamon tiptoed into the room ahead of Oriel, but neither that nor her soft melody elicited any reaction from Gareth. She sank to his side, flames pooling around her, and reached for his hand, only to backtrack before making contact.

Gareth rolled his head toward her, a slight gleam in his eyes despite the death shroud that seemed to hang around him. "I'm . . . dust, not . . . porcelain."

Oriel intertwined her slender fingers with his calloused ones. His hand was hot, much too hot.

Maggie changed the cloth on Gareth's chest again, revealing a black handprint burnt into the fiery skin, four slashes oozing blood. Oriel grimaced. Gareth squeezed her hand. "Not . . . bad . . . as it looks."

"No, the wound's appearance is fair compared to the damage caused." A male cantor glided into the room, the warm scent of mulled cider and a rocking lullaby accompanying his entrance. Jaki and Iris followed close behind.

Oriel's eyes followed the healer. "Is there no help for him?"

The cantor bowed slightly, blue swirling through his dimmed flames. "My condolences, Key, but his healing requires a different touch than mine. The guardian burns with our fire, which my ministrations fuel, not douse. In essence, my songs worsen his condition."

"Then do those things that hurt us!" Thunder accompanied Jaki's outburst, lightning flashing around him. "It doesn't seem all that difficult to figure out."

"What you suggest seems good and true, Warrior." The cantor kept his voice low and even, well acquainted with grief in its many forms. "However, the fire burns too near his heart, and the water we have is the water of death, water that kills flame."

Brandon rose from his corner to join the half circle around Gareth. "But isn't that what we want—to kill the fire?"

The cantor folded his hands before him as he faced Brandon. "As fire dies it releases smoke. Smoke expels the breath you require to live."

"In short, he'll suffocate." Jaki's wings rustled in agitation.

Oriel lowered her head, the blinding light of her hair hiding her face. "He needs the water which brings life."

"Key, no such water exists except—"

"In the Vault." She rose.

Gareth's fingers locked around hers, preventing her from pulling away. "You can't . . ." He doubled over in a coughing fit. "Juliet . . ."

Gliding to the bed, the cantor put his hands over Gareth's head and hummed a soothing tune. Gareth's breathing eased. "Can't . . . let . . ."

"All's well, Gareth. We've neutralized Levioth. She can no longer use the Key to find the Vault." Jaki folded his arms as he faced Oriel. "You know it's forbidden, an Adam in the Vault."

She matched his stance, her fire taking on a hard, crystalline sheen. "Not by Creator."

"But we are to obey those Creator set above us."

"Do the laws of the Ishir nullify the commands of Creator? For Creator has also commanded us to serve the Adam and seek their good."

Jaki held his imposing stance for a moment longer, then a chuckle escaped from him, making his flames dance and sparkle. "Gareth, my old friend, you are indeed a bad influence among the Ishir. All who work with you become rebels, it seems."

The cantor drifted up to Oriel and Jaki. "Then you are set on this course, Key of Everything?"

"Is there another option?"

The cantor lifted his face in petition. The crackle of fire and the intertwining songs of the three Ishir filled the room as everyone waited for his judgment. He opened his eyes, wings drooping. "I know of no other way." He beckoned Jaki closer. "Are you willing, Warrior, to lend your fire to this cause?"

Jaki inclined his head. "I am."

Resting one hand on Oriel's head and the other on Jaki's, the cantor spread all six of his wings as a sheltering canopy over and around them. Then he began to sing.

"Reflection of Creator's endless light,
"Burn brightest in this, the darkest of night,
"Impeded not by this world's broken plight
"Nor hindered by evil opposing the right.

"Flame hotter with Creator's holy fires,
"Nevermore to crave the viler desires,
"Seeking instead the truth as He requires
"With fervency burning that shall never tire."

As the cantor sang, the trio's fire grew brighter, changing from golds to yellows and finally to an intense white. When the song finished, Jaki and the cantor retreated, the fire of each muted and their size diminished. But Oriel continued to burn brilliantly, as if she absorbed the fire they lost. Yet that didn't fully explain the change either, for her sunny brilliance exceeded the sum of the parts, and Creator Himself seemed to place His seal of approval upon this mission, filling the room with a holy hush. Time ceased to have any meaning. The moment simply was.

Then Maggie sighed, and the spell broke. Oriel bent over Gareth, who recoiled against the bed, his thick shadowiness accentuated by her light. "Fear not, Mighty Prince." Oriel's voice rang with the clarity of a silver bell and the warmth of a summer breeze. "You are marked by the Adam blood which Creator's Son took as His own, and the flames will not hurt you. Will you allow me to carry you as you have often carried me?"

Gareth swallowed. Protesting would be foolish. Body tensing, he nodded. Oriel spread her wings over both of them, hiding them from sight, and when she straightened, Gareth was cradled in an orb of flame. Nearby Iris smiled at the sight. Jaki crossed one arm over his chest. "Go, carried on the wind of Creator's own Spirit."

Oriel's fire wavered. "You are not coming?"

"I will come, but I cannot carry all these." He waved his hand toward Maggie, Iris, and Brandon.

At this reassurance, Oriel stabilized. "Then Creator speed you on your way also." She glided toward the entrance, tightening her hold on Gareth. "Ready, Mighty Prince?"

Gareth's eyes remained closed, breathing shallow.

"Mighty Prince?"

"Go!" Jaki propelled her toward the door. "Fly with all you have!"

Oriel unfolded her wings, then, like a bolt of lightning, streaked out of the door.

JULIET MADE HER WAY UP THE ROCKY PATH AWAY from the river, back toward the gateway through which she arrived in Echoing. The golden light of day chilled to muted blues and purples of night as the sun dipped below the horizon, cooling the air as well. In the dimming light, the renewed gold streaks webbing her skin shone brighter than ever, but this time smoke coiled around her, testifying the mixture of blood and fire in her veins was an unholy one. The tips of her hair were also charred, and her fingers curled, as if a crippling disease prevented her from straightening them.

Juliet paused at a fork in the path, the left leading back to the gateway, the right continuing on a flatter route around the plateau. Far down that right path, a bolt of lightning darted from a cavern into the deepening night toward the north.

"The Key, headed for the Vault." A bass voice rumbled behind Juliet, its overtones clashing.

"Balai." Juliet turned and bowed to the towering giant.

Freed from the smoke he wore to talk to her in Terrestrial, Zarbal resembled most Echoing Ishir, wrapped in brilliant flame and sporting three pairs of wings. At first glance, few Adam would recognize anything different about him. But a closer examination revealed an unusual turbulence to the Rishi's green-hued flames, and violet-black lightning rippled through them. Two of his wings, a smoky gray, also drooped as if broken, and black smoke pooled around his feet, his fire failing to burn cleanly like the Ishir. Zarbal's beauty was stunning—in a distorted, almost grotesque way.

Juliet rose out of her bow. "Yes, all goes according to plan."

"Yet I find you alone." Zarbal flared out his four good wings, even more imposing in the growing darkness. "Where is the girl?"

"Witless will be here."

Sparks spewed from his flames. "The blood moon is four days away."

Juliet's voice hardened. "You'll have her in time."

"So you've assured me again and again."

"Perhaps if you'd be a little more forthcoming with all that wisdom and strength you *claim* to possess, it wouldn't be a problem."

The already towering Rishi grew another three feet, his size double of Juliet's. "You seem to forget, Adam's Dust, to whom you speak."

"How can I?" A sneer curled her lip. "You never cease to speak of it, O Mighty Zarbal, Prince of the Rishi."

A molten hand struck her face, hurtling her to the ground. "For your insolence." Zarbal shrank to his original stature. "Now obtain the Spliced and the key to the Bottomless Regions, or I shall find one more worthy to be my DragonRider." He lowered his voice, slipping into an alluring croon. "The one loved and adored by all nations."

Juliet placed a hand to the burned flesh of her face, as if

remembering a very different touch. "Your wisdom once more proves supreme, great balai; you need not seek another. I will accomplish what you ask this very night." She rose to her feet, head bowed. "However . . ."

"However what?" Zarbal layered a threat beneath his question.

"The Ishir move fast." Juliet examined her fingers, a forced casualness to her voice. "I have no wings or car."

"Very well." Zarbal clapped his hands, and two Rishi warriors materialized out of the shadows. "They can take you as far as the Vault's dome." He stretched out his wings. "I will await your return at the gateway." He flew away, a smear of light against the night.

When he vanished from sight, Juliet turned to the two warriors and pointed at the cliff. "The Key came from that cave, and Witless most likely remains there yet."

"As you wish." Without waiting for her permission, one Rishi wrapped her in his flames.

She inhaled sharply and arched her back, twisting within the flames licking around her the entire journey to the ledge. When the warrior expelled her back into air, her skin was red and blistered from the fire. Her breath hissed through teeth clenched against the pain.

Footsteps scuffled inside the cavern, headed their direction. Juliet plastered herself against the cliff in a shadowy crevice.

Iris crept out and scanned the horizon. Oriel's lightning bolt was long gone. Iris sighed, shoulders drooping, as she fingered a delicately carved flower—the iris Gareth had whittled for her.

Juliet crept up behind her. "Hello, Witless."

Iris spun, the wooden iris slipping from her fingers at the sight of a blistered Juliet flanked by the two Rishi. She opened her mouth. A warrior leapt forward and wrapped his flames around her, silencing her scream.

27

ORIEL COULD NOT MAINTAIN HER INITIAL BURST of speed.

Reaching the rim of mountains along Anatroshka's northern border, she slowed her pace as she navigated their crags, then the foothills beyond. Still, rocks and brush blurred together. Weathered villages passed in a blink of an eye. Cities, dark from electricity restrictions, were circled within seconds. Forests cropped up among the hills, and rivers and streams crisscrossed the land, slowing her further. Oriel checked on Gareth. "Mighty Prince?"

There was no response, but his chest rose and fell regularly. Creator's breath yet lingered, and while that lingered, so did hope.

Oriel tugged him closer. "We are almost there. Hold onto your breath a little longer." She leapt from ledge to ledge down a cliff and arced over a river.

As she landed on the other side, the ground heaved upward, raining clods of dirt upon them. Oriel skidded to a halt. A wall of snow, dirt, and dead leaves curled over her head. She dove sideways. The wave crashed onto the tail of her flames, snuffing them out. She hurtled to the ground, and Gareth tumbled away from her.

"Mighty Prince!" Pushing up on her hands, Oriel flapped her wings, trying to dislodge the smothering dirt, and lurched toward Gareth.

Tree roots shot out of the ground and over her like a cage, trapping her in a crater of dirt. A clear, sticky sap filled the spaces between roots and ground. A few feet away, a second root coiled around Gareth's body.

Oriel touched the sap with a finger and jerked back; the clear ooze instantly doused her flames, her fingertip turning charcoal black and gray smoke twining toward her palm. She shook her hand and blew flames on her finger. Its glow reignited. Breathing a sigh of relief, Oriel brushed a hand against the nearest wood. Roots contracted tighter around her *and* Gareth. He would be crushed before she could burn her way out, much less free him.

The ground heaved again, and a trio of leafless oaks tilted back. Mossy eyes half opened in the outer trunks. The middle tree made a nose of sorts while the carpet of dead leaves and snow created a long beard.

The trees rose higher, a mouth forming between roots and leaf-shrouded ground. "Be gone, leave, turn back from here, trespassing flame." The Yerek's words overlapped each other, filling in meaning like the foliage on a tree. "You who burn and destroy, neither welcome nor invitation nor embrace will you find here."

Oriel bowed her head, placing a fist over her firecore. "I do not seek to cause harm or pain, Ancient One. I wish only passage to the Vault."

Tree branches creaked, derisive in tone. "Likely story, a tale of lies and nonsense. No one, none at all, has sought out or traveled to the Vault that is neither here nor there, but is between all spaces. At least not in many a year, not since long ago." Roots tore out of the soil with a deafening groan, spewing massive amounts of dirt before diving into the ground again mere inches from Oriel. "The Key of Everything and All Things there dwells, only and alone there to reside." Sorrow muddied the earthy voice further.

"I *am* the Key, Ancient One, though I do not beseech or petition you for my sake. I know the Yerek's feud against the Ishir goes long and deep, longer than even your long memory. Rather for the sake of this Adam, this Guardian Prince, let us pass."

"The Key?" The Yerek blinked slowly, and the trio of trees tipped to one side. "There have been rumors and whispers, but . . . No, this cannot be. It is impossible. The Key has never left or abandoned her post."

Her flames flickered at his wording. "I did not abandon my post, Ancient One. Creator called me forth."

"Prove it. Show me you are the Key, the one who unlocks the Vault and guards all things. Tell me things she alone would know."

Oriel leaned toward the sap as near as she dared. Gareth lay so very still. "The Vault contains the Water of Life . . ." Her gaze flicked to the Yerek. "The Tree of the Everlasting . . . the Fruit of Knowledge . . . jars of the Heavenly Wafers."

"These things are known by many."

Oriel paced her small enclosure, lightning rippling through her flames. "Snow and hail are stored there. You can see all things past and all things present." The sap hissed at the charge building in the air, and she stilled herself to calm the swelling electrical storm. "All things future are there too, though Creator hides their truths from mortal eyes."

"Those who have visited the Vault and spent time in Creator's storehouses have whispered of these things." The roots contracted, threatening to smother her beneath a mound of dirt.

She muted her flames further, condensing her wings against her body. "What else can I offer you? I know nothing else to . . ." The nearest root caught her gaze. Unlike the rest of the wood, which emitted an uninterrupted brownish gleam, this one was disrupted by a black scorch mark. "Can it be?" She leaned closer. The scorch mark was about the size of her hand.

Oriel peered through the sap at the Yerek. "When the Ishir brought the Key to the Vault, she was very young, not more than a child. Terrified by this strange place, she ran away from the warriors escorting her and hid among the roots of your tree that snowy day, waking you from your winter slumber with her heat. You could have crushed her that day, but you did not. And before I returned to the warriors, I thanked you and named you, Ancient Yerek. I called you Gedol Menish."

"One mightier than fire." His eyes stretched past half-mast.

She nodded. "That day you also gave the Key a name—not a role to fill." Her words caught. "You called me—"

"Oriel, the Light of God." The Yerek bent forward, his roots retracting from around her and Gareth. "It has been too many days, little one."

"I wanted to come back." She leapt out of the earthen crater. "But I am the Key and—"

"Posh and rot. You are Oriel, Light of Creator's making. Anyone can be a Key . . . or a warrior . . . or an ancient one. There is only one Gedol Menish. There is only one Oriel. Your role, your job, your task is not you."

Colors cascaded through Oriel's flames. Spreading her wings, she bowed before him. "Thank you, Gedol Menish." Then she hurried to Gareth's side and gathered him up again. "I cannot stay . . ."

"I understand and comprehend. But promise me, Oriel, Bearer of Creator's Light. Vow to me one thing."

"Yes?"

"Return and talk to me. Tell me of where you have been. Tell me of what you've seen. The days are long, the nights are longer, and I tire of the sameness."

"I will, Gedol Menish. If I can return, I will."

"I wait for you." The eyes drooped close, and the oaks lowered, roots sinking into the ground. "Your return I will anticipate."

Oriel dipped her head once more toward the old trees. "Thank you," she whispered. Then she looked down at Gareth.

His chest no longer moved.

JULIET CLIMBED TO THE BOTTOM OF YET ANOTHER cliff, her gloves providing minimal protection against the jagged rocks. It would have been easier to ride the Rishi to the Vault's doorstep, but like the gateways and cracks, an invisible dome protected the entrance, prohibiting the Rishi from traveling farther. So she left them behind with Witless and entered the dome, pausing only long enough to inject herself with another dose of fireblood to heal her wounds and increase her strength.

At the bottom of the cliff, a river tumbled by. Juliet located an old log and crossed over the foaming water. Frankincense and cinnamon spiked the air. The Key had been here and not long ago. But her scent was scattered hither and yon, amidst churned-up earth, as if a great battle had been fought.

Keeping to the edges, Juliet circled around the disturbance. She didn't have time to engage another opponent, nor did she need to investigate what happened here. Where the Key went next—that alone mattered. On the opposite side, Juliet stooped and rifled through a few leaves. "There you are."

She pushed onward, occasionally sniffing the air or checking the ground. Oriel's trail led into a cliff cave. Juliet entered without hesitation. The rock glimmered just enough for her to navigate the narrow passageway, which twisted and turned and branched off in different directions again and again. Without Oriel's path, she would have become lost.

The passageway bent into a large room. There, Oriel stood before six pillars, forming a semicircle along a curved wall. Juliet pressed against the passageway.

Oriel placed her hand on the fourth pillar from the right.

Her flames brightened, and the pillar reddened into a lava-like substance. *"On the day, the fourth one, Creator molded fire and music, the Ishir His song to sing. And it was good, so very good, as only Creator could do."*

As she sang, an ancient script etched around the pillar glowed golden, a rune at a time. When the script and the song reached their end, a brilliant light flashed. Juliet covered her face. The light died, and stillness shrouded the cavern. She lifted her head. Oriel was nowhere in sight, and the pillar had returned to normal stone.

Juliet crept forward, eying the room. All was quiet. She rested her palm on the fourth pillar. *"On the day, the fourth one, Creator molded fire and music."*

But instead of light, a shadow mushroomed from the ground, blacker than the deepest darkness, icier than the coldest winter. Juliet choked and wrenched away from the pillar. The shadow dissipated.

When the specter didn't reappear, Juliet stepped forward again. This time she examined the pillars before touching them. Etched into the top of each was a picture—a star, a raindrop, three wavy lines, a flame, a leaf, a heap of rocks. Oriel's pillar bore the flame. At the pillar on the furthest left, the one with the heap of rocks, Juliet traced the ancient runes circling the base, nearly indiscernible to the naked eye. She nodded to herself.

Placing her palm against the top, she recited, *"On the sixth of all the days, Creator molded the greatest of all."* She stumbled over *Creator* but managed to get it out with a shudder. *"He fashioned dust into the Adam and breathed Himself into them."* The pillar grew dusty and cracked like parched ground as the runes lit up. *"His very nature to reflect."*

At the pronouncement of the final word, Juliet vanished in a flash of searing light.

28

BRANDON MOVED RESTLESSLY ABOUT THE CANTOR'S dwelling, the wooden iris tight in his grip.

Found on the ledge outside, the dropped token was the first sign of something amiss. A quick search soon verified Iris was nowhere in the immediate vicinity, which meant she had not wandered off on her own.

Taking his bow, Brandon held the iris with his fourth and fifth fingers while pulling the string taut with the first two. He had tried to join the search, but Maggie couldn't be left unprotected, and the two Ishir could travel faster than he could. Aiming the imaginary arrow at the entrance, he released the string. It twanged loudly but unsatisfactorily.

Maggie, who sat calmly in the corner with eyes closed, smiled at the sound. "Yer jest like him. Strong . . . brave . . . impatient."

"I should be out there helping." He leaned his long bow against the wall next to his quiver and sank onto the floor beside her. "They could be doing anything to her . . ." His hand closed around the iris.

Maggie opened one eye. "How do ye know she didn't walk away?"

"She couldn't have gotten that far. She was gone only five minutes."

"And . . . ?"

Brandon stroked the petals, carved so intricately—far more intricately than time should have permitted. In light of such time-bending evidence, his argument indeed seemed insufficient. "The air tasted burnt. And a . . . darkness lingered. I'm not sure how to describe it."

Maggie nodded. "Ah, yer learning."

He studied his grandmother's face, wrinkled with age yet aglow with contentment. He had once said that such contentment was only additional proof of her addled mind, since no lucid person who had faced the *real* world could look that way. Yet despite the day's strains and the present uncertainties, Maggie sat there as contented as ever. "I'm sorry, Grandmama."

"What for, Brady?"

"For not believing you. For thinking you were crazy."

"No shame in thinking the truth," Maggie told him, a twinkle in her eye. "Everybody's got a little crazy in them. Jest make sure it be the right kind of crazy."

"But all the things I said, the way I treated you—"

"Stung. I won't be denying it. But I also knew yer heart were true." She patted his knee. "That's why I gave ye the Star."

Brandon's hand went to his pocket. "How? How could you possibly know?"

"Creator. He knew He would call ye to be a protector." She nodded toward his quiver, where Oriel's arrow poked out above the rest. "So He had me give ye the Star."

Her reminder of his call creased his face with consternation. "But why *me*?"

"Why not?"

"The things I've done, the things I've said. Surely there are others better qualified."

Maggie clucked her tongue. "Creator chooses not by our goodness or none would be His choice. Creator chooses by *His* goodness."

"But I don't deserve—"

"Didn't you hear what the Jewel said?" Jaki's booming voice hailed his entrance into the room. "Not one deserves it. This is why it is called grace."

Brandon sprang to his feet. "Did you find her?"

Jaki's arms hung at his sides, one hand a tight fist. "I am sorry, son of dust. I did not find the Spliced."

His grip on the iris tightened to a white-knuckled hold. "She has a name."

Jaki raised an eyebrow at the younger man. "Yes, she does. But we Ishir also understand the power of a name, so we avoid speaking them—sometimes, I admit, to the detriment of all."

"You have no problem calling Gareth by name."

"It took many years and dire battles to teach me that."

"And what about—"

The cantor entered the cave. "I heard your summons, Warrior. What tidings do you bring?"

"I have found the Spliced's"—Jaki inclined his head to Brandon—"Iris's path. Moreover, she does not travel alone. Levioth is with her—and they head north."

Brandon moved closer. "So?"

"One of the entrances to the Vault lies north, son of dust."

A second passed before the implication hit Brandon. "I thought she couldn't track anymore."

"We underestimated her resourcefulness." Jaki opened his hand, revealing two empty vials. "When I realized where Levioth had gone, I circled back to where we met. Levioth did not drink all the Key's blood, as most would have, but held some in reserve."

"But if she's tracking Oriel again, why take Iris?"

Jaki's fire transformed to a purple-streaked red. "I do not know, son of dust—and that is what concerns me most of all."

ENDLESS LIGHT.

The Vault Between Spaces was permeated with light that

revealed nothing except more light. No floor. No ceiling. No walls. Just endless light with no beginning and no end, no matter the direction, and the heavy aroma of frankincense, cinnamon, balsam, and myrrh.

Oriel released her flames from around Gareth, and he floated where she left him in the midst of the endless light. She raised her voice in a cascading triplet melody reminiscent of a tumbling stream.

> *"Gurgling, bubbling, flowing life,*
> *"Endlessly pouring out, springing up,*
> *"Granting joy,*
> *"Stirring hearts,*
> *"Bringing light,*
> *"No more death, eternal victory."*

A water skin materialized beside Gareth.

Oriel grabbed it with shaking hands. "Please, Creator." She tipped Gareth's head back and poured the liquid into his mouth. Much of the silvery water dribbled out of the side, but she got some down him. The redness of his chest diminished, and the handprint faded to a scar. Still she poured. When the water skin produced no more, she set it aside. Then she clasped one of Gareth's hands, her flames a subdued orange, the white-hot fire from the cantor's blessing long gone.

"Please, Mighty Prince, don't leave us. We need you." She bowed her head, cracks of deep blue spreading through her flames. "I need you." The last words were a faint whisper, but in the vastness of the Vault it rang out.

Gareth remained unmoving, floating densely in the light of the Vault. Life had abandoned the old man's body.

Oriel compressed her fire into a small ball and wrapped her wings around her. "Creator, what have I done? This is all my fault."

"I'd say you did the world a service." Juliet's voice smeared the holy hush of the Vault with brazenness.

Oriel twisted around, flames growing her to an imposing height. Behind her, wings extended to hide Gareth from Juliet.

"How sweet. Even in death you seek to protect worthless dust." Juliet walked through empty space, seemingly unbothered by the phenomenon of walking on light. But despite her confident stride, which never brought her any nearer to Oriel, sweat dotted her forehead, and her breaths were labored.

"Be gone." Neither Oriel's stance nor her flames wavered. "You are not welcome."

"Not welcome?" Juliet placed a hand over her heart in mock surprise. "After you led me here?"

Oriel's wings flickered.

"Did you really think I didn't reserve some of your blood? Especially after I *let* you escape for this very purpose?"

Colored sparks cascaded through Oriel's flames.

"I suppose you thought that was due to some grand deliverance." Juliet's lips twitched in amusement. "Disappointing, I'm sure, but that was all me."

"That Creator chose to use you doesn't eradicate the truth that the deliverance came from His hand."

"Then if you serve such a powerful Being, make me leave."

Oriel held her position.

"That's what I thought. Because I pose no threat to him"— Juliet gestured to Gareth's body—"you can't harm me, for I too am an Adam." She laughed but with a forced edge. "Even here your precious *Creator* has crippled you, making you subservient to an inferior race."

Lightning ricocheted through Oriel's fire. "Creator crippled nothing."

"Yet He endowed you with great power and won't let

you use it."

"He didn't shackle us. We shackled ourselves. Just as you sought knowledge and became blind to the truth, we chose control rather than submission, and Power is a terrible taskmaster, enslaving all who serve it." Oriel blanched, her flames cooling to a sickly green. "That is what I have done, isn't it? Control rather than . . . oh Creator, mercy."

Juliet snorted. "You'll be waiting a while for that."

Oriel stood statuesque, face covered. The light of her flames alone churned, revealing the turmoil within. Then it steadied into a continuous glow, and her music's lament settled into a calming melody. "As You desire." Oriel raised her face, the light in her eyes as radiant as the Vault's. "What do you want, Juliet Kasam?"

Dark rage twisted the woman's face. "That's Levioth to you."

"To exchange one's name for a role is a terrible thing." Oriel glanced at Gareth's still form, a fresh strain of lament rippling through her song. "But as you wish. Why are you here, Levioth?" She fluttered her wings, bringing her closer.

Juliet turned her body sideways, in a defensive posture. Despite her own claim that Oriel could not harm her, suspicion darkened her visage. "The key to the Bottomless Regions."

"You know not for what you ask. Keys open doors, and some doors are best left shut."

"So say you. Now the key." Juliet stretched out her hand.

"You are determined?"

"What do you think?"

Oriel bowed her head, and her melody morphed again, this time into a dark, off-cadence march.

> "Bottomless, eternal dark
> "Smokiness, tormenting fire
> "Calling forth, evil freed.
> "Sovereign Lord, rescue us!"

When Oriel finished singing, she lifted her head.

Juliet scowled. "Well, where is it?"

"In your hand, Levioth."

Sure enough, on her outstretched palm rested a plain metal box as black as ebony. Juliet opened its lid, and on silver satin sat a thick, wrought-iron key, unadorned and unimpressive, yet leaching darkness and a sulfuric scent.

"Careful, Levioth. Some things, once unlocked, cannot be locked again."

Juliet snapped the lid shut and clutched the box to her chest. "Some things should have never been locked in the first place." She whirled, took a step, then hesitated. There was no door or clear pathway out. Just endless light that went on and on and on in every direction.

Oriel folded her hands, flames subdued. "The way you seek is before you."

"Why should I believe you?" Though Juliet snapped at Oriel, the saltiness of barely constrained panic tainted the air.

"Because I serve the Lord of truth, not a master of deception."

The pity which softened Oriel's voice stiffened Juliet's demeanor. Clenching her jaw, she strode forward. Light flashed. She blinked several times. She stood once more in the night-lit cave with its semicircle of pillars.

Freed from the burning purity of the Vault's light, Juliet relaxed. "Fools. Every last one of them." She withdrew the key from its box; unlike everything else around her, it emitted no light. She began to laugh. "Let my coronation begin!"

29

THE VAULT WAS DEATHLY STILL.

Oriel knelt beside Gareth's lifeless body, her head bowed, wings drooping. The calm granted with Juliet's visit dissolved with her departure, and all of Oriel's flames burned a yellow green, including her hair and skin, in sharp contrast to the Vault's golden light.

"Did I do right, Mighty Prince, in giving Levioth her desire? Especially when I know it shall lead to destruction?" She curled over, wings spread out to either side. "Creator of All, what am I to do? I sought to prove myself powerful and able to defend myself. Instead, I have fulfilled the worst fears of my people." Anguished dissonance intertwined with her melody. "Is giving Levioth the key my punishment? Do You intend to destroy the world because of my greed?"

"The desire for control indeed controls the desirer." Jaki's voice rang out like a gong, though he spoke normally. "This is the lesson our people must learn over and over, is it not?"

She shuddered at his words, dark purple bolts streaking through her flames. Rising, she wrapped her wings about her and faced him. Behind him Brandon poked at the golden air and watched as the air rippled, as if the light were as tangible as water.

"Valiant Warrior." Oriel bowed deeply to Jaki, then Brandon. "Son of dust."

Jaki frowned, his fire deepening to burnished orange. "Do not bow, Key of Everything."

"I can do nothing else, Valiant Warrior." Oriel's flames writhed around her. "My failure extends deeper than the Bottomless Regions themselves. I led Levioth to the Vault. I gave her the key. I didn't even attempt to withhold it from her. Moreover, I was not fast enough. The Guardian Prince is dead and—"

Jaki rested both hands on Oriel's head. "Harpah!"

Her writhing flames rippled into solid brightness, as if a turbulent wind, which had been stirring up her flames, suddenly died. Oriel took a deep breath, and Jaki drew his hands away. "Arise, Key. I extinguish no flame, for I am not without my share of blame. I've added brokenness to the world too. But Creator is gracious and merciful, and upon that mercy we must all cast ourselves."

"Upon His mercy I fall." Yellow and orange strands spread around Oriel in an intricate pattern, and her wings retracted again as she straightened.

Jaki glided past her to Gareth's body. A wave of blue spilled through Jaki's flames, his melody modulating into a minor key. At the change, Oriel's song shifted into a counterpoint, her fire acquiring threads that matched Jaki's melancholy color. "My heart grieves your loss, Warrior. Your bond with him was evident."

Fire pooled about him as he crouched beside his old friend. "No matter how many years Creator gives, death always comes too soon, forever unnatural, forever inescapable. This world is indeed broken." Pain filled his voice. "Gareth, you will be missed far beyond what you ever thought." He rested a hand on Gareth's chest . . . and frowned, a rainbow of colors swirling through his flames in sudden confusion. "Key, when did his breath depart?"

"Shortly before entering the Vault." Oriel picked up the water skin she'd tossed aside at Juliet's arrival. "I gave him the Water of Life, but it was . . . I was too late."

"Yet his body still lies warm."

"I do not understand, Warrior."

"When Death steals an Adam's breath, his body grows cold.

Yet warmth lingers within Gareth, as if—"

"He lives." Oriel gasped, flames sparking in surprise. "Creator, forgive my blindness." Clutching the water skin to her chest, she whirled toward Brandon. "Blow on him, son of dust."

He startled. "What?"

"Blow on him. The Water of Life doused Levioth's flames and sustains his life, but smoke still chokes him. He needs breath."

"But . . . why me?"

"We're Ishir; Creator made us of fire and song." Jaki glided up behind Oriel, hope brightening his flames. "Our breath would be as smoke to him. But you are Adam. You carry Creator's breath."

Oriel nodded. "Warrior speaks true. Creator breathed *into* you."

Brandon swallowed. Gareth lay so deathlike that Oriel's suggestion seemed ludicrous. Then again, he stood in the most impossible of places. He slung his bow on his back, and Jaki and Oriel parted before him. As he knelt at Gareth's head, a touch of crimson tinged his cheeks. "I'm not sure how to do this, so I'm sorry, Creator, sir, if I'm doing it wrong . . ." He stopped and began again, his voice firmer. "He needs Your breath, not mine. Give it to him. If You please, sir." Brandon bent over Gareth and blew across his face.

The light of the Vault quivered, and from nowhere a mighty wind rushed in, unstoppable in force yet tender in its touch.

Oriel stretched her arms above her head, wings unfurled and flames swirling around her. "Creator." She breathed the word in rapture.

Opposite of her, Jaki crossed both arms over his chest, wings folded around him as he sank into a prostrated puddle of fire. "My Liege."

Brandon stood, mouth agape, eyes wide, like one encountering what he scarcely believed was real.

The wind died.

Gareth bolted upright, doubled over, and coughed violently.

Brandon staggered backward as Jaki and Oriel came forward. The coughing fit subsided. Gareth inhaled a deep, cleansing breath, and with its exhale, his eyes slowly opened. He smiled faintly at the trio staring at him. "What? Never seen a dead man cough?"

"Mighty Prince, you're back." Oriel sank before him, flames puddling around her. "Creator be praised!"

"May He be praised indeed."

"Forever and ever," added Jaki, his bell voice ringing out.

Ever and ever and ever and ever. The words resounded throughout the Vault from every direction.

When the antiphonal echo faded, Gareth rose and refastened his shirt. "We've work to do."

Oriel looked at him quizzically. "Work?"

"Levioth has the key to the Bottomless Regions, does she not?"

Oriel wilted, threads of smoke weaving through her fire. "Yes, she does."

"Oriel." He waited for her to lift her eyes to him before continuing. "You've nothing to be ashamed of. Creator is pleased."

"Pleased? But—"

"You passed His test. You relinquished power, obeying rather than controlling." His mouth twitched, trying to hide a grin. "In fact, He's gloating right now over His victory through you."

The shadow diminished in her eyes, and the smoke dispersed.

He faced the other two. "But the time for the Bottomless Regions to be open has not come. We need to retrieve the key and return it to its proper place."

"Then you'll want these." Oriel extended the long knives she'd retrieved during the battle with Juliet.

Gareth took one and examined it. The battle with Juliet had left the blades smudged with sooty streaks. "I think it's time to retrieve my guardian daggers."

Jaki's flames sparked in surprise. "And what makes you think they will give them to you after their last refusal, my friend?"

"I died." Gareth sheathed both knives. He drew himself to full height before them. "Which means the council's requirement has now been fulfilled, and I can resume my guardianship."

Jaki chuckled. "Sarish's face should be quite the sight at such an announcement."

"A sight you'll see, for that's where we head first. Juliet will summon every force she can, both in Echoing and Terrestrial, and we will need all the help we can get."

"You believe Sarish will supply that assistance?" Jaki's skepticism sharpened the edge of both his voice and his melody.

"No. But I must ask." Gareth gripped the knife hilt and exited the Vault.

"Creator, help us all." Shaking his head, Jaki also left, and Brandon followed. Oriel was left alone.

Sighing, she retrieved the water skin, which had once again slipped from her grasp. She tried to smile, but it wobbled. "And thus it ends." She hummed a few notes, and the water skin vanished as mysteriously as it appeared.

"Tidiness is admirable, but time works against us."

Oriel spun to find Gareth once more present, watching her. "What can I do for you, Mighty Prince?"

"Haste would be nice."

Colors cascaded through her flames before settling into the muted orange of understanding. He was expecting her to come with them. "I am the Key, Mighty Prince. I am where I am supposed to be."

"You are not *just* the Key. You are Oriel." Gareth waved at the Vault. "This place does not need Creator's light. The world does."

Oriel turned away, her wings tucked against her. "But my strength is insufficient."

"It doesn't have to be otherwise. Creator is more than

sufficient, is He not?"

"But how can I leave?"

Gareth's mouth twitched. "By walking. Unless you want to be carried. Then I suppose I can carry you." Sobering, he placed hands on her slim shoulders, warmth radiating from him as if he were the one made of fire and not the other way around. "Forgetting is easier, but it is not better. It shrivels the heart, fogs the mind, cripples the will, and destroys the soul. Do not let yourself become imprisoned as I did."

"But I am the Key. The Key's place is in the Vault."

"Isn't a key for unlocking? And it's hard to unlock anything from the inside. Besides, more things need unlocking—and locking—than the Vault."

Oriel studied his face, which showed no glint of humor. "You truly believe this, Mighty Prince?"

"Of course. After all, you are the Key to Everything."

THE RISHI WARRIOR GLIDED TO A HALT WHERE THE gravel road split, Juliet riding on his back like a conqueror returning from battle. She leapt to the ground and scanned the area as the second warrior, still carrying Iris, stopped beside the first. About thirty feet away a gateway shimmered, an invisible barrier preventing the Rishi from drawing nearer. The rest of the landscape was brightening from the bluish night glow to daytime yellows, and between the eastern mountains peered the rising sun, as if it was afraid to witness the coming encounter.

"Do you have it?" Zarbal drifted out of the lingering shadows, the ground and air shuddering around him. He folded his arms and spread his wings to their full extent, black smoke boiling around him.

Juliet bowed before him. "I have obtained all you required, mighty balai."

The second warrior unceremoniously dropped Iris. She tumbled to the ground, flushed and trembling, like she had spiked a fever. A black webbing wound around her body, pinning arms to her sides. She lurched forward only to be yanked back by a leash held by the Rishi.

"And the key to the Bottomless Regions?" asked Zarbal.

"You can have it when we reach HopeWell."

Lightning crackled around Zarbal. A bolt seared the ground inches from her toes. Juliet blinked with catlike boredom at his theatrics.

"I should . . ." Zarbal cocked his head, then nodded once, snapping his wings shut. The electrical storm around him subsided. "Never mind. Prepare for my crossing."

"With pleasure, balai." Kneeling, Juliet took out the wood case and opened it.

Zarbal extended his hand. "The tears of a Jewel."

She handed up the jar of clear liquid.

"The blood of the Key."

A vial of Oriel's fireblood was given over next and poured into the jar.

"The heart of a guardian."

Juliet slowly unfastened her necklace and held it out by the chain, the intricately carved heart dangling from it. In Echoing's strange light, the pendant seemed to pulse with a reddish glow like a heartbeat. Along one edge was the inscription, *To Jul, all my love. Gareth.*

For several seconds, she held the necklace above Zarbal's palm, her fingers tightening around the chain. Then her pupils contracted, and her hand sprang open, releasing the heart to Zarbal. He crushed it in his fist, incinerating it to ash. A shudder ripped through Juliet.

Then the ash was added to the jar, causing the liquid to boil before congealing into a greasy black substance. Zarbal toasted Juliet with the jar and swallowed the liquid. An oily film oozed across his body. He tossed the jar away, which shattered against the rocks, and sailed toward the gateway. As he passed through the invisible barrier, a high-pitched squeal rent the air. Then with a thunderclap, he crossed the threshold, turning transparent.

Juliet strapped the black-bladed knife to her side, grabbed the wood case, and yanked Iris to her feet. "You won't want to miss this, Witless."

Digging in her heels, Iris thrashed against the older woman's grasp, and when that failed to slow their approach to the gateway, she dropped into dead weight. Juliet merely adjusted her grip and towed her through.

Zarbal waited a few feet away, an inky splotch among the rocks' shadows, elongated in the early morning light. "I thirst." His gravelly words, though lacking the rumbling power they held in Echoing, remained thick with slime.

Iris, still bound by the black webbing, tried to scoot away.

Flicking out the black-bladed knife, Juliet grabbed Iris by the hair and leaned down to place her mouth near the younger woman's ear. "I would tell you that this won't hurt, but I suspect it will. Very much." Then yanking the hair aside to expose Iris's neck, Juliet raised the knife.

30

"DID YOU SEE THAT?"

Brandon's four simple words charged the air with tension. During the past two days, travel had been uneventful, and vigilance had relaxed. But now it snapped back to high alert. Brandon rose from the rock near the campfire and reached for his bow.

"I saw." Gareth's tone commanded silence, and he noiselessly unsheathed his knives.

The campfire crackled. The stew cooking above it hissed and popped. Along the forest's edge, the bluish night glow of Echoing distorted every murky form into a lurking monster. A hunched shadow darted between the trees.

Maggie lowered her head, and the spicy aroma of her prayers mixed with the scent of food. Oriel extended her wings over Maggie and herself, creating a shield of fire. Gareth waved for Brandon to stand back—his bow was of little use in tight spaces— and Jaki circled around. As he moved forward, he grew taller, his glow brightening to the blinding whiteness of purifying fire. Gareth moved diagonally toward the trees, preparing to confront whatever Jaki flushed out.

As Jaki glided toward where the shadow disappeared, a stooped, limping figure scrambled away, a tattered coat flapping in its wake. But it was so intent on escaping, it crashed headlong into Gareth. The figure scuttled backward, then screeched upon seeing Gareth's face. "You! You're dead! You're supposed to be dead!" A wrinkled, claw-like hand struck out at him.

He ducked the strike and parried with the flat of his knife against his attacker's wrist. She howled and turned to flee. He flung his arms around her and pulled her against his chest, careful not to nick her with his knives. The woman squirmed and writhed but could not break free. Finally she collapsed against him, and Gareth eased his hold. She crumpled to the ground.

"Go ahead. Do it." Her wheezing morphed into a hoarse cackle. "Finish what he began."

As Jaki drew closer, his flames cast light over the shadowed figure. Gareth stepped back in shock. "Juliet?"

She had deteriorated into a hag more ancient than Maggie, almost past recognition. Her disheveled hair hung in matted gray locks around a sunken face, eyes wild and lips cracked. A crone's claw, its red nails ragged, clutched a tattered coat closed at her chest. "If you're too much of a coward, I'll do it," she rasped. "Just don't hand me over to *them*." She yanked her head toward Jaki.

"Gareth . . ." Jaki drew nearer.

Juliet screeched again and lunged for Gareth's weapon. Holding his knives beyond her reach, Gareth gave Jaki a warning shake of the head. The Ishir backed off.

Juliet clawed at him. "How dare you deny me my right to die!"

"I deny you no right." Gareth tossed the knives over her; they thunked into a nearby tree trunk high above her head. "Life is a gift from Creator. We have no right to give it—or take it."

"Says the murderer." Spittle flew from Juliet's mouth.

"Just because I have taken life does not mean that I was right to do so. But you could find Death in a hundred ways. Why stalk us?"

"To help, if you can believe that."

Brandon, who had arrived to overhear most of the conversation, yanked up his bow, aiming for Juliet's heart. "Of all the double-tongued—"

"Enough." Gareth's glare stopped Brandon mid-pull, though he left his arrow nocked. Gareth loosened his grip on Juliet slightly. "Now why would *you* want to help *us*?"

She rocked back and forth, clutching her coat, her voice pitching higher and higher. "He took it from me. He tossed me aside. He has to be made to pay."

"Who took what?"

"The key. Witless. My beauty. My power. Everything. He has to be made to pay. He must."

"Who?"

"Zarbal."

Gareth froze. Jaki recoiled at the name. The tip of Brandon's arrow dipped in confusion "Who?"

"Zarbal, prince of the Rishi." A shudder ripped through Gareth, and he barely managed the next words. "Second only to the Fallen Star himself."

"Gareth, that's not merely *a* lord of the Rishi from Shirel's prophesy. She crossed over *the* lord." Jaki's flames morphed to a muted red. "Fighting hunters is one thing. But to face the greatest might of the Rishi . . ."

"Suicide. I know." Gareth pointed. "Tell the other two what has happened."

They hesitated, then retreated to the clearing where Maggie and Oriel waited.

Gareth watched as Juliet picked at the frayed edge of her sleeve. "You said you wanted to help. What help did you intend to give?"

She said nothing, only picked, picked, picked at her sleeve.

He shook her. "Juliet!"

"Levioth! I am still Levioth!" Her head jerked up.

"You may be Levioth to the rest of the world, but to me . . ." He sighed. "You said you wanted to help."

"I know things, many things." She tapped her temple with a gnarled finger, a twisted smile upon her face.

"Most of which I have no desire to know." He pushed her away.

Juliet snatched his pant leg, her fingers clenching with a strength contrary to her decrepit appearance. "You don't know what I have to offer."

Gareth stood still, staring straight ahead. "Be on your way."

"Then you know where the door will appear . . . and how and when?"

Silence.

"I thought not."

Gareth glanced down at her, his gray eyes cool and unemotional. "I wonder if even you know."

"Know? Of course I know—I'm the one who figured it out! With the blood moon the keyhole shall appear in the midst of HopeWell."

"HopeWell?" He raised an eyebrow. "How convenient."

"It's true; it's all true!" Strength crept back into her voice. "And when the key is set in that hole, the door to the Bottomless Regions shall appear."

"So you say." Gareth eyed her. "For all I know, this is a ruse."

Juliet spat at him. "Blind fool. How can Zarbal be made to pay if he's not there?"

Gareth retrieved his knives from the tree. "I will speak with the others." He walked a few steps, then said over his shoulder, "We have some bread and water flasks if you're interested."

Juliet sniffed contemptuously, but when he walked on, she trailed him at a discreet distance. At the edge of the woods, however, she choked and backtracked, covering her nose and mouth with her arm. "Putrid odor," she gurgled. "Disgusting, despicable, reeking, foul, vile odor." She huddled at the base of a tree, her back to the clearing, continuing to mutter her disgust.

Gareth glanced at Oriel and Maggie, whose prayers were infusing the area with a sweet aroma spiced with cinnamon and frankincense. There would be no coaxing Juliet farther. Taking a half of a loaf and a water flask, he placed them a couple of feet from Juliet. She snatched them and scurried back to the shelter of the trees.

He sighed and returned to the others, informing them of what he'd learned. Their faces grew grim as they absorbed the news. The blood moon was two days away. HopeWell was a two-day journey. And the prince of the Rishi possessed the key to the Bottomless Regions.

"Now what?" Jaki caused flames to spring up and snuff out repeatedly on his hand as they debated this latest development. "The prophecy is coming true. May have already come to pass."

"Which points to this being a trap," Brandon declared.

"She seemed genuine." Gareth sat hunched over, elbows on his knees, the situation obviously weighing on him. "And revenge fits her."

"Besides, why would she lie?" added Jaki.

"Revenge," Brandon repeated. "But just not on this Zarbal guy."

"She had all she needed to open the Bottomless Regions. Once that happened, she would have had more power, unstoppable power, to crush us."

"It still could be a trick."

Oriel rustled her wings uncomfortably, and Gareth glanced at her. "What is your opinion, Oriel?"

She shrank under the intense scrutiny of the others, her glow reddening. "My experiences with the Adam are few. My thoughts on the matter are of little import, Mighty Prince."

"But you have thoughts."

Oriel looked at Juliet, who picked at her sleeve's tattered edge, muttering nonsensical words. "Levioth is unstable of mind—so unstable that she cannot form a coherent lie."

"Then you believe she is telling the truth?"

"I believe she speaks the truth as she sees it." Oriel tilted her head. "No offense, Mighty Prince, but she is Adam. The Adam are oft blind when truth is at stake. The Rishi, on the other hand . . ."

"He did not cast her off but is using her to lure us in."

"A possibility we must consider."

Brandon waved his bow. "Does it matter? Either way it is a trap. We can't go there."

Gareth rubbed his eyes. How to make a choice when no good choice existed?

Oriel glided over and sank gracefully before him. "I am at your service, Mighty Prince."

Gareth raised his head, brow knitting.

"You plan to return, deception or no deception." She spread out her hands. "Tell me how I may best serve you."

"It will be death. I cannot ask you—"

"You are not asking. I am offering." She fisted a hand over her chest and bent her head. "What would you have me do?"

"I as well." Jaki mirrored Oriel's position.

Maggie rested a hand on Gareth's shoulder. "Ye haven't because ye've not asked."

Gareth gently squeezed her hand. "You are right as usual, Maggie."

"This is insanity." Brandon ran his hand through his hair repeatedly.

"You don't have to come."

Brandon dipped his hand into his pocket. "Is there any other way to stop this Zarbal?"

"There is always a possibility. Creator can do as He pleases. But we seem to be what He has chosen to use at the moment."

Brandon's fingers encircled the Protector's Star. "I'm coming."

Gareth clapped him on the back. "Sarish first, then on to HopeWell." He turned toward the woods. "Juliet . . ." The word died in his mouth. Juliet no longer sat near the trees.

"Quick," he ordered. "Split up and find her!"

They scattered to hunt for her, but after an hour of searching, they turned up nothing. Juliet was gone. With grim faces they reassembled in the clearing.

"Now what?" Brandon flopped onto the ground in defeat.

Gareth gathered his pack. "We proceed as intended."

"But we don't know where she is!"

Gareth raised his gaze to the treetops, where a purple haze marked gathering storm clouds. "I may not know where she is, but I know where she will be. She returns to her master."

Brandon frowned. "I thought you said she was telling the truth."

"She was. And now she returns with *our* plans in hopes of regaining her master's favor."

"And we're still going forward?"

Gareth set his face to the west. "Yes."

31

THE ISHIR'S CHAMBER OF DECISION AND JUDGMENT reflected little of its impressive title at first glance. The marble cave-turned-council room extended no more than twenty feet in any direction. Its smooth walls boasted neither gems nor precious metals, only the subtle striping of the light-colored stone from which it was carved. Yet the rounded curves of the chamber gave the room a graceful simplicity while the marble added a sense of solidness and solemnity, even as two dozen scorch marks warned of the occasional debates that took place there.

The twelve Ishir who gathered inside the chamber showed no sign of such dissension today. The eight men and four women stood in a loose ring, their stances poised but relaxed, and their individual melodies intertwined into a harmonious whole. Perhaps this meeting would proceed peaceably without disruption. Sarish, standing at the head of the room as the council leader, nodded to the Ishir opposite of him to begin.

A rosy-cheeked Ishir glided toward the center of the ring and bowed to Sarish. "Most esteemed Sarish, honored council, I bring the annual report from—"

A rumble from the wall opposite of Sarish vibrated the whole chamber, warning of a coming interruption. Sarish fanned his flames, growing to a daunting size, and drew his sword. The other eleven council members followed suit, each readying their weapons, ranging from long knives and clubs to bows and javelins.

The rock wall split open, and Gareth strode into the chamber flanked by Jaki and Brandon. Oriel and Maggie followed close behind.

At the sight of the banished guardian, a disparaging mutter broke out among the council, and then when the Key of Everything entered, the place fell deathly silent before erupting into querulous demands. What was the Key doing outside of the Vault? Hadn't they decreed it would be safer for her to remain there? Who had dared defy them?

Sarish slashed his hand through the air, silencing the growing outrage, and arced across the room to stand before the intruders. "I see you have found the Key. You have our thanks for her safe return." His words were filled with stiff formality.

Gareth crossed one arm over his chest and bowed. "Indeed we did. But that is not why we are here." Unsheathing his long knives, he held them out to Sarish hilt first. "I have come for my guardian daggers."

One of the councilmen surged toward the group, brandishing a diamond fighting stick with both hands. "Of all the audacity—"

Sarish raised a hand, stilling the councilman, and leveled a glare on Gareth. "A life for a life, slayer? Or do you think such a trivial task as this"—he gestured dismissively—"should be sufficient payment?"

At his words Oriel shrank several inches, her flames dimming, but Gareth lifted his chin in defiance of Sarish's attempted intimidation. "Saving a life, especially one as valuable and precious as Oriel's should count for something. But it is not that upon which I base my claim." He tugged open his shirt to reveal the handprint left by Juliet.

The Ishir's gasps echoed through the chamber.

"The council decreed my death as restitution for the life I took. I have died, thus fulfilling the requirement." Gareth extended the long knives once more to Sarish.

Sarish folded his arms, refusing the weapons. "Then how is it that you stand before us? The death required was physical."

"Creator Himself restored my breath."

More gasps and murmuring filled the chamber. "Difficult to prove, slayer."

"Difficult, but not impossible. I have three witnesses of my death." A sly smile quirked his mouth. "I believe that is one more witness than required by law to confirm the truth."

"The council shall have to investigate and discuss this matter further." Sarish turned in dismissal and glided back toward the rest of the council.

"Perhaps I didn't make myself clear." Gareth's words took on a menacing rumble, and he flung the long knives across the room, hilt over tip, barely missing three of the Ishir. The blades hit the far wall and clattered to the floor.

Sarish whirled, lightning crackling around him. "Is that a threat, slayer?"

"A clarification that this is not negotiable." Gareth stretched out his hand. "My guardian daggers."

"You have tried my patience long enough—"

"Sarish." Jaki leapt between them and bowed to his leader. "Even we Ishir, with all the power that Creator has bestowed upon us, desire the best weapons our skill can create. Would you fault an Adam for desiring the same for the upcoming battle?"

"Battle?"

"Have you not heard? Levioth has joined forces with Zarbal, aided him in crossing the Wall, and obtained the key to the Bottomless Regions."

A flurry of whispers and the crackling of fire rushed through the council as they bent their heads together in consultation. Sarish's hand closed around the pommel of his sword. "And how did Levioth accomplish all this?"

Gareth opened his mouth to respond, but Oriel glided

forward and spoke before he could. "I am responsible, Sarish. I gave her the key." A thread of smoke coiled through her flames. "*Gave?* With the blood moon less than two days away?" An electrical charge snapped and crackled around Sarish.

Gareth stepped in front of Oriel. "As the Key of Everything and Protector of the Vault, Oriel understands perhaps even better than you, Sarish, the potential repercussions of her actions—actions, I might add, Creator approved." He glanced over his shoulder at her, his last words for her benefit as much as for Sarish's.

A strand of warmth laced with cinnamon conveyed her gratitude for the reminder.

Gareth continued. "What matters is not the past, for it cannot be undone, but the future upon which we may yet act."

"That is assuming you speak true. Yet the vigils have reported no such disturb—"

An Ishir burst into the room. Flames dancing wildly from his haste, he dropped into a deep bow before Sarish. "Forgive my intrusion, but I bring the most distressing news. Zarbal, the prince of the Rishi, has crossed the Wall into Terrestial."

A councilwoman arched forward, landing only inches behind Sarish. "When?"

"Two days past, near dawn."

"Two *days*?" Another councilmember joined the cluster.

"We wished to confirm the disturbance, so unexpected was the crossing."

The rest of the council crowded forward, questions piling upon questions. Sarish silenced the clamor. "Where is he now, Messenger?"

"We tracked him to the western forest, near the Adam settlement called Koma."

Gareth exchanged a look with Jaki at this confirmation that Juliet had indeed told the truth, at least in part. "We were told the door to the Bottomless Regions will appear at HopeWell, a few miles outside of Koma." His hand automatically reached for his knife hilt, forgetting the sheath was empty. "Will you lend us the aid of your warriors that we might stop Zarbal and Levioth?"

Murmurs once again rippled through the council. "We can't. But how can we not? Maybe if we get there ahead and surprise them . . ."

Gareth raised his voice. "Zarbal is already aware we are coming. He may not know numbers, but you can be assured he will be well-prepared to the point of overkill."

Sarish's growl vibrated the marble cavern. "Any other surprises?"

"None that I can think of."

"Then we will give you our decision before the day's end." Sarish arched back to where he stood before the disruption, dismissing further debate.

Gareth and the rest of his group exited the chamber into a cultivated grove. The wall sealed behind them. Gareth's shoulders sagged. "Your read of the situation, Jaki?"

"Not as favorable as I would like."

"We'd best prepare to face this alone."

Oriel glided up beside Gareth. "Not alone, Mighty Prince. Creator is with us, and as a wise Adam recently reminded me, He is more than sufficient."

IN THE HOURS FOLLOWING, THE GROVE SEEMED TO hold its breath in anticipation of the council's decision. No bird chirruped, no twig twitched, no squirrel scampered by. Stillness permeated the air, infecting all who breathed it.

Near the center of the grove, Jaki and Oriel leaned against

a stone pillar with their eyes closed, though the serenity of sleep did not soften their features. Maggie's lips moved in silent petition as she poked her fingers into the barren ground of a nearby flowerbed, stirring up the comforting loaminess of tilled earth. Gareth, settled on a bench at the edge of Maggie's flowerbed, whittled a long tree branch, curls of wood accumulating around him.

Brandon alone displayed restlessness. Every attempt at conversation ended after a half dozen exchanges. He shot arrows until his arms grew shaky. He prowled the grove's path in an endless circuit.

After an hour of that routine, he ground to a stop in front of Gareth. "Why aren't we doing anything?"

His demand provoked a low-throated chuckle from Jaki and a wry smile from Gareth.

"Sounds like another young guardian I once knew." Jaki flicked a spark in Gareth's direction.

Gareth batted it away before it could land among the wood curls. "And he'll find the answers as unsatisfactory as I did."

"What answers?" Brandon's gaze darted between the more experienced men.

"We're not doing nothing. We're waiting." Gareth glanced up. "Well, we are. You on the other hand . . ." He shrugged a shoulder and dropped another curl of wood to the ground.

"What's the difference?"

"Waiting implies purpose and expectation and preparation as we ready ourselves for wherever Creator leads next." Gareth waved his knife toward Maggie. "Therefore, your grandmother seeks direction and protection while Jaki and Oriel"—he jabbed at the two Ishir—"are fortifying their fire with the review of the Ancient Writings."

"And you?"

"Trying to determine how to a guide a brash young man." He

tossed a wood chip at Jaki, who caught it and popped it into his mouth. "Any insights into the techniques of Guardian Revolin?"

"Breathe often, pray more . . . and grumble frequently about your protégé when he's beyond earshot."

Gareth's mouth twitched. "Surely I wasn't that bad."

"Worse." Jaki smiled at his long-time friend. "I think it is not coincidence that he lost his hair while teaching you."

Gareth rubbed his own head. "I may follow suit." Then his eyes narrowed at Brandon fiddling with something in his pocket. Setting aside his whittling, Gareth held out his hand. "May I?"

Brandon hesitated a moment before placing his Protector's Star on Gareth's palm.

"*Tolmone, Dynamis, Eleos, Elpis.*" Gareth fingered the outside ring of the Star. "Do you know what that means?"

"Boldness, strength, mercy, hope." A touch of pride tinged Brandon's voice. "I suppose you think I'm an idealistic fool," he added.

"Would that we all be such fools. For the heart that seeks to protect while maintaining justice is a noble heart indeed, honored by Creator." He offered the Star back.

Brandon pocketed it.

Gareth picked up the branch he had been working on, running his hand along the curve of a long bow in its earliest stages. "Jaki, get over here."

Jaki opened one eye questioningly, and when he saw the incomplete bow in Gareth's hand, he rose. "You believe he is ready?"

Gareth nodded.

"Then I will not hinder." Jaki swept over the short distance and wrapped his fingers around the unfinished weapon. Humming, he slid his hands apart, one toward each end, leaving blackened wood in their wake. When he reached the tips, he offered the bow back to Gareth.

"Thank you, my friend. Oriel, Maggie, I need your witness."

The two women rose and came alongside the three men, standing opposite of Jaki.

Gareth faced Brandon again. "Hold out your hands."

Brandon hesitated, but Gareth's compelling command didn't leave refusal as an option. He held out his hands.

Gareth laid the charred bow on his palms. "By Creator who made all things, giving man his breath; by His Son who redeemed all things, giving man his purpose; by His Spirit who directs all things, giving man his path—by the Three-Yet-One—I charge you to protect and to defend all that is good and holy against the Great Adversary and his servant Levioth, for as long as Creator sees fit to give you breath."

Jaki steepled his fingers. "How shall you answer this charge, son of dust and Creator's breath? Shall you answer His call or chose the path of Adversary's making?"

Brandon looked at the two men, down at the charred bow, then over at his grandmother, her lips moving in silent intercession. "I say aye. I will answer the call."

"Bear witness this day, all creation of Creator's making: He has answered the call." Gareth blew across the bow.

The black flaked off, leaving behind polished wood glowing as if internally lit by fire, a weapon both new yet ancient. Golden scrollwork wound around the bow, a single line of script intertwining with it: *Now faith is the assurance of things hoped for, the conviction of things not seen.*

Jaki clasped Brandon's shoulder. "I think a trip to the armory is in order." He guided Brandon out of the grove.

Gareth sat back on the bench, looking after them. "He has no idea what he just agreed to."

Oriel rested a hand on his back, infusing the air with her warmth. "He'll learn like every guardian does."

"He deserves a better trainer."

"Creator provided him the *right* trainer."

"Yet the one thing I want to give the boy is the one thing I can't—more time to prepare."

"His training did not begin with answering the call, Mighty Prince," Oriel said. "Creator knew this day would come and used every day to ready him for this moment."

Before Gareth could respond, the rock wall shuddered and split open. Sarish emerged from the Chamber of Decision and Judgment. Gareth rose to meet him, Oriel hovering behind.

Sarish extended a wood plank upon which rested two elegant daggers "Your weapons . . . Guardian."

Gareth's expression was unreadable. He grasped the hilts, and the daggers hummed in pleasure, the reunion long in coming. He turned the blades to read the words etched among the scrollwork. The left bore the words, *Not by might nor by power, but by My Spirit, says the Lord of hosts.* The right read, *For apart from Me you can do nothing.*

As he read aloud the quotes, the blades grew brighter and brighter until they burned white. Gareth swung a few practice strokes. The daggers flashed like lightning, his fluid movements unnaturally quick. The Mighty Prince of the Guardians was back.

He bowed to Sarish. "I thank you."

"You didn't give me much choice."

"Nonetheless, I am grateful." Gareth sheathed the daggers. "As for the other matter?"

"The danger is great—so great we cannot compel our warriors to fight."

"But—"

Sarish held up a hand, cutting off the protest. "We will send a message, however, to all our people, telling them of the danger. If any wishes to fight, they shall assemble at eventide at the crack nearest the place you call HopeWell."

32

IT SHOULD HAVE BEEN A DARK AND STORMY NIGHT
filled with thunder and lightning, torrential rains and ravaging
winds. Such meteorological fury would have better suited the
tension of the two Ishir and three Adam climbing out of the car
along the edge of the forest. Instead, tranquility dominated the
night as the world slumbered on, either unaware or unconcerned
about the battle lines forming around HopeWell.

A light breeze rustled pine needles, bringing with it a thread
of warmth and the damp earthiness of early spring. Four of the
small group looked upward at the full moon, the graying of its
face unnoticeable except to the most watchful of eyes. Maggie
alone seemed unconcerned that the second phase of the eclipse
had already begun, and the blood moon would start in less
than an hour.

Jaki turned to Gareth, holding his fedora in his hands. "This
is where I must leave you. I should be through the crack within
five minutes."

"We will await your signal."

"Don't wait too long. I don't know what I shall find on the
other side." He glanced sideways at Maggie.

Gareth shook his head. "Creator has given her remarkable
insight, but if she knew anything more, she would have said
something."

Oriel shifted nervously behind him, twining her braid around
her fingers.

Jaki clasped one arm across his chest and dipped his head to her. "And I beg your forgiveness, Key of Everything."

At his formal address, she straightened her posture, puzzlement wrinkling her brow. "For what do you seek forgiveness, Warrior?"

"For our people's blindness. We sought to protect through isolation, forgetting Creator is your protector. Your difficult road has once again reminded us that under His protection, no one can harm you, and if He chooses to remove that shield, not even the whole might of the Ishir can protect you. And you are shielded by Him indeed, for you are not just the Key of Everything. You are Oriel."

Her eyes glistened with unusual dampness rather than their normal fire. "Thank you, Jakkiel."

"Creator be with you . . ."

"His face turned with favor to you."

"Glory be to Him this night."

"Amen and Amen."

And with that blessing ringing in the air, Jaki strode into the woods, retracing the path Oriel treaded less than a fortnight before, when Maggie's cry turned her aside.

When Jaki disappeared from sight, Gareth led the way back to the car. But although he grasped the handle of the back-passenger door, he did not open it.

Oriel paused beside him. "Mighty Prince?"

"I am sorry as well, Oriel."

"Whatever for?"

"My hard-headedness, my refusal to heed Creator's call, my temper. If I hadn't killed a man, if I had yielded to Creator's call to remember Him, this night, this battle would have never happened. It is my fault that—"

"Enough, Mighty Prince. Creator knew all this would happen before time unfolded. He could have stopped it in a hundred different ways yet chose not to because He knows the end already.

An end which, whatever happens here, He has deemed perfect. Trust Him to bring perfection from the pain."

Gareth shook his head. "How did one so young become so wise?"

Oriel tossed her braid over her shoulder. "Young? I have seen at least two centuries beyond you, Mighty Prince."

"Two *centuries?*" Sputtering, Brandon peered at her over the car's roof. "You can't be more than . . ."

Oriel lifted her eyes to him, their ancient depths mocking his unspoken words. "Yes, Guardian?"

Brandon yanked the passenger door open. "Nothing."

"Smart answer." Gareth helped Maggie into the car. "Never attempt to guess an Ishir's age, especially by their Adam façade." He stooped beside her. "It's not too late. You can return home and stay there until all this is over."

Maggie shook her head, a smile hovering on her lips. "The fruit be ripe, and I won't be missing Creator's harvest." She settled in further and stared straight ahead, leaving Gareth little choice but to close the door.

Oriel slid into the back seat on the other side while Gareth pulled open the driver's door. Pausing, he glanced once more at Koma slumbering peacefully below. For years they had turned a blind eye to HopeWell's existence. Why should tonight be any different? Leave well enough alone and you will be left alone, that was the policy. Not so different from his own attempt to forget. Was it any wonder, then, that evil flourished in Anatroshka?

Gareth could not correct all the evils of his people, but tonight he could, with Creator's help, prevent Hell itself from invading. "Creator, have mercy."

He slid behind the steering wheel, slamming the door behind him, as the first sliver of the moon darkened to red.

THE BATTLE LINES HAD BEEN DRAWN.

Though officially abandoned, HopeWell revealed itself to be anything but deserted. Beyond the gate, secured by a new bar, a dozen hunters paced the perimeter, sporting both their usual guns and an array of other weapons, such as swords, daggers, bows, and clubs. Several statuesque figures in hooded robes also were stationed at regular intervals, moonlight glinting off the silver runic embroidery and red gems decorating the black fabric: the Alphas in their formal attire, each overseeing a pack of hunters. Neither Juliet nor Zarbal were in sight, but the heavy protection suggested that Juliet had indeed returned with Gareth's plans.

Gareth and Brandon scouted the entire perimeter of the camp but spotted no lapse in security. The Alphas and their packs were distributed evenly with a double force stationed at the gate. The men returned to Oriel and Maggie, who hid in the woods just off the road, and at their inquiring looks, Gareth confirmed the worst with a curt shake of his head. HopeWell seemed as impenetrable as it once seemed inescapable.

"Any sign?" he whispered.

It was Oriel's turn to shake her head. Jaki must have run into extra opposition as well. Gareth eyed the moon, only a sliver of gray left. "We can't wait much longer."

"And how do you propose we get in?" Brandon asked.

"By the front gate."

"Are you crazy? There's twice as many there."

"Look again."

Brandon did. While twice as many did patrol behind the gate, the hunters held their guns carelessly, their shoulders slouched. "They don't expect us to come this way."

"Exactly. It's a show to encourage attack elsewhere.

These hunters are inattentive, and look at the stitching on the Alphas' robes."

"Pretty plain."

Gareth nodded. "These are the lowest ranks, the least skilled in the black arts. If we can distract the more skilled Alphas, we might stand a chance."

Oriel rose. "Leave that to me, Mighty Prince." She turned to head deeper into the woods.

"Oriel." .

Gareth's raspy voice halted her mid-stride. "Please, I can do—"

"May Creator be your shield and your sword." He clasped an arm across his chest, half bowing to her.

For the second time that night, dampness glistened in her eyes. "Thank you." Then she disappeared into the forest.

Brandon transferred his bow from hand to hand. "Shouldn't somebody go with her?"

"Creator will be a better defense than a legion of guardians." Gareth led the others back toward where they'd left the car. "You, on the other hand . . ."

Brandon bristled, but Maggie clucked her tongue. "Don't tease the boy."

Reaching the car, Gareth sobered and eyed Brandon. "Your Protector's Star, please."

"What?" Brandon pressed his hand to his pocket.

"Easy, Brady." Maggie patted her grandson's arm.

He reluctantly gave up the Star. Gareth held it up, and moonlight glinted off the gem. "*Tolmone, Dynamis, Eleos, Elpis.* Boldness, strength, mercy, and hope. A worthy aspiration." He reached out and pinned it to Brandon's collar.

The official gesture seemed to embolden Brandon, and he drew himself to full height. "I will do my utmost to honor these words."

Gareth clasped Brandon's shoulder. "Let's start with

surviving the night." He reached for the car door.

Then Maggie gasped. She turned in a slow circle, eyes wide behind her spectacles. "They're here."

"Who?" Brandon looked about him. "The Ishir?"

Gareth's face grew grim. "No. The Rishi." He jerked open the door. "Our time is out."

DIVING DEEPER INTO THE WOODS, ORIEL SKIRTED the camp until she reached the northeast edge, kitty-corner from the gate. A few yards beyond the fence an Alpha watched the area. The amount of intricate embroidery on his robe sparkled brightly despite the waning moonlight, making him easy to see. On the other hand, not a hunter was in sight. No visible presence, however, didn't mean absent.

Oriel stepped to a tall tree near the edge of the woods and peered into the expansive upper branches. "Noble Yerek, our peoples have often quarreled, but tonight I ask that we set those differences aside to serve Creator together to stop the Fallen Star's plan to unlock the door that should not be open." She placed her hands on the thick trunk wrinkled with age. "I know I'm asking you to pay a terrible price, perhaps the most painful of all. I need to fell this tree of yours to cross the fence. This is not fair to you, and I will not proceed without your permission." She bowed her head.

The trees around her groaned and shivered, as if protesting her request. Then the tree she touched creaked, and all the others fell silent. With a shudder it leaned away from Oriel, toward the fence, its roots pulling up from the soft ground.

She touched it gently. "May Creator reward your sacrifice." She knelt, hands beginning to glow. "I will try to work quickly." She struck her hands against the roots.

The wood shrieked as she burned through the base of the tree. The Alpha on the other side of the fence raised his head. A half dozen hunters emerged from the shadows. A second Alpha joined the first.

The tree groaned and tilted, extracting smaller roots from the ground until one last root prevented the tree from crashing.

Oriel paused to thrust a palm toward the fence. A fireball flew from her hand and struck the upper beam, lighting it on fire. She turned back to the tree. "Thank you, Noble Yerek. I shall always remember you as Notan Chyim." Taking a breath, she slashed through the final root.

With a crack, the tree toppled, spraying dirt, and its trunk cleaved HopeWell's fence where the fireball had eaten through the upper beam. Hunters scattered, though the two Alphas remained unmoved. Oriel hopped onto the trunk and ran down its girth, crossing the wreckage into the camp.

Hunters snatched their guns and fired at Oriel. Several tree branches repositioned themselves protectively around her. Bullets slammed into wood. The hunters fired again, then again. Each time the branches blocked the bullets, sending a shudder and a groan through the tree. The hunters backed away, wide-eyed.

A roar of an engine split the air, followed by the crack of splintering wood and the screech of metal.

All heads swiveled toward the front of the camp from whence the noise emanated, but Oriel leapt to the ground, body aglow, heat rolling off of her. The Alphas stalked toward her, muttering strange syllables.

A black mist rose from the ground. It collided with Oriel's heat, hissing, crackling, popping. She shuddered, but her glow brightened and the temperature rose, burning a path through the mist. She charged forward.

THE IMPACT OF THE GATE JARRED THE CAR, BUT Gareth plowed ahead. Scraps of the fence clung to the vehicle, creating a horrible racket. Hunters scattered before him, and there was a sickening thud of flesh.

Suddenly, an Alpha blocked their way and raised his hand. The tires blew out; the engine sputtered and died. The car halted a few feet from the commandant's office. Brandon gripped the bow resting on his lap. "Now what?"

"Plan C."

"What's Plan C?"

"I'll let you know when I do." Gareth drummed his fingers against the steering wheel. "The Rishi can't touch us from Echoing, but they can manipulate the elements . . ." He stiffened. "Get out, get out now!" He bolted from the car.

Brandon scrambled out and yanked open the back door. Gareth rounded the rear of the car as Maggie poked her head out. He grabbed her arm and shoved her ahead of him. The car exploded, throwing them to the ground.

Gareth recovered first. Clambering to his feet, he whipped out his daggers. Brandon helped his grandmother up as hunters circled, guns pointed at them. He placed his back to Gareth's with Maggie sandwiched between. His hand twitched, ready to snatch an arrow, useless as it might be against bullets.

Maggie, seemingly oblivious to the standoff, straightened her dress and hat, then resettled her spectacles on her nose. She gave a cry of delight. "They're here!"

Warmth enveloped the trio, their weapons beginning to glow. Brandon's eyes widened at the transformation, but Gareth just half grinned and adjusted his hold on the daggers. "Your timing, old friend, is impeccable as always." He called out to Brandon, "Relax. Let the Ishir warrior guide you."

Brandon swallowed as his bow rose stiffly under compulsion. He changed his hands to grip it like a curved staff.

Gunshot exploded on the other side of HopeWell. A hunter jumped, accidentally discharging his weapon. Gareth's dagger blurred as it deflected the bullet.

Other hunters opened fire. Shot after shot rang out. Gareth's daggers darted side to side, blocking every missile within arm's reach, his movements fluid. Brandon's swing was jerkier, but his bow also blocked every bullet within reach.

They edged toward their opponents. The hunters fell back. Weapons clicked, ammo gone. Tossing the guns aside, the hunters withdrew various daggers and swords. Gareth bent his knees in preparation for the next wave of attack. "Brace yourself."

The words no sooner left his mouth than the hunters charged. Again Gareth's daggers and Brandon's bow blurred, and a minute later, bodies sprawled around them. The remaining three hunters backed away and fled. Sweat plastered Brandon's clothing and hair to his body. Gareth groaned and rolled his shoulders. "We'll feel this one tomorrow."

"Assuming we make it to tomorrow." Brandon pointed at the Alpha and his two apprentices coming toward them. Black fire surged ahead of them, smoke choking the air. Soon only the glow of the weapons cut through the gloom, all else reduced to shadowy forms.

"What ye doing, staying here? This way." Maggie hobbled forward, despite of the darkness encompassing them. She headed straight for the wall of black flames.

"Grandmama . . ."

Gareth raised a dagger, its glow illuminating his face. "Trust her." Then he turned to follow Maggie.

Brandon rubbed his hand over his bow, across the words inscribed there. *The conviction of things not seen.* He squared his shoulders and marched into the choking smoke and crackling flames.

33

MAGGIE'S FORM WAS LOST ALMOST IMMEDIATELY among the shadows. Not unexpected with all the smoke. Then the radiant blades of Gareth's daggers vanished, and two steps later the glow of Brandon's own bow began to fade. He paused. Nothing could be seen in the intense darkness—no surprise there—but neither could anything be heard. No footsteps, no breathing, no crackling fire, no creaks or rattles or bangs. He stood in a void, alone.

Brandon squared his shoulders. This was just another trick of the Alpha to induce fear; the other two had to be just ahead. But when he upped his pace, he bumped into a solid wall made of wood, rough-hewn. A cabin? Brandon followed it with a hand until he reached a doorway. He fumbled for the handle—darkness still shrouded everything—and flung open the door . . . stumbling onto the office's porch in *Echoing*.

Brandon grabbed a post and leaned against it as if dizzy. Here the muted aura of Echoing shed light upon HopeWell. Walls of black fire raged throughout the open compound. Ghostlike Alphas stalked among them, working their black arts in Terrestrial, each aided by two or more Rishi. At least one had five Rishi assisting him.

Stumbling from the porch, Brandon swiveled his head. No Gareth. No Maggie. Only more Rishi engaging the Ishir warriors. He edged along the building, keeping his back to the wall. Maggie was heading toward the prisoner cabins the last time he saw her, so that was the direction he headed.

All around him fires of every color flared, lightning bolts sizzled, and swords flashed. Several Rishi poured black sap across the ground. A couple of them hung a black spiderweb between two storage buildings to the south.

A Rishi spotted Brandon. He grinned and leapt across the open space between them. Brandon readied with his bow, but before he could shoot, the warrior arched his back with a shriek before crumbling into a charred mass and a wisp of smoke. Behind it stood Jaki, his sword still outstretched. His flames sparked in surprise. "Guardian? How did you get here?"

"No idea." Brandon swiftly raised his bow and released an arrow. It impaled a Rishi behind Jaki. Jaki spun, and with one slice from his sword, that one too became smoke and charcoal.

Jaki glanced back at Brandon. "I wonder . . ." Then he shook himself. "This way."

Brandon retrieved his arrow. "What do you wonder?"

"Tunneling. It's a rare guardian gift, one I've not seen in a couple of decades." Jaki cut through a wall of fire. On the other side, a ghostly Gareth walked behind a phantom Maggie, who navigated around three traps without hesitation. Jaki dispatched another Rishi in order to catch up. "Tunneling allows a guardian to travel between Terrestrial and Echoing without a gateway or a crack."

Maggie rounded the corner between two cabins. A silver film stretched between the buildings and above them as far as the eye could see. Maggie and Gareth passed unimpeded. Jaki pressed against the barrier. It refused him passage, impenetrable as stone.

Guarding the rear, Brandon backed toward Jaki. "More dark arts?"

Jaki tested the unyielding barrier again. "The darkness is not responsible for this."

"Then what is?"

"Creator."

Three passing Rishi spotted them. With leering grins they arced toward them, obstructing their exit. Brandon loosed an arrow. It struck the leading Rishi in the chest, and he disintegrated. "Why would Creator—"

"Don't know." Jaki leapt to meet the second Rishi, deflecting her sword with his. He flicked out a second blade and drove it into her exposed chest, severing her connection to her firecore. She dissolved into smoke and ash.

The third Rishi, hanging back, thrust fiery air toward Brandon. The young guardian stumbled backward. But instead of slamming into a solid wall, he popped through a gelatinous substance and sprawled onto the ground on the other side. "What the . . . ?" Brandon scrambled to his feet and stared at the barrier. From this side, the translucent film, seemingly made of water, allowed him to see through the barrier, albeit with distortion.

And what he saw was Jaki struggling to hold the Rishi at bay.

Brandon snatched up his bow and shot the first arrow he laid hold of. The arrow flew through the barrier and pierced the firecore of the Rishi, who stared at the arrow in disbelief. Then he crumbled like the others. Brandon pushed through the gelatinous film.

"Many thanks, Guardian," Jaki said respectfully. "But now you must go on." He nodded at the translucent wall. "For reasons known only to Creator, you alone can pass through. Perhaps it was for this reason Creator brought you to Echoing."

"What about—"

"It doesn't matter. Lend your aid to Gareth. If he fails to stop Zarbal, it doesn't matter how many Rishi we douse." And with that, Jaki thrust Brandon back through the film.

GARETH PLODDED THROUGH THE DARKNESS, AIR
roiling around him. Hot, putrid, choking. He covered the lower
half of his face with his arm and slogged on, each laborious
step met with the resistance of knee-deep muck, though
nothing tangible surrounded his legs. Darkness deepened to
abyss blackness, hiding everything and everyone from view. A
smothering sense of evil seemed to load extra weight upon him,
trying to pull him back, pull him down. Gareth tucked his head
and pushed on and on and—

Then it was gone. The smothering weight, the impenetrable
darkness, the clawing muck, the putrid smoke.

Unbalanced by the sudden change, Gareth steadied himself
against a cabin wall. Maggie was waiting for him a couple of
paces ahead. Behind him, darkness drew a definite line across
the space between the two cabins, prevented by some invisible
barrier from encroaching farther.

The hilts of his dagger grew cool in his hands, the blades
fading to metallic dullness. "Jaki?"

"He can't help ye." Maggie cocked her head, listening to the
inaudible. "Creator Himself has set a line. The evil ones can't
cross—but neither can the Ishir."

Gareth glared at the sky. "Must You make this harder?"
Heaving a frustrated sigh, he rubbed his knotted neck. "At least
we have . . ." Only he and Maggie occupied the narrow alley
between the cabins. "Great. He went and got himself lost."
Wearily shoving away from the wall, he headed back toward
the darkness.

"No good. Brady's crossed over."

Maggie's words arrested his steps. "Crossed over . . . he's

in *Echoing*?"

She nodded, her hat's brim bobbing.

"A tunneler. Great," grumbled Gareth, turning back. "Nothing I can do about it now, though."

"Creator knows what He be about."

"I'm glad He does because I certainly don't." He went past her and around the cabin's corner, then stopped abruptly. "No Ishir? Including Oriel?"

"She's here, not there, but . . ." Maggie raised a hand, fingers curled as if to catch the light breeze sweeping by, and shook her head. "Nay, I think not."

Agitated, Gareth flipped his daggers between his hands. Oriel was coming from the north. The garden, the most likely spot for the keyhole to appear, was south. He couldn't be in two places at once.

Maggie shuffled up beside him. "It be Creator's choice."

He flipped his daggers again. Light glinted off one of the blades. *Not by might nor by power.* Gareth closed his eyes and took a deep breath. "Creator equipped her. He can save her." He lifted his eyes heavenward. "Please save her."

Then he turned south, the last of the moon sliding beneath the shadow, its whole face the dark red of dried blood.

WITH LIGHT STEPS, ORIEL ANGLED ACROSS THE north section of HopeWell. Past the soldier's eastern barracks. Past the mass graves for prisoners. Around her, bullets continued to fly. A black ground fog nipped at her heels.

Reaching the easternmost row of prisoner cabins, she darted between two of them and crashed into an invisible barrier. Stumbling back, she shook her head, trying to clear it. A bullet whizzed past her ear and embedded itself in the cabin *past* the obstacle, as if nothing were there.

She tried the next gap between buildings. Again an invisible but solid barrier obstructed her path. She thrust out a glowing hand. Sparks flew. She yanked her hand away, shaking it.

A bullet slammed into her shoulder. Oriel winced and pressed a hand over the wound to heal it. Her pursuers were closing in. She sprinted southward, searching for an opening into the inner part of camp. Faster and faster she pushed herself, movements blurring as she circled the south end of HopeWell, then the western side. More Alphas joined the pursuit. Still no opening.

As she neared the northeast corner where she began, three shots struck her back, near her fire core. She faltered, jerking at the impact, fireblood oozing from the punctures. She lost her momentum. A tall, hooded figure emerged from between the cabins ahead of her.

Oriel tried to reverse her course, but an Alpha stood behind her. Three more moved in from her side. She flattened her back against the rough cabin wall.

As the hooded figure loomed before her, the Alphas formed a half circle behind. Their garments' elaborate stitching and studded gems only emphasized the utter blackness of the leader's robe. A dark mist crept along the ground.

The leader shoved back the hood, and Juliet, fully restored to her former self, regarded Oriel with supreme disdain. "Not so strong without a human to protect, are you?" She flicked her wrist.

An icicle impaled Oriel in the stomach.

34

THE GARDEN APPEARED DESERTED. NO BLACK-ROBED Alphas. No menacing Rishi. Not even the terrible door leading to the Bottomless Regions. Just a few dried, broken stalks poked out of the clumpy earth. That was all.

Gareth held out his arm to prevent Maggie from entering the clearing. Had they come to the wrong place, despite the Ishir's confirmation of the location? As they peered between the buildings that yet sheltered them, there was no sign of pursuit by either the hunters or the Alphas. With so much power connected to the Rishi, who couldn't cross the barrier, perhaps they were content with simply blocking any escape route.

Ground squelched.

Gareth snapped his attention back toward the garden, his hands tightening around the hilts of his daggers. Near the garden's center, darkness solidified into a giant dressed in a black trench coat. A wide-brimmed hat shadowed his face, obscuring its features except for the eyes. Those glowed with the dark red of coals.

"Welcome, Guardian Prince. Welcome, Jewel." Zarbal's bass voice added an oily film to the air, making it hard to breathe. "Come to witness my triumph?"

Maggie pressed closer to Gareth as she murmured indistinguishable words. The air cleared. Gareth stood straighter, daggers poised. "We've come for the key."

Zarbal chuckled, a foul sound of slime and tar. "Then come and get it." He extended a hand, the ebony box atop the palm of a black-gloved hand.

"I said key, not box."

"You doubt I possess the key to the Bottomless Regions?"

"I doubt the box still contains the key."

"Very astute." Zarbal tossed the box at him, and it clattered to the ground.

Gareth nudged the lid open with his toe. The box was empty.

"A man with such a mind deserves more than this." Zarbal waved at HopeWell. "You should be leading armies, determining the course of nations." His eyes flickered, and his mouth widened. "I can give you that."

Placing one foot behind the other, Gareth crossed his daggers before his chest. "Invisible chains still imprison."

"Then perhaps you'd like to consider another proposition. A life for a life." Zarbal edged aside.

Iris knelt on the ground, head bowed, shivering like one unable to get warm. Chains shackled her ankles and wrists. A black, sticky webbing bound her to a wooden stake. Worst of all, her blouse had been slit in several places to allow vine-like tentacles to grow out of swollen gashes cut into her upper body and neck. The tentacles wound around each other into a thick rope, leading back to Zarbal. He snapped the tentacle rope. "Be polite and say hello."

Iris gasped and arched her back. Her hair fell away from her face. Tears streaked her cheeks, the ashy skin veined with black. Face terse, Gareth advanced toward her.

"Not so hasty. You've not seen the best part." Light streaked up half of the tentacles from Iris to Zarbal. He grew several inches, his eyes brightening. "Ahh." He smacked his lips. Iris paled further, and sweat dotted her face.

Gareth reddened and his nostrils flared. Zarbal was feeding off Iris, using her fire to strengthen his.

"So what will it be, Guardian? Join me, save her. Refuse, and

I'll drain her dry."

A light hand settled on Gareth's back; Maggie bent her head toward him. From under her hat, her murmuring patter rose and cut through the haze. Gareth blinked several times and shook his head as if trying to dislodge something.

Zarbal snarled. "Silence, old woman."

Maggie kept on, her murmuring sharper, more punctuated.

Gareth clenched his jaw. As much as he wanted to rescue Iris, such a bargain would not save her but condemn them all.

"You've chosen death. So be it." Zarbal tossed his gloves aside and raised his hands, a miniature electrical storm crackling around them.

BRANDON SURVEYED THE GHOSTLY TABLEAU. GARETH guarded Maggie at the garden's north end. Near the center stood a massive Rishi—Zarbal—his transparent human façade shrouding a raging fire. Beside him knelt Iris, her glow weak and flickering.

It seemed words were exchanged. At least, Gareth's lips moved, and the Rishi's shoulders shook as his mouth opened wide. The whole scene played out in eerie silence. But no one seemed to notice or sense his presence. Brandon nocked an arrow and took aim. The arrow flew true, straight for Zarbal's firecore—and passed right through him.

Brandon snatched a second arrow from his quiver and shot it. Then a third and a fourth. Each flew harmlessly through the Rishi.

Light streamed along the tentacles. Zarbal's flames leapt up brighter than ever. Iris slumped to the side, her luminescence dimming.

"No!" Brandon charged forward. He swung his bow at Zarbal; he whacked at the tentacles—anything to break the Rishi's connection with Iris. All without effect.

He collapsed to his knees and yelled into the dark heavens. "Why bring me here if I can't help them? What do You want from me? I don't care how dangerous or impossible or—or ridiculous. Just show me what to do!"

A golden mist surged from the ground, enveloping the scene. Brandon scrambled backward. The mist congealed to reveal a Brandon-like image cracking open the water tower. Then the vision disappeared.

"Release the water? How's that supposed to help?"

The mist darkened and dissolved as if in chastisement.

Brandon fingered his bow, tracing the scrollwork that melded into words. *Now faith is the assurance of things hoped for.* After a moment, he got to his feet and retrieved his arrows. "If this helps save them, I promise I will do as You ask, no matter what."

THE ICICLE WAS ONLY THE BEGINNING.

As soon as Oriel doubled over from Juliet's initial attack, the Alphas behind her conjured more of the same. She raised her arms, creating a shield of heat for defense, while she sheared off the penetrating icicle. She then pressed a glowing hand to the spot to finish melting the ice and heal the wound.

When she failed to counterattack, the Alphas tightened their circle, forcing her to contract her heat shield to avoid harming them. A few missiles failed to completely vaporize, and water droplets splattered Oriel. She winced. The water didn't penetrate her human skin, however, so her firecore overcame their dampening with ease.

Juliet held up her hand. The barrage ceased. Lifting her face to the blood moon, she basked in the moment. "The time has come for the door to be open. The time has come for me to reign, loved and adored by all."

"Love born out of fear is not truly love." Oriel's arms trembled from maintaining the delicate balance of self-defense without causing harm. Her shield shrank another notch.

"And love that imprisons and chains is?" Juliet's lips curled into a sneer.

"It is our choices that chain and our pride that imprisons."

"So your *choice* prevents you from destroying us?" Juliet waved at the half circle of Alphas. "Because we both know you can."

"A restriction is not the same as a chain." Oriel tapped the cabin behind her, sparks flying from her fingertips. "Chains prevent us from what we ought to do. A restriction protects us from what we ought not to do." She frowned; the wooden wall refused to burn, producing instead a few tendrils of smoke.

"Yet you are here rather than helping Gareth like you ought to."

"Creator's ways are not my ways." Oriel pressed her palm against the wall; moisture softened the wood.

The glee of success glittered in Juliet's eyes. Soaking the buildings ahead of time worked; Oriel could not pass through the damp wood. "So Creator desires for you to die at my hands? How *loving*."

A flicker of a smile crossed Oriel's lips. "As you once reminded me, death is not the worst that can happen. Besides," she said calmly, "how better to keep you and Zarbal apart?"

"Then I won't keep him waiting." Juliet clapped her hands and swung them above her head. "Kabat."

The Alphas did the same.

The ground bubbled, and a thick tar oozed out, a Terrestrial manifestation of Rishi sap. It crept along the ground toward Oriel.

THREE ARROWS BURST THROUGH THE BARRIER, announcing Brandon's return to the Ishir fight. Each arrow found its Rishi mark, and they successively disintegrated. Brandon nocked a fourth and pushed through into the narrow space between the cabins.

Jaki and the female warrior with him whirled around, and Jaki's face grew stern, flames churning. "You're not supposed to be here!"

"Yes, I am." Brandon reclaimed his arrows.

Jaki yanked his knife from the wall where it embedded itself during the fight. "Explain yourself, Guardian."

"I have to open the water tower." Reaching the corner of the building, Brandon peered around the edge, bow at the ready. Only two small knots battled in the immediate vicinity, but smoke and fire choked the area around the tower near the gate.

The flames of the female warrior flashed green and purple. "That could douse every Ishir out there—if you can get there at all!"

"It doesn't matter. I have to go." Brandon leaned his head against the wall, eyes closed. Sweat glazed his soot-streaked face, and he kept readjusting his grip on his bow. Of course the tower would be in the center of the thickest battle.

The warrior stretched her hands out to Jaki. "The Adam's touched, his senses driven from him."

At the charge of insanity, Brandon chuckled dryly. "No surprise there," he quipped. "It's hereditary. I got it from my grandmama." He swiped a sleeve over his face, smearing the soot and adding a touch of wildness to his expression.

Jaki raised his eyebrows. "You won't make it on your own."

"I have to."

Jaki shoved his knife and sword away, and from the midst

of his flames, pulled out two, double-bladed daggers. "Then I will come with you." Gripping each weapon in the middle, he glided up beside Brandon. "Two fools will have a better chance of breaking through than one."

"You cannot mean to do this." The female warrior rustled her wings.

"Don't you smell it?" Jaki gave each dagger a quick test flip. "He's been with Creator Himself. Creator never commands without reason."

"Creator commanded *him*, not you."

"He has commanded us to protect the Adam. He is Adam. I go."

Conflicting colors swirled through her flames, then the Ishir clasped one arm over her chest. "Creator go with you."

"May He turn His face toward you with favor." Then Jaki nodded at Brandon, and the two of them rushed toward the water tower.

GARETH TACKLED MAGGIE A SPLIT SECOND BEFORE the lightning struck. The air rippled with electricity, and the bolt charred the corner of the building. A mini boom of thunder rattled the sky.

Gareth kept moving. Leaving behind his fallen daggers, he clutched Maggie to him and rolled into the shadows of the buildings, out of Zarbal's immediate range. Gareth knelt and helped Maggie into a sitting position. She patted her bare head; she'd lost her hat. "I be getting a mite old for this."

"You and me both." Gareth leaned back for a glimpse of the garden, but too many buildings impeded the view. He pushed up onto one knee and hesitated.

She patted his cheek. "Go on. Creator can hear me here as well as there."

"Thank you, Maggie." He kissed the top of her head and rose.

"But before ye go . . ." She offered him Oriel's spectacles.

He pushed them back to her. "They won't fit me."

"Nonsense. Ye need them." She wobbled to her feet and slid them on Gareth's face. He blinked. Through the lens the world became fuller, more complete, as Terrestrial and Echoing overlapped. "Now shoo. Ye can't be letting him unlock that door." She fluttered a hand at him and turned away, her face raising heavenward. "Creator . . ."

With no time to waste, Gareth left Maggie and crept toward the garden again, keeping to the shadows of the buildings as much as possible. Metal clanked against metal. He hastened his pace. Maggie's spectacles revealed that Zarbal stood before a small keyhole hovering midair. The key was already inserted into it, suspending the key and hiding the inserted part from sight.

Then the air rippled. Metal materialized around the keyhole, swelling outward to form the door to the Bottomless Regions.

THE RISHI LINE REFUSED TO BREAK.

No matter where Brandon and Jaki tried to cross, every path swelled shut. A change in tactics didn't help either. Both frontal assault and sneak attack met with reinforced resistance.

With the other arrows gone, Brandon shot Oriel's over and over, the weapon faithfully returning to his hand after striking each intended target. Beside him, Jaki spun his daggers at speeds that blurred the blades into a deadly smear. Yet the chances of success diminished with every passing second. For every Rishi who combusted, three Ishir were doused. For every Rishi that crumbled, two replaced him whereas none replaced the fallen Ishir.

Jaki rushed ahead to block a strike, crossing a black puddle in the process. Rishi sap. It surged up him, extinguishing his flames. He burned off strand after strand clawing toward his firecore, but they multiplied faster than he could destroy them. He collapsed onto to the ground.

"Jaki!" Brandon dropped to his side.

The Ishir pushed him away. "Leave me, Guardian."

"No, I won't. I can't—"

"Creator will be your strength." Sap snaked around Jaki's chest, and his breaths shortened. "Now . . . go." Rousing, he flung his daggers, destroying two more Rishi and opening a space for Brandon.

Blinking rapidly, Brandon briefly pressed his hand on Jaki's arm and then sprang to his feet. Swinging his bow onto his back, he charged ahead and snatched up Jaki's daggers. He slashed, stabbed, and sliced at anything that crossed his line of sight, pushing onward, ever onward. His hands reddened, then blistered from wielding Ishir weapons. More and more Rishi converged on him, surrounding him. One dagger was knocked from his grasp, the second ripped from his fingers. He swung about his bow and nocked Oriel's arrow, swinging the tip from target to target. But there were too many, too close. The Rishi closed ranks, leering at him. Brandon dropped Oriel's arrow at his feet and extended the bow from its end, spinning in a circle.

The Rishi jumped back, except one who ducked beneath the bow and swung his fighting stick at the guardian's legs.

He crashed to the ground, bow flying from his hand. The other Rishi swarmed forward as he tucked himself into a ball. "Creator, help us."

35

"ENOUGH." JULIET PULLED HER HANDS APART, silencing the Alphas' chanting. The oozing tar seeped back into the ground, damage done. Oriel lay in a fetal position, her skin ashy and eyes dull. Tar clung to most of her lower body, and several cords twined around her chest. Though she still breathed, it came in sporadic bursts.

"How does it feel, flame, knowing your Creator put you here?" Juliet sauntered over to her. "That His restrictions will now kill you, all for want of a human to defend?"

Curling tighter, Oriel shivered violently, her fire on the verge of being extinguished.

Juliet pulled out a syringe and stooped beside Oriel. "Any final words before I silence your song forever?"

Her brow wrinkled, her mouth soundlessly repeating the words.

"What's that?" Leaning forward, Juliet mockingly cupped a hand around her ear. "I can't hear you."

Oriel opened her eyes. The tiniest flame flickered within their depths.

> "I sing forever of Creator's love
> "In the brightest of days, in the darkest night.
> "He reigns eternally from above,
> "The Ruler of all life, the Champion of right."

The light within her eyes strengthened, and a glow swelled across her skin, burning away the tar.

"No!" Juliet stabbed the syringe into Oriel's neck, draining Dr. Minio's flame-dousing potion into her.

Oriel gasped, her back arching. But still she sang.

> *"I sing forever of Creator's might*
> *"In the brightest of days, in the darkest night.*
> *"He endlessly is my great delight,*
> *"The Lover of my heart, the Song in my plight."*

With teeth gnashing, the Alphas and Juliet fell back, hands clamped over their ears. Oriel rolled onto her hands and knees and staggered onto her feet.

> *"I sing forever of Creator's name*
> *"In the brightest of days, in the darkest night."*

Her skin glowed brighter and brighter as her voice crescendoed, and pity glistened in her eyes for the group that tried to kill her minutes before.

> *"He shall remain the unchanging same,*
> *"The Music of my song, the Fuel of my light!"*

At her final note, the earth began to quake.

THE COMPLETED DOOR TO THE BOTTOMLESS REGION glowed the same dark red as the eclipsed moon. Metallic in sheen, its unadorned surface matched the key fitted into the lock at its heart. Sulfuric fumes leeched along the door's edges, and Zarbal inhaled deeply as if relishing the corrosive scent.

At the corner of a cabin, Gareth shed his bulky coat and eyed his daggers laying only a couple of yards away. His fingers tapped a countdown. Three . . . two . . . one. He sprang forward, grabbed the weapons, and sprinted for Zarbal. He flung a dagger at Zarbal's back.

The Rishi spun from the door. He knocked the spinning blade away and lobbed a ball of black fire.

Gareth dodged, but the fireball nicked his shoulder, its flames colder than ice. Zarbal tossed another fireball at him. Gareth regained his balance in time to evade it. Scooping up the thrown dagger, embedded in the ground close to his original position, he ducked past Zarbal and backhanded a third fireball away. He now stood between Zarbal and the door to the Bottomless Regions.

"Not bad, Guardian." Zarbal juggled a half dozen fireballs with one hand. "Let me see if I can't make this a bit more . . . challenging." He flung them at Gareth one after another.

Gareth blocked each one.

Zarbal yanked on the tentacles. Iris cried out. Gareth's daggers dipped as he glanced over at her. She bit her lip, tears streaming down her face, hands clenched. Zarbal blasted another pair of fireballs at him.

Yanking up his guard, Gareth blocked one, but the second slipped past and smashed into his shoulder, knocking him backward. His right arm struck the door, and the metal seared through his clothing. Gareth's daggers plunged to the ground as he slumped to his knees, cradling his arm.

Zarbal chuckled. "'How have the mighty fallen in the midst of the battle. How have the mighty fallen and the weapons of war perished!'"

At his quote, a wisp of light flickered across the blades of Gareth's daggers.

Zarbal drew his own sword for the first time and circled, pointing the tip at Gareth's neck. "But this should come as no surprise to you. For those who take up the sword shall perish by the sword."

A brighter curl of light streaked up Gareth's fallen daggers from hilt to tip. Gareth shoved Maggie's spectacles higher on his nose. "You're right. Yet the Ancient Writings also say He is faithful to cleanse us from all unrighteousness, removing transgressions as far as east is from the west."

This time the blades lit up and held their radiance.

Zarbal tracked his gaze.

Gareth seized the nearest dagger with his left hand. Flipping onto his back, he raised the weapon. A downward cut from Zarbal slammed into the flat. The Rishi's sword shattered, the shards vaporizing into mist.

Gareth rolled onto his feet, once again planting himself between the door and Zarbal.

Tossing aside the broken blade, Zarbal rolled his hands together to form another fireball. "Well played, Guardian. But no matter how powerful your weapon is, it can't protect forever." He raised his hand.

A melody rang through the air. "... *In the brightest of days, in the darkest night. He endlessly is my great delight.*"

Color rushed into Iris's face. Gareth tensed. But Zarbal didn't retreat or cover his ears. Instead, the song seemed to refresh him, and he smiled sardonically. "Natural immunity. Another advantage of feeding. Whatever I don't need I shunt back to her to hold in reserve. But time is ticking, and I'm done playing. Step aside."

Gareth held his position.

"So be it." Zarbal launched a volley of fire.

A SINGLE VOICE, PURE AND CLEAR, RANG OUT IN song like a bell tolling in the mountains. The sound stilled the fighting as both Ishir and Rishi turned their heads toward the source, weapons and hands lowering.

When the imminent Rishi attack failed to fall upon Brandon, he lifted his face.

The second verse of the song began, growing in power. All around the camp, Rishi retreated from the voice, hissing vehemently. The fire of the Ishir, however, brightened with every note. Brandon uncurled. This was impossible. Oriel fought in Terrestrial. There was no way they should be able to hear her. Yet the voice, though different from normal, remained unmistakably hers.

At the start of the third verse, Ishir after Ishir joined in, the swelling music vibrating the air. *"I sing forever of Creator's name . . ."* Fallen Ishir rose, black sap burning away, dying flames reigniting. The air brightened and the warmth of a midsummer's day permeated HopeWell. *"In the brightest of days, in the darkest of nights."*

The Rishi shrieked, each twisting within their own private vortex of flame and lightning. The song fed their fire as well, fanning it into an uncontrollable firestorm.

"He shall remain the unchanging same . . ."

No longer in control of their own fire, the Rishi found themselves immobilized, unable to flee. They tried to drown out the song with their screeching, but the tidal wave of music could not be held back.

"The Music of my song, the Fuel of my light!"

At the final climatic note, the earth quaked, and several Rishi combusted in a shower of sparks, leaving behind nothing but a few cinders and some ash.

"Charge, for He who made all things fights for you!" sang out an Ishir voice.

"For His Glory!" replied a chorus of warriors, who swept past Brandon after the retreating Rishi. Within the crowd, a voice started a new song, and soon others joined in.

> *"Praise Creator who dwells above;*
> *"Praise His Glory shown in love;*
> *"Praise His Power that made what is;*
> *"All glory, pow'r, and honor His!"*

Brandon breathed deeply, filling the entire capacity of his lungs for the first time since entering HopeWell. "Thank You."

"Indeed, thanksgiving is due Him, but the battle is not yet won." A warrior glided out from among the others, his flames brilliant and so solid that they resembled a suit of armor.

Brandon shielded his eyes, unable to look at such radiance. "Jaki?"

"It is I."

"But you—I saw . . . How's this possible?"

"We forgot—*I* forgot—our greatest strength lies not in our fire but in our song, because Creator planted His song within us to sing His praises. Therefore, when we sing His praises, it is the all-powerful Creator who is acting, and no one can stand against Him." He extended Brandon's bow to him. "But have we not water to loose, Guardian?"

Brandon took his bow before retrieving Oriel's arrow. Jaki unfurled his wings and skimmed across the ground, cutting a path through the battle with ease. Brandon sprinted to keep up, and by the time they reached the tower, he panted from the exertion. Resting his hands on his knees, he winced. His palms and fingers were raw and blistered from handling Jaki's daggers.

He looked up the ladder he had to climb, then back at Jaki. But his vision had shown *him* releasing the water, not Jaki. He steeled himself, and using the tip of Oriel's arrow, he cut off the hem of his shirt. He wrapped a strip around each hand and hauled himself onto the first rung. "Move the Ishir away!"

Jaki sounded a warning to the nearest warriors, and they retreated.

Reaching the top, Brandon pushed on the levers and yanked on the chains. The door opened, and water gushed out. A cascade of giggles followed as Dachi tumbled over each other. "We're out, we're out. Let's play!"

Brandon scrambled down to the ground, the water continuing to pour forth, far more than the tower could possibly contain.

Jaki pointed to the Dachi racing away. "Go on, Guardian. See where they lead. We'll finish here." He blended into the crowd, his voice ascending in song. *"Omnipotent—He rules o'er all."*

"Omnipresent—there when we call," responded the Ishir.

Fitting Oriel's arrow into his bow, Brandon chased after the Dachi as they somersaulted their way toward HopeWell's heart.

THE EARTH CALMED, AND QUIET DESCENDED ONCE more. Still Juliet and the Alphas pressed hands over their ears. Oriel moved forward. Though her human shell remained intact, her song had stoked her Ishir nature until it was visible through the façade, her hair flaming white-hot, her skin glowing with a burnished gleam, flames burning bright in her eyes.

The Alphas yelped and fled, scrambling through the opening Oriel had torn through the fence. Beyond it the forest swayed in the bloody moonlight, though the earth no longer quaked and no wind blew. Shouts and screams broke out, only to be cut off, leaving behind an eerie silence.

"Cowards." Juliet whirled toward Oriel, chanting guttural words low and fierce. She stretched out her hand, palm up, and elevated it slowly.

The ground cracked, and the tips of a dozen black vines burst forth. Larger and larger they grew, wriggling, writhing, more animal than plant as they snaked across the earth. Oriel held her position, neither advancing nor retreating. "Even now you do not see." Deep sorrow, somehow both ancient and fresh at once, laced her voice.

"It is you who fails to see," Juliet retorted. At the flick of her wrist, the vines reared up in a circle around Oriel. They swayed hypnotically, interweaving with each other as they drew together tighter and tighter.

Oriel spared them no glance, her attention wholly upon Juliet. "Yet in our servitude we find greater freedom, in surrender greater power."

"Showing how deluded you are." Juliet snapped her fingers shut. The vines constricted around Oriel, binding her from shoulder to foot.

She glanced down with the disinterest of discovering a minor annoyance. "Power lies not in fire nor might in dust."

"I suppose you think it lies in song and breath then."

"Song and breath are gifts from Creator, and as such, power comes with them. But they are not the spring from which the power originates." Her voice glided into a new melody.

> *"Before the start of time, alone and only He.*
> *"He spoke His word and it rang forth;*
> *"All things began to be."*

As Oriel sang, light streaked through the vines until they too gleamed. Leaves sprouted and flowers blossomed along their length.

Juliet resumed her chanting in louder tones. The vines uncoiled anyway and wove an imposing wall. Then they parted, forming an archway. Scarlet blossoms sparkled and the leaves glowed, thorns glistening with Oriel's fireblood.

In contrast, a shadow swelled behind Juliet, blacker than the darkest night or deepest pit.

"Even if the Rishi succeed this night, they cannot give what you desire." Oriel entered the vines' archway and plucked one of the vibrant flowers, now as large as a dinner plate. "Power yes, beauty maybe, the adoration of the world perhaps. But not real, abiding love, the kind that faced Death himself for your sake. This is what Creator offers you." She extended to Juliet the glittering blossom in her cupped hands.

Juliet wavered, a finger reaching toward the flower. Then she jerked her hand back, barking a laugh. "Love? He is a dictator, selfishly manipulating everything for His own ends! I will never bend knee to such a tyrant."

The declaration had barely left her mouth before the shadow crashed over her. With a scream, Juliet vanished from sight.

The blossom in Oriel's hands withered, then disintegrated, the shadow dissipating with it. Oriel bowed her head.

Juliet's body lay on the ground, hand to her throat, breath gone.

GARETH WARDED OFF THE FIREBALLS, GIVING UP NO ground but not gaining any either. Sweat poured down his face, and his chest heaved.

Zarbal cast a glance at the blood moon and increased his force.

Grunting, Gareth sidestepped the next three fireballs and

splattered a fourth with the flat of his dagger. But his reactions were turning sluggish, and he wouldn't be able to hold off Zarbal much longer.

In the distance Oriel's voice raised again in song. Light rushed through the tentacles, and Zarbal soaked in the renewing energy. "Impeccable timing."

Gareth lunged forward, slicing at the tentacles connecting Iris and the Rishi. Zarbal thrust his hand out, and a blast of scorching air knocked Gareth backward. He crumpled in a heap with a groan, away from Iris, away from the door. She released a gargled cry and strained against the webbing that bound her to the stake.

Zarbal patted her head. "Terrible, isn't it? Without a voice, you are robbed of both word and song." He turned to the door.

"Don't listen to him." Gareth pushed up with his good hand, still grasping his dagger somehow. "They may have stolen your tongue, but they cannot take your voice, for Creator both discerns the thoughts and hears the unuttered."

Iris nodded and bowed her head, beginning to hum. Zarbal whipped around as molten white light surged through the tentacles. He doubled over with a roar, and he jerked on the tentacle rope. Iris tensed in pain but continued to sing, a spicy aroma filling the air. Zarbal twisted in torment, his body fattening, his eyes bulging. He yanked harder, but the tentacles seemed welded in place. His growth accelerated, and cracks threaded through his human façade. He unsheathed a knife and hacked away at the connection, but he couldn't dent or fracture a single one. He raised the knife to fling it at Iris.

Water gushed from between the buildings, the ground softening to quicksand. Zarbal staggered, throwing his aim off, and his knife went wide. He twisted back toward the door to the Bottomless Regions, but his weight dragged him down. He grabbed for the key. He knocked it loose; the door faded away.

Water swirled and steamed around him, cooling the fire Iris's song stirred. The cracks in Zarbal's skin started to reseal. A tidal wave rolled toward them.

Gareth raised his dagger. "By His Spirit!" He threw the dagger like a javelin.

The blade sliced between two cracks, striking Zarbal's firecore. Light seared through the tentacles. Iris writhed. Zarbal exploded, the curling wave crashing over all three of them.

The water calmed and drained away. Gareth surfaced, coughing and spluttering but unharmed from Zarbal's detonation due to the engulfing waters. He staggered to his feet, then stilled.

His dagger lay at the base of an empty stake, a muddy pile of ashes where Zarbal and Iris had been a moment before.

AS BRANDON REACHED THE BARRIER CIRCLING THE interior of HopeWell, an explosion rocked the world. The air convulsed. The ground quaked. He slammed against the wall of a nearby cabin. The translucent barrier bulged, then popped, plastering him with water and protecting him from the blast of fiery air that raced by.

Brandon lurched a few steps before regaining his footing, then ran for the garden, spraying water and mud in his wake. But the scene at the garden stopped him in his tracks: a pile of ashes was heaped beside an empty stake, Gareth kneeling before it. His head was bowed, tears falling from his face.

"No!" Brandon dove for the ash heap. Iris couldn't have survived whatever happened here. He clawed at the pile helplessly. "Please, please, please . . ." His voice broke. But when his fingers started flinging more mud than ash, he slowed to a stop. He fell onto his hands, trembling, his breaths heavy and ragged.

"Surprise!" A water geyser shot upward, splattering Brandon with water and ashy mud. Startled, he scrambled backward. The water coalesced into giggling Dachi. "Surprise, surprise!" Brandon raised his head, and his mouth fell open. The Dachi's geyser had left behind a crater, in the middle of which sat Iris, soggy but very much alive. The Dachi's water had cooled the backlash of Zarbal's explosion, preventing her death. Gareth rushed to her.

"Are you surprised? Are you, are you?" The Dachi pranced around the younger guardian. "Creator said you would be if we hid around the Fire-Dust."

Brandon began laughing despite himself. "Yes, very surprised." He couldn't take his eyes off Iris. "The best surprise I have ever had."

That set off a new round of giggles from the Dachi. "Best surprise, best surprise, ever, ever, ever!" They tumbled around and arced over him.

Brandon closed his eyes and lifted his face heavenward. "Where to now?"

36

WHEN THE SUN ROSE OVER HOPEWELL, FEW TRACES
of the previous night's battle remained. The front gate was a
tangled mess of wire and splintered wood. A tree sprawled over
the fence. Two dozen buildings bore scorch marks. A broad
channel cut a path through the softened ground from the water
tower to the garden. Hardly the signs of an epic battle.

Along the north fence, Gareth knelt beside a fresh grave, his
last—and hardest—task of the long night. From his coat pocket he
removed the half-finished heart he had carved while overlooking
Juliet's home and pressed it into the dirt mound. "I wish it could
have been different, Jul." Using the shovel as a crutch, he climbed
to his feet. "Be merciful, Creator, if possible." Then resting the
shovel against his left shoulder, he walked back to the gate, his
bandaged right arm cradled against his chest.

In the forest, birds chattered and the sky lightened from gray
to pale blue. Robins snatched at worms brought to the surface by
an early morning shower. Gareth paused by the steps leading to
the commandant's quarters. The scent of damp earth mingled
with the rain-washed breeze thick with the promise of spring.
He inhaled deeply. "His mercies are new every morning. Great,
indeed, is His faithfulness."

A dozen birds burst into flight as two men came up the road.

Gareth altered his grip on the shovel to a defensive one, but as the
men neared, he relaxed. Digging the tip of the shovel into the ground,
he leaned on the handle. "Still refusing to let your song die, I see."

Jaki laughed, the merry sound echoing through the compound and disturbing another dozen birds. He tipped his hat over his eyes. "And you, old friend, have the longest dying breath of anyone I know." Gareth gave a short burst of laughter himself. Then he raised bushy brows at Brandon. "You managed to not get yourself killed." Jaki slapped a hand against Brandon's shoulder, making him wince. "I told you he was worth training."

"We'll see." But a twinkle of approval ruined the noncommittal answer.

"At least when he masters his tunneling, I won't have to spend half the night traveling to a gateway to return him to you."

A grin sneaked onto Gareth's face. "I'll make sure to teach him about that last then. I wouldn't want to deprive him of valuable time with the Ishir."

"Gareth—"

The door creaked open. Brandon's face lit up. "Grandmama!" He bounded onto the porch and picked her up in a bear hug.

"Careful . . ." warned Gareth.

"Oh hush." Maggie waved away Gareth's concern. "I'm not going to shatter. Creator knows I've too much to be doing yet."

Iris hovered in the doorway behind her. Though darkness still haunted her eyes, bandages covered her gashes, and a rosy tinge colored her skin.

Brandon crossed over to her, rummaging in his pocket. "You, ah . . . dropped this." He held out the carved iris.

She accepted the token with a smile of thanks and twirled it between her fingers, the pink in her cheeks deepening.

Maggie clicked her tongue at the pair, head bobbing in approval. Gareth wagged a finger at her. "Don't go there, Maggie."

"Go?" She studied the brightening sky. "Aye, I need to be going. So many things to be planting, so many seedlings to nurture." Plopping her recovered hat on her head, she returned her gaze to Brandon, who was whispering something to Iris.

"Aye. Much to do."

Gareth rolled his eyes.

Jaki angled for a better view through the doorway. "And the Key . . . ?"

"Present and accounted for, Warrior."

Jaki spun around. Oriel stood behind him, bodily whole, hair neatly plaited, and dressed in a fresh set of prison clothes scrounged from a supply shed. They still swamped her slim frame. He clasped an arm over his chest and bowed deeply to her. "The other warriors have told me of your battle with Levioth. You've proven yourself more powerful than any of us thought."

Oriel shook her head with a smile. "You honor me, Warrior, but if anything was proven, it is that Creator is more powerful than any of us remembered."

"Well spoken, Key of Everything."

Gareth propped the shovel against a post and removed from a pocket the ebony box. "I believe this belongs with you."

Oriel took the box and opened the lid. The key to the Bottomless Regions was once again nestled upon the silver satin.

Jaki placed a hand on her shoulder. "It is time to return."

"I suppose it is." Resignation twined with wistfulness as she closed the box and tucked it away.

Gareth and Jaki exchanged glances. Jaki nodded. "I'll escort the Guardian and the Jewels to their home." He waved Iris, Maggie, and Brandon toward the gate.

"One thing."

Jaki paused at Gareth's words.

"Don't let Maggie's imagination run away with her."

"Of course not." His eyes sparkled brightly beneath his fedora's brim. "An imagination properly directed is far more effective."

Maggie slipped a hand into the crook of the arm Jaki offered her. "I knew ye were a wise one." And their hats converged conspiratorially as they trailed Brandon and Iris out of HopeWell, leaving Gareth to shake his head.

Oriel hung back, as if she knew she should be going as well but was uncertain of which way to go. A robin flitted by, and the fence grated in the light breeze.

Gareth rubbed an ear. "That is one sound I won't miss."

"Is that so, Mighty Prince? Because I think I shall miss it very much."

"Really."

Oriel nodded and smiled impishly. "It reminds me of you, being both old and rusty."

Gareth stared at her, then burst into a full-chested laugh. "Well played. Jaki would be proud of you."

Oriel's eyes danced, then her expression changed, and her smile faded. She looked down at the ground, blinking rapidly.

Gareth walked over to stand shoulder to shoulder with her, his gaze roaming over the camp. The commandant's office where every new prisoner was informed that he would never leave. The drafty cabins with their hard beds. Rock piles that filled the prisoners' days with labor. The isolating Cellar that was used to break the strongest-willed prisoner.

But it was also at that Cellar that Gareth first saw Oriel and she him. And Cabin Twelve's table would forever bear the scar of their initial meeting. Then there were the commandant's quarters where they'd each challenged HopeWell's dictator, the bench from which Oriel declared her intent to escape, and the healers' cabin where he'd tended her after that escape failed.

"A happy ending is still an end, isn't it?"

Oriel swallowed hard. "I didn't know it could hurt so much."

"Regret coming?"

"No, never!" Her emphatic shake of the head dislodged a few wisps of hair from her braid.

"Good. Then I won't have to tell you how you brought light into our lives and how I would have probably died here without hope, Iris would have remained trapped nameless, and Brandon would still be seeking his purpose while Maggie mourned the hardness of his heart, but this all changed because of your incredible bravery."

Oriel's breath caught. "You think me . . . brave?"

Gareth faced her, his gray eyes misty. "One of the bravest I've ever had the privilege serving beside." Crossing both arms over his chest, he bowed deeply to her. "I am in your debt, Oriel, Bringer of Creator's Light."

She pressed a hand to her mouth, and a hot tear escaped her eye.

Gareth caught it on his finger. The tear sparkled gold and red as if water encased fire, and as it cooled, it hardened into a tiny gem. "The tear of an Ishir, the rarest of all gems." He placed it in her palm, wrapping her fingers around it. "May you never forget to live your name."

"Never, for as long as Creator sustains my song." She clutched the gem, renewed fire illuminating her eyes. Then lifting her chin, she faced HopeWell's gate. "I'm ready now, Mighty Prince."

He adjusted his sling and strode toward the road. "Then onto the next mission."

"Next mission?" Oriel came to a halt.

Gareth smiled to himself but maintained his steady pace toward the exit. "Did you really believe Creator's call would stop after one?"

Oriel quickly caught up with him, and as Gareth crossed HopeWell's threshold, she circled in front of him. "You think Creator has more for me?"

"Think? I know. There are many other prisoners out there needing to be shown the way, needing light. This"—Gareth waved at HopeWell—"was just the beginning."

"The beginning." Her words floated on the air, upborne by whispered awe. "I like the sound of that. It's full of . . . hope."

Gareth inhaled deeply, freely, as the sun crested the roofs of HopeWell. "That it is. That it is."

THE END

A NOTE FROM THE AUTHOR:

THE DEVELOPMENT OF A LEGEND

What if are probably the two most dangerous words to cross a writer's mind. At least for me, they tend to lead down long meandering trails, far from conventional paths, with no clear sense of where I will end up.

Such it was for me when writing *Vault*. I suspected from the moment that Oriel stepped onto the page that she was . . . different. That suspicion was confirmed when she grasped Gareth's whittling knife and slid it out from the table. There was definitely something not human about her.

That naturally led to the question of what was she? Although *Vault* is set in an imaginary land, the setting felt more historical than fantastical. The obvious answer—and one that some may assume—is that she is some sort of angel.

But early on I knew this wasn't quite right. For if I was to maintain the pseudo-historical feel of this world, then Oriel would have to conform to the biblical revelation of angels—which she doesn't. For one thing, she struck me as long-lived but not immortal; she could and would eventually die. So while Oriel was sweet, she was no angel. (Sorry if that disappoints!)

Indeed, she was more like the old faeries or Tolkien's elves than biblical angels. But to call her a faerie didn't work either as that contradicted the historical-styled setting. Therefore, I found myself in a quandary. What was Oriel?

About this time I realized that the pseudo-historical setting, the narrative voice, and the supernatural events gave the story the feel of a legend or myth. Legends and myths, while fantastical, are also often rooted in a seed of truth. That is, they are based, however loosely, on real people and real events. And this was when the what-ifs began.

What if Oriel wasn't a faerie—but the race that the myth of faeries came from? What if the stories about nymphs and dryads and faeries contained a seed of truth? What if the strange "faerieland" that the old tales speak of, the one into which travelers sometimes crossed accidentally, really did exist? Moreover, we know there are different races of what we traditionally call "angels": cherubim, seraphim, and messenger angels like Gabriel. What if God had created other races too, races that the legends call faeries and nymphs? Then I bumped into verses like Psalm 104:4 (also quoted in Hebrews 1:7) which reads, "He makes the winds His messengers, flaming fire His ministers." What if the psalmist meant this *literally*?

From there my imagination took off, the wind messengers becoming the Qolet and the ministering fire becoming the Ishir. Since much of mythology revolves around the four elements (wind/air, fire, earth, and water), and since man is made of dust, the Dachi soon evolved for water. Angels, of course, are also real, and they became the Melekah (a play on the Hebrew for "messenger," which is frequently translated as "angel" in the Old Testament). Then seeing a connection between my races and each day of creation, I filled in the sixth race with the plant-based Yerek.

By this point my myth gained a life of its own, growing and developing as I wrote the story and new questions emerged. Which races were immortal? (A: The Melekah, Qolet, and Dachi, since light, wind, and water cannot "die.") How did the Fall recorded in Genesis affect each of the races? (A: Each was tempted, fell in some way, and was punished accordingly, although only with Adam and Eve's fall did creation go into bondage because, as those made in God's image, they were to have dominion. So when they sinned, they handed their entire realm, which God had given to them, over to Satan to control.)

Some of these answers show up blatantly in the story. Others are only hinted at. But at all times I tried to remain true to the biblical accounts and descriptions, only filling in the cracks—those things about which Scripture says nothing—with imagination.

For while the Bible does not say God created the Ishir, Qolet, Dachi, and Yerek, neither does it say He didn't. ☺

CHAWNA SCHROEDER

About the Author

CHAWNA SCHROEDER IS A MINNESOTAN WRITER WHO enjoys snow, chai tea, and playing "what if?"—even if that game occasionally gets her into trouble. She also loves stretching both her imagination and her faith to their limits and helping others to do the same. As a result, her writing explores the vastness of God, His multifaceted nature, and the potential of a life lived with Him. This means both learning the boundaries He created for our protection as well as demolishing the human boxes that restrict both God and people.

When she isn't reading or writing, a variety of other activities fill her "free" time: practicing piano for church, preparing Sunday school lessons, studying the biblical languages, or working on one of her handwork projects while enjoying a movie.

Chawna's other books include *Beast*, a coming-of-age fairytale for teens and adults, and the Bearing the Sword curriculum, which teaches the basics of discernment to teens through in-depth Bible study and media analysis. You can connect with Chawna through her website (www.chawnaschroeder.com), blog (www.chawnaschroeder.blogspot.com) or Facebook (www.facebook.com/ChawnaSchroederAuthor).

ACKNOWLEDGMENTS

VAULT WAS STARTED AS A "SANDBOX" STORY—A PLACE to play, to experiment, to even break all the writing "rules" if I so chose. I never expected, at least initially, that this story would actually find its way into print. That it has done so is a testament to the efforts, enthusiasm, and endless encouragement of dozens of people, of whom I can list only a few.

I am greatly appreciative of the comments, corrections, and suggestions of my various critique partners, including (but not limited to) Brenda Anderson, Beth Goddard, and Stacy Monson.

I'm especially indebted to the collective genius of Angela Bell, Michelle Griep, and Sharon Hinck, critiquers extraordinaire. These three amazing ladies graciously poured into my writing, volunteering precious hours of time to comb through the entire manuscript. I am so blessed to be able to call you three friends!

My family deserves an award (or two or a dozen) for the hours listening to me, whether I was gloating over an unexpected plot twist, bemoaning the difficulty of the work, or working through problems that probably made no sense because I'd dug myself into another hole. I'm so glad your ears are still (mostly) intact!

Nor would *Vault* exist without the tireless efforts of Steve Laube, efforts done not only on my behalf, but also for this genre and those who write stories that don't quite fit anywhere else. Moreover, he has personally sunk additional time into this story to see it polished to a sheen. Some may call you an ogre (or HOGR), but I personally suspect that's just a façade hiding a knight in shining armor.

I am also grateful for the rest of the Enclave team that have helped with everything from copy edits to cover art to marketing.

I'm convinced you must possess some kind of magical fairy dust that turns words into books.

My parents, Jim and Barb, deserve special credit. I am only an author because they challenged me to be who God wanted me to be, instead of worrying about social conventions and norms. Nor would this book exist twenty years later without their unflagging support of every sort. One of the greatest blessings in my life is having you two as my parents!

And of course, my deepest gratitude belongs to the Lord Jesus Christ. You provided words when I had none, creativity when the well ran dry, focus amidst distractions, ideas amidst blankness, calm amidst panic, and hope amidst despair. You taught me afresh the joy of play, how to write with You (rather than merely for You), and the value of *all* writing as worship—even that which will eventually be scrapped. May this story bring You joy and honor.

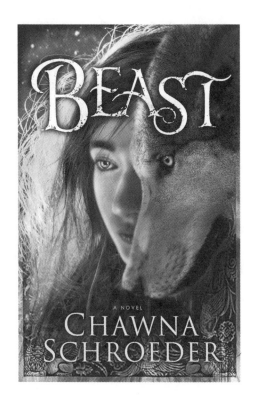